# Contents

Part I

- Tragedy - The Death Of Two Loves



Part II

- Rebirth and Revenge - The Reincarnation of Love and the
Fulfilled Destiny

# The Love They Could Not Share

**Copyright Edition**

Mars Avelino

Translator - Rossel Peras
Photographer - Majellia Zosa & Karen Reyes
Director Nonprofit Association - Edy Whidden
Finance Photo trip to Baguio city - Joseph Avelino
Photographer - Lilimar A. Ruhlmann
Photographers - Emerson Lot, Miguel and Milagros Avelino

Printed in the United States of America
ISBN: 978-1-959483-78-6 (sc)
Library of Congress Control Number: 2023913412

# Dedication

This book was written in dedication to my only son, Joseph Zosa Avelino, and his family; and to my only daughter, Lilimar Zosa Avelino-Ruhlmann, and her family. They were my inspirations in writing this beautiful story of life and a living memory of the unselfish love of two souls who would not leave this mother earth for the sake of the ever faithful love they could not share.

# Epigraph

When you fall in love with someone, you
would dare whatever is to come,
to nurture the love even when you are gone.

With your accidental death without warning,
your spirit would stay on earth to keep on telling
the dangers to the person on earth you keep
on loving.

When your life is taken away
without warning, your life is gone
without your say.
Your soul on earth would linger and stay
until your wish is met one day.

# Preface

The book portrays the hospitality of the Filipino people, the traditional way of courtship, and the Rite of Marriage in the Philippine culture. The book also mentioned some historical events of World War II related to the main character of the book. There were sketches of maps of the provinces of Bataan, Bulacan, Rizal, Laguna, and Quezon to make the portrayal of the stories more realistic and visually understandable. The summary of the book is as follows:

Mary Scarlet after nine years of waiting finally gave birth to a son. She named him David. Mary Scarlet became so obsessed with David. He was the apple of her eyes. David growing up knew how much his mother loved him. He likewise loved his mother very much. But the turn of events would shatter their love with the unsuspecting bullet that would pierce the heart of Mary Scarlet. Mary Scarlet was shot accidentally by Brutus Diablo on his way out after robbing a store. Young David promised to kill Brutus Diablo when they meet someday. The spirit of Mary Scarlet worried of the safety of David when he would meet Brutus and elected to stay on earth until their deadly meeting. David after graduation from high school was drafted by the U.S. Army. Trained as commando, he was sent to the Philippines. During the Japanese invasion of the Philippines, David was assigned in the front line in Bataan. With the Fall of Bataan, David, together with more than seventy-five thousand Filipinos and American soldiers, surrendered to the Japanese. In the death march, because of exhaustion, hunger, and lonesomeness with the death of his two friends killed during the Fall of Bataan, David collapsed in the line. A Japanese soldier from a distance saw him fell. The Japanese ran charging toward David with a fixed bayonet for the kill; but David was snatched by an American marine, who carried him on his shoulder, preventing the Japanese from killing him.

David, the American marine, and two Filipino officers—Capt. Joseph Lee and Alex Torres—escaped from the death march in the darkness of the night. The four with the help of Mang Pedro, the barrio captain of a village in Bataan, formed the Silent Killers. Their group killed their enemies by matching them one-on-one; from behind they slashed the throats and stabbed the hearts of their enemies. The group became hunted in the province of Bataan after killing hundreds of Japanese. They escaped the province of Bataan by route of Pampanga River to the Sierra Madre Mountain Ranges. On top of the Sierra Madre overlooking the province of Bulacan after a fierce battle with the Japanese, the group moved southward of the Sierra Madre Mountain Ranges. On top of the Sierra Madre Mountain overlooking the province of Laguna, David met Rosemarie, the only daughter of Commander Borromeo, by the waterfalls. David and Rosemarie fell in love. But the turn of events came to test their love. Commander Borromeo was captured by the Japanese. The group of Captain Lee, with David, came to rescue Commander Borromeo. In their escape route, Rosemarie was shot on the back. Rosemarie was killed. The spirit of Rosemarie felt sad watching the anguish of David and chose to stay on earth to guide him in finding the woman he would love and marry.

*Twice in the story, Mary Scarlet saved the life of David, while Rosemarie also saved his life two times—during and after the war. Both of them loved David very much, and after they have accomplished their wishes, both of them left earth with **the love they could not share**.*

# Acknowledgment

I would like to acknowledge the services of Rossel Peras in translating from English to Japanese, the instruction of the Japanese lieutenant general to his officers in the Death March in Chapter V – The Daring Escape.

I would like to express my gratitude to Edythe Whidden, for her evaluation of the two chapters of this book, while giving me the encouraging words to go ahead with the contentious Chapters XXIII and XXIV while ensuring that the sensitive contents of the two chapters are within the modern standard of today's social norm.

I would like to recognize the join efforts of Majella Zosa and Karen Joy Reyes in their untiring two days-two nights effort to take some beautiful pictures in Baguio City and a weekend travel in the city of Manila for more pictures relevant to Chapter XXIV The Honeymoon and Chapters that needed pictures of churches in the City of Manila.

I would like to express my thanks to my son Joseph Avelino, for his donation to finance the photographic trip to Baguio City for the pictures vital to the publication of this book. He also convinced his mother, my wife Lil, to fully understand my effort and dedication to writing this novel.

I would like to acknowledge the full effort of my daughter Lilimar Avelino-Ruhlmann in producing pictures relevant to the publication of this book.

I would like to acknowledge my brothers Amado and Miguel Avelino, his wife Milagros, and my nephew Emerson Lot for the pictures they contributed to this book.

And finally, I would like to express my heartfelt gratefulness to my wife **Lilia Z. Avelino**, for her understanding, consideration, and tolerance in the so many long hours I spent in so many nights, staying very late in my computer while writing this novel, and for her permission to let me publish this book.

# THE LOVE THEY COULD NOT SHARE

*The acacia tree by the waterfalls witnessed the love, faith, and hope of two lovers, David and Rosemarie, with the wish of a beautiful and glorious life together after the war. Under the acacia tree they fell in love and dreamt together of a beautiful tomorrow, but with the twist of unexpected events, Rosemarie was killed during the rescue operation of her father, Commander Borromeo, from the Japanese prison. The tragic death of Rosemarie was very hard for David to take. He was so devastated; a man who was a fierce fighter, trained to kill their enemies without fear, learned to shed his tears in deep anguish, grieving for the loss of an unfulfilled love. He loved Rosemarie very much. Rosemarie was buried under the acacia tree, the fervent wish of David to her father.*

*Feeling tormented watching David grieving, whom she loved very much, the spirit of Rosemarie chose to stay on earth to watch and guide him during and after the war until the time he would find the woman he would love and marry. David was faithful and true to his love for Rosemarie. He would not fall in love with another woman and dedicated his career to his business until Rosemarie appeared in his dream and told him, "David, I am at peace with God. I am giving you the freedom to fall in love again."*

# Part I
## - Tragedy
## - The Death Of Two Loves

# Chapter I

## The Scarborough Family

IT WAS A beautiful spring in the picturesque mansion of the Scarborough family. The surrounding roses around the house were blooming. The fruit trees behind the house—pears, plums, apples—and the grapes were starting to show healthy leaves, a revival of life after a long snowy winter. From the gate and along the driveway were line of well-kept pine trees and in front of the house were evergreens and blooming red, pink and white roses.

**The Scarborough Residence**

John was the dedicated gardener of the family. He had a green thumb, nurturing the plants around the house. He saw to it that the grass around the house was well trimmed and all the trees and flowering plants were well taken care of. Meanwhile, Anne took good care of the cooking and cleaning and all other household activities.

Dr. Frederick Scarborough and his wife, Mary Scarlet, enjoyed the weekend morning sunshine in their backyard's well-trimmed grass, over a cup of coffee. They talked about those days they first met in the hospital. Dr. Scarborough was a surgeon, and Mary Scarlet was an operating room nurse. They enjoyed being a team through all the delicate operations they worked on together until the time they felt they were meant for each other, so they decided to get married. It had been a long nine years waiting and wanting to have a child, until one day, Mary Scarlet called John.

"Hi, John, would you please get me the first harvest of your apples and grapes. I have a strong craving for your apples and grapes."

"Madam Mary, the apples and grapes will not be ready in three weeks.

You can just ask Anne to get some for you from the grocery," answered John.

"No, I want the first harvest from our backyard. Thank you," was the demanding reply by Mary Scarlet.

Not long after that exchange, Mary Scarlet had morning sickness. She felt like throwing up, was sleepy, and would sometimes feel dizzy. After thorough checking, Dr. Scarborough confirmed that Mary Scarlet was finally on the family way. It was a very big celebration for the couple. After a long nine years, finally they were going to have a baby.

Nine months after, the day they have been waiting for finally arrived, the birth of their firstborn. It was a baby boy.

"I will call him David. David is a powerful biblical name that sounds authoritative and just," Mary Scarlet told Dr. Scarborough.

"It is your choice, so let it be," answered Dr. Scarborough.

To have an extra hand to take care of little David, they hired Martha to babysit. The main duty of Martha would be to give Mary Scarlet a hand in taking care of little David. When Baby David was born, he had his own room. Martha was assigned to stay with the baby to answer to all his needs at night. But Martha was instructed that she could call Mary Scarlet if she needed some help.

Mary Scarlet still had the first hand in caring for little David, but when she was not around, Martha should take good care of the baby. After a very long wait to have a baby, Mary Scarlet became so obsessed with their new member of the family. At work the only thing she was thinking about was Baby David, and she could not wait to get home to play with him and kiss him. When she arrived home, she would change to her housedress, washed her hands, and right away went into the room of Baby David.

"Martha, my dear, how is my baby?" she asked Martha.

"He is doing well. He just woke up and is drinking his milk," answered Martha.

Mary Scarlet picked up the baby and danced with him, singing a lullaby. She put him down, then played with him. A little later, Dr. Scarborough arrived.

"I am home!" yelled Dr. Scarborough.

"Daddy, I am here in Baby David's room," answered Mary Scarlet. "Come here and look at Baby David."

Dr. Scarborough came to Baby David's room, pulled a chair, and watched Mary Scarlet playing with their child.

"Do not get used to carrying the baby. He may get used to it and may expect to be carried every time you come near him," warned Dr. Scarborough.

"No, I am not spoiling him. I am just playing with him to show my love and attention to him," answered Mary Scarlet.

The full attention and care of Mary Scarlet to little David continued until he was thirteen years old. She wanted to take good care of all of David's needs. She would bring David to school and drive him back home. She would leave work and attend to whatever she had to do for David.

"David, my son, come on, let's work on your homework. I want you to be the best in your school," said Mary Scarlet.

"Yes, Ma, I am coming. I am just changing to something comfortable. I just came from school," answered David.

On weekends, Mary Scarlet would make their time together memorable. She would sit in the piano and play. She would call Dr. Scarborough and David to join her, and they would sing together love songs. After they got tired singing, Mary Scarlet would take Dr. Scarborough and David to their lawn, and they would eat their brunch, prepared by their housekeeper Anne, under the shade of the trees. Mary Scarlet wanted to make every moment she was with David and her husband memorable.

Growing up, David knew all the time how much he was loved by his mother. The first thing he would look for every time he woke up was his mother. When he needed something or anything, he would call his mother. For any decision he had to make, he had to consult his mother. His mother was the tutor who guided him in all his school needs. David was a mama's boy.

Mary Scarlet had been the light and life of the family. On Saturdays, she attended to all the needs of the family and would go out with Anne and Martha, not only to shop for all their needs, but also to take them out to give them a little break. When they came back, they would bring something for John. Sunday was church day for the family. From church Mary Scarlet would initiate to eat out with David and Dr. Frederick. In spring, she would make an early plan for their summer vacation, touring places here and abroad. Mary Scarlet was very busy doing everything for the happiness of her family.

One of the traditions of the family that Mary Scarlet started with David growing up was their unique celebration of Christmas. Just after Thanksgiving Day, Mary Scarlet would order John to install their family Christmas tree already. She would decorate the Christmas tree with the help of Anne and Martha. They would continue decorating the tree and the house in preparation for Christmas. Every time Mary Scarlet would come home, she would have a gift wrapped for somebody in the family, which she would put in a big red bag, then tied with a yellow string. She would do this several times until she had gifts for everyone already. The red bag would always be sitting under the Christmas tree. The night before Christmas, it would be very dark in the house, and at exactly twelve midnight, a loud alarm would wake up everybody. Then Mary Scarlet would run to the piano and play "Joy to the World." Everybody would wake up, and she would ask David to open the red bag and pour the contents to the floor. Mary would ask everybody to look for their name in the box. Then she would ask one by one to open their box. Mary Scarlet would then play "Hark! The Herald Angels Sing" and invite everybody to eat. Unlike during ordinary days, Mary Scarlet would require John, Anne, and Martha to sit with them at the Christmas Eve dining table.

One Christmas night after they had finished eating the midnight dinner, Mary Scarlet invited David to sing a Christmas song.

"Come on, son, I want you to sing for me a Christmas song. I love to hear your tenor voice. How about singing for me 'O Holy Night'?"

"OK, son, I will be listening too," followed Dr. Scarborough.

"OK, Ma, hit the key," said David.

David sang "O Holy Night" accompanied by his mom while his dad was listening. After he sang a few more Christmas songs, they decided to go to bed. But David, as he was getting ready to go to his room and put off the light, glanced at the window, and it was bright. He came close to the window and looked at the sky. He was so surprised that it was so bright, and yet there was no moon in the sky. He called the attention of his mother.

"Look, Ma, there is no moon that I can see, and yet the sky seems lighted with all the stars shining so bright. And look there is a shooting star!" David pointed to his mother.

"You know, they say that if you see a shooting star, make a wish, and what you wish will usually happen," explained Mary Scarlet to David.

"Oh, I did not know that. Anyway, it happened so quickly, I would have not thought of anything to wish."

One afternoon from work, on her way home, Mary Scarlet called Dr. Frederick to inform him that she had a taste for Italian cooking and had to pass a corner store along Pennsylvania Avenue.

"Hello, Frederick, I am going to pass by the corner store to buy some cheese and Italian herbs and spices. I may be a little bit late coming home."

"OK," answered Dr. Frederick. "I'll just head home from the hospital in a few minutes after I finish what I am doing."

As Mary Scarlet approached the door of the corner store, she was not aware that the store was being robbed, and before she could reach the door, the robber rushed out, which she tried to avoid. As she was standing by the door, surprised of what was happening, she decided not to go in and turned around to leave, but the robber fired a shot and hit her on the chest. The robber was shocked to hit Mary Scarlet because his intention was to fire a warning shot so that he would not be followed. He stood astonished when he saw Mary Scarlet fall to the ground. A police car just passing by witnessed what happened. The police officers apprehended the robber right away. Mary Scarlet was rushed to the hospital but was pronounced dead on arrival.

The news of the death of Mary Scarlet was like a ton of dynamites that exploded in the center of the home of the Scarborough family. The young David cried uncontrollably, and Dr. Frederick Scarborough was so shocked, he felt numb and could not speak a word. John, Anne, and Martha were so devastated that they felt lost. They loved Mary Scarlet so much. She was caring, loving, understanding, and motherly and attended to everything in the house, and suddenly without any warning or sign, she was gone.

The picture of Brutus Diablo, the criminal killer of Mary Scarlet, was published in the local paper, and David looked at the face so intensely and remembered almost every mark on his face—the scar under his left eye, the mole on the right nose, a birthmark between his eyes, thick lips, big nose, and the deformed right ear. For the young age of twenty-five, Brutus looked old—a sign that he must had so much criminal experiences. David, after looking intensely at the face of Brutus, crumpled the newspaper, tore it into pieces, and whispered, "When the day has come when our paths meet, I will crush your head. I will not give you a chance the way you did not give a chance to my mother."

*Watching the anguish of David who promised to avenge her death, Mary Scarlet decided to stay on earth until the inevitable meeting of David and her killer Brutus.*

**The front area of the Scarborough residence**

# Chapter II

## The Bully

AFTER THE DEATH of Mary Scarlet, David became depressed and felt alone. He totally missed his beloved mother. There were times when he would cry and would meditate on memorable moments he had with his mother. At school, he had been very quiet and seemed lost in his lessons. When he arrived home, he would look at the picture of his mother, and then he would cry silently and whisper, "Mom, I missed you. Why? Why do you have to die?"

From a very quiet young boy, he became so affected by the death of his mother. His behavior changed. He started pushing other kids on his way. He did the pushing to his classmate Bert Haynes. Bert, who understood the situation of David, said, "No, David, no! . . . I understand your situation, David. I could feel the anger in your heart because of the death of your mother. But please, be reasonable. You just have to move on, and don't take your anger on others."

Bert Haynes also warned their classmates of the change in the attitude of David because of the death of his mother and asked them to ignore him if he showed his tormenting attitude to them. When

David tried to intimidate and shoved some of his classmates, he got no response, and they just proceeded to where they were going.

David felt alone and seemed lost, when one day, he noticed a young boy running away. Their eyes accidentally met. He stood still and did nothing, but when he saw the young boy ran, it excited him. He remembered that that young boy was his classmate the year before in section I; he was moved to section II. The name of the young boy is Kevin Smith.

One morning, as David was coming to school, he accidentally met Kevin at the door of the school. "Kevin, why are you trying to avoid me? Why are you running away when you see me?"

"Nothing, David!" Then Kevin just walked past straight to his classroom.

One day, David saw Kevin alone in the hallway walking ahead of him. David walked past and pushed him on the back a little bit. Kevin ran to his classroom, and David was left alone, looking.

One time, David was standing in the school hallway when he saw Kevin coming. Kevin saw David standing, looking at him, so he turned around and walked out the door, then came back with other students and a teacher.

The relationship of David and Kevin was like that of a hunter and the hunted. David was enjoying running after Kevin. David did not know why Kevin was avoiding him, but all he knew was he got exited running after Kevin. David was so thrilled at the ability of Kevin to find a way to escape his chasing mood. It was like a game of hide-and-seek. But this came to a point when Kevin got tired of running away from David.

One afternoon, Kevin stayed later than usual as he had some questions on their lesson, so he had a conference with his teacher. On his way out, he stayed in a corner to check if David was still around. To his surprise, David came from his back and tapped him on his right shoulder. Kevin, so surprised at seeing David behind him, just ran and ran to the school bus, which was waiting for him in front of the school. David just laughed and laughed and did not follow Kevin.

One day, David was eagerly waiting to see Kevin. But there was no Kevin. Days became months, and there was no Kevin. Kevin got tired of being followed and transferred to another school. David missed Kevin so much.

One afternoon after class, David felt weak, tired, and not feeling well. He would normally go to the kitchen to get some snack, but this time he went straight to his bedroom. He lay down and fell asleep. In his sleep, he dreamt that he was walking in a path leading to a flowery garden. At the end of the path was a patio with a table and a chair. After appreciating the flowers around him, he sat on the chair and put both his hands on the table. He then heard the voice of his mother:

*"How are you David? What is going on? You seem tensed, and you bully to your classmates. You are not the same David I used to know and loved. I want to see the same David I used to love—happy, caring, and loving and a well-liked young boy. Be a good boy, David. Be a good boy. Be nice to everyone."*

David was about to answer when he was awakened by the sound of the grandfather clock. It was six o'clock. He heard the call of his father.

"David, come down. It is dinnertime."

"Yes, Dad, I am coming down in a minute," answered David. He stood up and walked to his study table and picked up the picture of his mother, looked at it intensely, and embraced it. Then he whispered, "Mom, I miss you. I love you." He slowly put down the picture on his study table and then proceeded down to the dinner table with his dad.

The words of David's mother in the dream changed his behavior and attitude toward life. He became friendly, welcoming, and well-focused on his studies. After the dream, the first thing he did was to apologize to Bert, who had been understanding of him all the time that he was struggling to let go his mother.

"Bert, I am very sorry for my behavior due to the death of my mother. I let go my emotion and should have lived my life the way my mother wanted me to live," David said to Bert, who was surprised with the tone of David's voice, expressing sincerity in his statement.

"It is OK, David. I very well understand your miserable feeling after the death of your mother. Let us move on," answered Bert.

That apologetic gesture of David was noticed by most of his classmates. Not only was he more friendly to everybody, but he was also very focused on his study. Because of his changed attitude, he got more friends who became very close to him until their high school graduation. They were Arthur Silver, Steven Cohen, and Vincent Brown. After their graduation ceremony, the five friends had the chance to get together and talked about their plans for the future.

"Hi, Steve, what are you planning to take in college?" asked Bert.

"I am planning to take medicine. How about you?" asked Steve to Bert in return.

"I think I am going to take up law," answered Bert.

"How about you, Art, what are you planning to take in college?" asked Bert.

"I am thinking of taking BSEE. I like to teach young children. I love teaching," answered Arthur.

"How about you, Vincent, what are planning to take in college?" asked Arthur as he turned toward Vincent.

"I think I will take engineering, maybe, electrical engineering. I like numbers, math, and physics," answered Vincent.

"How about you, David, what are your plans?" asked Vincent as he turned toward David.

"I am not sure yet. Right now all I want is to visit the grave of my mother with the hope that in some way she would give me some hints of what I have to do with my life," answered David.

Sunday after David's graduation, Dr. Frederick woke up early and went to David's room to tell him to get ready for church.

"David, dress up now," called Dr. Scarborough. "We might be late for the eight o'clock Mass. From church we still have to pick up a floral arrangement from a flower shop to bring to your mother's grave. We have to get some candles and offer prayers for your mother. Get ready."

"Yes, Dad, I am getting ready. I will be out in a second," answered David.

David and Dr. Scarborough went to the eight o'clock Mass, picked up the floral arrangement from the flower shop, bought some candles, then proceeded to Mary Scarlet's grave.

In front of Mary Scarlet's grave, David knelt and prayed and whispered, "Mom, I miss you. I will forever remember your guidance and the loving care you have shared with me during those days when we were together. You took care of me and wanted me to be a good boy and a good Christian. Your memories will always be with me in my heart. I love you, Mommy."

# Chapter III

## The Call for Duty

BEHIND THE SCARBOROUGH property was a wooded area with a path leading to the Potomac River. The distance of the trail from the property was around a mile. Along the trail were tall oak trees, pine trees, vines, and some white dogwood trees. Closer to the riverside were grassy areas, where deer could be seen grazing and running around.

It was one hot summer when David was wondering around their backyard when he noticed the tall gate and the tall concrete fence behind their backyard of fruit trees.

"Hi, John, what is this gate for, and why do we have a very tall fence with barbwires on the top of the fences in our backyard?" asked David to John, who was then busy sweeping the leaves under the apple trees.

"The gate could be opened and leads to the Potomac River. We have a tall and well-protected property fence because outside of this property are wild animals, like raccoons and groundhogs. Those wild animals are a nuisance, and you do not want them to enter here, or else everything here will be a mess. There are times during the weekend when I go out through that gate to go fishing in the river, but I always see to it that the gate is well closed to prevent those wild animals from coming in."

"Hey, John, let me go with you fishing one day. I want to experience how to catch fish. Please let me know when you will go fishing, and I will go with you."

"I'll let you know when I'll go fishing, but be sure to dress well, like long-sleeved shirts and long pants and rubber shoes. There are a lot of insects that bite, like mosquitoes, fleas, ticks, and even flies, they do bite. You also need a hat with a wide brim because it is hot near the water."

"Yes, John, let me know when you are going fishing, and I'll prepare for it."

Early morning after a couple of weeks, David and John went out to go fishing. John checked if everything of what he told David were all met. When all his requirements were all met, they started their way out to the gate.

"David, hold on to our hook and lines. I have to see to it that the gate is well secured before we go, to prevent those wild animals from going into our property."

"OK, John, I also got the bucket for our catch," answered David.

While on the way, David noticed a big animal hanging on a tree, looking at them.

"Hey, John, what is that big black animal climbing on that tree?" David asked John as he pointed to the animal climbing on the tree.

"That is raccoon. That is harmless. Just ignore it."

Then as David was looking down in the wooded area, he noticed a weird-looking animal.

"Hey, John, look, what is that weird-looking animal in the wooded area?"

"Oh, that is a groundhog," answered John. "Let me lead the way. There may be some snakes on the trail," commanded John to David.

"Go ahead, John, I'll be behind you," answered David.

As John and David walked the path coming closer to the river, on the left of the trail opened up a grassy area, where a herd of deer were grazing, which amazed David.

"Hey, John, look at that big deer. This is the first time I have seen a deer that big. It is as big as a cow. This is the first time I have seen a group of deer tamely roaming around," pointed David to John.

"Those deer are afraid of humans. They run away as soon as they feel the presence of humans around. But the bull would attack with its horn when it is cornered, for self-defense," declared John to David.

When they reached the side of the river, John assigned David a spot, showed him how to put the bait in the hook of the fishing line, and taught him how to throw the line and how to remove the catch from the hook to be placed in the bucket. John did not leave David until he had a catch. He watched him handle the catch, put back the bait, and throw the line back to the river.

"OK, David, you know now how to fish with the hook and line. Yell at me when you caught the fourth one. We do not want to catch too much. We have to do this just for fun. We have to catch only the amount we can eat."

When David caught the fourth catfish, he yelled at John. By then John had already caught four catfish.

"Hey, John, I have already caught four big ones. I am set!" yelled David to John.

"Good, David, we are set. We can head home. I have also caught four big catfish. We are going early."

John and David headed home. When they reached home, John dug a hole of one foot wide by two feet long and one foot deep under an apple tree.

"John, what are you going to do with the hole on the ground?" asked David.

"The water that we used to clean our catch and their parts, like gills and fins, we have to bury them so they will not invite flies and other insects and at the same time serve as fertilizer to the plants."

John showed and demonstrated how to clean the fish—removing the fins, gills, and internal organ of each fish; rubbing each fish with salt to remove the slime of catfish; washing the fish; and then salting and peppering them and letting them stay for thirty minutes before grilling. He then showed him how to grill the fish using the charcoal grill.

"The first thing we have to do before we can start the fire is to collect small twigs and dry leaves of trees because they burn quickly. Then you put the charcoal on top of the pile when the fire is building up. When the charcoal is starting to burn, you help the spread of the heat in the charcoal by fanning using a cardboard. Continue fanning until most of the charcoal is burning. Then you can put the fish on the grill one at a time," John said to David as he continued showing the process of grilling.

When they finished grilling all the fish, they invited Anne and Martha for a backyard picnic. This pastime of David and John continued every summer vacation, and john always looked forward doing it.

It was a hot summer after David's graduation from high school. David and John had just returned from their fishing venture at the Potomac River when Martha approached them.

"David, you have a mail," said Martha as she was approaching David.
"Who would send me a mail?" questioned David to Martha.
"It looks like the letter is from the U.S. Army," answered Martha.

David opened the letter, and he was surprised when he read the letter.
"Wow, I am asked to report for military duty. I am drafted by the U.S. Army."
When Dr. Scarborough arrived that evening, David right away talked to his dad about his call for military service in the U.S. Army.
"Hi, Dad, I received a letter from the U. S. Army. I am asked to report to the U. S. Army enlistment office as soon as possible. I am drafted by the U.S. Army, Dad," explained David to his dad as the latter came to the door.
"That is still a long process, David. You have still to undergo physical and medical examinations. You will undergo training. Who knows, you may not even pass the screening test. Do not worry. Just report to the U. S. Army. Present yourself and see what happens," answered Dr. Scarborough.

The following day, David went to the draft office of the U. S. Army along Fourteenth Street, NW, Washington DC, and presented the letter. He was given personal and biological forms to complete.
"Mr. Scarborough, please complete the forms. Sign and return the forms to me," instructed by the desk officer.
"Yes, sir, thank you," responded David.

After David completed the forms, he handed them to the desk clerk.

"Sir, I have already completed the forms," said David to the desk clerk. The desk clerk looked through the completed forms and instructed David to have a seat and wait to be called.

"This looks good. Have a seat and wait for your name to be called." After thirty minutes of waiting, an officer came out of the door.

"Mr. David Scarborough!" called the officer as he looked at the form clipped on a lectern.

"Yes, sir, that is me," answered David.

"Please come follow me," instructed by the officer.

David was led to an interview room, and in the room the officer offered his hand for a handshake.

"I am Sergeant Green. How are you doing?" asked the officer to David. "I am doing fine, sir, and ready for whatever you want me to do."

"OK, Mr. Scarborough, let's go through your personal and bio data." The officer went thought David's personal and bio data. He asked some confirming questions and then explained what to expect in the military life. The officer emphasized that he was called to serve his country and he must be ready for the rigid and rigorous training to prepare him to become a good soldier.

"OK, Mr. Scarborough, if you have no more questions, I would like to hand this order to you to report for the U. S. Armed forces physical examination. Take this form to our U. S. Army hospital along Independence Street, NW, at the Selective Service Section. Be there tomorrow morning at 8:00 AM. The guard will show you the way as soon as you get into the U. S. Army hospital," instructed by the officer to David.

"Great! I'll be there first hour in the morning," answered David.

"Good luck," responded the officer to David.

"Thank you, sir," answered David as he turned around and headed to the door.

The following morning, David went to the U. S. Army military hospital for a physical examination. He passed the physical examination and was ordered to report for induction to military service in the U. S. Army. But before he reported for military duty, he talked to everybody in his family.

"Hi, Dad, I am ready to serve our country. I'll write and send you a message of what is going on," said David as hc looked at his dad.

"Take care, David, I will pray for you. Be careful and always pray," responded Dr. Scarborough.

"John, Anne, and Martha, I'll miss you all. I'll see you when I come back from my military duty," said David to John, Anne, and Martha. Then David headed to the door, where an army jeep was waiting. He waved his hand as the jeep drove away.

After the induction to the military, David was ordered to claim his military supplies and gun for training.

"Soldier, you follow the line to claim your military supplies, uniform, and rifle and ammunition," a military officer commanded David.

"Yes, sir," responded David.

David was then assigned the barracks for his lodging, and in that barracks he met two new recruits, Andrew Keller and Josh Darren. They became very close friends as they belonged to the same unit and the same squad. Being in the same squad, they drilled together, trained together, and underwent rigorous military training together. The three excelled in the firing range as marksmen and sharpshooters and developed mentally and physically as perfect soldiers, ready to face adversity and whatever the training would bring them. The three, after passing all military physical and mental tests, were transferred to Special Forces training. They had snipers training, hand-to-hand battle, and underwater resistance—swimming under and over the water in cold and warm streams and in both calm waters and those with a strong current. The three were ready for whatever challenges, hardships, or any mission they have to face in the line of duty as soldiers.

# Chapter IV

## The Fall of Bataan

FROM THE SAN Diego Military Base, David, Andrew, and Josh boarded a transport ship carrier going to the Philippines. As they journeyed through the Pacific Ocean, they enjoyed watching the vastness of the great blue ocean and watched the beauty of sunrises and sunsets as they moved closer to their destination. They were surprised with the beauty and grandeur of the Philippines as they came closer to the shore of Subic Bay in Olongapo, Zambales, Philippines. The military boat of the navy transported them to the shore, and they were greeted by military officers and led to their military quarters for briefings. That evening as they were walking around the base, Andrew invited David and Josh to check what they can see outside the base.

"Hi, guys, let's have some drink outside the base. I heard there are some clubs that are open late nights," Andrew suggested to David and Josh.

"OK, let's go, let's paint the night red," was the simultaneous answer of David and Josh.

"Hey, taxi!" called Andrew to a passing empty cab. "Please take us to one of the bars outside the base. We just want to have a good time."

The three hopped into the taxicab and proceeded outside the base to have a good time. They were taken by the taxi driver to the Bay View Night Life and Bar. They went in and were received at the door by a waiter, and they were assigned a table.

"Can I take your order now, sirs?" asked the waiter as the three were seated comfortably around the table.

David answered, "Please give us three beers to start with and a serving of peanuts, thank you."

"Do you want to order some food?" followed up by the waiter.

"No, thank you," answered David.

The three had just three sets of beers and two servings of peanuts when a trouble started between two military men who probably had too much to drink. The two started fighting. When the other guys who were trying to stop the fight also got hit, the rumble started, and everybody started hitting anybody. David, Andrew, and Josh started their move to the door, and they were hitting anybody on the way. They got hit too, but they finally were able to get out of the door, and as they were walking out and heading to the boardwalk, several U.S. military police arrived and entered the bar.

"Wow, that was crazy. Our first night of outing was a rumble," said David. "Well, don't complain. We had free drinks and free snacks," answered Andrew.

"Where are we heading?" asked Josh.

"We are just going for a walk along the boardwalk, and we will head back to our station," answered David.

The following day, the three were back to their military drills, the firing range, and practice of hand-to-hand combat. The routine went on for weeks, then months, with military activities and having fun going to bars and clubs at night.

One evening, the three friends decided to go out and have fun and had a couple of drinks. On the way, inside the taxicab, Andrew started talking about having fun—not only to have a drink but to get a girl for the night. In the bar, they started drinking, and after a few drinks, Andrew stood up and invited David and Josh to go out for a walk to get some fresh breeze from the bay.

"Well, I think I will try to have fun. I'll get a girl and go to that hotel nearby. Would you like to join me?" insinuated Andrew to the two.

"I'll join you, Andrew," responded Josh.

"No, I'll just walk around and wait for you here at the boardwalk," answered David.

The two went ahead and picked up some girls and brought them to the nearby hotel, while David remained walking in the boardwalk, thinking more of his mother and the home he left, which he loved so dearly. He thought of the good time he had with John and the backyard cooking he had with Anne and Martha, with John providing the fire. It was already very late when the two came back to meet David. They then headed to their barracks to rest.

Then came the most unexpected and unnerving news—the Pearl Harbor was bombed by the Japanese, and World War II began. With the destruction of Pearl Harbor, their unit was ordered to be transported to Bataan to be the front defense of Manila against the invading Japanese. Their unit was assigned in the front line in Mariveles, Bataan, overlooking Manila Bay. They dug foxholes to protect themselves from the possible bombing of the Japanese. It was a beautiful sunny morning, calm, and the front line was very quiet. Then around noontime, they heard the sound of a thousand fighter planes coming to their area, heading toward the city of Manila. These were the planes they had to intercept and stop. Before the planes came closer to their site, the firepower of the Filipino and American soldiers started. Some fighter planes flying low got hit. Andrew, who was firing his .50-caliber machine gun, with Josh feeding the cartridge of bullets, got excited.

"Come on, come on, I'll kill you all!" Andrew yelled with emotion. "Take it easy, Andrew, this is going to be a long fight. We have to reserve our energy," advised Josh. But the more Josh reminded Andrew, the more he became aggressive, and he picked up the .50-caliber machine gun, stood up, and ran toward the firepower of the Japanese.

"Andrew, Andrew, come back. Come back, you are going to be killed. Take cover!" yelled David to Andrew.

Andrew did not hear the yell of David because of the loud exchange of firepower between the Japanese and the Filipino American defense units. Andrew got hit and killed by the firepower of a Japanese fighter plane machine gun flying low, visualizing the location of the defending soldiers beneath those trees dug in deep foxholes that were covered with net and grass along the Bataan ridges.

David picked up the .50-caliber machine gun dropped by Andrew and ran firing toward the edge of Manila Bay. He fired at the coming Japanese boats that were ready to land on the shore, killing them all. Some boats started to retreat when they were met by bullets, and David saw to it that none of those small landing boats could come back to their mother ship. He finished them all until he ran out of bullets with his .50-caliber machine gun. He was on his way to his foxhole, when waves of fighter planes came and started bombing their position. A bomb hit the foxhole where Josh was hiding. He was killed instantly. David was on his way to the foxhole but just missed the bomb that was dropped as he was going back to get more ammunition.

David dropped to his knees in disbelief; two of his best friends, who had been the vital part of his military life, were both gone. With so much emotion, he could not hold his tears coming from his eyes. It was the first time he experienced such feeling of loneliness from his friends that for so long had been like brothers to him. He carried the dead body of Andrew and put it together with the dead body of Josh in the foxhole. He loaded his .50-caliber machine gun and started firing to any fighter plane that flew low to their area. He would celebrate after hitting and downing planes.

Day and night, David, alone, tirelessly fought for the sake of his two friends until he ran out of ammunition. Tired and hungry, he just leaned back in the foxhole and closed his eyes. Then there was complete silence. No more firing. Nothing could be heard, and everybody who might have survived just waited for something to happen. Then there was the order of surrender. Everybody was ordered to come out and surrender to the Japanese.

David arranged the burial of his two friends. He put the dead bodies of Andrew and Josh side by side and covered them with dirt. He made two crosses out of branches of trees and stacked them on the graves of the two. He hung their dog tags on each cross. He then staked the rifles of Andrew and Josh with the barrels to the ground and butts pointed to the sky, then put their helmets on the butts of the rifles. He then knelt down and said his prayers. After saying his prayers, David just sat down and meditated on the good times that the three of them enjoyed together. After a while, he grabbed a handful of dust and showered the dust onto the graves of the two soldiers, who had been like brothers to him since their military training began. He then stood in front of the two crosses and the rifles bearing their helmets. He stood straight and gave two respectful salutes to honor his buried friends as a gesture of good-bye. He turned his back from the grave and headed to the open field to surrender to the Japanese.

# Chapter V

## The Daring Escape

APRIL 9, 1942, the rays of the morning sun were peeping through the leaves of the trees in the vast peninsula of Mariveles, Bataan, overlooking the Manila Bay, when David started his journey to the open field to surrender to the Japanese soldiers. David, who was emotionally drained because of the death of his two closes friends, was so surprised of the number of Filipino and American soldiers who survived after the constant bombing and machine gun firepower of the low-flying Japanese fighter planes. When David arrived in the open, he noticed over seventy-five thousand Filipino and American soldiers surrendering to the Japanese—a ratio of ten Filipino and American soldiers to one Japanese soldier—who were busy harassing the helpless surrendering prisoners of war. They were showing off that they were powerful men with their guns and fixed bayonets, ready to kill whoever would commit an unnecessary or provocative move.

Lt. Gen. Masaharu Homma, who was the Japanese highest commanding officer, discovered that there were more prisoners of war than he had anticipated, and he had no means of transporting the prisoners by truck to their holding point at San Fernando, Pampanga.1 He decided that the only way he could get the prisoners to the concentration camp was to make them march the seventy- to eighty-mile distance from Mariveles, Bataan, to San Fernando, Pampanga. Lt. Gen. Masaharu Homma called all his officers and ordered them, "We do not have enough trucks to transport all these many prisoners. Form them into a single file and have them march from here to our concentration camp in San Fernando, Pampanga. Any problem prisoners, kill them. Understand?" ( "Wareware wa, subete no korera no ōku no shūjin o yusō suru no ni jūbun'na torakku o motte iru tan'itsu no fairu ni sorera o keisei shi, karera o koko kara San Ferunando, Panpamga, shūjin no izure no mondai de watashitachi no kyōsei shūyōsho ni kōshin shite inai, karera o korosu. Wakaru?")

The helpless prisoners of war were asked to line up single file under the guard of the vicious Japanese soldiers showing off their brutality. With the signal from Lt. Gen. Masaharo Homma, the death march of the Filipino and American prisoners of war began.

David was holding very well for the first day of marching toward the concentration camp, but the following morning at around eleven o'clock, just ahead of him were around thirty prisoners of war who attempted to fill their canteens on the side of the road from the water buffalos' bath canal. As the men were filling up their canteens, the Japanese set up machine guns and fired at them, killing all of them like dogs. After around three hours of that incident, ahead of David was a Filipino prisoner who was trying to get some clean drinking water, but he was shot without provocation. A little later on, as David walked following the line of prisoners, one Filipino soldier just fell to the ground in exhaustion, was bayoneted, shot, and beheaded by a Japanese soldier with his samurai sword.

The second day of the march, David was still holding on very well, but at around 2:00 PM, he was starting to feel weak and a little dizzy and hungry, and the torturous temperate heat was becoming unbearable to him, but he kept on going on because he knew what would happen to him if he fell down; he would be killed. Around 4:00 PM, David just felt so weak, his knees started to buckle, and he just rolled down on the road helplessly. From a distance, a Japanese soldier saw him fell down and ran toward him with a fixed bayonet, ready for the kill. David saw the Japanese coming toward him, but he was so helpless to do anything. He could not even stand. He just closed his eyes and waited for his painful death, then lost consciousness.

*(The spirit of Mary Scarlet was watching the fall of David and the charging Japanese soldier with the fixed bayonet on his gun, pointed toward the direction of David for the kill. The spirit of Mary Scarlet put a stone on the path of the Japanese soldier, which caused him to trip up and stumble. The Japanese soldier fell forward chest down, then stood up and continued his attempted attack on David but . . .)*

A few yards before the Japanese could reach David, one tall American snatched David from the ground and carried him on his shoulder and whispered to himself, "No American soldier shall be left behind."

The Japanese just scratched his head in disbelief; he thought he could have another victim. The American soldier kept on walking with David sleeping on his shoulders, across his back, behind his head.

At around 6:00 PM, David woke up and regained consciousness. He tapped the shoulder of the brave American and told him to bring him down.

"Hi, soldier, I am OK now, please put me down. I feel better after I had a good rest. Thank you very much," said David to the American soldier.

"As an American soldier, it is my duty to save you." The soldier continued walking to follow the march. Then without looking, he instructed David to listen. "Now, soldier, you listen to me very carefully. It is getting dark. Look at that wooded area to our left just ahead of us. The guards are a little far from us. We have to walk innocently until we come close to that wooded area. You follow me. We will escape from this death march. Do you read me?"

"Yes, I read you," answered David in a very low tone of his voice.

When they came close to the wooded area, the two ran to it, and because it was starting to become dark, no Japanese soldier noticed their escape. Without the knowledge of David and the American soldier, two Filipino soldiers followed their escape. After an hour of running and walking into the woods, one Filipino solder shouted, "Soldiers, that is not the right way! That is going to the bay. Come and follow us."

David and his companion soldier followed the Filipino soldiers. It was almost midnight when they reached a small farmhouse in the middle of a field.

The Filipino officer told the three to stay put and that he would check around the house just to be safe. He walked around the house, then entered the rear and came out in front.

"The house is empty. You can come up," instructed the Filipino officer.

When they were in the house, the Filipino officer instructed them to each take a corner and rest.

"OK, guys, we will rest here for tonight. Take your corners, and tomorrow we will look for food. It is too dark and dangerous to be out this time of the night."

The following morning, the two Filipino soldiers left very early to look for food. David and the American soldier were left still sleeping. David was the first one to wake up of the two. He stood up and was about to walk to the door to look for the two Filipino soldiers when something caught his eyes—the name tag of the American soldier and his dog tag on his chest. It read, "Cpl. Kevin Smith, United States Marine." David could not believe it. The guy whom he bullied in high school was the one who saved his life. David knelt at the side of Kevin and woke him up. Kevin was so surprised of the behavior of David kneeling before him as he was waking up. As Kevin sat down, David hugged him with tears in his eyes.

"Thank you, Kevin, for saving my life. I am David, the bad boy when we were still very young. I am very sorry for my attitude then. I am very sorry."

"David, forget it. We are here together for the call of duty. We are here shoulder to shoulder to fight for our country," answered Kevin.

Not long after they have shaken hands, the two Filipino soldiers arrived with fruits for their breakfast. They had ripe papaya, a bunch of ripe bananas, ripe guavas, and young coconuts.

"OK, good that both of you are already awake. I am Capt. Joseph Lee of the Philippine Army, and this is Lt. Alex Torres. He is with me in the same unit."

"I am David Scarborough of the U.S. Army. Just call me David."

"I am Kevin Smith of the U.S. Marines. Just call me Kevin."

Capt. Joseph Lee was 5'10", 170 pounds; Alex Torres was 5'8", 150 pounds; David Scarborough was 6'1", 180 pounds; while Kevin Smith was 6'4", 195 pounds.

"OK, let's eat our breakfast. There is a little table in the kitchen. There is also a knife and bolo we can use to open the papaya and the young coconut for water. You see in a war like this, you have to get used to any kind of food to survive," said Capt. Joseph Lee.

The four ate together in the little kitchen and consumed everything, having nothing to eat for several days.

"OK, we are heading to Mount Mariveles from here. We will form a guerilla unit to fight against the Japanese. We will recruit some capable young Filipino volunteers, and we will train them to be good soldiers ready to fight for our freedom. Are you going to join us?" asked Captain Lee to David and Kevin.

"Absolutely," said Kevin. "We are here for the ride."

"Yes, we are here together. We will fight against the brutality of those Japanese soldiers," followed up David.

"OK, we will take these bolo and knife with us. We may use these in cutting something," said Captain Lee.

The four started their journey toward the mountain, when along the way Captain Joseph got reminded of somebody he knew in the area.

"I know of a barrio captain in this area. Let's go and pay him a visit."

After a one-hour walk, they came to a wooden house in the middle of a field surrounded by vegetable plants and a well-cared-for garden. There was a dog howling, and chickens were running around.

"Hello, anybody home!" yelled Capt. Joseph Lee.

A man came out, wondering who were calling. When he saw Capt. Joseph Lee, he right away came down and greeted them.

"Hi, Joe, good that you were able to come by. I have not seen you for years.

How can I help you? Come in. It is almost lunch now. We will eat together.

You just have to pardon me. We still have to cook." Then he yelled to his wife, "Bertha, we have visitors. Prepare the table!"

Captain Joseph Lee was a close friend of Antonio, the son of Mang Pedro, when they were classmates in Manila. He used to visit the family when they were studying together. His son was killed in an accident while in the middle of the farm tending his cow, caught by strong rain and was hit by lightning.

Captain Lee introduced David, Kevin, and Alex to Mang Pedro and to Aling Bertha. Mang Pedro invited the four to the living room and asked permission to go to the kitchen to butcher a chicken. Aling Bertha prepared the dressed chicken and boiled water for the parts of the chicken for their soup, with young papaya and pepper leaves. Some parts of the chicken were fried and were served with rice on the side. They had a good lunch together in the little dining area. Then they headed again to the living room for a heart-to-heart conversation.

"Mang Pedro, we came here to ask for your help. I know as barrio captain in this area, you are very influential to your community. We need some volunteers to train with us to form a guerilla unit to fight against the Japanese," explained Captain Lee to Mang Pedro.

"Yes, I have heard of the cruelty of those Japanese soldiers. We really have to do something. You all stay here tonight, while I go around and recruit some volunteers. OK, agreed?"

"Yes, Mang Pedro. Thank you very much for your help," answered Captain Lee.

That night, while the four were staying in the house, Mang Pedro went around the barrio and looked for some able young volunteers who can be trained as fighters. He explained to them the purpose why they were being recruited. Mang Pedro was able to recruit twenty able men. And he invited them to come to his house to meet with Captain Lee. Mang Pedro butchered a goat and cooked the meat using their native recipe called spicy *caldereta* and then served the men with their local wine called *tuba*.

Mang Pedro introduced the twenty volunteers to Captain Lee, David, Kevin, and Alex.

"Let me introduce to you our men volunteers, from left to right. This is Simon, then Andrew, Jim, Juan, Felipe, Roberto, Tomas, Martin, Jun, Ted, Patrick, Pablo, Victor, Angelo, Diego, Carlos, Julian, Marco, Daniel, and Isaac."

Captain Lee explained to the recruits that they would be trained as guerillas to fight the Japanese to serve the country.

"Tomorrow when you come back here, be ready to come with us to the mountain. Have an extra shirt and extra pants. Have a sharp knife and a bolo. You will need those for your training. Be sure that the knife that you will bring is pointed and very sharp. If you have horses, we will need them to carry our things. Also if you have ropes and some threads and big needles, take them with you. We will need them in the camp. Do you have any questions?" asked Captain Lee.

"No, sir," answered simultaneously by the group.

Everybody had a good time eating together and drinking together. When the party was over, the recruits left. Captain Lee with David, Kevin, and Alex stayed overnight in the house of Mang Pedro.

"Thank you very much, Mang Pedro, for your help. Now we can proceed with our plan. We will head to the mountain tomorrow and train there our new recruits," uttered Captain Lee as an expression of appreciation, while David, Kevin, and Alex were just listening and just nodding their heads.

"I have a couple of goats you can take with you and a pig. That will at least help you to start with. You may just as well bring a sack of rice and some chickens. Good luck to your journey," said Mang Pedro.

"Thank you again, Mang Pedro," responded Captain Lee. "By the way, Mang Pedro, do you still have some shirts and pants of Antonio that I can have? I do not have any shirt to change clothes," asked Captain Lee.

"Oh yes, I still have some shirts and pants of Antonio that you can wear. You are of the same size as Antonio. Let me get them for you," answered Mang Pedro.

"Also, Mang Pedro, my two American friends with us also have no clothing to change into. Do you have any that you can spare for them?" asked Captain Lee.

"Oh yes, I have a couple of big and tall shirts and pants I bought from the GI store, which I was then intending to repair for hunting. I can give them to you for their use. You can also spare some extra shirts and pants of Antonio to Alex, OK? Let me get them now," answered Mang Pedro.

Mang Pedro got the shirts and pants left by Antonio and the shirts and pants that he bought from the GI store and handed them all to Captain Lee. Captain Lee put them aside to pick them up in the morning when they were ready to depart for Mount Mariveles.

The following morning, the four woke up very early to prepare for their journey. After they have eaten their breakfast, they put the pig in a sack and secured the two goats with a long rope to be tagged along. They tied the legs of the chickens together, and they just carried them by hand. Then they waited for the arrival of the recruits. They were so pleased to see that the recruits had two horses with them. Mang Pedro offered his cart to load the rice and pig, goat, and chickens for their long journey. They hooked the cart to one of the horses. Then Capt.

Joseph Lee accounted for the men that would be in his command in forming his planned guerilla unit in Mount Mariveles.

Mang Pedro and Aling Bertha were standing near the stairs of their house watching the crew as they prepared for departure, loading the animals in the cart and other things they have to bring with them in their journey. When all the things were ready and the crew was set to go, Captain Lee turned around to the couple and hugged them and then bid good-bye.

"Mang Pedro and Aling Bertha, thank you for everything. Thank you for your hospitality, for all the things you gave us and for sharing to us the comfort of your home," said Captain Lee to the couple.

David and Kevin likewise approached Mang Pedro and Aling Bertha and shook hands with them and expressed their thanks for the accommodation they have shared with them.

David and Kevin noticed an excellent display of leadership of Capt. Joseph Lee, who expressed himself with calmness and control of what he wanted to do. He demonstrated a characteristic of a well-trained officer ready to lead. David and Kevin knew they were in good hands.

(1) Bataan Death March (Wikipedia, the free encyclopedia)

# Chapter VI

## The Journey to Mount Mariveles

IT WAS A bright sunny morning. The group was preparing all the things they have to carry on their long journey to Mount Mariveles, when Angelo and Diego approached Captain Lee, David, Kevin, and Alex.

"I have to take with me my wife, Maria, so that she can help us at least to do some cooking. She is safer with me than to be left alone in our house, most especially with the coming of the Japanese to our province. We also brought with us a wok and a big pot for our cooking and some coconut shells we can use as serving dinner plates in the mountain," said Angelo.

"I also have my wife, Ana, with me to help us in the camp. She can give us a hand on anything. She is safer with me than to be left alone in the farm. We also brought with us two big pots for cooking," said Diego.

"That's great. The more hand we have, the better. We need help on anything. We will let the two women ride the cart, and all of us men will have to walk," answered Captain Lee.

"Sir, is it OK to bring my guitar?" asked Daniel.

"It is fine. You take it with you to the mountain," answered Captain Lee.

Captain Lee turned around to face Mang Pedro and Aling Bertha.

"Mang Pedro and Aling Bertha, we have to go. We still have a long journey to Mount Mariveles. Thank you very much for everything, for the accommodation, food, and for the help in finding volunteers. We have a lot of work to do forming our guerilla group to fight the Japanese regime," said Captain Lee to the couple.

Captain Lee extended his hand to shake hands with the couple, then gave them a hug. David, Kevin, and Alex did the same, expressing gratitude for the good dealing the couple had accorded them. The group moved on, waving their hands as they departed, heading to Mount Mariveles.

On the trail going to the mountain, in a remote area on their way, the horns of a water buffalo were caught between the branches of trees and vines. The poor animal was trying to get loose, but the only thing it can do was growl. Simon volunteered to untangle the animal. He first tied the horn of the animal in a way he could rig or control the animal's movement. Then with his bolo, he removed the tree branches and vines that were holding the head of the poor buffalo. Everyone was watching what Simon was doing. Juan and Pablo came to help clear the entanglement of the poor animal. Simon rode the water buffalo, locally called "carabao," and they all moved on going to Mount Mariveles.

On their trail, David noticed something in the grassy side of the path a little away from their trail, an anaconda swallowing a big animal that it just constricted and killed.

"Hey, Captain Lee, what is that thing in that corner near that tree. It looks like a big snake eating something big," asked David.

"Watch out, that is not a snake. That is an anaconda, a boa swallowing a big wild pig. Don't come too close to the animal. You may get into trouble," answered Captain Lee.

Captain Lee leading the way noticed a little ahead of them some banana trees bearing fruits.

"Hey, Angelo, would you please get at least two bunches of banana fruits that are matured? We can eat them in the camp. Diego, will you help Angelo, and you may as well get some banana flowers. Cut whatever you can carry," instructed Captain Lee to Angelo and Diego. The other members of the crew also followed Angelo and looked for what they could bring to the camp for food. After a while, the group was able to get some young bamboo shoots, green papayas, root crops, banana flowers, mushrooms, and some yellow squash (*calabasa* in Filipino) from a vacant farm and loaded them all into the cart hauled by a horse.

As they came closer to the foot of the mountain, Captain Lee noticed some guava trees along the trail. He led everybody to get leaves to put into their pockets, which can be boiled as tea. They also grabbed some fruits and ate them on their way to the foot of the mountain.

As they were coming close to the foot of Mount Mariveles, they noticed a group of deer grazing around, and when the animals heard them, they just disappeared into the wild.

"Wow, it looks like I'll enjoy it here. We can have some hunting to keep us busy," said David.

"No, David. We are here to train and form a guerilla unit strong and capable of fighting the well-equipped Japanese Army," interjected Captain Lee.

"You are right. I am just carried away of the things I am seeing," answered David.

The group started climbing the slope of Mount Mariveles until they reached the fresh running water of the Papaya River.

**Picture of the section of Papaya River, courtesy of Amado Avelino**

"OK, guys, this is where we are going to camp. There is a clean supply of water here and plain surface, where we can build shades for our shelter. We will have our kitchen near the river for easy access to the water. The water here is drinkable, clean, and no impurities coming from the falls from up the mountain. This will be our camping area, but our training area will be up the mountain in the Tarak Ridge. Now let's begin working. Maria, Ana, Angelo, and Diego, the four of you can start cooking for all of us. You can start with the chicken and rice we brought. Cook them the way you know. OK?" instructed Captain Lee.

The group started collecting materials for building their shelters—bamboo, woods, and palm leaves for their roofing and shades. They cleared the area, then started putting their structures together. They built several little shelters with floorings because there were scorpions and snakes crawling most especially at night. It did not take long for them to complete their temporary shelters as they were working together. Their first day was very rewarding. They accomplished a lot of things. They ate together on an improvised table made of bamboo and felt like they were having fun having a picnic together. They had a small bonfire in the middle of their camp to give light and also to drive away mosquitoes and other biting insects. After that long journey, everyone fell asleep early and soundly except Captain Lee, David, Kevin, and Alex. They had to plan how they would do the training. They were all military soldiers and trained well, but they have to put together a good plan that would be suited to the new recruits they have to train.

While the four of them were seated around the bonfire planning what they had to do the following day to start their training, David cracked the questions to Captain Lee.

"Captain Lee, how and where did you get training? You seem to know almost everything we need to do. You are always in command of the situation. You have a very good sense of direction, even locating this very remote area. You have that sense of anticipation of what to come and what to prepare for. I am amazed of your display of leadership. You are calm, and yet you are in control."

"I grew up in Mainland China with my grandfather Chong Lee. He taught me physical, mental, and spiritual control of myself. My grandfather was a master in our native martial arts. He trained me in my very young age so that when I grow up I'll be ready to face the world. When my father Bing and mother Wu immigrated to the Philippines, they took me with them. Together with them I became a Filipino citizen. They sent me to a Chinese school in Binondo, Manila, but after a year I transferred to a parochial school so that I could learn more the native language and the culture. It was in the parochial school where I met Father Francis Montemayor. He baptized me to become Catholic and gave me the name Joseph. My original name was Song Lee, and now I am Joseph S. Lee. After graduation from high school, I qualified to enter the Philippine Military Academy. That institution is similar to your West Point. I belong to the 1936 graduates of the Philippine Military Academy. I learned mapping and military tactics in the PMA."

"Wow, you have a long journey from Mainland China to the Philippines.

A very long and interesting story of your life," responded Kevin.

"That's why I keep on following him," Alex followed up.

"Well, we better go to sleep now. We have a long day tomorrow. We have to start very early because it is hot at the ridge. Good night," said Captain Lee.

The four went to sleep with the anticipation of the big day they were facing the following day. What was the condition of the training ground, and how would they start the basic training leading to advance guerilla tactics? There were lots of questions in their minds as they went to sleep.

# Chapter VII

## The Guerilla Training

IT WAS FOUR o'clock in the morning. Angelo, Diego, Maria, and Ana woke up early to prepare the group breakfast. They boiled the guava leaves to make tea and boiled bananas for their breakfast. At around five o'clock, Capt. Joseph Lee woke up everybody to get something to eat and to prepare to head up to their training area at the Tarak Ridge. Diego volunteered to go with the group to train. Each member of the training crew prepared the bamboo node water container for a long day's work up the ridge. At six o'clock, Joe led the group up the top of the mountain to the Tarak Ridge. On the way there were fallen trees along the trail, which they have to clear. Some ground lizards were jumping and running from the trails to the woods. They were very careful as they moved up for fear of any venomous snakes or constrictors hanging on the trees as they followed the trail up to the Tarak Ridge. It was already 7:00 AM when they reached the ridge. It took them longer than they expected because they had to clear their way going up the mountain so that the next time they come up, it would be an easy climb.

**A picture of the section of Tarak Ridge, courtesy of Amado Avelino**

The first day in the Tarak Ridge was spent more on clearing. They cleared one hectare of land and removed any possible objects that might cause accidents or somebody getting hurt. They removed stones and sharp objects that might cause injury during the training. They selected to clear the grassy area for their tumbling and other military exercises. It took them one day just to prepare and clear the area for training. It was late afternoon when they finished clearing without eating their lunch. They headed down to their hideout very tired and hungry.

While the group was busy in the clearing of the Tarak Ridge training ground, Angelo butchered a goat, cleaned and cut the meat into pieces, and gave them to Maria and Ana for cooking. They spread the skin of the goat to dry for future use. While Maria and Ana were cooking the meat of the goat and the rice, Angelo made a bow and arrow using a matured split bamboo trunk. He wanted to go hunting while the other members of the group were training up at the Tarak Ridge.

The first day of training was very demanding to test the stamina and resistance of each of the members of the crew. Everyone including Captain Lee, David, Kevin, and Alex ran ten miles. They all ran together to see who would be able to complete the course. Then each was required to jump over five feet high to develop the ability and to have grace while jumping. They all rolled over the training course and practiced how to fall with soft landing. The training went on for a week. Then Joe, David, Kevin, and Alex made the evaluation of the group as to who among the twenty could qualify to be trained as Silent Killers.

Based on speed, agility, stamina, and resistance, six out of twenty volunteers were reassigned to a different guerilla assignment. Victor and Carlos were assigned as lookouts. Julian, Marco, and Daniel were assigned as guards. Felipe and Diego as reserved back up, with Diego helping Angelo in the kitchen. Captain Lee became closer and confident with David, who had been calm and in control and was a better communicator, while Kevin was bold, aggressive, but more secretive.

After the selection of the possible members of the Silent Killers Squad, they took a break from training in preparation for the things they needed in operations. They had to mend shoes from the skin of a goat or a sheep, with carabao skin as the sole. They had to dye their shirts, pants, and bandanas black. They had to sharpen their knives as sharp as razor. The twelve selected volunteers including the two back-ups, Joe, David, Kevin, and Alex took no time preparing for their needs. It was Captain Lee who showed them how to make the shoes. Alex led in helping them dye their uniforms black so that they would not be seen at night. While everybody was very busy preparing their attires, Captain Lee sat down with Victor and Carlos of what to do as lookouts, to do the surveillance of the towns close to Mount Mariveles and familiarize them with paths and trails. Captain Lee asked Victor and Carlos to get some wire cutters and watches and also survey for any Japanese sentries, stations, or headquarters.

The training of the eighteen continued with strengthening their wrists by jumping from the top of a tree downward without using their feet. They transferred from branch to branch downward by grabbing branches to strengthen their arms and biceps. They did hundreds of push-ups and developed their speed and timing. They had to be physically strong and mentally ready for the mission.

Captain Lee started talking about the technicality of their mission.

"Element of surprise is everything. Attacking our enemy to be 100 percent successful must be like dancing. Each enemy must have a partner, and our approach must always be from the back of our enemy. Timing is the name of the game. When we strike, it must be 1, 2, 3, and everything must be done in two seconds with no sound. You approach the enemy from the back. Your left hand covers the mouth of the enemy to prevent any sound. With your knife, slash the throat, then stab the heart. Do not release the mouth of the enemy until you are sure he is dead. We will practice this one hundred times or more until we perfect the move."

To relieve the group of the stress, they went down to the Mariveles River; they swam and practiced somersault dives to polish their moves in the air. They needed speed and grace in their mission to accomplish 100 percent success.

They started practicing the moves with Captain Lee, David, Kevin, and Alex demonstrating how the silent killing could be accomplished. Kevin and Alex acting as Japanese soldiers, then Joe and David were to attack from their backs. They showed them how to approach the enemy, then jump for the kill. Then Joe and David pretended to be Japanese, and Kevin and Alex came to attack them from behind. The fourteen divided into two groups of seven, then practiced the act. They practiced the act a hundred times to see to it that they had mastered the moves—of covering the mouth, accurate slashing of the throat, and the stabbing of the heart of the opponent. Element of surprise, timing, and speed were the keys that they had to master very well in preparation for their first mission as Silent Killers. After six months of continuous training, with the last month concentrated on mastering their moves in the darkness of the night, Capt. Joseph Lee announced the completion of the training and declared that they were ready to go to military secret missions.

"Men, you may not have experience to kill. In our missions, we have to be brave and strong to accomplish them. You have to put your hesitations aside and do what we are supposed to do, to fight for our country for the sake of freedom and democracy. We will be the Silent Killers."

While waiting for the report from Victor and Carlos for the possible first mission that they had to launch, they practiced all their moves in the darkness of the night at Tarak Ridge. They wanted to have a perfect mission—no mistake in timing and delivery of their deadly strike to the Japanese Army. In the early morning before they did the drill, they sat down with crossed feet, facing the sunrise, and meditated on the action they had to do when they faced the enemies in a secret mission as Silent Killers.

Victor and Carlos had been very busy going around the back roads and trails to have a good feel of travel, especially at night, of the different towns close to Mount Mariveles. They then came with the detailed report to Capt. Joseph Lee, who was seated by the side of David. "There were four Japanese camps that we observed—Camps Mariveles, Limay, Orion, and Pilar—along the main road of Bataan. There are around twenty Japanese personnel in each location. The places were surrounded with barbwires. There were four guards at the gate, two guards in each side of the barracks, no guard at the back of the compound, but there are horses fenced in the back. We observed that the best time to attack is around 2:00 AM, when everybody seems tired and inside the housing complex is very quiet," reported by Victor and Carlos.

"Of the four Japanese camps you observed, I prefer Camp Mariveles to be our first mission, because it is the last town of the provincial road and it would take days before other Japanese would know what happened. Also those Japanese in the Mariveles Camp would be very complacent and careless having just won the war. They would think that nobody would dare to harm them," said Captain Lee, explaining his motivation why he prepared the town of Mariveles over the other towns along Manila Bay.

"I think you are right, Captain Lee. I also like Mariveles to be our first target," exclaimed David.

"David, you come with me tonight. We will check our first target place to be sure that our first mission will be successful in the Japanese Mariveles Camp. I want 100 percent success in our first mission. No mistake."

Captain Lee, David, Victor, and Carlos observed the Japanese Mariveles Camp for two nights. They have confirmed that at two in the morning, it was really very quiet, and everybody was sleeping soundly except the two guards on each side and the four guards at the gate, but they also seemed tired and sleepy. They also took note that the front and the back doors of the housing were not locked and that they could enter the place without anybody knowing it. When they were sure of the timing and got all the needed information, they met with the group and prepared for their first mission.

As planned and agreed, David and Kevin would be at the corner of the front fence, and in the opposite corner would be Captain Lee and Alex at 2:00 AM. They would start to crawl toward the guards slowly and carefully. At 2:00 AM, the teams of Simon and Andrew must have entered already the back fence of the compound by cutting the barbwires. The men under the command of Simon would be Jim, Juan, Felipe, Jun, Ted, and Patrick. The men under the command of Andrew would be Roberto, Tomas, Martin, Pablo, Isaac, and Diego. Simon and Jim were to take care of the guards on the left side of the building, and Andrew and Robert were to take care of the guards on the other side of the building. The attack must be at exactly 2:30 AM simultaneously. When all the guards were killed, David's and Captain Lee's team would enter the front door carefully while the teams of Simon and Andrew would enter the back door silently. All would crawl toward the sleeping Japanese soldiers, one-on-one, and in one signal from Captain Lee, at one time, slash their throats and stab their hearts, covering the mouth of each victim.

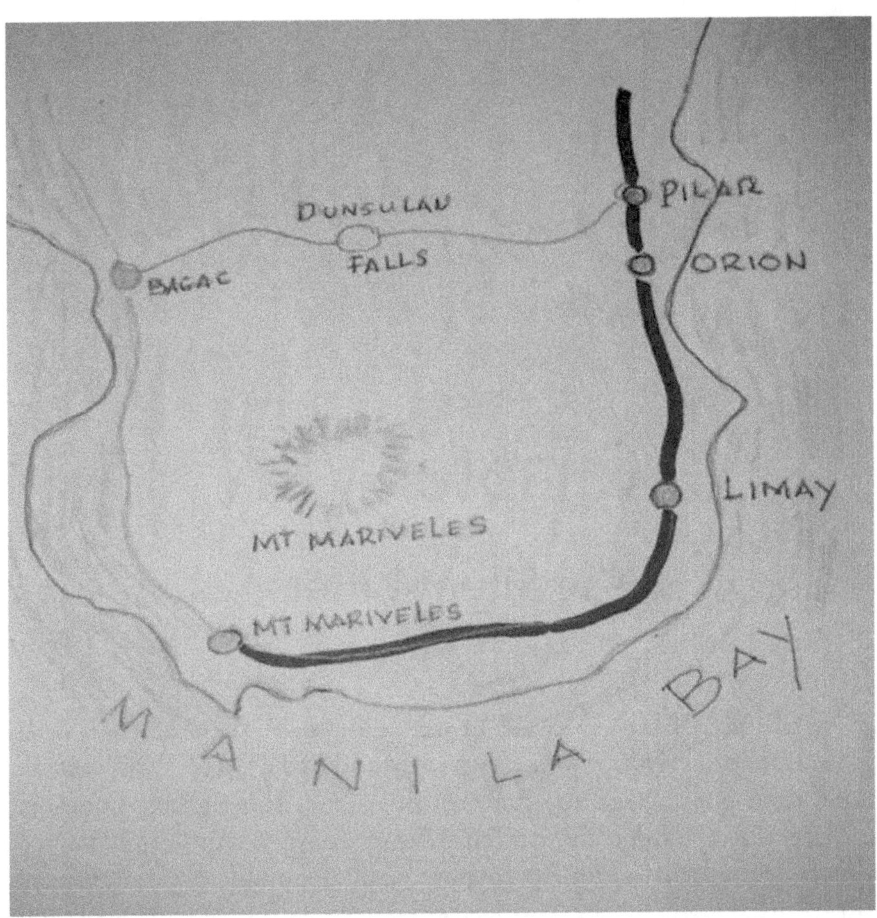


**Sketch of the Southern Part of the Province of Bataan**

# Chapter VIII

## The Silent Killers

**B**EFORE THE DAWN of the scheduled date of their first mission, everybody woke up early and had a sip of warm tea and then got dressed for the morning drill. The eighteen-member team went to the ridge and started their morning sessions. They started with morning meditation to prepare them mentally, psychologically, and spiritually. Then they practiced their acts, with speed and accuracy. Their main intention was to have a 100 percent completion of the mission with no mistake—soundless killing of the enemies. After a short break, they went down to their area and had a light meal of rice and meat. Then they proceeded to the Mariveles River and swam to calm their emotions. They wanted to feel fresh and composed. They all went back to their place and had lunch; prepared their black attires, black shoes, black pants, black shirts, and black bandanas; and checked the sharpness of their knives. When it was late afternoon, they all dressed up. Captain Lee, David, Simon, and Andrew—who would lead each assigned attack—synchronized the time in their watches, and they all waited for sundown. While they were waiting for nightfall at the edge of Mount Mariveles, they watched the beautiful sunset in Manila Bay as the sun slowly lost the glaring lights and the yellow-orange color of the horizon turned blood-red, and then little by little the darkness covered the wideness of the sky. When the sun disappeared from their sight, everything around them turned dark. They all did the sign of the cross, and they all started to go down the mountain, heading to their target Japanese camp in the town of Mariveles—the last town along the main road of the province of Bataan, overlooking Manila Bay.

Led by Victor and Carlos, who had observed the camp for several days, they arrived at the site almost midnight. They stayed behind the camp, silently watching the movement of the Japanese inside, counting the heads and planning their precise move and action. At around 1:00 AM, Simon and Andrew moved to start cutting the barbwires behind the camp. At precisely 2:00 AM, the team of Simon and Patrick got inside the back of the compound, and Captain Lee with Alex and David with Kevin were in the corners of the front fence and started crawling toward the four guards. At precisely 2:30 AM, they moved for the kill. The four guards and the two guards on each side of the building were all silently killed in seconds. Their throats were slashed, and they were all stabbed in the heart. The team of Simon and Andrew entered the back door of the building, while the team of Captain Lee and David entered the front door, and they all silently crawled on the floor to have a one-on-one victim to kill. In one signal of Captain Lee, they all covered the mouth of each victim, slashed the throat, and stabbed the heart. In one fast and swept action, all the Japanese were killed. With the first accomplished swift and deadly mission, the Silent Killers were born.

Slowly and silently, they collected .50- and .30-caliber machine guns, firearms, handguns, hand grenades, and ammo and loaded them into a cart behind the building. They also collected telescopes, flashlights, lighters, watches, clocks, canvases, samurai, and folding tables. They also took lots of food supplies, bread, cookies and crackers, and canned goods from the stockroom and kitchen. Using a cart hooked to a horse, they loaded all they collected and took with them all the six horses in the backyard, and they exited at the back of the compound, then turned back to the main road so that they would not be traced. They travelled a mile northward along the main road and then changed direction toward Mount Mariveles, heading to their headquarters.

On their way back home, from a distance, Patrick noticed two stray carabaos grazing around fifty yards from their way home.

"Simon, look at those carabaos. It looks like they are lost and abandoned," said Patrick to Simon.

"You are right, Patrick. Let me ask Captain Lee if he is interested to get those carabaos."

"Captain Lee, have you noticed those two carabaos that seem lost."

"Oh yeah, I did not notice them. This area had been a battlefield, and I don't think there is any civilian in this area. Come on, let's get those carabaos. We can use them in the future."

The group caught the carabaos and had them tag along on their way back to their hideout.

In the main headquarters of the group, Angelo, Maria, and Ana woke up very early to cook. Angelo slaughtered a pig and cut it into several parts for cooking. Maria boiled root crops while Ana boiled guava leaves for tea. The three prepared the table for the coming of the group.

On the left side of the path going up the mountain was a wooded area, and behind the trees was a wide grassy area. When the group arrived at the foot of the mountain, Marco and Daniel were there to welcome them. They led the horses and the two carabaos through the wooded area to the open verdant field for grazing. Around ten feet from the foot of the mountain along the trail going up the mountain was a flat surface of around five feet in width by twenty feet in length. On the right side of this plateau, they assembled the .30-caliber machine guns and on the left side the .50-caliber machine guns in preparation just in case they were attacked. They brought the boxes of hand grenades to their hideout, and everybody was provided with a rifle, ammunition, and a handgun to be used when necessary.

After they finished the inventory of their firearms, they joined together for a warm breakfast of pork *adobo*, boiled root crops, and warm tea.

After their big meal, Captain Lee asked his team to form a circle and sit down for a little conversation regarding their first mission. "Let me start with you, Simon. Tell us what you think about our first mission."

Simon answered, "We had a good training, and I accomplished what I was asked to accomplish."

Jim commented, "That was the first time I killed somebody. I had to pray for forgiveness."

Juan said, "I was very nervous at the beginning, but after I killed my subject, I felt OK."

Jun commented, "My hand was shaking even before and after I have killed my man."

Patrick said, "I was mentally prepared, so everything was OK with me. It was just like a game."

Ted said, "I was praying all the way going and coming back. I am very thankful that everything went well." Felipe spoke – I was so nervous when we entered the compound but after we had accomplished our mission, I felt relieved and thankful.

Roberto added, "We were all together in this big mission. I felt OK all the way."

Tomas commented, "We had a very good training, and we worked together, and I believed from the very beginning that everything will go well. I knew from the very beginning we can do it."

Martin said, "I was nervous when we entered the back of the compound, but after we all came inside the building, I felt better. I knew we would accomplish what we had planned to accomplish."

Pablo said, "I have never doubted our capability after our rigid training. I knew we could do it."

Diego said, "I was there to do my duty for our country. I did not have any fear at all. I was ready."

Isaac said, "I have prayed and prayed all the way, most especially when we entered the compound. I was praying that they wouldn't notice us. I was praying that those horses would not make a sound that may cause the guards to go to the back of the building, which would complicate our timing and plan. I was very happy that everything went as planned."

Andrew said, "I was there for our country. I was ready all the way." Alex said, "Looking back at what we have experienced in the death march,

I was ready for revenge."

Kevin commented, "The atrocity of the Japanese soldiers to Filipino and American prisoners of war and their disrespect for human dignity prepared me to fight a battle to win this war."

David commented, "I remember those helpless Filipino soldiers who just wanted some drop of water to drink but were machine-gunned by the Japanese. A soldier who fell down in exhaustion was shot and beheaded by a Japanese, who then laughed as if he owned the world. My experience in the death march made me feel stronger and a prepared warrior to win this war."

Captain Lee commented, "I am here as a soldier performing my duty to fight for our county. We are all together in this war, and I know we will win this war. We will fight to the end."

The final words of Captain Lee to the group were, "OK, guys, we had a very successful first mission. Have a very good sleep. Have some rest because tomorrow we will attack the Japanese camp in the town of Limay. We have to take advantage while the Japanese have not yet discovered what we did to the Japanese camp in Mariveles."

After eating, the group dispersed and looked for a place to have a good rest. At 5:00 PM, Captain Lee and David called all the members of the group to prepare for their second mission. They all dressed up with their dark shirts and pants and black shoes and tied their black bandanas on their heads. They synchronized their time and checked their knives. When darkness started to cover their camp, the group started to descend, led by Victor and Carlos, who were very familiar with the area. Julian, Marco, and Daniel stayed back as guards of the camp.

When they reached their target, the Limay Japanese camp, they stayed quietly behind the place, watching the movement of the Japanese inside the compound. There were five horses in the back of the building, quietly standing and eating. Like in Camp Mariveles, the Japanese seemed so complacent, not concerned of anything or any danger that might harm them. They felt so confident that they had won the war and nobody would dare to attack them. At 1:00 AM, the Japanese compound was already quiet, and guards seemed sleepy and unconcerned. The group started to move. Simon and Andrew started cutting the barbwires behind the compound. They were so very careful not to make any noise that might make the horses do some annoying sound. At 2:00 AM, everybody was in their assigned position. Captain Lee and David's group was already in the corners in front of the compound to kill the gate guards, while the group of Simon and Andrew was already inside, behind the building, ready to attack the side guards. At two thirty, in one fast and swept move, all the guards were killed, slashed on the throat and stabbed on the heart. The team of Captain Lee and David entered slowly the front door of the building, while the group of Simon and Andrew entered the back door. The group crawled inside the building slowly and carefully, and each picked a Japanese soldier to be killed. In one signal of Captain Lee, all the Japanese were killed, and their second mission was accomplished. Like what they did in Camp Mariveles, they gathered more guns, ammunition, and food supplies from the storage and the kitchen. They loaded the ammunition, more gadgets—like telescopes, flashlights, lighters, radios—and more food supplies to a cart in the back of the building, hooked to a horse. Like what they did in Camp Mariveles, they exited at the back of the compound, turned toward the main road and went half a mile northward, then turned to the direction of Mount Mariveles. They tried to erase their footmarks on their path with the use of a tree branch so that they would not be followed.

On their way back to Mount Mariveles, they saw an abandoned cow. Captain Lee called the attention of Victor and Carlos to get the cow.

"Hi, Victor, Carlos, I don't think anybody owns that cow. This area here had been a battleground, and I am sure there is no civilian in this area. Secure the cow and have the cow tag with you. We can use the cow in the future."

Victor and Carlos went ahead and took care of the cow and had it tag with them on their way back to Mount Mariveles.

When they reached the bottom of Mount Mariveles, they led their horses and the cow behind the woods in the grassy flatland to eat. Julian and Marco were there to welcome them and took care of the horses and the cow. Daniel was the guard assigned in their headquarters. The group went up their camp carrying ammunition and food supplies they collected from their second mission. When the group arrived in the camp, the hot meal was ready. Instead of root crops, they had rice, and instead of tea, they had coffee, with sugar and cream. Everybody seemed happy for the success of their mission, and now they had good food—the fruit of their success.

After their big meal, Captain Lee called Julian, Marco, and Daniel for a short briefing.

"We have many horses to take care. We always need two persons to guard and take care of our horses. We always need two guards down there, and you must be fully equipped with heavy weapons just in case there will be people who will dare to come and steal our horses. In addition to your rifles and handguns, we will provide you with a .30-caliber machine gun. I will show you how to use it. The three of you must switch assignments, where one of you must be a guard with a telescope to check for any incoming intruders to our area and watch the surroundings below to check for any hostile visitors," explained Captain Lee to the three guards.

Daniel responded, "We will arrange our schedule of who will be guarding the horses and who will be staying here to watch for intruders. After you have shown to us how to use the machine gun, we will proceed to our respective assignment."

After Captain Lee showed how to use the .30-caliber machine gun to the three, the three had a brief meeting to do their scheduling, then proceeded to their respective assignments, while Captain Lee called David, Kevin, and Alex together for a brief meeting.

"Guys, I would like to ask your opinion of my plan on our third mission and please let me know what you think. The Japanese camp in Orion is less than an hour's walk to Pilar's Japanese camp. I am thinking of attacking both camps simultaneously tomorrow early morning. What do you think?" asked Captain Lee to the three.

Kevin responded, "I think that is a brilliant idea, but we have to make adjustments to our timing in a way that we should be back before dawn."

"I think if we are in our positions at one thirty in the morning at the Orion Japanese camp, kill the guards at 2:00 AM, and complete the mission at 2:30 AM, we have plenty of time to go to the Japanese camp in the town of Pilar. In Pilar's Japanese camp, we must be in our positions at three thirty, kill the guards at four, and complete the mission at four thirty," explained David to the team.

"I agree to the suggestion of David," interjected Alex.

"OK, if you agree to what we have talked about, I'll bring this matter to our group. Also, I am thinking of resting for a couple of days after this hectic mission we will undergo. Come on, let's talk to our guys," said Captain Lee to the three as they started walking to call for a meeting.

After they have assembled the group, Captain Lee explained their mission the following morning.

"Our mission tomorrow would be hard, tough, but I believe it can be accomplished. The key to the accomplishment of our mission is our timing. We must all be in the back of the compound of the Orion Japanese camp by twelve midnight. Simon and Andrew, you must start cutting the barbwires at 1:00 AM for the entry of your group in the back, and all of us must be in position ready for attack at one thirty, and at two we attack the guards. Simon and Andrew, your group will enter the back door of the building, and our group will enter the front door. We have to complete our mission here at 2:30 AM. Our timers must all be synchronized before we leave our area. From Orion we will go to the Japanese camp in Pilar. It is not far from Orion. Simon and Andrew, your group must be in your position inside the compound by 3:30 AM, and our group will be in our position at that same time in front of the corners of the compound, and we move to kill the guards at 4:00 AM. Simon and Andrew, your group will enter the back door of the building, and our group will enter the front of the building, and at four thirty our mission must be complete," explained Captain Lee to the group.

"Captain Lee, our guys are a little bit overwhelmed. When are we going to have a little break?" asked Simon to Captain Lee.

"After this mission, I am contemplating of having a couple of days of rest for all of us to invigorate our strength and health, eating good food and having good rest," answered Captain Lee. "OK, if you don't have any more questions, you can go and have a good rest. We have a long night tonight until tomorrow morning."

At around 5:00 PM, everybody started to get ready, dressing up with their standard uniform. But unlike before, each one of them had a handgun in a holster, secured by a belt around their waistline. They double-checked the sharpness of their knives. They synchronized their watches and waited for sundown. Led by Victor and Carlos, the group headed to their destination, the Orion Japanese camp. On their way to their mission, Captain Lee kept on telling everybody to be calm and be focused on the mission. At twelve midnight, they were in the back side of the Orion Japanese camp. They first observed the movement inside the compound, and when it was very quiet at 1:00 AM, the crew of Simon and Andrew started opening their way to the compound, and at one thirty everybody was in their respective position, ready for the kill. At 2:00 AM, they simultaneously attacked and killed the guards. Like cats without sound, the group entered the compound, and at two thirty, their mission was complete, killing all sleeping Japanese inside the building.

"OK, guys, let's keep moving. We will come back here after we finish our mission at the Pilar Japanese camp," instructed Captain Lee to the group.

The group proceeded to the Pilar Japanese camp, and they were in the back of the compound at 3:00 AM. First they observed what was going on inside the compound, and then the crew of Simon and Andrew cut the barbwires to enter the back of the compound. At 3:30 AM, the crew of Simon and Andrew entered the backside of the compound, and Captain Lee and David's crew was already positioned in the corners of the front fences and started crawling toward the guards at the gate of the compound. At four, all the guards were killed, and the crew slowly entered the building for the last stage of the mission. At four thirty, silently they were able to kill all the sleeping Japanese without any problem. They started collecting any valuables that they might use in their camp. They got more ammunition, food, and gadgets—like watches, radios, telescopes, knives, samurai. They loaded everything into a car attached to a horse, in the back of the compound. They took all the five horses in the back of the compound and then headed back to the Orion Japanese camp to collect more war ammunition, machine guns, a few reserved rifles, food, ropes, matches, more telescopes, and the five horses in the back of the compound. After collecting all their needs in the Orion Japanese camp, the group headed home to Mount Mariveles. On their way home, they passed through an abandoned farm with lots of yellow squash (locally called *calabasa*) on the ground. Captain Lee summoned Victor and Carlos to pick some for their food.

When the group arrived at the foot of Mount Mariveles, they were welcomed by Julian and Marco. They were the guards assigned to look after the horses in the mountainside. The two led the ten horses to the grassland with the help of ten members of the Silent Killers. After they have secured the horses in their respective feeding areas, the group headed up to their headquarters, hungry and very tired.

After their heavy meal, Captain Lee called to meet everybody and told them, "Guys, I know you are all very tired. We will rest for several days to get a good rest and sleep. We have been working very hard, with very few hours of sleep and long hours of journey. We need to revitalize our energy to regain our weakening strength. I understand all of us are overwhelmed, and it is about time for us to have a good rest. I know that when we come back to attack our enemies, we have to use a different strategy because by then they would have already discovered their casualties. But we will make adjustments. OK, guys, have a good rest. Thank you."

It was morning of the third resting day when from the top of a tree, Daniel, who was assigned as lookout, using his telescope saw a convoy of Japanese military trucks coming to their direction.

"Captain Lee, we have company!" yelled Daniel as he was going down from the tree. He ran to warn everybody. "Guys, there is a convoy of Japanese military trucks coming to our direction. Get ready," warned Daniel as he went around telling everybody of the danger approaching their camp.

Captain Lee jumped and ran toward the edge of the mountain behind the bushes to confirm and view the military convoy of the Japanese coming to their direction. What he saw in his telescope were the Japanese flags waving, as if saying, "We are here to get you. We are coming for revenge."

**A sketch of the cart used by the guerilla unit headed by Capt. Joseph Lee**

# Chapter IX

## The Journey to the Sierra Madre Mountain Range

CAPTAIN LEE WANTED to be coequal with all the members of the Silent Killers group. They fought shoulder to shoulder to kill their enemies. But this time was a different situation; he had to assert himself as a leader in command to fight the incoming enemies. He had to assert his leadership as Capt. Joseph Lee in this forthcoming firepower battle with the Japanese. He had to use his military training, ingenuity, and tactical knowledge of confronting the coming Japanese Army. After his confirmation of the arriving convoy of Japanese Army, he right away met with his men and asserted his commanding leadership.

"Daniel, you get a box of ammo for the .30-caliber machine gun and hurl down the side of the mountain using a rope and join the team of Julian and Marco in the woods guarding the horses. Now tell them to hold their fire not unless your team is in danger. Wait for me. I'll be the one to fire first. We will wait until they are very close to us before we start firing. Go!"

"Big Kevin and Alex, take care of the boxes of hand grenades. When you hurl the grenades, aim at the trucks. We will take care of the men. Got it?"

"Yap," replied Kevin. "Let's go, Alex," as the two left to take their position closer to the edge of the mountain with boxes of hand grenades.

"David, you go with me down to our position in the lower level, and you handle the .50-caliber machine gun while I'll fire the .30-caliber machine gun."

Then Captain Lee faced the other members of the team and told them to get more ammo for their rifles.

"Guys, have a good practice with your rifle."

"David, come on, let's go to our position."

Everybody was in their respective position waiting for the coming of the Japanese convoy, unaware of the trap waiting for them. Captain Lee and David, the lead gunners, were holding their breaths behind their covering of twigs and dried leaves and branches of trees, where only an inch of the barrels of their machine guns was coming out, waiting for the Japanese to come closer. When the Japanese dismounted from the trucks, everybody got ready, and when the lead group of the Japanese army was about ten feet from the position of Captain Lee and David, Captain Lee commenced firing, followed by David with his .50-caliber machine gun. The team of Julian, Marco, and Daniel from the woods started firing too, while Kevin and Alex started throwing grenades, aiming at the Japanese trucks. Everybody continued firing at the unsuspecting Japanese soldiers, who did not have the chance to fire their guns as they were overwhelmed with firepower from the waiting guerillas. The hand grenades thrown by Kevin and Alex were like bombs coming from the sky. And the bullets from the waiting guerillas were hitting them like rain, and when the firing of the guns was over, there was a complete silence, and all the Japanese soldiers were all down and dead.

"Hold your fire!" yelled Captain Lee. "I think we got them all."

Capt. Joseph Lee and David with their drawn handguns went down to check the fallen Japanese soldiers to be sure they were already dead. Kevin and Alex went down and followed Captain Lee and David to help check the trucks and the dead Japanese soldiers. Kevin followed the direction of David, while Alex followed Captain Lee, checking each fallen body. Kevin was a little careless and did not notice a Japanese soldier pretending to be dead as he passed him, and the soldier was ready to stab him with a samurai. At that time, David turned around to check on Kevin. He saw Kevin about to be stabbed by the Japanese soldier.

David Yelled to Kevin, "Kevin, run!"

Then David sidestepped to have a clear view of the Japanese and fired his handgun, hitting him in the head, neck, and chest. The Japanese fell to his back dead.

"Kevin, that was close. Be very careful with your steps," said David to Kevin as Captain Lee and Alex came to check what was going on. When Captain Lee was assured that everything was OK, he told David, Kevin, and Alex to go to the campsite and tell everybody to get ready. They had to abandon the area before more Japanese came for revenge.

"Guys, you tell everybody to prepare to leave. We have to evacuate this area. I'll check with the team of Julian, Marco, and Daniel to prepare the horses and carts. We have to leave as soon as possible. Also please tell Victor and Carlos to come down and guard this area while we are preparing to evacuate."

Capt. Joseph Lee proceeded to see Julian Marco and Daniel. He instructed them to prepare the horses for evacuation—the horses to ride on, two carts to be rigged to carabaos, one cart to be rigged to a cow, and the other cart to be rigged to a horse. The heavy weapons, boxes of ammo, and boxes of hand grenades were to be loaded to the carts towed by the carabaos because they are stronger. The sacks of rice, livestock—pig and goat—and other food elements were to be loaded into the cart towed by the cow, and the cooking wares and other cooking materials were to be loaded to the cart towed by the horse. There were enough horses to ride on by everybody.

The team of Simon helped carry all the heavy weapons down to load into the carts, while the team of Andrew helped Angelo, Anna, and Maria bring down their food subsistence and cooking materials.

Diego dragged down to the foot of the mountain, to the loading area, a pig and two goats to load into one of the carts. At the meeting place at the foot of the mountain, on the ground behind the wooded area where the horses were, Captain Lee instructed the team to which cart the weapons, ammo, food, and cooking materials must be loaded and then turned around and met with Victor and Carlos and showed them the map of Bataan, then told them, "Victor and Carlos, you are very familiar with this province. We cannot go north because we might be intercepted by the Japanese. We have to go around Mount Mariveles, then go north, and then we turn east between Mount Natib and Mount Mariveles. We will target to rest near the Dunsulan Falls. OK? We will lead the group. You will be the advance party, and I'll be behind you. Let's go and talk to the group!"

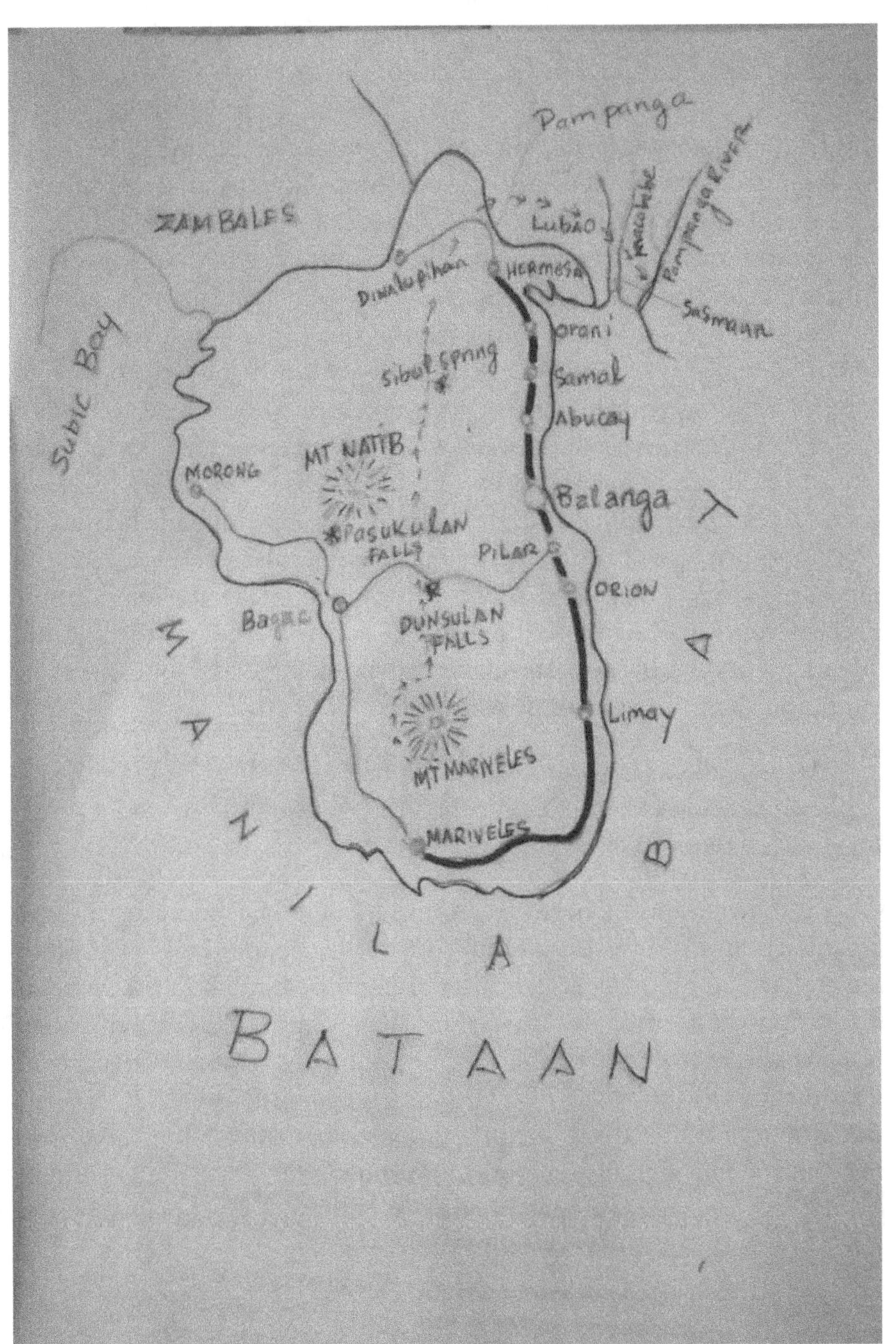


**to the Pampanga River on their way to Sierra Madre**

Capt. Joseph Lee assembled the group to assign the placement of the cavalcade and the proper sequence of the carts and horses: "Patrick and Julian, you ride the first cart carrying our heavy weapons. Marco and Daniel, you ride the second cart carrying boxes of ammo, boxes of hand grenades, and other heavy metals. Simon, your horsemen follow the carts of our heavy weapons. Keep an eye at the two carts in front of you as we move on. Angelo, you ride the cart carrying our food with your wife, Maria. You steer direct the cart following the horsemen of Simon. Diego, you ride the cart carrying our cooking materials, pots, and others. Take your wife, Anna, with you and follow the cart of Angelo. Andrew, your horsemen must take care of our back, following the cart of Diego. Keep an eye on what is happening in front of your line and listen and be sensitive to your behind as we move along. Have some of your men put some dried branches on our path behind to prevent the enemies from following us. Victor and Carlos, you lead the caravan. David, Kevin, and Alex, we stay behind Victor and Carlos. Each of you was issued a flashlight. Please at night when it is lighted, do not point it upward. The light can be detected by our enemies. Point your light downward, forward, or to your back."

"Are you all set? Let's go!" yelled Captain Lee as he took his position in the line, with David, Kevin, and Alex behind Victor and Carlos, who were leading the way.

The caravan moved on to go around Mount Mariveles to avoid the Japanese patrol and travel closer to the foot of the mountain to prevent being detected by the enemies. They tried to be hidden in the wooded side along the foot of the mountain as they moved along until they reached the north edge of the foot of Mount Mariveles. The caravan then turned east until they reached the Dunsulan River. They traveled along the Dunsulan River until they were about three kilometers from the Dunsulan Waterfalls, behind the wooded area along the Dunsulan River. They selected the spot because of the small springwater by the side of the river, good for cooking and drinking.

**Picture of the section of Dunsulan River, courtesy of Amado Avelino**

"OK. We will settle here for a few days of rest to regain our strength. I am sure everybody is tired and hungry," Captain Lee told Victor and Carlos.

Captain Lee signaled to the caravan that they had to stop. He assembled the group to update his plan to get out of the province of Bataan and head to the Sierra Madre Mountains.

"Bataan is a peninsula and a very small province. There is not much place here to hide against the powerful Japanese Army. We need a bigger space where we can have our freedom of movement without getting caught. We are going to the Sierra Madre Mountains. There is a secondary road near Dunsulan Falls that divides this province crosswise. We will cross that secondary road at night to prevent getting seen by our enemies. From there, we will travel toward the foot of the eastern side of the Natib Mountain. From Natib Mountain, we will go near the Sibul Spring, where we will rest for a day before we cross the boundary of the province of Pampanga. As soon as we cross the province of Pampanga, we will be safe," explained Captain Lee to the group.

"Guys, we will stay here for a days to regain our energy and to prepare our plans. There are bread, cookies, and crackers in the third cart hooked to the cow. Go ahead and serve yourselves while we are waiting for our hot meal. Do not forget to feed your horses and the two goats," continued Captain Lee as he turned to Angelo.

"Angelo, you can go ahead and cook our food with Ana and Maria. Diego, please give them a hand," instructed Captain Lee.

"Ana, please prepare the rice for cooking. I'll gather some firewood and get some stones to form a stove. Maria, please get the container of the pork adobo we cooked but did not eat because of our encounter with the Japanese," pointed Angelo to the two women as he left to gather stones and firewood.

"I'll pick some green papaya, and go along the riverbank to gather edible ferns and some mushrooms. We can boil them with ginger and garlic for our vegetable," said Diego as he headed to the river.

After they had eaten their heavy meal, everybody felt so contented and dispersed to different corners to have a good rest. Some took canvases from the cart and used them as bedsheets. Some just leaned on trees and went to sleep. Julian, Marco, and Daniel switched guarding the area with the help of Victor and Carlos. They watched around to check for any incoming intruders. While Angelo, Anna, and Maria saw to it that there was warm coffee with sugar and cream for everybody to keep those guards awake.

Captain Lee called David, Kevin, and Alex and showed them the map of Bataan. "You see, this is the secondary road I was talking about," as he pointed to the map. "Here is the Dunsulan Falls. Now, David and Kevin, you take the .50-caliber machine gun. David, you will be the gunner. Kevin, hold the case of the ammo. You guard the direction toward the west. Alex and I with the .30-caliber machine gun will guard the direction toward the east of the secondary road. When we know it is clear, we will let our caravan cross the road one by one, slowly and silently. What do you think?" asserted Joe to the three.

"I think that is a brilliant plan. What do you think, Kevin?" answered David as he turned the question to Kevin.

"It looks good to me," said Kevin. "How about you, Alex, what do say?" asked Kevin to Alex as he turned to him.

"It is fine with me," answered Alex.

"OK, if you don't have any more questions, let's have some rest. I am also very tired," said Captain Lee as he left the three and looked for a corner under the tree to rest. Alex took a canvas from the cart and offered it to Captain Lee to sleep on. David and Kevin went their way to have some rest.

The following morning after a night of rest along the Dunsulan River, Capt. Joseph Lee assembled everybody for further instructions on how they would cross the secondary road on their way to Sibul Spring: "Guys, today we will leave this area heading to Sibul Spring. Prepare what you have to prepare. Put back the canvas you may have used where you got them from. Check your rifles and see to it that you have enough ammo. Check your flashlights. Be sure to fill up your bamboo drinking water container before we leave this area. We will eat our supper very early today, around 4:00 PM. You have an hour to prepare. By 5:00 PM we should all be ready. That is the time when I will leave with David, Kevin, and Alex to check the secondary road that we will pass through. Victor and Carlos will be with us. If everything is clear, we will send Carlos to get you all, and Victor will cross the road and start clearing our path to Sibul Spring. We will start to cross the road at around 6:00 PM, one by one, not to create too much sound. Do you have any questions?" explained Captain Lee to the group, ending with a questions.

"OK, if you have no more questions, go ahead and prepare yourself and be ready for our departure tonight," followed up Captain Lee to the group, then turned to Angelo. "Angelo, do you think you can be ready by five after we have served supper to our crew?"

"I'll ask the help of Diego, and with Anna and Maria, I think we can do it. Anyway you said we will cross the road at 6:00 PM. I am sure we can make it. We will just put everything in the river for easy cleaning of all our utensils, and with the help of Diego we can easily load them into the cart," answered Angelo.

Captain Lee left and met with David and asked him to go with him to prepare their machine guns to be brought to the road crossing. They walked together to the cart that contained their machine guns and ammo. The two called Kevin and Alex to follow them.

"Come on, David, let's prepare our machines," said the captain as he continued walking.

"OK, I'll follow you to the cart. I'll get Kevin and Alex to join us," answered David.

David checked his .50-caliber machine gun, then asked Kevin to get their horses to load the machine and the ammo. While Alex, who was guiding the two horses of him and that of Captain Lee, led said horses closer to the cart to prepare them to be loaded with the .30 caliber and the ammo. David loaded the .50-caliber machine gun onto his horse, while the ammo was loaded onto the horse of Kevin. Captain Lee loaded his .30-caliber machine gun onto his horse, and Alex loaded the ammo of the .30 caliber onto his. They prepared their horses, ready to go.

At 5:00 PM, Captain Lee called everybody to get ready and check everything and be prepared to move on, waiting for the return of Victor and Carlos, who would get them, to lead them going to the road they would cross.

When everything was ready, Capt. Joseph Lee signaled to David, Kevin, Alex, Victor, and Carlos to start moving. Headed by Capt. Joseph Lee, they proceeded to the road the caravan had to pass through. When they reached the road, Captain Lee and David went ahead and checked their positions, and when everything was clear, they set their machine guns, with Captain Lee pointing to the east and David pointing to the west of the road. After they felt that it was safe to call the group, they sent Carlos to get the caravan, and Victor crossed the road and started clearing the path for its clear passage.

When the caravan arrived, Captain Lee stopped them for a moment and waited for the surrounding to dim a little bit, then signaled Patrick and Julian to go ahead and cross the road with their cart, followed by the cart driven by Marco and Daniel. When the two carts passed the road, Captain Lee asked all the horsemen to dismount and lead their horses across the road to avoid too much noise.

After the horsemen crossed the road, the sets of cart driven by Angelo and Maria and the cart drive by Diego and Ana slowly crossed the road. Like what the first group of horsemen did, Captain Lee asked them all to dismount and just lead their horses across the road slowly and silently. When all the groups of the caravan were able to cross the road, Captain Lee, David, Kevin, and Alex loaded their machine guns and ammo on their respective horses and crossed the road silently. The four went back after they had securely tied their horses to the tree on the other side of the road and put dried branches on the path to avoid them being detected, that they used the path. They also put dried branches of trees onto their entrance path going to the wilderness to avoid being followed. After they felt satisfied covering their path, they rode their horses and followed the caravan.

It was a long journey from the Dunsulan Falls to Mount Natib. They were trying to travel under tall trees of the heavy forested area of the land to avoid being detected by the Japanese. When they were approaching the foot of Mount Natib, the horses of Victor and Carlos, who were leading the caravan, started jumping and doing some distressed sound. Captain Lee, David, and Kevin right away checked what was going on. Victor and Carlos were almost thrown from their horses when their horses jumped in distress. When Captain Lee came closer, he noticed a very big anaconda on the way. Kevin right away pulled out his handgun and was ready to fire at the snake, but Captain Lee yelled to Kevin.

"No! Don't! Do not make any noise. We have to be careful not to be detected in this part of the forest. Those Japanese are looking for us. With the number of Japanese we killed, I am sure they wanted to turn this province upside down to find us. Let us try to drive the snake away."

Kevin and David got a piece of wood and tried to drive the snake away, but the snake was so stubborn and was even biting their piece of wood. The snake was fighting back and looked very hungry for some prey. Kevin got tired of pushing and shoving the snake; he got his samurai and in one swing cut off the head of the helpless snake.

They continued their journey along the edge of the foot of Mount Natib, then turned toward the direction of the Sibul Spring. When they were about fifty yards away from the spring in the wooded area along the Sibul River, Captain Lee stopped the caravan. He assembled everybody for an update of their plans.

**Picture of the section of Sibul River, courtesy of Amado Avelino**

"We will not go near the Sibul Spring because it is accessible to the town of Abucay, where there may me Japanese soldiers wandering around. We will easily be exposed to the Japanese who are hunting us. We will use the water from the river to cook our food and just get water from the spring at night for some water to drink. We will stay here for a couple of days to rest to prepare for our long journey to the Sierra Madre Mountain. Angelo, Maria, Anna, and Diego you can prepare to cook. Everybody, you just wait around and get snacks in the cart if you are hungry. Do not forget to feed your horses and provide them water to drink. We need all of them healthy for our long journey to the Sierra Madre Mountain Range."

"I'll get the stones we used at Dunsulan Falls and set the stove for cooking. Diego can help secure some firewood. Maria, please prepare the rice for cooking. You can use the water from the river to wash the rice, and, Anna, would you please peel the green papayas, squash, yam, and some mushrooms. We will boil them with ginger and garlic to have some soup. We will sauté some canned meat in onion to have some protein," Angelo told the cooking crew.

Captain Lee called Victor and Carlos and instructed them to survey their way to cross the provincial road and the boundary between Bataan and Pampanga. They have to pass the towns of Lubao, Sasmuan, and Macabebe in Pampanga Province to reach the mouth of the Pampanga River. The caravan had to follow the Pampanga River northward to get to the Sierra Madre Mountain Range. The headwater of the Pampanga River is located in the Sierra Madre Mountains. Captain Lee told them he would be with them up to the provincial road of Bataan to see to it that they were safe as they cross the boundary to Pampanga Province.

At around 6:00 PM, Captain Lee called Victor and Carlos to get ready. They had to proceed with the plan. Captain Lee summoned David and Kevin to go with him to escort Victor and Carlos and take their .50-caliber machine gun and ammo, and he instructed Alex to take with him a box of ammo for the .30-caliber machine gun. Before the group reached the intersection, Captain Lee, David, Kevin, and Alex dismounted and with their machine guns walked to the provincial road. Captain Lee told Victor and Carlos to hold back and wait until he received the signal from him. Captain Lee and David with their machine guns pointing to the direction of the provincial road looked and waited to check everything was clear. When the two were sure of their safety, Captain Lee signaled Victor and Carlos to proceed across the provincial road and to travel between the towns of Dinalupihan and Hermosa and enter the town of Lubao in Pampanga. It was already 7:00 PM when Victor and Carlos crossed the Bataan Provincial Road leading to the Bataan–Pampanga provincial boundary. The two had to survey the trail that the caravan had to travel in going to the mouth of the Pampanga River. Captain Lee, David, Kevin, and Alex stayed behind the provincial road to wait for the return of Victor and Carlos. It was early and a quiet night when from the northern direction of the provincial road they heard sounds of incoming trucks. They sounded like thunders as they came closer to their position. The four ran and hide in the tall thick cogon grass and waited for the passing of the vehicles. Captain Lee and David held the triggers of their machine guns as the convoy passed, rushing a few yards from their hiding place. The loud sound of the crushing tires of the trucks on the unpaved provincial road was like thunders as the six trucks loaded with Japanese soldiers passed through. The four were almost not breathing as they watched the rushing loaded trucks of Japanese soldiers. When the sound of the rushing vehicles was gone, it was completely silent, and the four stepped out from their hiding place.

"Those Japanese soldiers must be reinforcement to hunt for us. They probably discovered already the pile of dead Japanese soldiers at the foot of Mount Mariveles. We really have to get out of this area as soon as possible," Captain Lee told the three in a very low-toned voice.

The four stayed steadfast waiting for the return of Victor and Carlos, who crossed the Bataan Provincial Road to Pampanga Province to survey their trail going to the Pampanga River. They would use the Pampanga River as their guide to reach the Sierra Madre Mountain Range. They stayed alert, dozing once in a while. It was around 5:00 AM, ten hours of waiting, when they heard the sound of the horses of Victor and Carlos. The four prepared to welcome Victor and Carlos while alert with their machine guns just in case something unexpected happened. When Victor and Carlos crossed the provincial road, heading to their direction, they, too, got onto their horses and headed to their camp area. When the six arrived in their camp area, breakfast was ready, prepared by Angelo, Maria, and Anna. The six went ahead and ate their breakfast, then went straight to take some rest.

It was noontime. Some members of the crew were napping. Some were resting. Some were eating their lunch. While Captain Lee, David, Kevin, Alex, Victor, and Carlos were in deep sleep, low-flying fighter planes passed above their camp's position. Then a little later, they heard sound of bombs being dropped in the southern part of their camp—*boom, boom, boom, boom*. The sound of the fighter planes and the sound of bombs being dropped awoke and alerted everybody. Capt. Joseph Lee right away called everybody to alarm them and to prepare for their next plan.

"Men, it looks like they have already found the dead bodies of the Japanese army at the foot of Mount Mariveles. They probably bombed our campsite on top of Mount Mariveles. Last night we have seen six trucks of Japanese soldiers going south. Most likely they will comb this province hunting for us. So tonight prepare yourself. We have to leave this campsite and cross the provincial boundary going to Pampanga Province. It is not safe here in Bataan. We have to leave while there is still time. At 6:00 PM tonight when our surrounding starts to dark, we will leave this camp. As usual we will guard the provincial road before our caravan could cross it. You will wait for our signal before you start moving. The caravan will be led by Victor and Carlos because they are familiar with the area. You have to eat well because this will be a very long journey. By 5:00 PM, we must all get ready and please double-check to see to it that we have not forgotten anything. At 5:30 PM, you must all be in proper formation and everything must then be loaded to our carts ready to move. Do you have any questions?"

After the briefing of Captain Lee, everybody started getting ready, putting back the canvases they had used. They checked their rifles, ammo, flashlights, samurai, and knives, getting ready for the battle if they encounter the Japanese. They filled up their bamboo drinking water containers from the spring by the side of the Sibul River. Then they all silently waited for the final moment—the caravan assembly formation and the departure signal from Victor and Carlos.

At 6:00 PM, Captain Lee, David, Kevin, and Alex headed to the provincial road on horseback, with their machine guns and ammo, together with Victor and Carlos. When they reached the provincial road, David set his .50-caliber machine gun pointing northward, and Captain Lee set his .30-caliber machine gun pointing southward of the provincial road. After they were sure that everything was safe, Captain Lee instructed Victor to go ahead and cross the provincial road and wait for the caravan and instructed Carlos to get the caravan and start the journey.

When Carlos arrived in the campsite, he signaled to start moving, for them to follow him. Carlos led the caravan toward the provincial road. With the signal from Captain Lee, group by group the caravan crossed the provincial road, moving toward the provincial boundary, where Victor was waiting. When the complete formation of the caravan had passed the provincial road, Captain Lee, David, Kevin, and Alex abandoned their position and carrying their weapons mounted their horses and followed the caravan. It was a long night of journey, and finally at around 4:00 AM, they were near the mouth of the Pampanga River. They rested for two hours, ate together, and then proceeded moving upward along the riverbank to the direction of the Sierra Madre Mountain Range. They traveled very close to the riverbank mostly under the wooded area and avoided confrontation with the Japanese. After four days of continuous journey with few hours of stopover to eat and have a little rest, they finally reached the top of the Sierra Madre Mountains, tired and very hungry.

# Chapter X

## The Entrapments

THE CARAVAN HEADED by Capt. Joseph Lee finally reached the top of the Sierra Madre Mountain Range late afternoon. Upon reaching the top of the mountain range, Captain Lee called his men for a briefing:

"Men, you are all very tired. We are now in a safe place. Get some rest, sleep, and for some of you who are hungry, we have cookies and crackers in the cart. Be sure to clean the area you are going to rest on because there are a lot of snakes here in this part of the mountain. Tentatively, we will rest here, but we have to move as soon as we find a spring. We have to locate our camp closer to a spring for cooking and easy access to water for all our drinking and cleaning necessities. We have canvases in the cart you can use to sleep on. Angelo and Diego, you come with me to look for a spring. Julian, Marco, and Daniel, stay and guard our area here. Alex, you also come with me."

"I'll join you," said David.

"I am coming," said Maria.

"So am I," followed up Anna.

"OK, let's go," commanded Captain Lee.

Walking southward on top of the mountain range, they found a spring by a riverbank near a wooded area, very good for shelter building to hide their location.

"OK, Angelo, you can start building a tripod stove here for cooking and gather some firewood for our fuel. Maria and Anna, please help Angelo prepare this site. David and Alex, stay with them, and, Diego, come with me. We will get the cart that we loaded the cooking materials onto and the cart where we loaded our food supplies. Let's go," instructed Captain Lee.

When Captain Lee and Diego arrived in their tentative camp, Captain Lee summoned the help of Patrick to give them a hand in bringing one of the carts to the site near the spring so that they can cook their meals. They did not bother anymore the other members of the crew to give them a longer rest. After Angelo, Maria, and Anna with the help of Diego cooked their evening meals, they told Captain Lee that they were ready to serve the food.

"Thanks, Angelo, Diego, Maria, and Anna. David and Alex, you stay with them, and, Patrick, you come with me, and we will wake up everybody. I am also very hungry."

After Captain Lee and Patrick left to get everybody for supper, Angelo, Diego, Maria, and Anna set the folding tables side by side and put banana leaves on top of the tables and filled them with rice and viands. They were to eat together the native way, with bare hands, elbow to elbow, side by side.

When Captain Lee and Patrick arrived on their tentative site, Patrick right away sought the help of Julian, Marco, and Daniel to prepare the loaded carts of guns and ammunition to be hauled by carabaos. Captain Lee woke up everybody and told them it was time to eat. They told them not to forget to carry with them the canvas they slept on because they were not coming back to the place.

"Men, we have to move to a location near a spring for convenience. Let us all go together to our new selected site, where we can be conveniently located near a fresh supply of water. Take everything with you because we are not coming back here. That area near the spring will be the area where we will build our camp."

All the men were so surprised when they reached the spring site, when they saw the food was ready, served on banana leaves set on the folding tables, arranged side by side.

"Men, go ahead and wash your hands. We will eat all together on this long table to celebrate our first supper here on top of the Sierra Madre Mountain Range. We can finally have a very peaceful rest with no fear of the Japanese hunting us. Come on, guys, let's eat," commanded Captain Lee to all the members of the crew.

After their supper, Captain Lee assembled everybody and talked to them to have a very good sleep because the following day they had to build their camp.

"Tomorrow, we have to build our camp here near this spring under those tall trees so that we will not be seen by our enemies from the air. We will use cogon grass for our roofing, and there are lots of bamboo plants in this area that we can use as materials. There are also plenty of strong wood materials we can get and rattans we can use for tying in joining together woods and bamboo and cogon grass for roofing. So have a good night's sleep, and tomorrow we have plenty of work to do. Thank you," explained Captain Lee to the group.

The group dispersed to the wooded area using their flashlights and looked for some place to spend the night with their canvas, while Angel, Diego, Maria, and Ana stayed to clean up and throw away the trash and feed the only pig they had carried from Bataan. They were busy cleaning up when Captain Lee came and approached them.

"You know, Angelo and Diego, I am thinking that tomorrow we will be very busy building our camp, and since this is the first time that we could really say we are safe and could sleep soundly here, let's serve our group good food tomorrow. Let's roast our only pig and cook our two goats into spicy *caldereta* (native Filipino recipe). What do you think?"

"OK, sir," answered Angelo. "I'll take care of the pig, and Diego will take care of the goats. I'll ask the help of Patrick in turning the pole during the roasting of the pork. I can cook other recipes using the internal parts of the pig."

"Do you agree with that, Diego?" asked Captain Lee to Diego.
"Yes, sir, we can handle it," answered Diego.

"OK, so we are set. Let's start cooking tomorrow early in the morning, good?" followed up by Captain Lee.

Early morning the following day, after the cooking crew finished cooking their breakfast of coffee with cream, tea made from boiled lemongrass, and boiled sweet potatoes and green bananas, they started preparing to butcher the pig and the goats. Angelo took care of butchering the pig, and Diego took care of the two goats. Maria and Anna helped out boiling the water to remove the skin of the animals. Patrick later on came to help in rotating the pig stuck in a pole, the two ends resting on Y-shaped branches of a tree rooted to the ground. The charcoal was maintained burning and hot until the skin of the pig was crispy and brown. Diego took care of cooking the two goats.

The crew after eating their breakfast started gathering the materials for building their camp in the wooded area to prevent from being seen from the air by the passing Japanese planes. Everybody was busy, so they did not break the crew for lunch, and instead they just invited them to eat as they become hungry. Captain Lee was anxious to finish their shelters so that when it rained, they would not get wet. The project was done smoothly because of the availability of materials in the site. They were able to install posts of the housings and attached roofing materials. Before dark, they already had a housing standing, built to protect them from the weather. Captain Lee ordered everybody to assemble and proceed to the spring, where the cooking crew was waiting to serve. On the center table of the arranged folding tables was the roasted pig. Captain Lee asked Alex to get the box of Japanese wine (sake) from the cart. They all ate together, laughing, exchanging stories, and later on drinking wine. Daniel brought his guitar and played with the other members of the crew, who joined him singing serenade songs. The celebration turned emotional and touching, and everybody was silent when Daniel with his guitar sang "Bayan Ko" (My Country).

*Pilipinas kong minumutya (Philippines my beloved)*
*Pugad ng luha ko't dalita (Nest of our tears and simple life)*
*Akin adhika makita kang (My only wish is to see you)*
*Sakdal, laya. (Completely free)*

The following day after breakfast, Captain Lee asked Victor and Carlos to go down to see what province and towns they were overlooking from their campsite and to do some spying.

"Victor and Carlos, I want you to check the areas below our campsite and spy for Japanese stations, sentries, camps, garrisons, buildings, or any Japanese installations. You carry with you telescopes but do not carry any weapon and avoid confrontations with the Japanese. Use secondary roads if necessary and use telescopes in a hidden place to spy on the activities of the Japanese. You may do day-and-night surveillance of the Japanese stations and activities, then report to me so that we can plan our actions," asked Captain Lee to Victor and Carlos.

"Yes, sir, we'll do as soon as possible," replied Victor and Carlos.

After three weeks of surveillance and spying, visiting towns of the province of Bulacan, Victor and Carlos reported to Captain Lee what they had observed in the lowlands below their mountain camp.

"The province we are overlooking from our camp here on top of the mountain is the province of Bulacan. We have explored four towns that are close to us: San Miguel, San Ildefonso, Dona Remedios Trinidad, and Norzagaray. The last three days we concentrated our attention on the towns of San Miguel and San Ildefonso. In San Ildefonso there is a sentry manned by few soldiers, around nine men. In San Miguel there are barracks, a bigger force of maybe fifty to sixty Japanese, well equipped. I think we can handle the sentry in San Ildefonso of only nine men, but we may have a problem with the Japanese defense force in San Miguel," Illustrated by Victor, seconded by Carlos.

"OK, tonight we will observe the activities of the sentry in San Ildefonso, and we also need to find out what is going on in the garrison in San Miguel. Maybe we can plan a good approach to the puzzle of one shot hitting two birds. We will see," said Captain Lee to Victor and Carlos, who were listening very carefully.

The following day, Captain Lee, guided by Victor and Carlos, went down to see the sentry in San Ildefonso from a distance and the Japanese garrison in San Miguel to find out their activities during daytime, using a telescope from a distance. He observed the changing of the guards in the sentry, guards from the main Japanese garrison replaced the guards of the sentry during daytime at around noon. The guards in the sentry were not permanent and were relieved by guards coming from the Japanese garrison, their main fort.

When Captain Lee returned to their camp with Victor and Carlos, he called David and Kevin and Alex and explained his observation. He suggested that the four of them come to the sentry at night and observe them until morning before dawn to find out the best plan of action to attack the sentry and to lure the Japanese from the main fort to an entrapment after they killed the guards in the sentry.

Riding on their horses, the four went to observe the sentry. They confirmed the report of Victor and Carlos of nine guards in the sentry. They noticed that after midnight, the sentry was very quiet, and the guards looked inactive, sitting lazily and unconcerned of any possible danger. There were always four guards in front of the sentry, and another five were inside the small housing. They changed four guards at midnight. But 3:00 AM, there was no activity going on at all at the sentry. And the four guards were just seated, unconcerned of any possible danger.

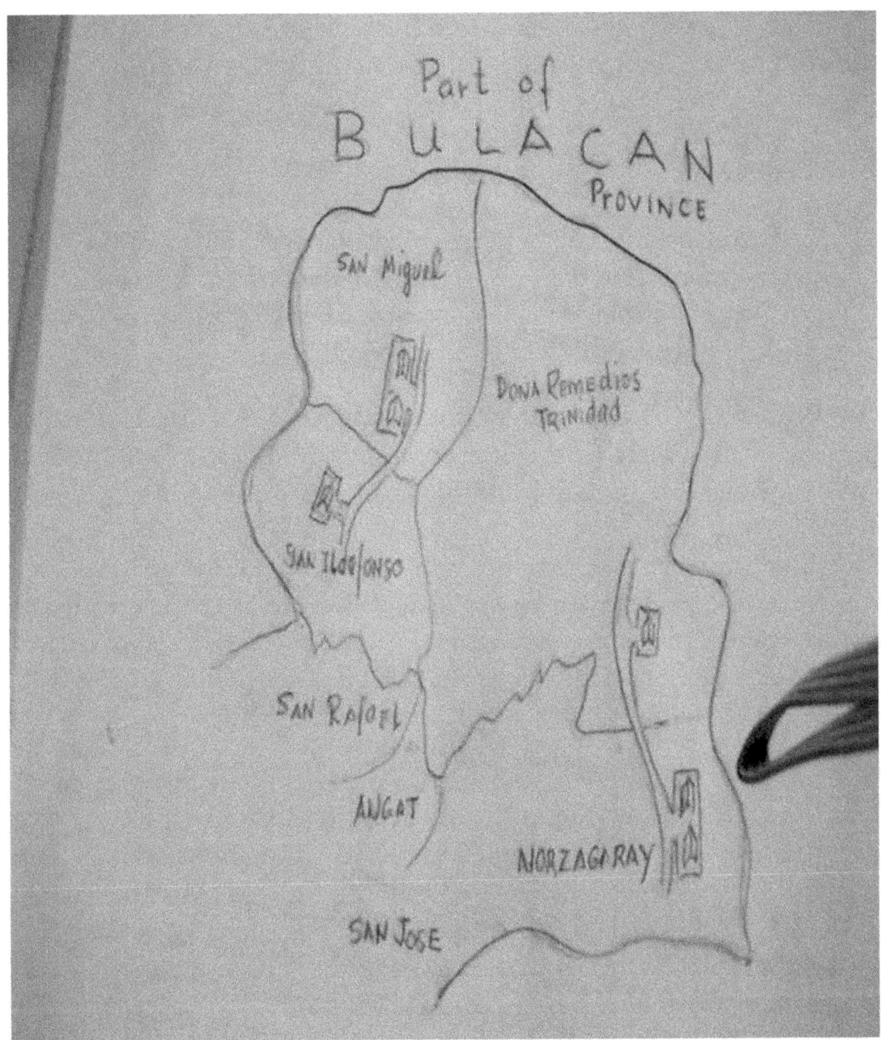



**Sketch of the small housings in the picture were the Japanese sentries and the two enclosed housings were Japanese garrisons**

"You know what I am thinking? We can lure the Japanese from their main fort after we have killed the guards in the sentry. We will set the sentry house on fire to lure the Japanese while we are waiting for them with our heavy weapons. What do you think?" asked Captain Lee to David, Kevin, and Alex.

"That is a very good plan. But let's talk to our men so that we can plan our action properly so that we will have no mistake in the execution of the plan," replied David.

"I agree," followed up Kevin.

"That's right," answered Alex.

The following day, Captain Lee called all the members of the team to explain the military plan of attack that they had talked about the night before, after their final observation of the Japanese camps. He presented the sketch of how they would do their mission.

"OK, men, we have a mission to do tonight. We will travel down to Bulacan, the province we are overlooking from our camp, and we will leave our horses far enough from the Japanese sentry in a wooded area. Then we will just walk and stay close to the sentry until about 2:00 AM. Our attack must be smooth and silent. Do not fire any gun. We will kill all the guards with knives. David, Kevin, Alex, and I will take care of the guards at the gate. Simon, Andrew, Patrick, Robert, and Tomas, take care of the guards at the sides the sentry housing. We will attack and kill all the guards simultaneously at exactly

3:00 AM. Simon and Andrew, use the back door for your entry. Jim, Juan, Felipe, Jun, Ted, Martin, Pablo, Diego, and Isaac, you take your position along the road on the left-hand side of the sentry building around ten feet from the road. After we successfully killed all the guards in the sentry, Victor and Carlos, you burn the sentry house and fire your guns upward to call the attention of the Japanese in their main fort so that we can lure them to come to the sentry. We will prepare for our line of fire on the left side of the road. Julian and Marco, you will be firing a .30-caliber machine gun in our leftmost column. And in the middle, David and Kevin will be firing their .50-caliber machine gun. And in our rightmost column, I will be firing a .30-caliber machine gun, when the Japanese are lured to our entrapment. In between us will be all the riflemen. Be sure that we all have more than enough ammo for this mission. When we start firing, Marco, throw a hand grenade to the last truck. Kevin, you throw a hand grenade to the middle truck. And, Alex, you throw a hand grenade to the first truck so that the convoy will be paralyzed. Do you have any questions or suggestions?" explained Captain Lee, followed by a question.

"If you do not have any more questions, prepare your black uniforms, prepare and clean your guns, have enough ammo. Have a good rest. We leave at exactly 6:00 PM tonight. Thank you," followed up by Captain Lee as his final instruction to his crew.

At exactly 6:00 PM, the crew left on horseback, completely prepared for their mission. As planned, they left their horses in the wooded area away from the sentry, then just walked to the sentry to wait for 2:00 AM. At two thirty in the morning, they were already in their assigned position, ready for the execution of their plan. At 3:00 AM, they simultaneously moved on and executed their plan. The four guards at the entrance were killed, and the guards inside the sentry housing were all killed. Captain Lee ordered Victor and Carlos to burn the housing and fire their guns to lure the Japanese from their main fort. Captain Lee ordered all men to be in their respective positions and wait until he called, "FIRE!"

Victor and Carlos poured gasoline around the housing of the sentry, then ignited the line of gasoline to start the fire. Then they started firing upward to the direction of the big Japanese installation, while the column of the firing squad headed by Captain Lee was anxiously waiting. A little later, they could hear the thundering sound of trucks coming to their direction along the road, coming from the direction of the big Japanese garrison. When the Japanese convoy passed in front of them, Captain Lee ordered to fire. Marco, Kevin, and Alex threw their hand grenades as planned. The convoy went on a sudden stop and was riddled with bullets coming from the waiting column of gunfire headed by Captain Lee. Everybody in the convoy was killed. Then Captain Lee ordered his team to attack the main garrison of the Japanese since there should not be many soldiers left there.

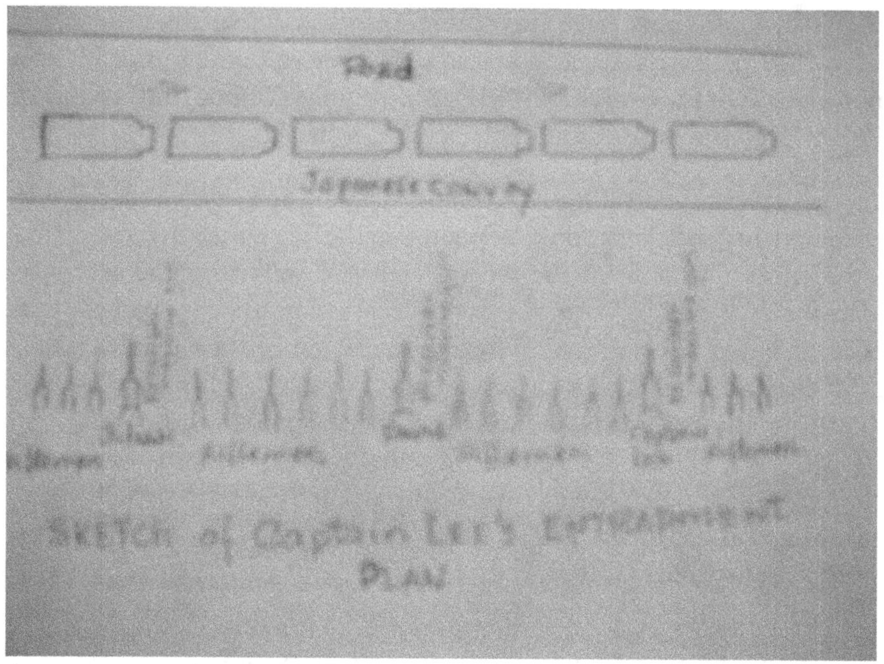


When they reached the front of the garrison, they right away fired their machine guns and riddled the front of the building. The team entered the compound without so much resistance, surprised with their firepower. They entered the compound firing and killed all the unsuspecting Japanese. The team checked around to see to it that everything was under control. When they were inside the weapon stockpile of the building, Captain Lee noticed a big cannon on the side, with some big ammo.

"Hey, Alex, would you please call David or Kevin so they can identify what this big thing here is? Thank you," instructed Captain Lee to Alex.

When David and Kevin arrived inside the stockroom, David and Kevin were so surprised.

"That is a bazooka. We will need that to fire against the big weapons of our enemies. Let's take that with us together with the ammunition. Also I have noticed some gasoline tanks. Let's get some and some bottles so we can make some Molotov bombs," answered David, followed with a suggestion.

They took a carriage from the back of the building and loaded them with plenty of food supplies and more ammo for additional supplies for their future missions. They burned the Japanese garrison, and at 6:00 AM, their mission was complete, and they all headed back to the mountain with no casualty. When they arrived in their camp on top of the mountain, Angelo, Maria, and Anna were ready to serve their breakfast. There was coffee and cream, tea extracted from lemongrass, boiled yam and *camote* roots, and broiled tendered meat of deer just caught the day before near their camp. It was a beautiful morning for the guerilla unit, who for the first time in their missions used heavy weapons in an offensive way. It was the first time they experienced attacking a well-equipped Japanese military garrison, which they overwhelmed with heavy firepower.

After a couple days of rest, Victor and Carlos approached Captain Lee about the two towns in the province of Bulacan, which had the same setting as the one they just demolished successfully.

"Captain Lee, there is a similar installation on the other side of the province of Bulacan that we can probably look at for our next mission. The Japanese sentry is located in the town of Dona Remedios Trinidad, and the Japanese garrison is a mile away in the town of Norzagaray. We will go with you to do a surveillance to take note of their activities and to find out the best time for us to attack them," explained Victor.

"Yes, Captain Lee, I think we can handle this mission similar to what we did in San Miguel and San Ildefonso," followed up Carlos.

"OK, let us watch their activities day and night so we can prepare the best planning to accomplish a successful mission. When we do our mission, I do not want any commission of mistake. I want a perfect execution of the plan without any casualty. Let's leave very early tomorrow morning. Do not carry any weapon, just your telescopes. We will observe them at a distance. OK?" instructed Captain Lee to Victor and Carlos.

The three left very early in the morning, riding their horses to do surveillance for their next military mission. When they reached the town of Dona Remedios Trinidad, where the sentry was located, they stopped far behind the sentry in the wooded area. They climbed the tall trees and used their telescopes to check the activities in the sentry. They noticed that there were twelve guards that manned the sentry, and there were times when there was exchanging of guards, coming and going to the garrison a mile away. They then went to observe the Japanese garrison located in the town of Norzagaray, a mile away from the sentry. They noticed that there were more soldiers in this garrison compared to that in San Miguel. After looking and observing the strength and the number of the enemies to be encountered, Captain Lee was so hesitant to order the mission without consulting his team. When the three went back to their camp, Captain Lee called David, Kevin, and Alex for a meeting and explained what he observed with Victor and Carlos.

"I want you to go with me to do an evaluation of the Japanese installations in the towns of Dona Remedios Trinidad and Norzagaray. The setting is similar to that of San Miguel and San Ildefonso, but this has more soldiers in the sentry and in the main garrison. I want you to go with me tonight, and let's observe closely their activities. We have to wear our black uniforms so that they will not see us in the dark. Let us see if we can successfully do a mission in this location. OK?" instructed Captain Lee to David, Kevin, and Alex.

"Do we have to take with us weapons?" asked David.
"No, just telescopes and your samurai for cutting hindrances on our way," answered Captain Lee.

The four left the camp after 6:00 PM and rode their horses in the darkness of the night. When they were half a mile away from the sentry, they left their horses tied to the trees and just walked to the back of the sentry. They watched the movements of the guards inside the compound, and they crawled to the side of the sentry in the dark to observe the activities of the guards in the front of the sentry. They noticed that at 2:00 AM, the sentry was already very quiet. They proceeded to assess the road between the garrison and the sentry to check where they can position their columns of gunners. Then they proceeded to observe the activities in the Japanese garrison. The garrison was well guarded in the front, back, and both sides of the compound. There were six trucks inside the compound, but it was so quiet that you could not hear anything. After their thorough observation, they walked back to their horses and headed back to their home base to discuss what action they had to do.

It was already late morning when they reached their home base. Everybody had already eaten their breakfast. The four went straight to the breakfast table, where they were served by Angelo, Maria, and Anna. After they had eaten their breakfast, the four went to the drawing table to discuss the feasibility of pursuing a mission. If they had to do a military mission, how would they do it in a way that the mission would be successful? They sketched the plan based on their observations the night before.

"OK, this is what I think what we must do so that we can be sure of 100 percent success in our mission. Like we did in San Ildefonso, we will kill all the guards in the sentry without using guns. We have to silently kill the guards in the sentry so as not to alarm the soldiers in the garrison. We need exactly twelve men to do the job. After we have killed the twelve guards, we have to position our machine guns and riflemen on the left side of the road between the sentry and the garrison. We will wait, holding our fire until the Japanese from the garrison arrived. Victor and Carlos will burn the building of the sentry and fire their guns upward, pointing to the direction of the garrison, to attract their attention to the entrapment. We are expecting more Japanese soldiers in this operation, so we must have lots of ammo with us to be sure we will not run out of firepower."

"I think that is a very good and sound plan," said David.

"I do not see any problem even though there are more Japanese soldiers in this mission. We just have to execute our plan the way we did in San Miguel and San Ildefonso. We should be OK," followed up Kevin.

"Yah, that's right. Let's just follow what we did in our last military mission, and I think we will be all right," followed up Alex.

"OK, let us call everybody so that we can prepare our action plan," said Captain Joseph.

Captain Joseph called everybody to assemble, to plan and give their respective assignments in this very delicate mission.

"This military mission that we will carry out is more dangerous than the last one that we successfully accomplished, but I believe with proper coordination, execution, and timing, we can accomplish our mission successfully without any casualty. First thing we have to do is to kill the twelve guards in the Japanese sentry. You will see the sentry when we arrive there at night. We will wait until two thirty. Then we move to our position, and we execute the killing of the guards at exactly 3:00 AM. David, Kevin, Alex, and me will kill the four guards at the gate. Simon and Patrick, you take care of the guards on one side of the building. And, Andrew and Roberto, you both take care of the guards on the other side of the building. Jim, Juan, Tomas, and Martin, you take care of the four guards inside the sentry building. Felipe and Pablo, you follow Jim, Juan, Tomas, and Martin just in case they need help. Jun, Ted, Diego, Isaac, Julian, Marco, and Daniel, take your position with your rifles along the side of the road around fifteen feet from the road between the sentry and the garrison. Julian, set your .30-caliber machine gun toward the direction of the garrison. We will join you when we have accomplished our mission of killing the guards, with me setting my .30-caliber machine gun, and David will be firing his .50-caliber machine gun. Victor and Carlos will burn the sentry building and will create noise to lure the Japanese soldiers to come to the aide of the burning sentry. Please hold your fire until I yelled, 'FIRE.' When we start firing, Alex, you throw a hand grenade to the lead car. Marco, you throw a hand grenade to the last car. And, Kevin, you throw a hand grenade to the middle car. By this, we will paralyze the Japanese line, and we will trap and kill all the Japanese without giving them the chance to fire a shot. Are you all clear with your assignments?" explained Captain Lee, followed up with a question.

"If you do not have any more questions or clarifications, set your time. We will leave at 6:00 PM tonight. Eat well your dinner. This coming operation is more daring than the other operations we have experienced. Be sure you have enough ammo. This will be a big operation. Those who are assigned to kill the guards in the sentry must wear black uniforms, and the other team members, whatever is more convenient with you in firing your guns is OK with me. Have your handguns ready just in case you may use it. OK, let us go ahead and get ready," instructed Captain Lee.

At exactly 6:00 PM, the group left on their horses, heading to the sentry located in the town of Dona Remedios Trinidad. They arrived in the area almost midnight and left their horses in the wooded area twenty yards from the Japanese sentry. The personnel assigned to execute the guards in the sentry closely observed the activities in the compound. Those who were assigned to be part of the column to entrap the incoming Japanese help surveyed the area where they had to position. They were all so very careful not to make any unnecessary noise. At 2:30 AM, the assigned assassinators to the sentry guards were in their respective positions, and at 3:00 AM, they executed the plan, silently killing all the guards in the sentry without firing a gun. Captain Lee right away called Victor and Carlos to prepare burning the sentry building. He told the two to pour gasoline around the building but not to start the fire until he gave the signal. Captain Lee then proceeded to the column of his men to check their assignments and readiness. He checked the gunner and ammo supplies, then the positions of the gunners and the riflemen and personnel responsible for throwing the hand grenades to the first, middle, and last Japanese military truck. After Captain Lee completely checked everybody in the column for their readiness, he signaled to Victor and Carlos to burn the Japanese sentry building to lure the Japanese in the garrison to come to the aide of the sentry. They fired their guns upward toward to the direction of the Japanese garrison to be sure that they would hear them and give attention to the fire they created.

The group of Captain Lee waited patiently with their fingers on the triggers of their guns. They were anxiously waiting, and every minute seemed like a day, when finally after around fifteen minutes, they could hear the thundering sound of the trucks rushing to their direction. Everybody was holding their breath. Then when the convoy of Japanese trucks was passing in front of them, Captain Lee yelled, "FIRE." The convoy totally stopped when the hand grenade was thrown by Alex to the lead truck, which gave the column of gunners the opportunity to completely annihilate the convoy, killing all the Japanese in the trucks, giving them no chance to even fire a single shot. All the five cars were on fire, ablaze due to the explosion when the gasoline tanks of the trucks caught fire.

Captain Lee ordered his group to move toward the direction of the garrison, with their guns pointing to the road. He was expecting more Japanese support, which would be coming after they had heard explosions and shootings. A little later, there were Japanese soldiers on foot running to the direction of the flaming convoy of trucks, with their guns drawn. Captain Lee told his men to hold their fire until they came closer. When Japanese soldiers on foot were within reasonable distance, Captain Lee ordered, "FIRE," killing all the Japanese soldiers.

Captain Lee then ordered his men to proceed to the garrison in the dark without using the road, on foot, along the grassy and wooded side. When they were near the garrison, they could see that there were already a few Japanese soldiers left in the garrison, and they were all out in front of the garrison building, ready for a shootout. The group entered the back of the compound by cutting the barbwires, then surprised the Japanese with the volley of firepower coming from the side of the garrison building. Some members of the group entered the back door of the garrison and found nobody inside. All the Japanese soldiers were all in the front of the compound, expecting that the attack would come from the gate, but they were surprised when the volley of fire came from their side and behind.

Captain Lee ordered to check the garrison of what they could commandeer to bring to their camp. Captain Lee went to the stockroom of the garrison and noticed something in a case. He called Kevin, who was just passing by to check on what was going on.

"Hey, Kevin, do you know what is in this casing? I do not want to open it because I am not sure what is in it," asked Captain Lee to Kevin.

"Oh, that is a chain saw. Let us take that with us. We can use that in our camp. Let us also take some boxes of nails there in the corner and a couple of hammers. They will be useful in the camp. There is also a medicine cabinet here. Let us take that as well," said Kevin with an expression of delight.

"Captain Lee!" yelled Simon from another room.

"What, Simon, what do you have there?" questioned Captain Lee. "Look, Captain, I opened this steel cabinet, and I found a drawer full of

Japanese money. What shall we do with these?" questioned Simon to Captain Lee.

"Get the whole drawer and all the money in it. We may use the money when we go down the mountain to buy anything," suggested Captain Lee.

"Hey, Kevin, come here. I am here in the closet!" yelled David from a nearby room.

"What do you have there?" Kevin walked to the room where David was. "Look, there are some civilian shirts and pants that may fit us. Do you want some?" asked David to a surprised Kevin.

"Yeah, let me have some. I have not changed my clothing for a while now," answered Kevin.

"I'll take some myself. I'll change after I took my bath in the camp," replied David.

"Come on, guys, let's go!" yelled Captain Lee.

"Let's go, Kevin. Get what you want. I have selected already what I want," instructed David to Kevin.

Some members of the group who went to get the horses they left a few yards from the sentry were already back. They loaded into a cart what they had gathered from the garrison and hooked the cart to one of the horses. They were able to confiscate more ammo and more food supplies and took some guns and handguns. After they had emptied the stockroom and kitchen with food supplies, they all headed back to their hideout on top of the mountain.

Without their knowledge, a Filipino "*Makapili*" (a Filipino spy for the Japanese) spied on their location and reported their activities to the Japanese central military operation in the province of Bulacan. It was a sunny morning while everybody was resting, when the three guards—Julian, Marco, and Daniel—noticed from a faraway road a convoy of trucks that appeared to be Japanese military soldiers coming to their direction. Julian asked Marco to right away report to Captain Lee that the enemies were coming. Upon receiving the message, Captain Lee right away grabbed his telescope and went with Marco to have a clear view of the coming convoy of the Japanese. After confirmation of the danger, Captain Lee told Julian and Marco to go with him, and they all right away ran to their campsite, and Captain Lee ordered everybody to prepare for battle.

"Men, a big convoy of the Japanese is coming. Get ready with your guns, ammo, and hand grenades. We have to use everything we have to stop their advance to our territory here on top of the mountain, or else we will be in big trouble. David and Kevin, get ready with your .50-caliber machine gun. Julian and Marco, get ready with your .30-caliber machine gun. Everybody, prepare your semi- and automatic rifles, and I will get ready with our .30-caliber machine gun. Kevin, Marco, and Alex, do not forget to take with you some hand grenades. David, you position your .50 caliber with me in the front line behind those bushes. I'll be with you with my .30-caliber machine gun. Do you have any questions?"

"Captain Lee, I'll bring with me the bazooka and some ammo. I also have some prepared Molotov bombs ready," said Kevin to Captain Lee.

"Good job, Kevin. OK, let's go, and take your positions to counterattack the coming Japanese military might."

The group took their battle positions—David with his .50 caliber and Captain Lee with his .30 caliber in the front line, hidden behind the bushes along the path leading to their camp on the mountaintop. Captain Lee ordered to hold their fire until he commenced firing. They had to wait until the Japanese convoy was close enough for an easy and effective target. Everybody in the firing line was on their triggers, breathlessly waiting for Captain Lee's order to fire. Then when the convoy was close enough, Captain Lee shouted, "FIRE!" and he commenced firing, followed by a volley of firepower from everywhere, overwhelming the incoming Japanese convoy. They were so surprised that they did not have any chance to prepare to respond. Kevin fired his bazooka with the help of Daniel and hit the front of the lead truck, which caused the Japanese convoy suddenly stop, then explode. Kevin put down the bazooka and hurled the Molotov bombs, and one hit the fender of a truck, which caused the gasoline to scatter, causing fire everywhere—some dried grass, leaves, and trees. The fire became so big that it created a big wall. The wind coming from the top of the mountain caused the fire to blow downward toward the convoy, which caused the Japanese to retreat. The blazing fire was so huge and was coming closer to their front line. Captain Lee ordered all his men to back away and return to their hideout to prepare for evacuation.

"Men, let us evacuate from here. There is no way we can control that big inferno. That fire is too huge that we need firefighters and a lot of water to control it. We have to abandon this campsite and move farther where we will not be reached by this huge fire. Let us load our things into the carts. We have to move quickly toward the south of this mountain. Marco and Daniel, get ready with our horses. We have a long way to travel. Angelo and Diego, take good care of our food supplies and cooking materials. Victor and Carlos, please help Angelo and Diego. Simon and Andrew, please supervise your men with the loading of our guns and ammo into the carts. And, Kevin, we will leave behind those canisters of gasoline. They can cause us a lot of trouble. David and Alex, please help hooking those carts to the two carabao— the carts hauling our guns and ammo and other military equipment. Use the cow and the horse to haul the food supplies and other food service materials."

Because of the huge uncontrollable fire blazing in their campsite, the group of Captain Lee was forced to abandon their camp and head south of the Sierra Madre Mountain Range. To all the members of the group, including Captain Lee, they did not know what was waiting for them in the southern part of the Sierra Madre Mountain Range

# Chapter XI
## Christmas 1943

THE CONVOY OF the guerilla unit led by Captain Lee hurriedly evacuated their camp on top of the Sierra Madre Mountain Range overlooking the province of Bulacan. They headed southward of the mountain range with the plan to reach that part of the mountain range overlooking the province of Quezon. The terrain of the mountain was very challenging, rough, and uneven, with many hills and thick forest, rivers, and brooks that they had to pass and overcome. After several days of challenging journey, they finally reached the point of the mountain overlooking the province of Rizal. In a nearby freshwater spring, Captain Lee ordered their caravan to have a stopover for several days so that they can have a good rest and recover after the grueling and punishing rough travel from their burning camp on the top of the mountain overlooking the province of Bulacan. He assembled his men for a short briefing.

"OK, men, we have to station here for several days to regain our strength. We are already tired running away from that gigantic blazing fire. We still have a very long way to go. We need to reserve our energy. Let us have some good rest and good sleep here since we have clean drinking water in this spring. I also checked my calendar and noted that today is December 21, 1943, five days before Christmas. We will spend our Christmas here in our temporary camp rather than on the trail so that we can enjoy the food and drink together on Christmas Day. Julian, Marco, and Daniel, take care of our horses. Angelo, Maria, and Anna, prepare for something to eat. Diego, please give a hand to Angelo, Maria, and Anna in cooking our food. Simon, Andrew, Patrick, and Tomas, see if you can hunt for deer or wild hogs. We need some meat for dinner. Jim, Juan, Felipe, Jun, Ted, Roberto, Martin, Pablo, and Isaac, you gather some materials we can use to build a temporary shelter. David, Kevin, and Alex, help the crew to build the temporary shelter. Victor and Carlos, please survey the trail going south. We have to have a clear way of traveling to the south. Check the best route we are going to follow with less hassle. For the meantime, get something to eat from our food cart while we are waiting for some cooked and warm food. OK, let us keep moving," instructed Captain Lee to his crew.

Angelo, Diego, Maria, and Anna right away proceeded to the cart where the cooking materials were loaded, unloaded the cooking pots, and gathered the needed provisions for cooking. Angelo set up tripod stones for a stove, while Diego gathered some firewood. The four got busy helping each other to cook their meals of rice and vegetables and some canned meat. They boiled water for their coffee, served with sugar and cream. They also served tea extracted from lemongrass and guava leaves. There was no formality in serving the food because everybody had something to do, so whoever was hungry came to the table, where the food was always ready to be served hot.

Jim, Juan, Felipe, Jun, Ted, Roberto, Martin, Pablo, and Isaac went to get their materials for building their temporary camp. They gathered some cogon grass and bunched them in tiled arrangement for the roofing of their temporary quarters. They also gathered some bamboo trunks to be used as materials for different parts of the house. They also cut some woods to be used as posts, and they used split bamboo to hold the tiled bunched cogon grass to hold their roofing.

Victor and Carlos left to survey the trail that they would use in going to the southern part of the mountain range. They would like to see to it that their carts would have no problems moving through those trails, usually blocked by thick bushes and branches of trees.

Captain Lee, David, Kevin, and Alex went around and looked for a flat space close to the spring, where they can install their temporary housings. After they selected the area, they summoned the group of Jim to deliver the materials to the site. Then they worked together to put the posts, the studs, the braces, and the wood pieces holding the roof made of tiled cogon grass.

Simon, Andrew, Patrick, and Tomas left to hunt for deer and wild pigs. They went to the place they felt was the feeding place of the deer, not far from their camp. When they reached the deer's feeding place, they hid behind trees, trying to have a clear view of the feeding area, when Simon saw from a distance a big deer with long horns.

"Guys, do not move. I could see one big deer standing in the grassy area near that tall tree. You all stay here. I'll try to come closer for a better view of the head of the deer."

Simon carrying his rifle slowly moved, transferring while hiding from tree to tree to have a better view of the head of the deer. When he thought he had a clear view of the neck and was close enough for a good shot, he fired his rifle, hitting the deer on the side of the neck. The deer tumbled sideward, and Simon ran to check the fallen deer. The deer was dead in one shot. Andrew, Patrick, and Tomas followed Simon, and all cheered when they saw the lifeless deer. They went back to their camp area carrying the big deer on the shoulders of Patrick and Tomas. They handed the deer to Angelo and Diego to dress and to prepare for cooking for their dinner. When Angelo and Diego received the big deer, they started dressing it, cut it to manageable sizes, washed the meat with salt, rinsed, then cooked the meat into their native spicy *caldereta*. Maria and Anna broiled the cleaned and washed internal organs of the deer.

David, Kevin, Alex, Jim, Juan, Felipe, Jun, Ted, Roberto, Martin, Pablo, and Isaac worked till it was dark, trying to finish walls and something to cover their heads just in case it rained. The cold breeze could already be felt as the wind blew in the mountaintops. For the whole day, they were able to build at least three housing units. They had been used to building temporary shelter, so it did not take them long to assemble three from scratch.

It was already very late when Victor and Carlos came back from their mission to survey and clear their path going to the southern part of the mountain range, locating the best terrain, where they could easily pull their cart without so much hassle and effort. They had to continue their mission the following day. They were back tired and hungry, ready for dinner.

Angelo set up the folding tables side by side, then covered them with washed banana leaves, where they served the warm rice, some root crops, and the broiled internal organs of the deer. On the side was a big pot of hot spicy caldereta. The crew started coming, tired from the day's work. After they washed their hands in the nearby spring, they fell in line, and each took a coconut shell, which served as their dinner plate. Each one took their food, then sat in a corner to enjoy them, eaten by bare hand and served by the cooking crew of Angelo, Diego, Maria, and Anna.

Angelo and Diego dug a small pit near their cooking area to serve as their garbage disposal for their dirty leftovers and other foodstuff that would attract flies. They made a matrix of bamboo sticks attached to a wooden frame to serve as cover of the pit.

During the second day, the crew of David, Kevin, Alex, Jim, Juan, Felipe, Jun, Ted, Roberto, Martin, Pablo, and Isaac easily finished the last and fourth housing they were building, so they decided to start working on the things they had to do in preparation for the coming Christmas Day. The crew went down to the lowland just below the mountain range within the area of Rizal Province, which had coconuts planted, bearing matured fruits. The crew just walked down the mountain to find the coconut plantation, where they could get matured coconuts to be used to extract coconut oil. When they found some coconut trees with some matured fruits,

"Who is going to start to climb the coconut tree?" asked Alex to the group.

"I will," answered Jim.

"I will also climb," responded Pablo.

"OK, the two of you would be enough. We just need a few matured fruits to extract oil. We will also need the husk to be used as wick to make torches," answered Alex, who was familiar with the making of bamboo torches.

The two climbed two coconut trees, and when they had hauled one dozen matured coconuts, Alex told them to climb down.

"Jim, Pablo, we have enough already. You can come down. We will head back to our campsite!" yelled Alex to Jim and Pablo on top of the coconut trees.

David, Kevin, Alex, Juan, Felipe, Jun, Ted, Roberto, Martin, and Isaac helped pick up the fallen coconuts. After they picked up all the matured coconuts, they headed to get some small bamboo trunks to be used as posts for the torches. They passed a group of bamboo plants along the way and secured the needed materials for their torches. Then the crew headed home to their campsite. When they reached their camp, they removed the husks from the coconut shells. They opened the coconut shells to expose the coconut meat, then handed them all to Angelo and Diego to extract coconut oil. The crew then cut their bamboo trunks to be six feet high. One end was sharpened, and the other end was made into a cup, which would hold a tin can containing the oil. They also shaped some coconut husks to fit the tin can, which would serve as wick for the torch. They made fourteen torches ready to be lit.

In preparation for Christmas, Simon, Andrew, Patrick, and Tomas left very early in the morning and headed to the nesting place of wild pigs. This time they had to take with them a horse to be used to carry their catch. When they arrived in the nesting place, they climbed the trees overlooking the nesting place of the wild pigs and waited. They had seen small piglets roaming around, but they were not interested because they were still too small. They waited for the male boar and the mother pig. After an hour of waiting, a big boar came out growling. Andrew, who was closer to boar, signaled to the crew to be quiet and not to move. Andrew aimed his gun to the neck, and in one shot, the boar fell down on its side. With the sound of the gun, all other animals in the area ran away. The crew went down from the tree and looked at their catch. They tied the two hind legs of the wild pig, then hooked the tied legs to a rope attached to the horse. They led the horse back to their camp and handed the wild boar to Angelo and Diego to be prepared for cooking.

The four were very happy and got excited with the experience and went back to hunt after lunch. They wanted to get more catch. This time they would like to hunt for a deer. They went to the grassy area where the deer usually roamed around, but after an hour, they failed to see any. The four decided to walk a little farther to a hilly wooded area, and from their location, Andrew could see from his telescope the tail of a big deer. Andrew advised the others to be quiet and not to move. Andrew advanced slowly, trying to circumvent the deer so that he would have a clear view of the head. He climbed to the other side of the hill and then moved slowly toward the location of the deer. There were three big deer eating the leaves of the lower branches of a tree. One deer was just resting comfortably, while another was looking to the other side of the hill. When Andrew came close enough without being noticed by the deer standing, eating some leaves, he aimed the barrel of his gun to the neck and fired. The sound of the gun caused the other deer to run away. The deer he shot fell forward lifeless and rolled a little downward on the hillside. Simon, Patrick, and Tomas, who were watching everything, came and looked at the shot deer. It was so big that they couldn't just carry it on their backs. They pulled down the deer to the bottom of the hill and got their horse so that they can haul the dead deer back to their camp.

On their way home, in the damp side of the hill just across the grassy land where they usually hunted for deer, Patrick noticed hidden on the side of the grassy area, with the back facing their direction, a wild pig pushing the ground looking for food. Patrick signed the other three to be quiet and not to move. Patrick slowly went to the wooded area where he could not be seen or heard by the wild pig but where he could have a clear view of the wild pig's entire body. When he was close enough and had a clear view of the wild pig, he fired a shot, hitting the wild pig in the lower neck, busting the throat region. The wild pig tumbled to its side. The crew left the horse and ran to the fallen wild pig.

"Wow, it is big enough for roasting. Good job, Patrick," said Simon.

"OK, let's tie the legs so that we can have it hauled by our horse," said Patrick.

After they had tied the legs, they attached them to the rope hooked to the neck of their horse.

"OK, let us head home," said Andrew.

"I am sure we are going to have a very merry Christmas, with plenty of food on the table. We must give a hand to Angelo and Diego in cooking all these meat. They will be overwhelmed," said Simon.

The four headed to their campsite excited with their catch—a deer and a wild pig.

Simon, Andrew, Patrick, and Tomas, instead of resting after hunting, gave a hand to Angelo, Diego, Maria, and Anna. They helped dress the deer and the wild pig that they had just caught. The first wild pig that they first caught was already cut into pieces by Angelo and Diego and was being cooked already by Maria and Anna. The second wild pig would be intended for roasting. They had to remove the hair with hot water and then remove the internal organs, and it would be prepared for roasting by sticking a long pole of bamboo through its mouth to the anus. The bamboo would be rotated over burning charcoal until the whole pig is roasted, cooked with crispy skin.

David, Kevin, and Alex selected a flat surface away from the wooded area, where they could hold their Christmas celebration. They would like to avoid the fire catching on trees, causing an uncontrollable blaze. The site they selected was not too far from their campsite, with an area of fifty feet by forty feet. With the help of Juan, Felipe, Jun, Ted, Roberto, Martin, and Isaac, they cleared the area. Then they stuck their torches on the ground around the area with a distance of ten feet apart, forming a rectangle of forty feet by twenty feet. They then built a center table made of wood and bamboo, measuring five feet by ten feet. After they finished building the center table, they secured banana leaves, which they exposed to warm fire so that they would not break. Then they put some clean bamboo sticks as weight so that they would not be blown by the wind while waiting for the food to be placed on the table.

Kevin noticed two big dried fallen trees. He went to the cart and got the chain saw. He then cut the trunks of the two trees to one and a half feet in length, to be used for sitting on. After cutting the trunks of the trees, he called Juan, Felipe, Jun, Ted, Roberto, Martin, and Tomas for help. They brought all the cut pieces to the Christmas celebration area to be used as benches.

Very early in the morning the day before Christmas, Captain Lee left on horseback and went down from their mountain campsite to the public market in the town of Antipolo, Rizal. Using some Japanese money they had confiscated from their raids in Bataan and Bulacan, he bought some fruits to be placed on the center table for the Christmas celebration. He bought apples, grapes, ripe bananas, and oranges. He loaded them into a sack, then headed back to their camp on top of the mountain.

**Above is a sketch of the Christmas Celebration area showing the roasted pig in the middle of the table**

Early on the night before Christmas, Captain Lee asked all except the cooking crew to stay in the campsite so that the cooking crew can prepare the table. Angelo, Diego, Maria, Anna, Simon, Andrew, Patrick, and Tomas stayed to prepare the table. Patrick and Tomas were charged of the roasted pork. Simon and Andrew with the help of Maria and Anna cooked the deer, cutting the meat for different recipes. Angelo and Diego with the help of Maria and Anna cooked the big wild pig they cut into pieces and using different recipes. They also added more coconut shells for additional dinner plates. They also had more drinking mugs made of bamboo nodes. After they had set the table, they put off all the lights. It was very dark in the site of the celebration. At exactly twelve midnight on Christmas Eve, David, Kevin, Alex, Juan, Felipe, Jun, Ted, Roberto, Martin, Isaac, Simon, and Andrew lighted each torch at the same time. At the end of the table stood Captain Lee, who then called the attention of everybody.

"Please all stand and come closer to the center table and let us pray for the blessing of the food.

"Father Almighty God,
please give the gift of peace to our beloved country the Philippines.
Please guide us to the path of freedom and liberty
in our battle that we have to fight.
Please shield us with your power and mercy
so that we will be protected against any harm
from the bullets and swords of our enemies.
And for the gift that we are about to receive,
we all dare to say,
'Bless us, O Lord, and these Thy gifts that we are about to receive
from Thy bounty through Jesus Christ our Lord,
amen.'

"OK, men, come on and let's eat!" commanded Captain Lee to all who were surrounding the table. This time there was no line to get food. Everybody had access to the food. In the center of the table, seated was the roasted pork, still hot. Around the roasted pork were different varieties of food recipes from the meat of the wild pig and deer. They also had a tray of fruits at the two ends of the table, symbolizing good harvest.

A little later, Captain Lee ordered Alex to get the box of sake from the cart. While everybody was busy eating, Daniel got his guitar from the cart and hummed some Christmas songs. When he was back in the celebration site, he played and sang "Silent Night." After Daniel sang, David, who used to sing when he was a young boy, sang "O

Holy Night." While singing the song, he was looking around at the faces of everybody to feel their sense of joy for the celebration, when he accidentally looked up to the sky. He saw stars in the sky, and it seemed well lighted. After singing, he stepped out of the celebration area, wanting to enjoy the brilliant stars in the sky. He was then reminded of his mother, the things they did during Christmas. Then he thought of the killer of his mother. He was trying to figure out how he looked, when a shooting star appeared in the sky.

"Wow. What was that? That was a shooting star. I just wanted to think of how the killer of Mom looks like, and the shooting star came from nowhere. Does it mean that somewhere in the future I will meet the killer of my mother?" There were lots of questions that were going on in the mind of David.

*(The spirit of Mary Scarlet was watching David as he was trying to figure out the face of Brutus Diablo, the killer of his mother, when from nowhere a shooting star suddenly appeared. The spirit of Mary Scarlet felt the inevitable. David and her killer would surely meet sometime somewhere in the future.)*

David decided to return to the celebration area, when he met Captain Lee.

"Hey, David, are you enjoying our celebration of Christmas?" asked Captain Lee.

"Yes, Captain Lee, I am just getting a little break. I would like to space my drinking and eating a little bit," answered David.

The celebration continued until morning—eating and drinking and exchanging of stories. On Christmas morning, Angelo, Maria, and Anna served some coffee with sugar and tea extracted from lemongrass. The whole Christmas Day, people were coming and going to the table to eat, while some went to sleep. Christmas Night was very quiet. Everybody were sound asleep. Angelo, Diego, Maria, and Anna took advantage of the quietness of the evening and started cleaning the mess left by the Christmas celebration. It was already 10:00 PM when they finished clearing the area and cleaning everything they used in serving the food. They went to sleep ready to wake up early the following morning to prepare the breakfast for the group.

The following day after Christmas, everybody seemed still disoriented from too much eating and drinking and sleeping long hours. Captain Lee decided to stay another day in the camp and required everybody to take a bath to renew their strength and vigor. Everybody needed to refresh to remove the alcohol and tiredness in their systems. Captain Lee ordered everybody to help prepare for departure. They had to leave the following day, the second day after Christmas.

Very early in the morning, Angelo, Diego, Maria, and Anna prepared their breakfast of grilled semidried salted meat of deer and wild pig, with hot coffee with cream and sugar and tea extracted from lemongrass. After breakfast, Julian, Marco, and Daniel took the two carabaos, the cow, and all the horses from their grazing place to prepare for their departure. David, Kevin, and Alex helped hook the carts to the animals. Other members of the crew cleaned up their camp area, removed all the trash, and piled them in one corner to avoid attracting insects. Simon, Andrew, Patrick, and Tomas helped Angelo, Diego, Maria, and Anna clean up their kitchen area, wash all their cooking materials and servers, and load them into the cart. At around 10:00 AM, they started their journey heading to the southern part of the Sierra Madre Mountain Range, guided by Victor and Carlos.

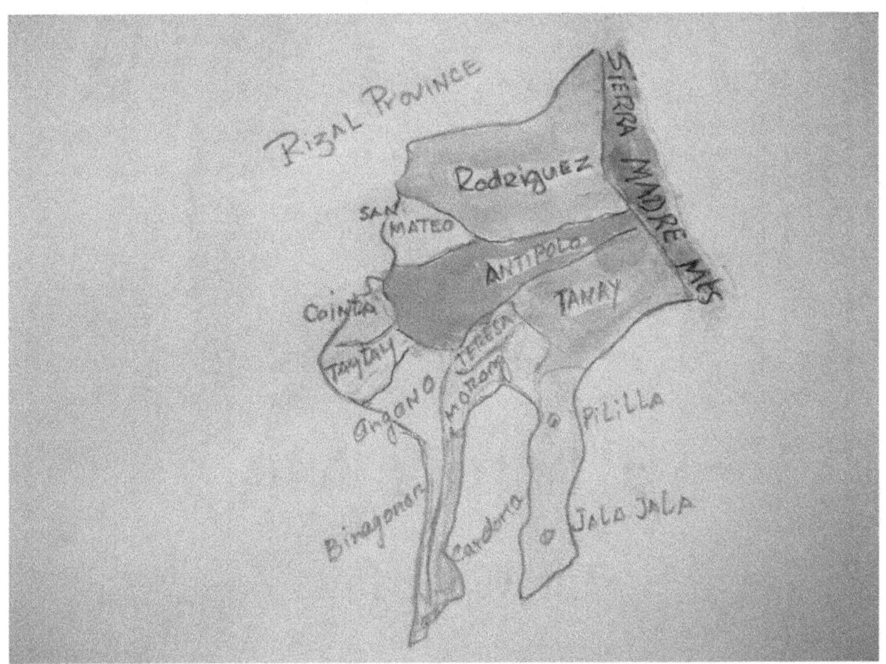



**Sketch of the Rizal Province showing portions of the Sierra Madre Mountain Range**

# Chapter XII

## The Waterfalls

**The acacia tree by the Waterfalls**

THE CARAVAN HEADED by Capt. Joseph Lee once again hit the trail going to an unknown destination, the southernmost part of the Sierra Madre Mountain Range. Once again they passed the trail of wooded and unfamiliar places they had never travelled before. Captain Lee was only using his instinct, a recollection of his map readings and military experiences, in directing his guerilla group in search for a much safer and better place to fulfill their military tactics for which they were trained. Captain Lee accompanied by Victor and Carlos were leading the caravan. They did not seem to feel tired in spite of the long journey that they had travelled. They continued their unstoppable journey until they were close to the boundary of Laguna Province, which covered part of the Sierra Madre Mountain Range, when from nowhere six armed men shouted, "Tigil! Saan kayo patungo? (Hold! Where are you going?)" shouted one of the armed men.

"*Patungo kami sa timog ng Sierra Madre* (We are heading to the southern part of Sierra Madre)," answered Capt. Joseph Lee.

At that point, David, Kevin, and Alex approached Captain Lee to join the conversation.

"*Sir, sumama po kayo sa akin para makausap ninyo and aming commander* (Sir, you come with me so that you can talk to our commander)," said the lead guard.

"*OK, tayo na* (OK, let's go)," answered Captain Lee.

"*Sir, si Antonio po ako* (Sir, my name is Antonio)."

"*Mabuti, ako si Capt. Joseph Lee* (Good, I am Capt. Joseph Lee)."

Captain Lee was escorted by the guard to the headquarters of the guerilla unit of the province of Laguna. David, Kevin, and Alex followed Captain Lee and the guard while the other five guards were left to guard their caravan. After one hour of walking, they finally reached the headquarters of the commander of the group. David, Kevin, Alex, and Captain Lee were surprised. There were many nipa huts built around the area, and the place was like a little community. Standing in front of the headquarters was a tall middle-aged Caucasian-looking man.

Capt. Joseph Lee right away approached the leader of the group to pay respects and ask permission to pass through their territorial coverage.

"Sir, I am Capt. Joseph Lee of the Third Brigade of the Philippine Army," was the introductory statement of Captain Lee as he approached the commander of the group.

"Welcome to our humble community. I am Cmdr. Artemio Borromeo." The commander approached the group and shook hands with Captain Lee.

Captain Lee introduced David, Kevin, and Alex to Commander Borromeo.

"Commander Borromeo, please meet David Scarborough of the U.S. Army, Kevin Smith of the U.S. Marines. The two of them escaped with me from the death march in Mariveles, Bataan. This is Lt. Alex Torres. We were all together when we escaped from the death march. We have formed a guerilla unit in Bataan, and we are transferring our unit to the southern part of this mountain range."

"Well, feel at home in our humble community. You can stay in our area as long as you want. By the way, come on, let's go and see your unit. I am anxious to see your group," requested Commander Borromeo.

Captain Lee led Commander Borromeo to his unit together with David, Kevin, Alex, and Antonio, the guard. When they reached the area where the caravan was located at a distance, Captain Borromeo was already impressed with the display of arms of the unit. He saw the load of guns and ammunition, and everybody in the caravan was well armed. He was impressed with the heavy guns loaded in the cart.

"Wow, you are really ready for a big battle," commented Commander Borromeo.

"We confiscated those arms from the different Japanese garrisons we have attacked. We started just with knives," answered Captain Lee.

"Well, you know you can stay in our community as long as you want. Also, I want to invite the four of you to dinner tonight, so that we can talk about your experiences, say around six o'clock," was the invitational comment of Commander Borromeo.

"OK, sir, I will first settle my group in an area close to a spring to have an access to water to drink. A little spring which I am sure you have some near your area because I could hear the sound of waterfalls," said Captain Lee to Commander Borromeo.

"OK, go ahead and let me know if you need anything," answered Commander Borromeo.

The convoy passed through the community and headed to a nearby spring not far from the house of Commander Borromeo. They selected the wooded area to have shade during daytime, most especially during the middle of the day, the height of sunlight in the mountaintop. Angelo, Diego, Maria, and Anna unloaded their cooking materials, while Angelo set up a tripod stove, and Diego gathered firewood in preparation for cooking their meals. David, Kevin, and Alex helped unhook the animals from the horses. Everybody helped out to bring all the horses to the grassy area, after they had them drink some water from the flowing spring.

After everything seemed settled, David approached Capt. Joseph Lee and asked permission to walk around the area to familiarize himself.

"Captain Lee, I'll just go around and see what is going on in this area. I would like to see the waterfalls that I can hear from here," said David to Captain Lee.

"Go ahead, but do not go very far. You may get lost. We are not familiar with this area," warned Captain Lee.

David walked away from their camp and was very amazed of the many nipa huts in this remote mountaintop away from urban civilization. He walked toward the sound of the waterfalls and was very anxious of everything around. When he was getting closer to the waterfalls, he could hear the sound of women talking and laughing. When he looked down the waterfalls, his eyes were drawn to a beautiful woman taking a bath with other women. When he looked around, the waterfalls was well guarded by armed men. David approached one of the guards as he came closer, getting a better view of the women taking a bath in the waterfalls. He asked the guard some questions.

"Hello, sir, excuse me, can you tell me who that beautiful lady is in the waterfalls?" asked David to the guard.

"Hands off, sir, she is untouchable. Her name is Rosemarie. She is the daughter of Commander Borromeo," answered the guard.

"Can I talk to her just for a minute, just to know her?" asked David.

"No, sir, I am just following orders. You can ask permission from our commander if you want to talk to his daughter."

"Yeah, I think that's what I will do. Thank you," said David to the guard.

David left the guard and headed to their camp. He then approached Captain Lee and told him his problem.

"Captain Lee, I saw a beautiful lady in the waterfalls. The guard told me that she is the daughter of Commander Borromeo. I am interested to meet and know her. What do you think is the best thing I have to do?" asked David to Captain Lee.

"Ethically, you really have to ask permission from Commander Borromeo, most especially that we just came here. You do not want to rush anything that will take away the trust of Commander Borromeo. You can go now and see him because we are not going to stay in this area very long," instructed Captain Lee to David.

David left their camp and went straight to the house of Captain Borromeo, who luckily was just outside of his house, apparently getting some fresh mountain air.

"Good afternoon, Commander Borromeo," was the greeting of David.

"Oh, Mr. Scarborough, what can I do for you?" asked Commander Borromeo.

"Sir, I hope you don't mind. I have seen your daughter, and I am attracted to her. I would like your permission for me to court her," asked David with humility.

"Well, Of course, why not. I just have to remind you that roses have thorns.

If you are not careful, you may get hurt," answered Commander Borromeo.

"Oh, thank you, sir. I will be very careful. Thank you, sir, and good-bye," replied David.

"Good-bye," answered Commander Borromeo.

David left excited and headed to their temporary camp area. He right away took a bath from the spring close to them. He changed his clothes to the one he took from the Japanese closet and fixed his hair and looked for Captain Lee.

"Captain Lee, I am ready when you are," said David to Captain Lee.

"I am still waiting for Kevin and Alex. I do not know where they are now.

We are supposed to leave in an hour," answered Captain Lee.

"There they are, with Angelo and Diego, eating."

"Will you get them and tell Alex and Kevin to get one set of a .30-caliber machine gun and a box of ammo. We will donate the set to Commander Borromeo. I could see that they have no big gun to protect their community just in case they get attacked by the Japanese," instructed Captain Lee to David.

"Yes, sir," responded David to Captain Lee.

David left to get Kevin and Alex. The three of them went to the cart and took with them the .30-caliber machine gun and a box of .30-caliber ammo. They went back to report to Captain Lee to let him know that they were ready to go.

"Captain Lee, we have the .30-caliber machine gun you requested and a box of ammo. We are ready to go," said Alex, holding the .30-caliber machine gun.

"OK, let's go. They must be waiting for us," replied Captain Lee.

The four left their camp and headed to the house of Commander Borromeo. On the way, Captain Lee looked at David and commented, "Hi, David, you look well dressed for the occasion. It looks like there is somebody you would like to meet to impress."

"Oh no, I just felt kind of warm and took my shower, then changed to get ready for dinner," answered David.

When they arrived at the house, Commander Borromeo and another gentleman was at the door waiting for them.

"Good evening, gentlemen. Come in, come in please," were the welcome words of Commander Borromeo. "By the way, please meet my town mate in Laguna, Cesar Amante," said Commander Borromeo as he introduced Cesar to the four.

Captain Lee, David, Alex, and Kevin shook hands with Cesar, introducing their names. Then Captain Lee turned his head to Commander Borromeo.

"Commander Borromeo, we have brought for you a .30-caliber machine gun and a case of ammo that you may use just in case your area is attacked by our enemies," said Captain Lee to Commander Borromeo.

"Oh, thank you very much. We will really need that," answered Commander Borromeo.

"Hey, Alfonso, would you please take this machine gun and case of ammo to our stockroom. I'll check on it next time. Thank you," was the instruction of Captain Borromeo to one of his guards, and then he turned to his guests.

"OK, let us all go inside. Let us talk while they are setting the table for our dinner," requested Commander Borromeo to the four guests.

"Please, have a seat, gentlemen. Petra, will you please serve us some egg rolls here in the living room. Thank you!" yelled Commander Borromeo to his helper.

To the surprise of everybody, it was not the helper Petra who came out carrying a tray of egg rolls. It was his daughter Rosemarie. And everybody stood up in respect. The heart of David almost jumped out of his chest when he saw Rosemarie close in person. She was very beautiful, tall, at 5'9", with a very sweet smile as she came out carrying the tray of egg rolls. David could not stop admiring the beauty of Rosemarie, with her long black hair flowing from her head to her shoulders like silk that made glitters with the rays of light from the lamps. Her eyes were beautiful, with long lashes projecting, making her eyes so tantalizing. Her nose was perfectly formed, her kissable red lips perfectly shaped, which covered the most beautiful white teeth, which sparkled when she smiled, and her well-shaped body curve was an image of the goddess Venus under the shirt tucked in a belted blue pants.

"Oh, this is my daughter Rosemarie." Commander Borromeo pointed to his daughter, who put the tray of egg rolls on the center table.

Rosemarie just waved her hand and sat down in one of the chairs. The five gentlemen sat down and one by one reached out for an egg roll from the center table.

"OK, Captain Lee, please would you tell me more about you? How were you able to form this group that you trained to accumulate so much guns and ammo from the Japanese?" asked Commander Borromeo to Captain Lee.

"Sir, I am a PMA graduate of class 1936 and selected the army as my branch of military service. We fought in Bataan, and we were part of the death march, and the four of us escaped the death march. We formed our guerilla unit in Bataan. We trained our unit to use and kill by knives because we did not have guns. We attacked several Japanese stations in Bataan along Manila Bay, and we confiscated all of the guns, ammo, and food supplies from the Japanese we killed. We are heading south of this Sierra Madre Mountain Range to give my unit a little break for the many battles we fought," explained Captain Lee.

While Captain Lee was telling his story, David was trying to catch the eyes of Rosemarie. He could not stop looking at her. Rosemarie was trying to avoid David's eyes. But when their eyes met, they stared at each other, with David seemingly needing to convey something. Rosemarie evaded the eyes of David and then stood up and politely asked permission to leave. Kevin from the corner of his eyes was smiling, watching David trying to connect his vision with Rosemarie. He could feel that his partner was falling in love.

"Pa, I am going to check if the table is ready for our dinner?" said Rosemarie to Commander Borromeo.

"Oh yes, you may go ahead," answered Commander Borromeo.

"Please excuse me," said Rosemarie to the five gentlemen, and then she turned around, heading to the kitchen to check the preparation of the food.

"We fought a big battle at the foot of Mount Mariveles, and we killed approximately one battalion of Japanese with our surprise attacked when they were coming. They did not have any chance to prepare with the volley of our firepower. After the battle, we escaped Bataan through the province of Pampanga and headed to the Sierra Madre Mountains. The big fire in our camp overlooking the province of Bulacan drove us to move south. That's why we are passing through your area here," continued Captain Lee.

"So what is your plan when you arrive in the southern part of this mountain range?" asked Cesar.

"Oh, I would like to give our unit a rest. We have fought so many battles, and I thought of giving them a little break. Depending upon the call of circumstances, we may do more missions to attack the Japanese installations in the province of Quezon that covers the southern part of this mountain range," answered Captain Lee as he turned, answering the question of Cesar.

"Thank you for your story, Captain Lee. I am also a graduate of PMA class 1930. Cesar was also a graduate of PMA class 1932, but he got out of the military and turned into a businessman. I was also a part of the death march in Bataan, but I was able to escape. I have seen the brutality of the Japanese to Filipino and American soldiers, so when I returned to our town, I invited some of our town mates to come with me here to establish a guerilla community. Our unit is more of a defensive unit. We do not attack. We formed this community just to be away from the ruling of the Japanese in our town, but if they come to attack us, we will fight. We do not have many guns. The .30-caliber machine gun you brought would be a big boost to our unit. Thank you for the .30-caliber machine gun you brought. We now have better firepower just in case we are attacked by the Japanese," replied Commander Borromeo.

A little later, Rosemarie came out to announce that dinner was ready.

"Pa, dinner is ready," was the smiling message of Rosemarie to his father.

"OK, come on, let's all go to the dining room and eat," was the invitation of Commander Borromeo as Rosemarie led the group to the dining room.

Rosemarie did not sit in the dining table but instead helped serve dinner to the guests. She went around serving whatever was needed to be filled—meat, rice, or water—and as she moved around, the eyes of David also moved around, following her. Rosemarie had really noticed the interest of David, and she tried to avoid his eyes. They served stuffed milkfish, fried chicken, and shrimp soup with tamarind extract.

"Wow, I have not eaten fish for a long time. This is wonderful," said Captain Lee.

"One of our guards went very early to the Laguna Bay shoreline, where they were selling newly caught fish, and bought some for us. They also picked up a couple of chickens from the market on their way back," said Commander Borromeo.

David broke his silence when he picked up a piece of fried chicken.

"Rosemarie, did you fry this fried chicken?" asked David to Rosemarie.

"Oh no, I just helped in the kitchen. Aling Petra did all that," answered Rosemarie as she turned to David and right away took her eyes from him to avoid eye contact.

"By the way, Commander Borromeo, I hope you don't mind my asking," asked Captain Lee to Commander Borromeo.

"No, not at all, go ahead. What do you want to know?" asked Commander Borromeo.

"Sir, are you an American? You have Caucasian features. You are tall and has white complexion," asked Captain Lee to Commander Borromeo.

"Oh no, I am a pure Filipino. I was born here in Laguna. My mother was a pure Filipina, but my father was mixed English/Spanish. Maybe the blood of my father was much stronger than my mother. That is why I inherited more the features of my father."

"I am five feet ten inches, and you are taller than me," said Captain Lee. "Oh yes, I am five feet eleven and a half inches tall. I am almost six feet tall," answered Commander Borromeo.

Everybody enjoyed the dinner and the exchange of stories about their journeys. Captain Lee, David, Kevin, and Alex finally bid good-bye to Commander Borromeo and to Rosemarie, who was there all along listening to the conversation but did not say a word. She just smiled once in a while—a very reserved and modest young woman. Cesar also left with them.

"Thank you very much for the dinner. That was very delicious food that you served. We enjoyed every bit of it. Good night," said Captain Lee to Commander Borromeo and to Rosemarie.

"Thank you and good-bye, sir, Rosemarie," David, Kevin, and Alex said to Commander Borromeo and Rosemarie simultaneously as they were heading out with Captain Lee.

"I am going home too," said Cesar to Commander Borromeo and Rosemarie.

Commander Borromeo and Rosemarie remained standing at the door as they watched the five men leave. Commander Borromeo turned to Rosemarie and said, "It looks like David is attracted to you. I have noticed the very affectionate look of David toward you."

"I don't know that, Pa. I just ignored him," answered Rosemarie.

The two headed inside their house and closed their door.

The following day, very early in the morning after breakfast, David decided to walk toward the waterfalls. The sun was shining brightly, coming from the east, with a slight fresh breeze coming from the Pacific Ocean. David felt refreshed for a new day, looking forward with the hope that he would accidentally see Rosemarie in his morning walk. He was right, because he saw Rosemarie walking alone toward the waterfalls. He walked fast, trying to close his distance to Rosemarie. He was walking like a cat, hoping he would not be noticed by Rosemarie, with the intention of jokingly surprising her from behind. But when David was a couple of feet behind Rosemarie, unsuspectingly he got a kick on the abdomen and the heel of the right foot of Rosemarie hit him behind his right knee, between his leg and thigh, which caused him to tumble backward like a log. Before he could react, the right foot of Rosemarie was on his throat, and he could not move. Surprised of what happened, David raised his two hands and said he did not mean any harm.

"Rosemarie, I am David. I did not mean any harm. I was going to surprise you, but you were very quick to hit me," begged David, with the expression of surrender to the unexpected power of Rosemarie.

"OK, stand up. Next time you have to be very careful before you get killed," said Rosemarie with an expression of authority.

David stood up and cleaned the dusts and leaves that stuck to his shirt and pants, then faced Rosemarie with an expression of humbleness.

"Rosemarie, you are good. I like you. I am ready to be your punching bag. Just please give me a few minutes of your time to listen to me."

"Your mouth is very quick, but I think my fist is much faster than you think," replied Rosemarie.

"I am very willing to be hit by your fist. Just please give me a moment of your time to talk so that I can know you more, please," begged David.

The two walked toward the waterfalls and stood not far from the edge of the river. They did not come close to the waterfalls because the sound of the waterfalls was so loud that it was very hard for them to hear each other. David noticed that Rosemarie settled down a little bit, and he started feeling safe from the power of Rosemarie, so he started asking questions.

"Where did you learn those moves? You were impressive. I have not seen that move ever. You surprised me," asked Dave with an expression of sincerity.

"I am a black belt in judo-karate and tae kwon do. My dad wanted me to be physically fit growing up. My dad does not want me to be like my mother, who was very heavyset. She passed away too early when I was just twelve years old of heart attack and kidney complications. My dad wanted me to work out every day to be physically fit."

"Rosemarie, you surprised me. You are amazing and beautiful, and from the very first time I saw you taking a bath in those waterfalls, I felt different. When I saw you up close in your house and when our eyes met, there was something within me that told me I have found the girl I want to marry. I know I am falling in love. Rosemarie, I love you," said David with an expression of sincerity.

"David, do not be carried away of what you see and what you feel. You do not know much about me. Love like a plant takes time to grow. Like the fruit of a mango tree, you have to wait until it ripens, or else it would be sour," answered Rosemarie.

"I am very willing to wait even to the end of time. I will be there waiting for you, with both my hands begging for your mercy to love me."

Rosemarie did not answer and instead politely asked permission to leave.

She said she had to do something at home and she had to go back home.

"David, excuse me, I have to leave. I have to do something at home," was the excuse of Rosemarie, with a little alienation, trying to avoid continuing the conversation about love. She tried to avoid the affectionate eyes of David and turned her back to him.

"Rosemarie, can we see each other here tomorrow? I'll wait," requested David.

"I'll think it over," answered Rosemarie as she hurriedly walked away from David.

David was left so excited that he was able to express the love that he had been holding in his heart since he saw Rosemarie in the waterfalls. He went straight to their campsite and looked for Daniel.

"Hi, Daniel, I would like to ask you a favor," said David to Daniel with a smile.

"Yes, David, what do you want?" answered Daniel.

"I want you to help me. I want to serenade the daughter of Commander Borromeo tonight. Can you help me please?" asked David to Daniel with a smile.

"Sure, just let me know what time you want us to go," answered Daniel.

"Around nine in the evening. Is that all right with you?" asked David.

"OK, nine in the evening is fine. I'll check my guitar to see to it that it is in tune," answered Daniel.

The two walked to the cart to look for the guitar. Daniel checked his guitar to see to it that all the strings were properly tuned. Then the two practiced singing. David tried his tenor voice and practiced the old songs he learned through the years. Daniel practiced his serenade songs.

When it was eight o'clock in the evening, the two went away from the group and started practicing again, and when they were ready, they started heading to the house of Commander Borromeo. Daniel started singing with his serenade songs in Tagalog.

*"Dungawin mo hirang* (Sweetheart look out your window)
*Ang nananambitan* (at the one serenading)
*Kahit sulyap mo man lamang* (even just your momentary look)
*Iyong idampulay* (would you please glance at me)."

With the song of Daniel, Rosemarie opened the window. She was surprised to see David right in front of their house, with a guitarist playing a serenade song. When Rosemarie opened the window, David right away sang his serenade song, "My Serenade." Then with his tenor voice, he lovely sang "If I Love You." Then David sang the song "Oh Rosemarie I Love You" with so much feeling that Rosemarie was touched.

*Oh, Rosemarie, I love you*
*I'm always thinking of you*
*Since that day I met you,*
*I keep on thinking of you*

*All the things around me are the image of you*
*You are everything to me*
*In the bottom of my heart, I have chosen you*
*To be the queen and I'll serve you*

*Oh, Rosemarie, please say you love me. I choose you*
*To rule my life forever*
*My beloved Rosemarie*

After the song of David, Rosemarie waved her hand to David and said good night.

"Thank you for the serenade. Good night," said Rosemarie as she closed her window while waving her hand, bidding good night to David.

The following morning after breakfast, David right away left and walked toward the waterfalls. The morning sun was peeping in between the leaves of the trees, and the fresh breeze of the wind coming from Laguna de Bay in the west and the breeze coming from the Pacific Ocean in the east made the morning so welcoming. David was so excited to go to the place near the waterfalls, where he hoped to see Rosemarie. When he reached the place, he leaned on a big acacia tree that was overlooking the edge of the river, supplied by the water coming from the waterfalls. He loved and appreciated the beauty of the scenery, the verdant surrounding and the continuous flowing from the waterfalls. There was a message of peace in the beautiful picture of nature in spite of the thundering sound of the waterfalls. David looked to the direction of where Rosemarie would be coming from, and there was no shadow of her. David was already worried that she might not come. There were many things that were going into his mind. He was already getting uneasy as the time went by. He looked to the waterfalls and then closed his eyes, imagining the beautiful face of Rosemarie, which he kept as treasure in his heart and mind. It was a different feeling within him; he was very much in love. He once looked again at the direction where Rosemarie was coming from, and there was no Rosemarie. He looked to the waterfalls, then closed his eyes and whispered, "Why, where is she? I love her, I love her very much." But with his eyes closed as he was imagining the beautiful face of Rosemarie that night in their window, smiling while he was serenading, a soft hand touched his right shoulder.

"Hi, David, have you been here long?" said Rosemarie, who surprised David in his daydreaming.

"Oh, Rosemarie, I will wait as long as forever because I love you," said David with emotion.

"I did not know you have a very beautiful voice. How did you learn to sing?" asked Rosemarie as if she did not hear the word "love" spoken by David.

"When I was young, our family used to sing together in our home. My mother trained me to sing. She developed my tenor voice before she passed away. She died in an accident when I was thirteen years old. I miss the love and care of my mother. There were times when I kept on thinking of her. My mother was beautiful, with a soprano voice. She played the piano in our house, especially when we had a get-together. I really miss my mother," explained David to Rosemarie.

"Come on, let's walk near the waterfalls. Let us wade in the water. I would like to feel the tenderness of the water flowing from the rushing of the falls," was the invitation of David to Rosemarie as he offered his hand.

Rosemarie gave her hand to David, and they both went down the side of the river, whose water was supplied by the waterfalls. They walked without speaking as if their hearts were talking and understanding the message of love. They felt different together. Rosemarie for the first time felt secure in the company of David. She seemed to accept the sincerity of the love that David kept on saying. She was starting to smile and felt submissive to the emotions of David. David embraced Rosemarie, and Rosemarie did not resist.

"I love you," David whispered to the ears of Rosemarie as he embraced her.

Rosemarie just smiled and looked at David and invited him to walk home.

"Shall we meet here again tomorrow?" asked David as they walked away from the waterfalls.

"I'll see," answered Rosemarie.

David brought home Rosemarie, but to his surprise, as they were coming in, Captain Lee was coming out of the house together with Commander Borromeo.

"Oh, Captain Lee, why are you here?" asked David to Captain Lee.

"I informed Commander Borromeo that we are leaving tomorrow morning. I was not able to tell you because I could not find you. I do not know where you were," answered Captain Lee.

David was tongue-tied and could not speak. Then he looked at Rosemarie and to Commander Borromeo, then spoke what was in his mind.

"I'll stay here for the meantime, Captain Lee. Let us talk about it in our camp," suggested David.

"OK," replied Captain Lee.

"Sir, we are going now. Thank you again for everything," said Captain Lee to Commander Borromeo.

"Bye, sir, Rosemarie," said David to Commander Borromeo and to Rosemarie.

The two left the house of Commander Borromeo, heading to their camp.

"Where were you? We were all looking for you. We looked all over the place, but we could not find you," asked Captain Lee to David as they walked heading to their camp.

"I was with Rosemarie in the waterfalls. We were just talking," answered David.

"Next time you should let us know or tell somebody where you intend to go so that we will know where to find you," replied Captain Lee to David.

"Captain Lee, I may stay here for the meantime. There is still something that I want to resolve with Rosemarie if you don't mind?" requested David to Captain Lee.

"That is fine. You can follow us to the southern part of this mountain range. You will not miss us. Just go straight southward. That is where we will establish our camp," said Captain Lee.

The following day after breakfast, everybody prepared for departure going south of the Sierra Madre Mountain Range. David helped load everything into the carts. Then he put aside his things—his rifle, handgun, knife, and ammo. Standing in the side of the caravan ready to leave, David was approached by everybody, shaking hands with him, and when it came to Kevin, he gave him a hug and held him by the shoulders and said, "It is hard to fall in love. Good luck, I'll see you in the south."

Captain Lee approached David and said, "David, your horse is in the grassy area in the back of our camp. Use it when you are ready to come to our camp in the south. Good luck. See you later." Then Captain Lee walked to the front of the caravan with Victor and Carlos and gave the sign to move forward. David watched the caravan move southward. He stood watching the caravan until they disappeared from his sight. David did not know that all the time two souls were watching what was going on.

"Sir, I am Isidro Belmonte, and this is my wife, Amanda. We have been watching you and your group. We overheard that you will be left behind by your guerilla unit, and we know that you have no place to stay here. My wife and I would welcome you to stay in our little house for the meantime," said Mang Isidro to David.

"That would be great, sir. I will be honored to be your guest in your house. Thank you very much. By the way, sir, my name is David Scarborough of the U.S. Army. You can just call me David," was the polite and thankful introductory answer of David.

"Come, let's go to our house. Just near your camp. It is just my wife and me in the house. You can bring your things with you," said Mang Isidro to David.

Mang Isidro and Aling Amanda led David, walking toward their little house. When they reached the house, Mang Isidro and Aling Amanda welcomed David into their home.

"Come in, David," Mang Isidro and Aling Amanda said. Led by Mang Isidro, they all went to the room they want to assign to David.

"This will be your room while you are with us, and for anything that you need, please let us know. You are our guest here in our house. We are not rich, but we are hospitable," said Mang Isidro.

The room is small but good enough for David to rest and to spend the night, more especially that he has no place to stay in the area.

"David, can we offer you something, coffee?" said Aling Amanda.

"No, ma'am, thank you very much. We just had our breakfast this morning. Mang Isidro and Aling Amanda, if you don't mind, I'll leave with you here in my room my weapons. I do not want to be carrying them around," said David to Mang Isidro and Aling Amanda.

"You can leave your weapons in your room. Nobody will touch that. That will be secure in this room. My wife and I are always here," said Mang Isidro.

"Thank you very much for your hospitality. I will go out for a moment to walk to the waterfalls. I have to meet somebody near the waterfalls. I'll be back later," said David to the couple.

"You go ahead. We will wait for you for lunch," said Mang Isidro, with Aling Amanda looking.

David left hurriedly to the direction of the waterfalls. He was not sure if Rosemarie would be there. There were so many things going on in his mind, with Rosemarie knowing their guerilla unit was supposed to leave that morning. He walked, ran, and jogged until he could see the acacia tree that was on the edge of the river overlooking the waterfalls, and under the acacia tree was Rosemarie watching the waterfalls. The sun was bright; it was a beautiful morning. David was relieved and walked normally with a smile. Then he slowly approached Rosemarie, who was unaware of his presence.

"Rosemarie, I am here," said David.

Rosemarie turned around and faced David, leaning her body onto the acacia tree, smiling.
"Oh, I thought your guerilla unit was leaving this morning. I thought you left with them," said Rosemarie.

"You know that I cannot leave without telling you, without even saying good-bye, because I love you," answered David.

David offered his hand to Rosemarie, and Rosemarie took the hand of David.

"Come on, let us go down by the riverbank and walk," offered David smiling.

"OK," answered Rosemarie smiling.

Hand in hand they followed the path, walking down toward the riverbank, with the thundering sound of the waterfalls. The waterfalls' sound was so loud that they could not hear each other, but their hearts seemed to understand the moment of joy of being together. Without even whispering the sound of love from their lips, their silence spoke more than enough expression of love. They both cared for each other, and with the sound of silence, their eyes communicated the sincerity and holiness of the occasion, witnessed only by the rushing water in the river and the swinging branches of the trees that surrounded the waterfalls. For the first time, David embraced Rosemarie, and Rosemarie put her right arm around David. For the first time they felt the warmness of each other's body. Then they walked together as if the world was theirs. After a while, Rosemarie suggested to go back to the acacia tree so that they could talk. Hand in hand they walked together, going up, following the path to the acacia tree. Under the acacia tree they sat down, their eyes watching the rushing water of the river and the waterfalls. For a moment there was complete silence, and then Rosemarie spoke.

"David, everything seemed moving so fast. Let me ask you a question, and I hope you do not give any meaning to what I will ask you."

"Yes, Rosemarie, what do you want to ask me?" said David smiling.

"You see, you came to my life so fast that it seems to overwhelm me. Have you ever fallen in love before, and to how many women have you said, 'I love you'?"

"I have never fallen in love before. You are the first woman I ever loved. I have been to so many places since I left my country, America, and I have seen many women in my life, but there had been no woman that made my heart fell in love until I saw you. I love you with all my heart," answered David.

"How about you, have you fallen in love before?" asked David with a smile.

"No, as a matter of fact you were the first man who ever said to me, 'I love you.' When my mother passed away, I grew up with my grandma Mamita and grandpa Nonito because my dad was in the military. My grandparents were well-to-do in our hometown, and they watched every move I did. My dad wanted me to be, well, physically fit, so through the guidance and supervision of my grandparents, they sent me to a school of martial arts, and so I became a black belt holder in different areas of self-defense. Maybe it is because of our family prestige or maybe because of my expertise in martial arts that men were afraid to court me or even dare to try to approach me. They probably knew that I can kill anybody with my bare hands," answered Rosemarie. "And you, are you not afraid of me?" jokingly followed up Rosemarie as she looked at David with a smile.

"All that I know is I love you and that's all I care about. I love you very much, and there is nothing that can stop me from loving you. I love you with all my heart and soul," said David emotionally. Then he pulled Rosemarie to his side. He embraced her and then kissed her so tenderly. Rosemarie was already carried away. Her heart already surrendered totally to David's invitation of love. David whispered to Rosemarie with all his heart, "I love you, I love you very much."

When suddenly as if Rosemarie was awakened to reality, she pushed David away and yelled, "Let's talk about love after the war." David almost stumbled at the strength of the push of Rosemarie.

David was stunned and surprised at what Rosemarie did. He stood in silence, asking himself what he did wrong. He looked at Rosemarie with his eyes asking why, a question that his lips could not say. He respected Rosemarie, and he did not want to hurt her. After a complete silence, Rosemarie spoke. "I am sorry, David. I am so confused. I am not sure of myself," Rosemarie spoke, looking away, trying to avoid the eyes of David.

"Rosemarie, I understand. Do not worry. I'll let you think about us. Tomorrow I'll leave to follow my guerilla unit in the south. I'll see you tomorrow to say good-bye. Can I hold your hand before I go, please?" begged David with emotion.

Rosemarie gave her right hand to David. David held it with his two hands.

Then he kissed it and then let it go and stepped back.

"Rosemarie, I'll see you tomorrow before I go south. I'll see you in the morning," said David with the expression of loneliness.

"I'll be waiting for you tomorrow in front of our house," answered Rosemarie.

David turned his back and walked away, while Rosemarie watched his every stride going away from her. Then she just felt two drops of tears flowing from her eyes, rolling on her rosy cheeks. Then all she could feel was herself walking unconsciously toward their home with tears in her eyes. When she got home, she entered the living room and sat crying. She could not hold her tears. She leaned forward with her two hands on her face and the back of her hands touching her lap. She cried uncontrollably. Her dad heard her and came out from the room.

"What's wrong, baby, why are you crying?" asked Commander Borromeo.

"Pa, I love David. I love him very much. My heart is telling me I love him, but my mind is telling me NO, it is too early to make a commitment. We have a very short courtship, and I do not know what kind of person David is. I am so confused, Pa."

Commander Borromeo gently touched the hair of her beloved daughter and then kissed it and embraced her and said affectionately, "Follow your heart. You can never be wrong when you heed whatever your heart tells you."

Rosemarie wiped her tears and looked at her dad and said, "Thank you, Pa," and stood up and walked to her room and closed the door.

Instead of going home to the house of Mang Isidro and Aling Amanda, David went to edge of Sierra Madre, overlooking the province of Laguna. His mind was so confused of what happened between him and Rosemarie. Everything was going well, when suddenly she changed without any hint. He looked at the vastness of the space covering the lowland of the province of Laguna, and the blue waters of Laguna de Bay seemed to tell him of the vastness of the unanswerable questions of his love for Rosemarie. His love was like travelling to that vastness of space, going to an unknown destiny. Then he asked himself, "Why? Why did she do this to me? I love her, and I know she loves me, but why? I thought she loves me, and that's how I perceived it. We spent some memorable moments together enjoying our company, our stories of love. We were holding hands, enjoying our moments along the waterfalls, the waterfalls that have been the witness of our time together. I could still feel the warmth of her body when I embraced her along the river by the waterfalls, which to me seemed an endless feeling of joy. I don't know. I could not understand." David lamented, holding his head as he looked beyond the vastness of the horizon. Without knowing it, time had passed, and the sun, which used to be up in the sky, was starting to set, saying good-bye to him. As he looked at the sunset with the feeling of grief, the darkness little by little covered the immensity of the horizon. Like a soldier who just lost a war, mentally weak and heartbroken, David stood up and walked home to the house of Mang Isidro and Aling Amanda.

"Oh, come on, David, we waited for you during lunch. We thought you were coming home. So we thought that you must have eaten your lunch with somebody. Come on and join us for dinner," was the invitation of Mang Isidro to David.

"Thank you, Mang Isidro and Aling Amanda, I am really hungry already," answered David.

The three walked to the kitchen and enjoyed dinner together. While they were eating, David told them his intention to leave the following morning. "Mang Isidro and Aling Amanda, I would like to let you know that tomorrow early in the morning I have to leave to follow our guerilla unit to the south of this mountain. I have already finished my business here, so I have decided to leave tomorrow. Thank you very much for your hospitality."

"Oh, that's OK. That is our culture here in the Philippines. Most Filipinos are hospitable. Anytime you would like to come here, you are always welcome," said Mang Isidro.

After eating, David went straight to his room. He was so surprised that there was a sheet, a pillow, and a mosquito net. That would be the first time for a very long time that he would be able to sleep on a pillow, with a sheet under a mosquito net. But the comfort of the bed he lay on was not enough to make him sleep soundly. It was still the picture of Rosemarie that dominated and occupied his mind. The whole night, he only slept a few hours. He woke up very early in the morning to get ready to leave for the south of the mountain. He was surprised when he woke up to see that the couple were already awaked and were cooking breakfast. David asked permission to go down to check on his horse in the grassy area near their camp area.

"Mang Isidro and Aling Amanda, I'll just go down to get my horse tied in the grassy area near our camp. I'll be back as soon as I got the horse. I would like to be ready for my long journey to the south," said David to the couple.

"Go ahead, and we will wait for you for breakfast," answered Mang Isidro.

After breakfast, David rode his horse, heading to the house of Rosemarie to bid her good-bye. On the way, his mind had full of questions and unknown expectations. At a distance, he could already see Rosemarie standing in front of their house, apparently waiting for him. Around ten feet away, under a tree he got down from his horse and tied the horse to a branch, then walked toward Rosemarie. Rosemarie was standing patiently, waiting as David walked toward her, not knowing what to expect.

When David was already in front of Rosemarie, he spoke with the expression of loneliness: "I came here to see you just to say good-bye. Can I hug you for a moment before I go?"

Rosemarie offered both her hands to David, and David embraced Rosemarie tightly, kissed her on the forehead, then whispered to her ears, "Good-bye. I hope to see you someday."

David turned his back and walked away from Rosemarie, heading to his horse, when Rosemarie called David, with her voice so gentle and soft, an expression of loneliness.

"David."

"Yes, Rosemarie," responded David as he turned around to face her.

"I have a sealed envelope I would like to give you. Please keep it and treasure it. Do not open the envelope until you reach your destination."

David walked back to get the sealed envelope. He put it in the pocket of his shirt near his heart, then turned around and rode his horse, heading to the south. Rosemarie was left alone in front of their house, watching David with tears in her eyes as he disappeared from her sight.

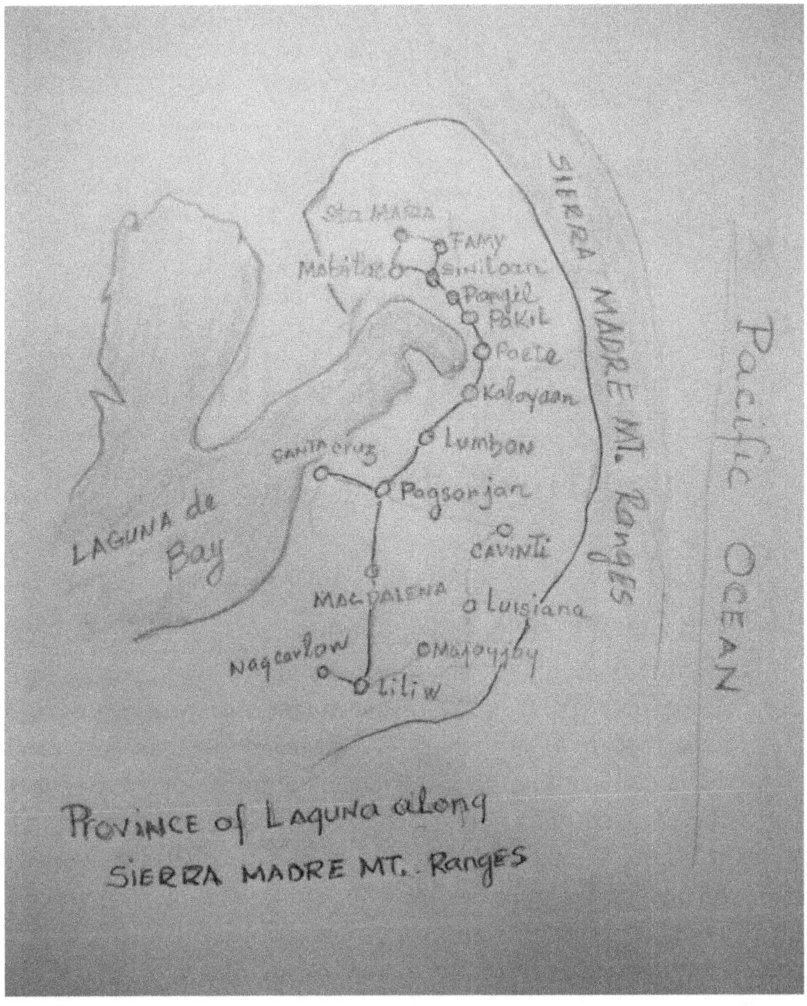


**Sketch of the province of Laguna along Sierra Madre Mt. Ranges**

# Chapter XIII

## The Deliverance

DAVID RODE HIS horse southward of the Sierra Madre Mountain Range with mixed feelings about his love for Rosemarie. All the time in his journey, the only thing in his mind was the picture of Rosemarie—her smile and the warm feeling when he embraced her. He still savored the memories of those beautiful moments he enjoyed with her under the acacia tree by the waterfalls. Through the long journey, he did not even notice that he was close to the campsite of his guerilla unit. When he saw at a distance the group working together to build their new campsite, he suddenly was awakened and rushed to reach them so that he could give them a hand.

"Hi, David, It is nice to see you back," was the welcome greeting of Captain Lee.

"Yes, Captain Lee, it is nice to be with the group. It looks like the work is in progress. I am back to give everybody a hand. Let me put my horse with the other horses and put my weapons down so that I can start working," responded David.

Kevin came to David and said, "Hi, buddy, nice to see you back. I missed you. We have already started gathering the materials and laid down the foundation of our housing complex. It was a design suggested by Captain Lee, with an open area for easy access to everything," said Kevin.

"Let me put my horse away to the grassy area, and I will join you. I'll see you later," answered David.

Everybody greeted David as he walked his horse to be tied to the grassy area of their campsite. He then put all his things under the shade of a tree and then walked to work with everybody in gathering materials for the roofing, woods for their post, and braces and bamboo trunks, which they split for their walling and roofing.

With the heavy schedule of work in building their housing complex, David momentarily forgot Rosemarie and focused his attention on helping the group in building their housing complex to protect them from rain and the direct heat of the sun. It had been a long day that everybody concentrated on trying to complete the construction of their housing shelter in a W shape, with the center as their cooking and kitchen area, and around would be their housing area, with the back completely covered, but the front was completely open. The chain saw they took from one of the Japanese garrisons helped a lot in the construction of their housing complex in cutting big pieces of wood and bamboo trunks. The boxes of nails they got from the Japanese garrison also helped in nailing and attaching one piece to another, the flooring, sidings, and more. Their housing was being built close to a spring, near a river flowing down the edge of the mountain, going to the lower area of the province of Quezon. While most of the crew was busy in the construction, Angelo, Diego, Maria, and Anna were busy in the kitchen. They saw to eat that the workers had something hot to drink and to eat while working. They came and went to the kitchen when they felt hungry. Simon, Andrew, Tomas, and Patrick went out hunting for wild catch. They needed wild catch for their meat. There were lots of deer and wild hogs in the area. There were also wild birds, rabbits, and monkeys that they hunted for meat. After a whole day of work, they finished the flooring of their housing and the framework of the roofing.

**_The Sketch of the house complex designed by Captain Joseph Lee for his Guerilla Unit_**

They then rested and waited for the dinner to be served in the center of their campsite. David finally had the time for himself to get away from the crowd. He walked away from the crowd and sat under the tree by the river and anxiously touched the pocket that held the sealed envelope given to him by Rosemarie. He then pulled out the envelope from the pocket with mixed feelings—of what was in it that seemed very important that Rosemarie told him to keep and treasure. He carefully opened the envelope, trying not to tear any piece of it. He was so surprised when he pulled the content of the envelope. It was a beautiful picture of Rosemarie. David could not help but kiss the smiling picture of Rosemarie, but when he turned it, he could not help but jump with joy. He almost cried in celebration. He could not believe what he was looking at:

*David,*
*Take good care of this picture.*
*I love you,*
*Rosemarie*

David put the picture close to his heart and whispered, "Yes, Rosemarie, I'll take good care of your picture, and I will come back to you to honor my promised love, the love that I have been telling you all the time. I sincerely love you with all my heart and soul. I hope I can see you soon to feel your embrace so that I can whisper to you once again that I love you."

It was before dinner when Simon, Andrew, Patrick, and Tomas arrived with their only catch, a big wild hog. They right away gave the catch to Angelo and Diego, who boiled water to remove the hair of the wild hog. Angelo and Diego helped each other cut the hog's lower portion and cut them into grill size and then handed the cut meat to Maria and Anna for grilling. It did not take long, and the dinner was served, which included grilled pork and rice served with hot mushroom soup. While everybody was enjoying the dinner, Captain Lee spoke.

"It looks like by tomorrow we should be finished with our housing project. We have already completed the major framework and flooring. We just need the roofing to be installed. I think we all did a good job. Thank you very much for the work well done. Tomorrow we will start early so that by early or late afternoon, we should have completed the roofing of our housing. But the most important part of today's accomplishment is we can sleep already on the product of our labor. We are no longer going to sleep on the ground. Let us all eat well, rest well, and get ready for another day of work. Thank you," was the explanation of Captain Lee of what had been accomplished of his planned housing and what was to be accomplished the following day.

Very early in the morning the following day, Angelo, Diego, Maria, and Anna woke up early and prepared breakfast for everybody. Simon, Andrew, Patrick, and Tomas ate breakfast ahead of everybody and left after with their guns to go hunting.

They already had a kitchen table, with the top made of split bamboo trunk, and all parts were made from bamboo. Breakfast was served in pots placed on the kitchen table, with clean coconut shells that served as their plates and cups. Breakfast included boiled root crops served with coffee with cream and sugar, and they also served tea extracted from lemongrass.

After breakfast, everybody went to work to finish their housing project. After they finished the roofing, Captain Lee suggested building the wall behind the housing so that the wind would not be passing through. He suggested using tiled cogon grass so that it would be cooler and would not absorb heat, most especially during high noon.

The housing was finally completed, and their vacation from the war started. They rested every day. Some would go hunting, and some would go down to the lowland to buy what they wanted; they had plenty of money, which they took from the Japanese garrison. But for David, it was a long waiting game. It was still fresh in his mind what Rosemarie told him when she pushed him so hard that he almost stumbled: "Let's talk of love after the war." But he was decided to wait however long it takes. All he dreamt and wanted for was to earn the love of Rosemarie. He was willing to sacrifice because he loved Rosemarie so much. Every day that passed seemed too long for David. His heart was somewhere, left near the waterfalls under that acacia tree, with the unforgettable memories of the beautiful face of Rosemarie. Day and night, the only thing he was thinking of was Rosemarie. Every time when he was alone, he would take out the picture of Rosemarie, look at it, and kiss it. He would then put it close to his heart and look up and whisper, "Rosemarie, I love you."

Meanwhile in the part of the Sierra Madre covered by the province of Laguna, a soul was lonesome for the memories that were left behind under that acacia tree by the waterfalls. Rosemarie once in a while would come and visit the acacia tree and savor the beautiful memories she had with David. The memories that she shattered because of her unsettled mind, her confused and doubting heart, and now she was alone with those memories of pain she caused for no valid reason. Every morning she would come to that acacia tree hoping that one day David would appear there and would hold her tenderly and would say to her, "I love you." The only thing left with her was repentance and the bitter memories of watching David walking away, leaving her with nothing but beautiful memories.

The days had passed, and days that passed became months. Then one day, her dad told her that he would like to visit their house in Cavinti, Laguna. He would like to check their house to see to it that everything in the house was all right, that they still had somewhere to go home to after the war.

"Pa, it is dangerous to go to Cavinti. There are many Japanese roaming around, and they may capture you."

"The Japanese do not know me. I will pretend to be just an ordinary civilian walking around to make an errand. I'll take with me Cesar so that I'll have company. It is hard to be alone without anybody to talk to along the way. It drives you crazy."

"Pa, please be very careful," followed up Rosemarie.

Commander Borromeo called Alfonso, his house guard. "Alfonso, would you please go to the house of Cesar and tell him to come over, please," requested Commander Borromeo.

"Yes, sir," answered Alfonso and right away left to get Cesar.

When Cesar arrived, Commander Borromeo requested that he join him in visiting his house in Cavinti, Laguna. Cesar without hesitation accepted to join Commander Borromeo. They decided to leave the following morning. Meanwhile, Commander Borromeo called all the members of his guerilla unit to give them a briefing.

Commander Borromeo assembled his guerilla unit in front of their house. Then he announced to them that they should be alert, attentive, and watchful because he was planning to go down to the lowland.

"I will be leaving to visit my house in Cavinti, and I want you all to be alert and on guard. Be always ready with your weapons and question any outsiders in our little community. We do not want any intruder in our area here. There are Makapili (Japanese spies) that are roaming around, and we do not want them here. Tomorrow I'll be going down to our town in Cavinti to visit our house. You take good care of our area while I am away. OK! You can take your post. Thank you," ordered Commander Borromeo to his guerilla unit.

The following morning after breakfast, Cesar left home and proceeded to the house of Commander Borromeo. When he arrived at the house, he knocked at the door, and Rosemarie opened it.

"Good morning, Rosemarie, where is your dad?" said Cesar to Rosemarie. "Good morning. Pa is coming down. He is just getting some cleaning tools. He wanted to clean the house. He said that there are probably already a lot of cobwebs around our house."

A little later, Commander Borromeo came down carrying the cleaning tools, a coconut midrib broom with a long handle, and some dirty rugs.

"OK, I am here, Cesar, let us go," was the invitation of Commander Borromeo.

"OK, let's go," answered Cesar.

"Pa, be very careful. Be alert on your way. Do not be climbing in the house, you may get hurt, OK?" requested Rosemarie.

Commander Borromeo and Cesar left their little community and headed to the town of Cavinti, a small town in Laguna Province. Without any problem, the two reached the house of Commander Borromeo safely. When they reached the house, they noticed the long growth of grass around it. So the first thing that the two did was to clear the surrounding, with the growing grass around, using their grass cutter and lawn mower. They were able to clean the surrounding of the house before noon. But they did not notice that while they were cleaning, a man was observing them, what they were doing, and trying to recognize them. Later on the man left, while Commander Borromeo and Cesar went to the house to eat their lunch. After eating, they started cleaning the house of cobwebs and sweeping the floor. Commander Borromeo was working in the living room, while Cesar was working in the kitchen area, when they heard a knock on the main door.

"Who is it?" asked Commander Borromeo.

"This is your next-door neighbor. I just want to ask you something," answered the man outside the door.

"OK, I am coming," answered Commander Borromeo, and he came to the door and opened it.

When the door opened, the Japanese soldiers rushed in and apprehended Commander Borromeo.

"We are arresting you. You guerilla," said the Japanese.

In the kitchen, Cesar heard the coming of the Japanese. He hid right away in the cabinet under the sink. He slowly closed the door of the cabinet sink, then listened to the noise outside. He heard the steps of the Japanese soldiers going around and checking. He was almost breathless and not moving at all. After around thirty minutes, there was complete silence. The Japanese soldiers left, arresting Commander Borromeo.

Cesar slowly opened the door of the cabinet under the sink and checked for any possible danger. When it was safe to go out, he stepped out of the cabinet and exited using the back door. He used the back door gate to go out of the property, then looked around how he could find where they brought Commander Borromeo. Cesar was not sure of the affiliation of the neighborhood, if they were pro-Japanese or neutral, so to be sure, he wanted to go to somebody whom he knew in town. He walked to the clinic of Dr. Alfredo Mercado to ask him if he knew what the Japanese would do if a person was caught suspected to be guerilla. When he reached the clinic, he knocked on the door.

"Come in!" Dr. Alfredo Mercado yelled from inside the clinic.

Cesar pushed the door and went into the clinic.
"Dr. Mercado, it is me, Cesar," answered Cesar as he entered the door. "Oh, what can I do for you? I have not seen you for quite a while now," replied Dr. Mercado.
"I have a very important question I would like to ask you, Dr. Mercado."
"What is it?" asked Dr. Mercado.
"Mr. Artemio Borromeo was arrested in his house today. Where do you think did the Japanese bring him, and do you know how I could see him or visit him?" asked Cesar.

"I am sure they brought him to the prison cell in the municipal building. The municipal building is already occupied by the Japanese. They are already the ones running the government here in Cavinti. I do not know how you can visit him because you may also be arrested. Some Makapili may recognize you as a guerilla. What you can do is look for somebody that may not be prominently recognized as a guerilla who can come close to see Mr. Borromeo so that we can evaluate how he is doing," answered Dr. Mercado.

"I think that is what I'll do. I'll go back to see his daughter and tell her what happened, and then we'll talk about how we can resolve this problem. OK, thank you very much, Dr. Mercado. I'll go and see his daughter and talk to her about it."

"OK, be very careful on your way. There are many Makapili around. You may be recognized. Just walk straight and proceed where you are going. Good luck," were the farewell words of Dr. Mercado to Cesar.

Cesar went straight to Sierra Madre to talk to Rosemarie. He did not know what to do, and he did not know how he could handle the situation. He needed to tell Rosemarie what happened to her dad, with the hope that she had the answer to the big problem they were facing—their commander was in the hand of the Japanese. Cesar was still approaching the house of Commander Borromeo when Rosemarie saw him coming. Rosemarie right away went down and opened the door and approached him.

"Tito Cesar, what happened? Where is my dad?" was the worried question of Rosemarie as he approached Cesar.

"Rosemarie, your dad was arrested by the Japanese. I was able to hide in the cabinet under the sink. They brought him to prison in the municipal building of Cavinti. I really do not know what to do. That's why I came over to tell you what happened."

Rosemarie cried and went inside the house. She did not know what to do—of how she could help his father escape from Japanese custody. With quick thinking, she called Alfonso, their trusted guard in the house.

"Alfonso, I have a very important mission I would like you to do. Take your horse and ride southward of this mountain and look for the camp of Captain Lee. Look for Captain Lee and David and tell them that Commander Borromeo was arrested by the Japanese. Please move quickly. I want to talk to them as soon as possible."

"Right away, Rosemarie," answered Alfonso as he left to go to the camp of Capt. Joseph Lee to tell them that Commander Borromeo was captured by the Japanese.

Rosemarie was so worried of what was happening to her father in the hand of the Japanese. She was crying and crying, for her dad was the only family she had. She did not want to be alone in this cruel war. She stayed by the window, waiting for the coming of help. She was waiting for the coming of the guerilla unit of Captain Lee. She was waiting for the return of David. She needed their help, care, and understanding. This was the time she could measure the love that so many times David had said to her and she believed. There were so many things going on in her mind, troubling and disturbing because of the capture of her father by the Japanese. She was becoming impatient. Time was so long for her. Pondering so many questions in her mind: "Where are they? Why are they not here yet? I hope they care?" Her eyes were focused on the window, looking at the direction where Alfonso disappeared to ask for help, her eyes with tears.

When Alfonso arrived in the camp of the guerilla unit headed by Captain Lee, he was approached by Julian, Marco, and Daniel.

"Who are you, and what are you doing here?" questioned Julian, while Marco and Daniel were listening.

"Sir, I was sent by Rosemarie to tell Captain Lee and David that Commander Borromeo was captured by the Japanese and they need help," answered Alfonso, who was almost breathless after a rushing journey to reach the camp of Captain Lee.

"OK, come on, let's talk to Captain Lee and David," said Julian.

Julian accompanied Alfonso to see Captain Lee, while Marco and Daniel left as guards on watch for the camp. When Alfonso met Captain Lee, he reported the capture of Commander Borromeo.

"Captain Lee, Commander Borromeo was captured by the Japanese when he went down to his hometown to check on his home. Apparently, a Japanese spy may have reported him when he was in his home. He was arrested without any incident."

"OK, I know you are very tired. You eat first, and we will do our best to help Commander Borromeo," responded Captain Lee.

"Angelo, Maria, would you please get something to eat for Alfonso!" yelled Captain Lee to Angelo and Maria, who were standing in the kitchen, in the middle of the housing complex.

David, who was at the end of the housing complex, overheard the name Alfonso—a name familiar to him when they first visited the house of Commander Borromeo, to whom they gave a set of .30-caliber machine gun. David walked to see Alfonso to inquire why he was in their camp.

"Hey, Alfonso, you were in the house of Commander Borromeo, I remember. What are you doing here?" asked David.

"Sir David, Commander Borromeo was captured by the Japanese, and Rosemarie sent me here to ask for help," responded Alfonso.

"What? Commander Borromeo was captured by the Japanese?" was the very surprised question of David.

David without asking quickly reacted to what Alfonso said. He right away approached Captain Lee and asked permission to leave as soon as possible.

"Captain Lee, I have to leave right away to see what is going on with Rosemarie. She is by herself right now. I am afraid of what she may do. I'll just get my things and leave right away," requested David.

"OK, go ahead, we will follow you. We have to do something to help Commander Borromeo. We have to prepare everything to see to it that we have everything we need to save Commander Borromeo. Please do not forget your black uniform. We might use it in saving Commander Borromeo," advised Captain Lee.

David prepared everything he needed, knowing the challenge they had to face in saving Commander Borromeo. His mind was already troubled, wondering what was going on in the mind of Rosemarie: "How is she taking all these?"

After he double-checked everything he needed for the trip, he took his horse from the grassy area and left.

Captain Lee right away called all the members of his unit. He asked them to prepare for a mission to help rescue Commander Borromeo.

"Men, we need everything in this mission. We cannot let our brother be taken prisoner by our enemies. We can do better. We will leave our camp for the meantime and go north to save Commander Borromeo. Prepare and load everything into the cart, all our weapons necessary for this mission. Do not forget your black uniforms. We may use the black uniforms for a certain special mission. We have to rush before they do something bad to Commander Borromeo. You go now and load everything into the carts, and we have to leave as soon as we are all ready. Go!" yelled Captain Lee to the group.

Alfonso after eating waited and also helped in the loading of all the cooking materials and food into the cart with Angelo, Diego, Maria, and Anna. The other men helped in loading the heavy weapons and military equipment, which they stocked in the housing quarters to protect against the weather. After loading was completed, all the carts were hooked to the animals. Captain Lee led the caravan heading north to rescue Commander Borromeo.

Rosemarie was by the window waiting when from a distance she saw somebody coming on horseback. She looked intensely, and when she saw it was David, she ran downstairs and to the main door to meet David. David dismounted from the horse and approached Rosemarie. They embraced. After a long time, they finally found each other's arms, but now in a different situation. It was not about love. It was about the challenge to their love, and they needed to find the answer. David and Rosemarie hand in hand walked back to the house.

"Come on, David, you must be hungry, after that long trip from your camp," requested Rosemarie.

"Aling Petra, would you please set the table. David is here. We have to serve him dinner!" yelled Rosemarie.

The two sat down in the dining table, while Aling Petra was setting the table and at the same time serving the food.

"So tell me what happened to your father. What was he doing in your hometown?" asked David.

"He went to visit our house in our hometown because it has been long time that he has not seen the house, and he was worried that it has become dilapidated without being attended to. Apparently, a Makapili, a Filipino working as spy for the Japanese, saw my dad and reported him."

After eating, Rosemarie invited David to continue the conversation in the living room. David was very careful with his language, of speaking about his love. He knew how sensitive Rosemarie was, most especially in the situation she was in, with her father in the hand of the Japanese. Though she loved David, Rosemarie was holding in her emotion, worried about the condition of her father in the prison cell of the Japanese. Both of them were so hungry for love, but only their eyes were communicating, holding their emotions, but their hearts seemed to understand each other. They could feel the sensation of togetherness at a time when their relationship was in a very challenging situation, which they both have to overcome.

Meanwhile the caravan of Captain Lee arrived in the area. He ordered his caravan to settle in the previous area they occupied, where they were the last time. While they were organizing their things, many members to the guerilla unit of Commander Borromeo came to see them. The commotion reached the attention of Cesar, and he joined the crowd welcoming the group of Captain Lee. Antonio, the guard who first met Captain Lee, spoke. "Sir, let us know what we can do to help rescue Commander Borromeo," asked Antonio.

"That's right, sir, we will come with you to fight the Japanese, sir, and my name is Elena Marques. Please give me a chance to serve with you. I am ready anytime," added Elena, a woman member of the guerilla unit of Commander Borromeo.

"Antonio and Elena, it is not that easy to resolve this problem. We have to study this very well. Then we react according to our findings. We have to find first the exact location where Commander Borromeo is being held, and then we have to evaluate their firepower before we can prepare what action we have to do," answered Captain Lee.

"Captain Lee, they said that Commander Borromeo must be held in prison in the Cavinti municipal building prison cell," added Cesar to the conversation.

"Well, we still have to be very sure that he is really held in that location. Elena, would you be willing to pretend to be a cousin of Commander Borromeo from the other town and that your cousin was arrested and you want to see him. Please dress well to look like you are a legitimate civilian," requested Captain Lee. "You report to me tomorrow your findings so that we can prepare our action to rescue Commander Borromeo," was the follow-up request of Captain Lee to Elena.

"Yes, sir. Let me go, sir, so that I can prepare for my trip tomorrow. Thank you, sir," answered Elena as she left the crowd.

"To all of you who are here, why don't you go back to your post and guard the whole area to prevent the intruders from coming and spying on us," instructed Captain Lee to the guerilla unit of Commander Borromeo. "Alfonso, can you stay for a little bit. Thank you," Captain Lee pointed to Alfonso.

When the crowd was gone, Captain Lee turned to his group to check if they had settled well in the camp, and then he talked to Alfonso secretly. "Do you know the location of the Cavinti Municipality that Cesar was talking about?" questioned Captain Lee.

"Yes, sir," answered Alfonso.

"Can you lead us to that location, and then just leave us. You have nothing to do except to point to us the municipal building," requested Captain Lee.

"Yes, sir, I'll go with you for the sake of Commander Borromeo," answered Alfonso.

"OK, you stay here for a moment. I'll just call two of my men," requested Captain Lee.

Right away he left Alfonso and went to his group and looked for Kevin and Alex.

"Kevin and Alex, we have a mission to do. We are going to make surveillance in the location of the place where Commander Borromeo is being held. We are not going to carry any heavy guns, just handguns, our black uniforms, and telescopes. I am sure we cannot come closer to the municipal building. We have to use telescopes," instructed Captain Lee.

"We'll just get our black uniforms and telescopes, and we should be ready any minute. We have our handguns already," answered Alex.

"OK, go ahead and get your black uniforms and telescopes and let's go," instructed Captain Lee.

Captain Lee took with them Alfonso to be the lead guide in locating the municipal building, but before they proceeded to their destination, they passed the house of Commander Borromeo. In front of the house looking at the window, Captain Lee yelled to David, "Hey, David, let's go. We are heading down to the lowland!"

David looked out the window with Rosemarie.

"Yes, Captain Lee, I am coming," answered David.

"You have to bring with you your black uniform, telescope, and a handgun.

Come on so that we can go," instructed Captain Lee.

David right away reacted and sorted his things and took his black uniform, telescope, and handgun and then faced Rosemarie.

"Rosemarie, I have to go," said David.

"David, please be careful, I'll wait for you," answered Rosemarie as she moved forward closer to David. "Please wear this miraculous medal and keep it always with you so that you will be safe. The miraculous medal is sacred and blessed. The miraculous medal will protect you from harm," added Rosemarie as she put the chain of the miraculous medal around David's neck.

The two embraced tightly. Then David kissed Rosemarie on the forehead. When Rosemarie looked up to David, David kissed her lips, and Rosemarie for the first time surrendered her lips to David. For the first time, Rosemarie felt the warm lips of David as they embraced tightly, as if they did not want to end their embrace, but David had to go.

"Thank you, Rosemarie, I'll see you when I get back," said David as he turned away from Rosemarie, heading to the stairs to join the surveillance team of Captain Lee.

The four rode their horses to the lowland, led by Alfonso. When the municipal building of Cavinti was in their view, Alfonso pointed the building to the team. At that point, Captain Lee instructed Alfonso to go back to the mountain so that they could start their surveillance. They did not need his help. Captain Lee selected a wooded area where they could hide their horses, and they stayed there until it was dark. Then they wore their black uniforms and just walked toward the municipal building.

"We have to stay in the dark far enough just to see what is going on around the building. We have to count the guards around the building so that we can match them with our men. I'll observe the front of the building. Alex, you observe the back. David, you observe the right side of the building. And, Kevin, you observe the left side of the building. We will observe the activities of the guards all night until morning. Set your watch. We will meet where we left our horses at exactly 4:00 AM," instructed Captain Lee to his team.

Using their telescopes, the team observed the activities of the Japanese guards around the building. They noted the number of guards around the building and the best time for them to execute their mission. It had been a tedious long observation, being very careful that no one would notice them in the area that they had first visited. In addition to observing the perimeter of the building, they also looked around for an easy exit if they had to rescue Commander Borromeo. They moved around to familiarize themselves around the area of the municipal building, far enough so that they would not be detected by the Japanese. They stayed late until morning after a long night of observation. Then they met in their set location around 4:00 AM and then headed back to the mountain. Captain Lee, Kevin, and Alex went straight to their camp, while David went to the house of Commander Borromeo.

"How was it?" asked Rosemarie as she opened the door for David.

"We just made surveillance. We observed the activities of the guards, how many they were, and when is the best time for us to execute our mission to rescue Commander Borromeo," responded David.

"Come on, you eat your breakfast, then have some rest. I am sure you are hungry and tired," said Rosemarie with an expression of concern.

After breakfast, Rosemarie showed the room of his father.

"This is the room of Dad. Please feel at home. Have a good rest, and we can talk when you wake up," said Rosemarie.

"Thank you, Rosemarie," answered David as he headed to the room to have some sleep.

Around 10:30 AM, David woke up. He went out of the room and asked permission from Rosemarie if he could use their bathroom to take a shower.

"Hi, Rosemarie, can I use your bathroom to take a shower. I feel hot and uneasy. I need to refresh a little," requested David.

"Sure, there is a water pump in the bathroom and a big basin you can use to fill with water. You can feel at home," replied Rosemarie.

After taking his shower, David changed his clothes and then went to see Rosemarie.

"Rosemarie, I have a family I want to visit here. Would you come with me so that I can introduce you to them?" requested David.

"Sure, why not. Who are they?" questioned Rosemarie.

"Mang Isidro and Aling Amanda, they were the ones who took care of me when our unit left me."

"Oh, Tito Isidro and Tita Amanda, sure, let's go."

The two went to the place of Mang Isidro and Aling Amanda for David to pay respects to them for keeping him when his unit left him in the area.

"Come on, David and Rosemarie," was the welcome message of Mang Isidro to the couple.

"Mang Isidro, as I have promised, when I come to this area, I'll pay you a visit," said David.

"Yes, of course, come in. Amanda, we have visitors!" yelled Mang Isidro to Aling Amanda, who was inside their home.

Aling Amanda came out and was so surprised to see David and Rosemarie together.

"Oh, Rosemarie and David, good that you can come. Rosemarie, you talk to your tito Isidro while I prepare the table so that we can eat together, OK?" said Aling Amanda.

"Yes, Tita," answered Rosemarie.

Rosemarie told Mang Isidro the reason why David was back—that her father was captured by the Japanese. She also mentioned that the guerilla unit of Captain Lee, which David was a member of, would try to rescue her father. They all ate lunch together, exchanging stories and talking of the sad situation of Rosemarie missing the company of her father. After lunch, David accompanied Rosemarie to their house and asked permission to leave.

"Rosemarie, I have to meet with Captain Lee and our team to decide what move we have to do to prepare for our mission to rescue your father," said David.

"OK, go ahead. I'll see you when you come back," answered Rosemarie.

David left Rosemarie and walked to see Captain Lee, Kevin, and Alex to talk about their planned mission. When they met together, they presented each finding and observation from their mission the other night. Unlike the other missions they had completed, the municipal building had no barbwires around. It was an open space. The only problem was they could not come close, not unless the guards were tired and so sleepy. They counted six guards in the front of the building walking around. But there were times that the six sat down around 3:00 AM talking. There were two guards on the two sides of the building, which also covered the back of the building in their guarding routine. They also seem to slow down and get tired by around 2:00 AM, and they start to sit down and talk and rest.

"In this mission we use knives. Each of us must have a handgun and only use it when necessary. OK, this is how we are going to match the guards against us, and it must be fast and swift. We must be able to bring out Commander Borromeo in one minute. We have to attack all at the same time. David and I will enter the prison cell and kill the guards who are guarding the prison area, and we will release and take with us Commander Borromeo and exit. Kevin, Alex, Patrick, Tomas, Juan, and Pablo will take the six guards in the front of the building. We assign the two guards on the right to Simon and Jim and the guards on the left side of the building to Andrew and Roberto. We will kill those guards silently with knives. We have Felipe, Jun, Ted, Martin, Diego, and Isaac to carry heavy weapons just in case we need firepower to support our mission. Julian, Marco, and Daniel will take care of our horses to see to it they must be ready after we rescued Commander Borromeo. Our exit must be quick. If Rosemarie insists to come, we have to ask Victor and Carlos to watch her. She must not come close to our mission. She can watch our mission from a distance using a telescope. She should be quick to exit after we have rescued Commander Borromeo. We cannot waste any time. After our meeting, I'll talk to our team to prepare for the execution of our plan," was the briefing of Captain Lee.

Just after the briefing of Captain Lee to the three, Elena just came in rushing.

"Captain Lee, I am back."

"What is your report, Elena?"

"Sir, it is confirmed. Commander Borromeo is being held prisoner in the prison cell in the Cavinti municipal building guarded by Japanese soldiers."

"Good. Thank you, Elena. We will take it from here. You can go now," responded and instructed Captain Lee, and Elena left right away.

Captain Lee assembled his team in a secret conference to present their plan of attack and to give each member of the team a specific assignment in the mission, to see to it that their mission would be executed to perfection. The team ate their dinner to prepare for departure at six in the evening. As planned, they had to travel in the dark until they reach the Cavinti municipal building.

In preparation for the departure of the team, David was begging Rosemarie not to come with them.

"Rosemarie, it is a dangerous mission. You are not part of the planned attack. Please just stay here and wait for us, please," begged David.

"David, please understand me. I want to be a part of this. It is my father whom we have to rescue. I want to go," insisted Rosemarie.

"OK, if you want to go, stay in the sideline. You can watch what we will be doing with the use of a telescope. I want you to be away from the action. We have to rescue your father in a speedy manner. We were trained for this. So please listen to me. Victor and Carlos will accompany you. Stay with them and just watch, OK?" insisted David.

"OK, whatever you say. I'll be with Victor and Carlos to observe. I just want to be near the action," answered Rosemarie.

At 6:00 PM the team departed on horses to execute their mission to rescue Commander Borromeo. The team was composed of three sections; the first were those dressed in their black uniforms, then Rosemarie escorted by Victor and Carlos, and then the team with the heavy weapons for firepower support just in case they have problems rescuing Commander Borromeo. The group settled in the wooded area away from the municipal building, where they left their horses under the care of Julian, Marco, and Daniel. At around 2:00 AM, they started walking toward the municipal building. Rosemarie with Victor and Carlos positioned where they could view the attack of the group. When it was exactly 3:00 AM, the team moved to execute the plan. It was fast and swift, like watching a dance. All the guards were killed simultaneously without any noise, and Captain Lee and David entered the municipal prison room and quickly brought out Commander Borromeo. They were rushing out, heading to escape from the municipal building.

At a distance, Rosemarie was watching the activities in front and at the side of the Cavinti municipal building. She was standing quietly and nervously, not knowing what to expect. She could see the Japanese guards lazily moving around, some sitting around, seemingly unaware of what was to happen. Then in a glimpse, the guards were overwhelmed by all the men in black, and all the Japanese soldiers were all on the ground, and all the men in black were standing in corners with their handguns drawn. It was fast and swift, like watching a dance. All the guards were killed simultaneously without any noise, and Captain Lee and David entered the municipal prison room and quickly brought out Commander Borromeo. The three were rushing out, heading to escape from the municipal building, when Rosemarie saw them come out from one of the doors of the building, Captain Lee and David with her dad in the middle, running together; she could not help but run to the direction of her dad. She followed them in their route to escape. Victor and Carlos were surprised when Rosemarie just ran without even giving them a little hint. They both followed her, but they saw one Japanese soldier who was lying on the ground, apparently wounded, pull a gun and point to the direction of the escaping group. Then he fired a shot.

*BANG!*

The Japanese soldier who fired the shot then collapsed. The sound of the gun fired shattered the silence of the night, where dead bodies of Japanese soldiers with a slash on the throat and a stab on the chest were scattered in front and at the sides of the municipal building. Victor and Carlos approached the Japanese soldier lying on the ground, who had a slash on the throat and a stab on the chest. The soldier was dead, and the gun used to fire a shot was on the ground. Victor kicked the head of the Japanese soldier, with no response. Carlos kicked the gun onto the ground. Then both of them ran to the direction of the escaping group. The two were worried of Rosemarie because she was behind the escaping members of the team. They worried that somebody in their team might have been hit by a bullet from the gun shot by the Japanese soldier, but they did not see anybody among their group fell to the ground. They could see Rosemarie running and riding her horse with ease and driving away. Victor and Carlos rode their horses and followed the group in their escape toward the mountain.

# Chapter XIV

## The Retribution
### *(The Precious Price of Freedom)*

ROSEMARIE RAN TO catch up with her dad, running between Captain Lee and David, leading to their planned escape route. Rosemarie running a little behind was hit by a bullet a little right on the back above the waistline. She almost stumbled but was able to regain her balance and continued running, following Captain Lee, David, her dad, and all the members of the rescue team. With ease she was able to jump and climb her horse and rode following her dad. Behind her were Victor and Carlos, who were observing her and following her to see to it that she was all right. After a long ride, they finally reached their home. Commander Borromeo got off his horse, followed by Captain Lee and David. A little behind was Rosemarie, who also dismounted from her horse.

"Pa!" yelled Rosemarie, smiling and walking away from her horse to embrace her father, but before she could reach her father, she lost consciousness and fell onto the ground. David and Commander Borromeo right away ran to assist Rosemarie, lying on the ground. David tried to carry Rosemarie when he felt that her back was wet with blood.

"Commander, she is wounded. Faster, we have to bring her in so that we can see her wound," said David to Commander Borromeo, who was stunned of what happened to Rosemarie.

David carried Rosemarie inside the house, then turned her around to see where the blood was coming from.

"Commander Borromeo, do you have any sort of Band-Aid we can use to block the bleeding? She is losing too much blood," requested David.

"Let's just put a piece of cloth to the wound and then put pressure to stop the bleeding," suggested Commander Borromeo.

"Cesar!" yelled Commander Borromeo. Cesar was around when they arrived.

"Yes, Commander Borromeo," responded Cesar.

"Would you please get Dr. Mercado from our town of Cavinti? We need his services to look at Rosemarie. She is seriously wounded. Please get him quickly," requested Commander Borromeo.

Without any word said, Cesar ran and took a horse and rode to get Dr. Mercado from the town of Cavinti. David requested Aling Petra to change the clothes of Rosemarie because her pants and shirt were wet with blood. David stepped out of the room while Aling Petra changed the clothes of Rosemarie, who was still unconscious. After Aling Petra changed the clothing of Rosemarie, Rosemarie regained consciousness.

"Pa, where is Pa? Pa, are you all right?" Rosemarie spoke, looking for her father.

"Rosemarie, I am here by your side. What happened? Where were you get shot?" asked Commander Borromeo.

"I don't know, Pa. I was following you while you were with Captain Lee and David when I got hit by a bullet. I do not know where it came from. I kept on running trying to catch up with you."

"I have asked Cesar to call Dr. Mercado from our town of Cavinti. He should be coming very soon," were the tender words of Commander Borromeo.

"Where is David, Pa?" asked Rosemarie.

"I am here, Rosemarie," answered David as he came close.

"Thank you, David, for rescuing my dad, and to Captain Lee and all the members of the rescue team, please express my thanks," said Rosemarie in a very low tone of voice.

"Rosemarie, it is our duty to your Dad and to our country to assist anybody who is fighting this war," answered David.

When Rosemarie started talking with David, Commander Borromeo walked away to give the two a little privacy and the chance to talk to each other. For a moment there was complete silence. Then Rosemarie spoke slowly and tenderly to David.

"You know, David, since you left that day, I have always been looking at the window, wishing that one day you would come back so that we could again walk by the waterfalls. You know I treasure the moments when we were walking together holding hands by the waterfalls. We do not talk or say a word, and yet I felt happiness and joy within me. I enjoyed the moments of our time together, talking under that acacia tree. It was a great pleasure for me to hear how many times you said, 'I love you.' I pretended I did not hear so that you would say it many more times," said Rosemarie in a very tender voice.

"That day that I left going south, you gave me a sealed envelope. When I reached my destination, I was so anxious to see what was inside the envelope, and when I saw that it was your picture, I put your picture close to my heart, and then I kissed your picture. When I looked at the back of the picture, you wrote on it, 'David, I love you.' I jumped in celebration. I was alone by the side of the river, but I was like crazy, dancing and jumping with joy. Rosemarie, I love you. Please be strong. I need you."

"David, I am getting weaker. I think I am dying," said Rosemarie in a very low tone.

"Rosemarie, try to be strong. Get well so that once again we can walk by the waterfalls. So that we can talk of our love under that acacia tree," begged David with tears in his eyes.

"David, I am cold, I am very cold. Please hold me, hold me tight," requested Rosemarie.

"Rosemarie, please be strong, please hold on, hold on for the sake of our love. Please," begged David with tears in his eyes.

David sobbed and was in tears. He embraced and held Rosemarie. Rosemarie was trying to say something in whisper to David as she was losing her breath, and David listened. David listened with all his heart and soul. With her last breath, Rosemarie whispered, "David, I love you." Then she passed away.

*When the spirit of Rosemarie separated from her mortal body, she watched David as he embraced her body with tears in his eyes. The spirit of Rosemarie was so touched that she wanted to come down to touch David, when she saw a beautiful lady in spirit coming to her. Rosemarie asked her a question: "Are you the Virgin Mary?"*

*"No, Rosemarie. My name is Mary Scarlet. I am the mother of David. Come with me," answered the spirit of Mary Scarlet as she held Rosemarie by the hand and took her away.*

When Dr. Mercado arrived, Rosemarie was already dead. She lost too much blood from the wound caused by the bullet shot by the Japanese soldier. David confronted Victor and Carlos, whom they assigned to take care of Rosemarie, and asked the two what happened. Victor explained, "When Rosemarie saw her dad coming out free from prison, she ran toward the municipal building to catch up with him. She was just behind you when a Japanese soldier fired a shot aimlessly. We did not know if anybody in our team was hit because we did not see anybody slowing down as we escaped, running to get to our horses. We were following Rosemarie, and we thought that she was OK. We did not see any sign of her slowing down. She was running and rode her horse with ease. We were just behind her, watching her all the time, and we did not see in her any sign that she was hit by the shot of the Japanese soldier. The Japanese soldier died after he fired the shot. I even kicked him on the head."

David left the house and walked with tears in his eyes. He did not want anybody to see him crying. He walked toward the waterfalls and under the acacia tree; he cried and cried, talking to himself. "Why? Why? Rosemarie, why did you leave me? I don't understand. I have a dream that one day we will be together. You said after the war, we will talk about our love, and now I am alone without your love. I love you, Rosemarie, I love you," whispered David, crying alone under the acacia tree.

A little later, David felt a touch on his right shoulder. He turned around, reminded of Rosemarie. It was not Rosemarie. It was Kevin.

"David, I understand your feelings. You love Rosemarie very much. Do not put too much pain in your heart. She is now in a better world with God. She is at peace. Let us just pray for her. She would appreciate your prayers. Express your love to her in prayers. I am sure she will be happier with your prayers, and your prayers will serve as her inspirations in her journey to a peaceful world," advised Kevin.

David was in complete silence because even with how much he craved for her love, for her beauty, for her kisses, for her embraces, for her smiles, they were no more. Their love, their dreams, and their faith for each other were gone, and David was left alone, lonesome, waiting for nothing in silence. David turned around and faced Kevin.

"You are right, Kevin. I have to be realistic. She is gone, and she is at peace with God. I must not cry so that she will not worry about me when we bring her to her grave, so that she will be in peace. Come on, Kevin. Let's go back to the house and see what funeral arrangements they have done so far."

The two walked back to the house of Rosemarie to check what they had already done about the preparation for the funeral. When they arrived in the house, there were floral arrangements and candles lit in the house. They were surprised that Rosemarie was already in her interment dress on a table in the middle of the living room. The two came in and came close to the body of Rosemarie. Kevin looked at the beautiful face of Rosemarie and whispered to himself, "She is so beautiful. That's why David became so crazy in love with her."

David could not help the two drops of tears rolling on his cheeks as he looked at the beautiful face of Rosemarie. He tenderly touched the hand of Rosemarie and whispered, "I love you. I will miss you." David was in deep thought as he stood in front of the lifeless body of the only woman he loved, when he felt somebody touch his shoulder. When he turned around, it was Commander Borromeo.

"David, I have already instructed one of our carpenters to build a coffin for Rosemarie. Hopefully the coffin should be ready by tomorrow afternoon," said Commander Borromeo.

"Sir, there is one very important favor I would like to ask you. Maybe if Rosemarie could only speak now, she would request you the same favor," said David.

"What is it, David?" asked Commander Borromeo.

"I would like to request, if you don't mind, sir, to have Rosemarie's body buried under the acacia tree by the waterfalls."

"Why do you want her buried there?" asked Commander Borromeo.

"Sir, under that acacia tree, Rosemarie and I found our love. That's the place we spent most of our time together. Under that acacia tree was our meeting place, where we spent our happy time together, where we laughed, where we embraced, where we would talk about our life together," explained David.

"If that is what you wish, and maybe the wish of Rosemarie, let us bury her remains under the acacia tree by the waterfalls," answered Commander Borromeo.

"Thank you, sir. Tomorrow I'll start digging the grave for Rosemarie. This will be the last thing that I can do for her. I love her very much," answered David with a smile.

"David, I am free, but my only daughter is dead. The precious life of my daughter was the price of my freedom," expressed Commander Borromeo, with a sigh of remorse.

The following morning, David and Kevin headed to the acacia tree by the waterfalls with digging tools and a spade. They selected the best location under the tree, one that would not be stepped on by people and yet would be accessible to anybody who would visit the grave. The two started to dig the grave for Rosemarie, when two men close to Commander Borromeo came to give them a hand—Alfonso and Antonio. Alternately the four dug the hole, with the head of the body to face east, and by early afternoon, the grave was ready. That afternoon, the coffin for Rosemarie was built, and Commander Borromeo with the help of David, Kevin, and Petra transferred the body of Rosemarie from the center table to the coffin.

Commander Borromeo requested one of his men who knew how to do letterings to make a marker for Rosemarie's grave. He also asked one of his carpenters to make a beautiful cross to be staked in front of the grave after the interment.

The following day, when everything was ready, they prepared everything to bring the body of Rosemarie to be buried under the acacia tree. It was a procession of the community from the house to the graveyard of Rosemarie, where women were praying as they walked. When they reached the graveyard under the acacia tree, they sang religious songs. Then Commander Borromeo led the prayer dedicated to her only daughter. After they dropped the coffin into the grave, David was the first to throw a flower. Then Commander Borromeo and the others followed. Mang Isidro and Aling Amanda were present and also threw flowers to Rosemarie's grave. Captain Lee, Kevin, Alex, and all the members of the guerilla unit that rescued Commander Borromeo attended the burial of Rosemarie. It was a very sad day for David. His heart was down, but his eyes and body were on fire. He wanted revenge.

After the funeral, Captain Lee talked to Commander Borromeo, asking permission to leave to go back to their camp in the south.

"Commander Borromeo, we have to go back to our camp in the south. We still have a lot of things to attend to."

"Thank you very much, for all your help and for the help of all your team. You are great. I do not know how I can repay you with what you have done for us," answered Commander Borromeo.

"That is nothing. It is our duty as soldiers of our country to help each other, most especially during the time of trouble," answered Captain Lee.

After Captain Lee turned around to leave, David approached Commander Borromeo and also asked permission to leave.

"Sir, thank you very much for everything. Now Rosemarie is in eternal rest. I am leaving, but my heart will remain here, thinking of those beautiful memories I enjoyed with Rosemarie. Thank you for being a good father to her. Good-bye, sir," said David.

Commander Borromeo extended his right hand for a handshake. David extended his right hand to accept the handshake with Commander Borromeo. David then stood straight. Then he saluted Commander Borromeo, then turned around and left. With due respect to Mang Isidro and Aling Amanda, David approached them on his way to follow Captain Lee.

"Mang Isidro and Aling Amanda, our guerilla unit is leaving going south. Thank you for coming to share with us the passing of Rosemarie. If and when I come back to this area, I will see to it that I come by to see you," said David. Then he hugged both of them and then turned around and left to follow Captain Lee, heading to their camp.

The caravan led by Captain Lee left southward to their home camp in the Sierra Madre Mountain Range, part of Quezon Province. David was riding his horse empty-headed with his mind still focused on the shattered dreams, love, and faith he had with Rosemarie. His life seemed to be moving without any sense of direction after the death of the only woman he loved. He felt so down, wondering what would be next in his life now that Rosemarie was dead. With the death of Rosemarie, there was a fire of anger in his heart toward the Japanese who ruined their beautiful plan of love. His heart was full of blazing hate, which was ready to explode anytime. How he would execute the revenge, he did not know yet, but he had to plan and organize his move when he reached their camp.

When the caravan arrived in their camp, Captain Lee assembled all the members of his guerilla unit. He talked to them about the plan of being independent and being able to sustain without buying or getting out of their camp.

"Men, we have killed so many Japanese already in the so many encounters we made with our enemies, I thought of giving ourselves a break. But let's use that break not just to sit down but to be independent from outside sources for our needs. Going down to the lowland is always dangerous, to be caught by the Japanese. Instead of going down to the lowland to buy what we need, let us produce them here. This is also a way to prepare us to a life after the war. With the money that we took from the Japanese, we will spend them to buy things that we need in farming, horticulture, poultry, and piggery. Tomorrow we will begin our project, securing all the needed materials, like tools, plows, seeds, and livestock. Are you in favor of my plan?" explained the captain.

"I think that is a very good Idea, sir. It is better to produce our food here in our area. We can eat fresh vegetable and fresh meat," answered Simon.

"We are all farmers. We should be able to do what Captain Lee is suggesting," followed up Andrew as he looked to his fellow guerillas.

"OK, if you have no objections to my plan and suggestion, I'll start giving you your respective assignments. Simon, Andrew, Jim, and Robert, you are assigned to get the materials from any town in the lowland down in Quezon province.

"Angelo, Diego, Maria, and Anna, you remain the masters of our kitchen. "Alex, you take charge of sanitation of our camp area. You are assigned to build a toilet system behind our housing complex. You can select your men. I guess it would be David and Kevin. They are the only two who have no farming experience.

"The remaining members should start clearing the area where we have to plant vegetable, plant corns, build a poultry housing and a piggery housing."

After a week of work building a sanitary toilet system enclosed in a nipa hut, with a small water pump, David approached Captain Lee.

"Captain Lee, I have a special request I would like to ask you," asked David.

"What do you want, David?" answered Captain Lee.

"Captain Lee, I would like to continue our mission of fighting the Japanese, and I want to do it alone."

"It is dangerous, David, to do it alone. But if that is what you want, I cannot hold you. With our experience together, I know you can do it successfully, but you got to be careful. Plan your action to perfection so that the execution will just be easy and safe, like what we have been doing. Good luck," advised Captain Lee.

"Thank you, sir, I'll be very careful," responded David.

"Captain Lee, I'll be using one of our .30-caliber machine guns in executing my plan," added David.

"Sure, you help yourself with whatever you want to use in your plan. I am behind you. Go ahead," answered Captain Lee.

Right away David went to see Daniel, who had been close to him since they serenaded Rosemarie. He had a big project that he wanted to ask Daniel to do so that he could execute his planned revenge against the Japanese. But before he went straight to see Daniel, he took a .30-caliber machine gun without ammo and brought it with him to Daniel.

"Daniel, I would like to ask you a favor. I remember seeing your guitar with a shoulder strap made of braided leather," said David as he held the .30-caliber machine gun.

"What do you mean, David? What do you want me to do?" asked Daniel. "If you don't mind, if you can braid me a strap for this .30-caliber machine gun out of the skin of a deer. Can you do that for me.?" asked David.

"Sure, but it may take a little longer. We have to get the skin of an adult deer, cut the skin into strands, and then dry the strands before we can braid the strand to a strap. With the weight of the .30-caliber machine gun, the strap must be strong, especially when the gun itself is loaded," answered Daniel.

"It is OK, I'll wait. I'll ask Angelo to reserve the skin of the deer for you so that you can start the work. Thank you," responded David.

David went right away to Angelo and Diego to make a reservation for the skin of deer or any animal that could be braided into a strap for his machine gun.

"Hello, Angelo and Diego, I would like to ask you something," asked David.

"What can we do for you, David?" responded Angelo.

"Simple thing only. If you can reserve for me a skin of deer or goat, because I'll need it to braid a strap for my .30-caliber machine gun," answered David.

"Well, we'll see tomorrow. If Simon and Andrew have a catch of deer tomorrow, we'll reserve it for you," answered Diego.

"OK, you can just give the skin to Daniel because he is the one who will braid the strap for me. I'll really appreciate it. I'll see you tomorrow afternoon. Thank you," said David.

David left and proceeded to check the condition of his horse. He rode his horse around, then went up and down the hill. He practiced his horse in speed and stamina, then led his horse by the river to have a good drink. Then he brought the horse to a green grassy area and fed him well.

The following afternoon, David was able to get the skin of a deer from Angelo and Diego, so he gave the skin to Daniel so that he could start the preparation to braid the strap for his .30-caliber machine gun. He continued his practice riding his horse every day, trying to improve the speed and develop the stamina of his horse. After a week of practice, he felt contented with the speed of his horse, which he called Lightning.

Meanwhile, the community project of Captain Lee to develop self-sufficiency in food was doing well. They had an area plowed, planted with corn. They had a vegetable garden planted with tomatoes, eggplants, peppers, peanuts, radishes, and other leafy vegetables. Around the vegetable garden were papayas, bananas, cassavas, and malunggay trees. There were also guava trees along the corn plantation. They did not do poultry and hog raising because there were many jungle fowl, locally called *manok labuyo*, and wild pigs and lots of deer roaming around the mountain, which were accessible for hunting.

The project of Daniel of braiding the strap for the machine gun of David was almost done. The skin of the deer was already divided into strands and dried. David was already braiding it into a strap wide enough to fit the shoulder of David when he carried the machine gun.

David was very anxious to start his mission to avenge the death of Rosemarie, the only woman he ever loved. This would be the first time that he would travel across the province of Quezon, so while the braided strap was not ready for his .30-caliber machine gun, wearing his black uniform he rode around the province from town to town to familiarize himself with the roads and paths that he might use as route in going in and out in the implementation and execution of his plan. The province was big, so he had to limit his focus to few towns where he could easily get in and out. He selected the close towns of Pagbilao, Padre Burgos, and Atimonan of Quezon Province. The execution of his mission must be perfect, with no mistake, so he did a careful dry run of what to do in the execution of his mission. He visited his targeted sentries at around 2:00 to 3:00 AM, when every soldier guard of the sentry would be sleepy, drowsy, and sluggish. He studied the best position to execute his plan. After a long observation, he left the area, contented of what to do with the actual execution of his plan.

After a thorough run of the selected town where he had to execute his mission, he went right away to see Daniel to check if the braiding for his machine gun was already done.

"Hi, Daniel, how is the braiding of my strap for my .30-caliber machine gun?" asked David.

"Oh, it has been ready. Come on, let me show you," said Daniel as he walked to his place to get the .30-caliber machine gun, with the strap made from the braided skin of deer already hooked, ready to be slung on the shoulder.

"Wow, this is great. I'll just remove the tripod to lessen the wait, and I am ready to go. Thanks, Daniel," said David as he retrieved the machine gun with the strap and then left.

That night, David prepared for his first mission. He checked his .30-caliber machine gun, his ammunition, put on his black uniform, then double-checked his handgun and sharp knife and rode his horse Lightning to execute his first mission in the sentry in Atimonan, Quezon, Barrio Tinandog, along the road leading to the Pacific Ocean shore. He used the secondary road instead of the main road, the route he mastered during his dry run of his mission. He arrived around 2:00 AM in Barrio Tinandog. Using the back road, he came close to the back of the sentry and waited until 3:00 AM, when the guards were all settled down and complacent in the quietness of the night. Then he slowly moved toward the front side of the compound to have a good view of all the guards. After he accounted for the guards, who were unaware of the coming danger, David fired his .30-caliber machine gun, killing all the guards in front and at the side of the building, and then he went inside the building and rapid-fired his .30-caliber machine gun and killed all the Japanese soldiers. As a signature point of his attack, he threw a hand grenade to the housing, causing it to explode and be destroyed. He then ran out to his horse and rode away and disappeared in the darkness of the night.

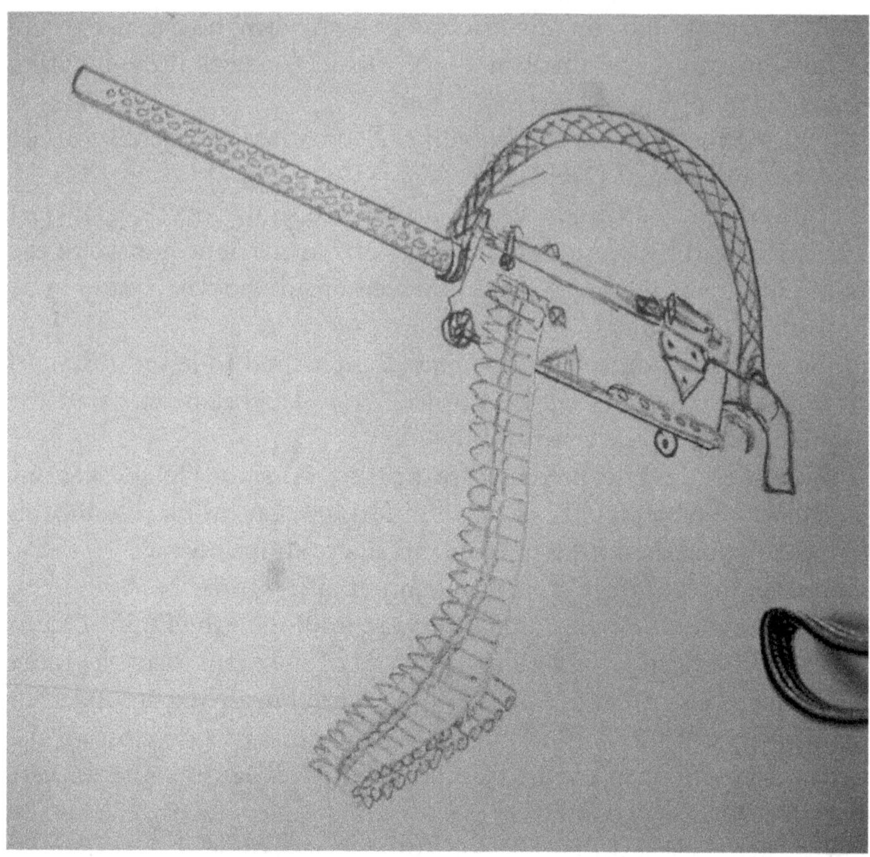

**A sketch of the .30=caliber machine gun with the shoulder strap made from deerskin**

When David arrived in the camp, after bringing Lightning to the grassy area to feed, he went straight to his quarters and changed to his civilian uniform and went to sleep as if nothing happened the night before. He woke up around 10:00 AM and went to the kitchen, where Angelo and Diego were.

"Hey, David, you woke up late today. Come have a cup of coffee. We have some root crops, young corn, and grilled meat of wild pig."

"Oh, thank you, I am really very hungry," answered David.

After eating his breakfast, he went back to his quarters and got some clothes to change and then walked to the river and swam to cool himself. After taking a bath, he proceeded to their stockroom and got more ammo for his .30-caliber machine gun. His next plan was to attack the sentry located along the Maharlika Highway in the town of Padre Burgos. David prepared all the things he needed to take with him in his next mission. He then went to sleep with the plan to wake up at sunset. When he woke up, he proceeded to the kitchen, where he met Angelo and Maria. They were cleaning up, and apparently everybody had eaten their supper.

"Hi, David, you were asleep soundly when I checked on you, so I did not bother to wake you up. Come on, get something to eat. We have hot rice, grilled meat of deer, and hot tea with lemon. We have ripe guava for dessert," offered Angelo.

"That's great. I am really very hungry. Thank you very much," answered David.

After eating, David went back to his quarters and put on his black uniform, then collected all the things he had to bring to his second mission. He saw to it that he had enough ammo for .30-caliber machine gun and replacement ammo for his handgun and hand grenades. He took Lightning from the grassy area, then rode toward Padre Burgos along the Maharlika Highway, Quezon Province. He rode in the dark, using the route that he mastered during his dry run. Instead of riding along Maharlika Highway, he used the road parallel to it. Then when he was close to the location of the Japanese sentry in the other side of the block, he got off and walked across the block and hid behind the bushes. He waited until it was around 3:00 AM and then behind the bushes tried to get near the electric transformer along the highway. He looked around, and when he was sure it was safe to climb the transformer, he left his .30-caliber machine gun underneath the post and quickly climbed the transformer post and put off the lights along the highway. He went down and picked up his .30-caliber machine gun and took advantage of the darkness. He ran toward the sentry, whose guards were in chaos looking for flashlights. He stood in front of the compound and fired his .30-caliber machine gun, killing all the guards outside the building. He entered the building, rapid firing his .30-caliber machine gun, killing all the unsuspecting Japanese who were awakened by the volley of firepower. As a signature point of his attack, he threw a hand grenade inside the building, which caused the building to explode and be destroyed. He then got out of the compound, ran to his horse, and rode into the darkness, following his escape route, leading to their campsite. When he arrived in the campsite, he brought

Lightning to the grassy area to feed, then went straight to his quarters and went to sleep. After a couple hours of sleep, he woke up to mingle with other members of the group.

"Hi, Captain Lee. Hi, Kevin. Hi, Daniel. Hi, Simon. Hi, Daniel. Good morning! Good morning to all," was the greeting of David. Everybody greeted David as they all went to eat their breakfast. After breakfast, David went again for a swim to take away the feeling of tension he had after a long night of journey and a dangerous mission well accomplished. After swimming, he proceeded again to their stockroom and took more ammo for his .30-caliber machine gun and additional hand grenades. Then he proceeded to his quarters and went to sleep. At around 5:00 PM, he woke up and went to the kitchen to eat his supper. He met Kevin and Alex there.

"Hello, Kevin, Alex," was the greeting of David.

"How are you, David? You seem to have been busy lately?" asked Kevin. "Oh, I have just been doing some mission alone. No big deal," answered

David.

"Do you need company?" asked Alex.

"Oh no, I am OK alone. Thank you," answered David.

The three ate together, and after eating, they went to their separate quarters. David on his way to his quarters was in deep thought about the number of Japanese soldiers he killed in Padre Burgos along the Maharlika Highway. He had second thoughts about doing the third mission in Pagbilao. Pagbilao is along the highway, and most likely they had already heard the news of what happened in Padre Burgos and would probably prepare for any possible attack. It would be dangerous and a big gamble if he attacked any sentry along the highway. As a change of plan, he decided to do a mission on the other side of the mountain, in one of the barrios of Atimonan, Quezon, the sentry along the road of Barrio Malinao Ibaba.

At 6:00 PM, he prepared everything he would need in his mission. He saw to it that he had enough ammo for his .30-caliber machine gun, hand grenades, a knife, and a handgun. He then put on his black uniform, then rode Lightning, headed to Barrio Malinao Ibaba. Along the way he was so calm and relaxed, without any feeling of danger. He had done this run several times, and he believed he always had an edge over the enemies because he attacked them during an ungodly hour, when they were vulnerable and unprepared. David was unsuspecting of any possible danger on his way en route to his third mission, but when he was crossing the road of Barrio Malinao Ilaya, a sniper was waiting for his arrival. David was so unsuspecting and calmly riding his horse when the sniper fired a shot.

*BANG!*

David was hit on the chest and fell backward from his horse, still holding his .30-caliber machine gun as he hit the ground. Lightning kept on running while David fell hard onto the ground, holding his chest in pain as he was hit by a bullet fired by the sniper.

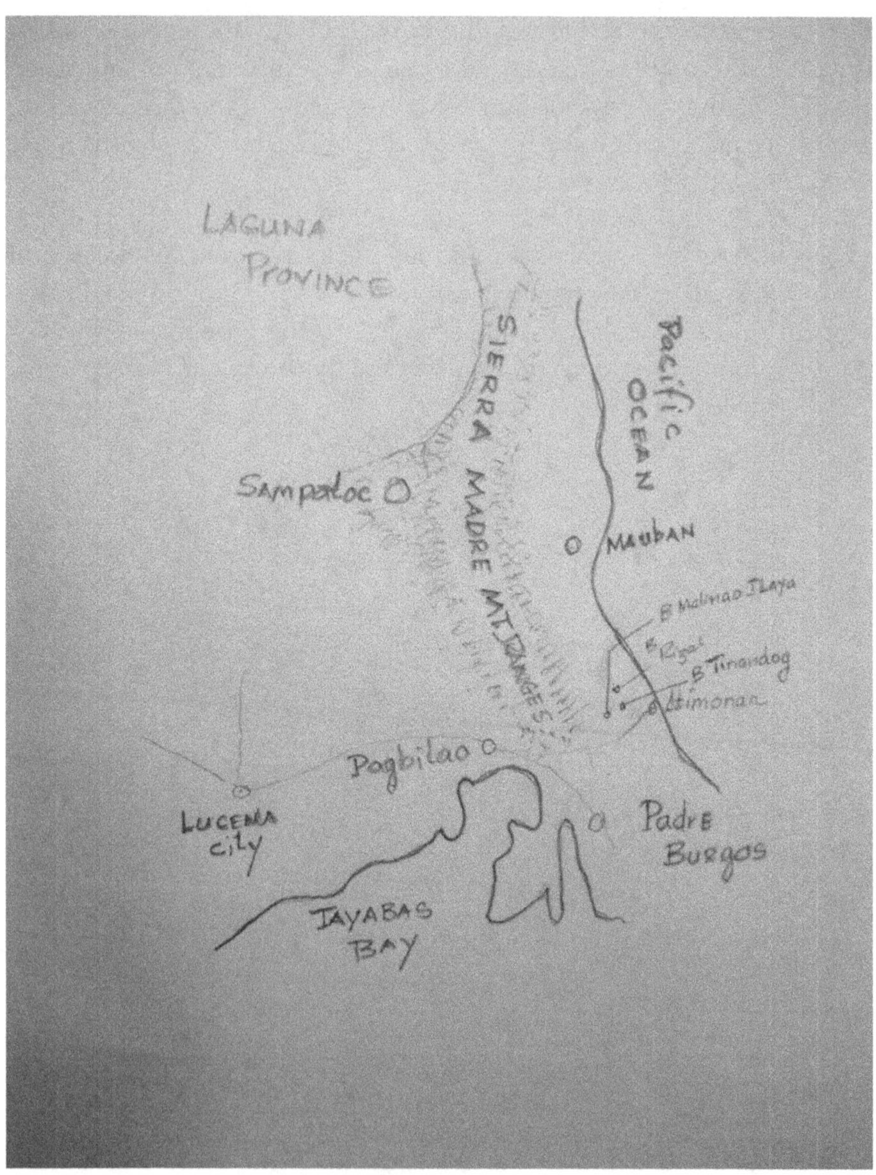


**Sketch of the map of Quezon Province showing the towns of Pagbilao, Padre Burgos, and Atimonan and Barrios Tinandog, Rizal, and Malinao Ilaya**

# Chapter XV

## The Emancipation
## *(The High Cost of Liberty)*

*(The spirit of Rosemarie and Mary Scarlet were there watching David when he fell from the horse.*

*"Rosemarie, David was shot. Did you see that? Is he wounded? I did not have a clear view of what happened."*

*"No, Mary Scarlet, he will not be wounded. He fell from the horse because of the strong push of the bullet to the body of David. He should be all right. The miraculous medal should have received the strong impact of the bullet to protect David," answered Rosemarie.)*

DAVID FELL FROM the horse with the impact of the bullet on his chest so hard that he almost lost his breath. He felt the pain of the strong impact, but when he touched his chest, there was no blood. He quickly reached for his .30-caliber machine gun and returned fire in the direction of the sniper, killing him. David stood and felt his chest. There was a hole on the chest part of his black uniform, and in the hole he felt the miraculous medal. He was saved by the miraculous medal. Lightning, who ran and ran after David was shot, came running back to check on his master. David instead of proceeding to his intended mission rode Lightning back to their camp. He brought Lightning to the grassy area. Then he went straight to his quarters to put away his weapons, changed into his civilian clothes, then sat down and removed the necklace hanging around his neck, the miraculous medal. He examined the medal, and there was no sign that it was hit by the bullet, and it looked very shiny. He looked up and thought of Rosemarie. He remembered her when she said, *"Please wear this miraculous medal and keep it always with you so that you will be safe. The miraculous medal is sacred and blessed. The miraculous medal will protect you from harm."*

He was sitting in disbelief. If not for that miraculous medal, he would have been killed by the sniper. If he were killed by the sniper in that last mission, nobody would have known what happened to him. He decided that in the morning, he would ask permission from Captain Lee to leave and pay Rosemarie's graveyard a visit. He went to sleep thinking of the unbelievable experience he had. If not for that miraculous medal he would not have been back, and nobody in their group would have known what happened to him.

The following morning, David woke up very early and went to their kitchen area. There he met Angelo, Diego, Maria, and Anna, who were busy preparing for breakfast.

"Hi, David, you are very early this morning," was the greeting of Angelo as he was arranging some coconut shells they use to serve food.

"Oh yes, I would like to leave early to visit the grave of Rosemarie," answered David.

"You can eat your breakfast already. We have coffee, some boiled yam, sweet potato, and grilled dried pork."

"I may as well while waiting for Captain Lee. I would like to ask permission from him to visit the graveyard of Rosemarie," answered David.

Not long after David ate breakfast, Captain Lee arrived in the kitchen area of their housing complex.

"Good morning, everybody," was the greeting of Captain Lee to all who were there eating.

Everybody who was in the kitchen area responded, "Good morning," to Captain Lee. David took the chance to talk to Captain Lee while he was drinking his cup of coffee.

"Captain Lee, I would like to ask permission to visit the grave of Rosemarie today. I'll try to be back this afternoon or early tomorrow morning," David requested.

"Yeah, you can go ahead. You just be very careful. It is getting dangerous now. I heard in the news over the radio in the international station that the Americans are already in the Philippine seas and are battling with the Japanese. The Japanese in different areas of the country are starting to brutalize citizens. Stay within the mountain range. I think you will be safe. Take your weapons with you just in case," advised Captain Lee.

"Yes, Captain Lee. Thank you very much for your advice. I'll go to my quarters and prepare my things. I will leave the camp in a few minutes. Good-bye, Captain Lee," was the farewell answer of David.

After talking to Captain Lee, David went straight to his quarters, a part of the housing complex, and secured the things to bring in his journey to visit the graveyard of Rosemarie. He first returned the .30-caliber machine gun to their stockroom and took instead a rifle and ammo. Then he was on his way out, when Kevin saw him.

"Hey, David, where are you going?" asked Kevin while David was getting his horse, "Lightning."

"I'll visit the grave of Rosemarie. I should be back tonight or maybe tomorrow morning."

"You still remember her. What a great love. Good luck and please be very careful," advised Kevin.

David took Lightning from the grassy area and brought him to the riverside to have some drinks. With everything ready for his journey, he rode Lightning and headed northward to visit the graveyard of Rosemarie. All the way, he had been wondering how he was able to survive the shot right on his chest. He was alive because of the miraculous medal that Rosemarie gave her. He wanted to visit Rosemarie to offer a prayer of thanksgiving to her soul, for without that miraculous medal, he would have been dead. Once again in his journey, riding the loyal Lightning, he tried to recall those beautiful moments he had with Rosemarie, those days when they were talking under the acacia tree, those days when they were walking hand in hand along the river by the waterfalls. It seemed just yesterday she was very much alive and loving. Everything disappeared like smoke, dispersing in the air, and the love that they shared together turned into just memories. Along the way, David picked up some flowers from trees and bushes, then bunched them into a floral arrangement.

After a long journey, David finally arrived at the graveyard of Rosemarie. He put the flowers he arranged along the way in front of the grave. As a safety precaution, he looked around to check for any possible danger. Then in front of Rosemarie's grave, he knelt and prayed. He could not help the tears flowing from his eyes as he recalled the loving face of Rosemarie and the caring words she said: *"Please be careful. I'll wait for you."*

> *(The spirits of Rosemarie and Mary Scarlet had been watching David all the way and were touched as David knelt and prayed with tears in his eyes. The spirits of Rosemarie and Mary Scarlet felt sad while watching David with such deep passion, praying in front of Rosemarie's grave.)*

After David finished his Thanksgiving prayers, he stood and leaned on the acacia tree, looking at the waterfalls. He looked at the path they both walked on going to the side of the river. He could still remember her sweet smile. After a while, he faced Rosemarie's grave and did the sign of the cross and rode Lighting, heading to the house of Commander Borromeo. At the front of the house was their guard, Alfonso.

"Hi, David, what are you doing here?" asked Alfonso.

"Oh, I just visited the grave of Rosemarie and brought some flowers. I am just passing along here," answered David.

Commander Borromeo heard the conversation of Alfonso and David, and he looked out the window to check.

"Hi, David, come in. It is nice you could visit," was the greeting of Commander Borromeo.

"Sir, I am just passing. I visited the grave of Rosemarie and brought some flowers I gathered on my way here and offered prayers for her," answered David.

"Come in for a moment and let's talk. We have not had a conversation since the death of Rosemarie. Please come," requested Commander Borromeo.

David got off from Lightning and handed the horse to Alfonso to keep away. He then entered the house of Commander Borromeo.

"Have a seat," was the invitation of Commander Borromeo.

"Oh, thank you, sir," responded David.

"Petra, would you please bring us something to drink here? David is here visiting."

"So, David, what have you been doing since you left our area here?" asked Commander Borromeo.

"Our guerilla unit stopped our offensive philosophy. Captain Lee was afraid that with the many battles we fought and the many Japanese we killed, we may not be so lucky next time. He did not want to have any casualty in our unit. So I did my solo mission of killing more Japanese with my .30-caliber machine gun. But I almost got killed when I was shot by a Japanese sniper on my way to my mission to a barrio in Atimonan, Quezon. I was saved by the miraculous medal that was given to me by Rosemarie. The bullet hit the miraculous medal, which prevented me from being killed. The miraculous medal absorbed the impact of the bullet that hit my chest. I owe my life to the miraculous medal. Without that miraculous medal, I would have been dead now, wounded by the direct heat of the bullet of the sniper aimed at my chest," explained David.

"Wow, what a miracle. You are still lucky," responded Commander Borromeo.

Aling Petra came in with two glasses of young coconut water on a tray and put the tray on the center table.

"Hey, David, how are you?" was the greeting of Aling Petra to David. "Oh, I am OK. I just came by to pay respects to Commander Borromeo."

"OK, enjoy the water from the young coconut. It has some young coconut meat. I put some sugar in it," said Aling Petra.

"Thank you very much, Aling Petra," answered David.

"OK, David, it is nice to see you," replied Aling Petra, and she turned around and left.

"So, Commander Borromeo, how have you been doing since we left?" asked David.

"Well, when you left, we had that nine days' novena that we offered for the repose of the soul of Rosemarie. That is a part of our traditional culture here in the Philippines. On the fortieth day of the death of

Rosemarie, we had a little gathering with prayer offerings, where we invited our neighbors here in our community. We ate together after our community prayers. Since then, I have just been alone and with nothing to do. I am just hoping that this war may be over so that we can go home and work in the farm."

After a long exchange of life experiences between David and Commander Borromeo, David asked permission to leave. He would like to visit Mang Isidro and Aling Amanda, who became close to him. He asked Alfonso to get Lightning, then turned to Commander Borromeo and waved his hand.

"Good-bye, sir, I still have to see Mang Isidro and Aling Amanda before I head back to our camp," said David.

"Be careful on your way back," advised Commander Borromeo as David rode away to see Mang Isidro and Aling Amanda.

When David arrived in front of the house of Mang Isidro and Aling Amanda, he got off from his horse and came closer to the door. The house seemed quiet, and apparently nobody was home.

"Hello, hello, anybody home?" yelled David as he came close to the house. From the back of the house, Mang Isidro heard the yell of David. He went around the house to meet David, who was about to leave.

"Hey, David, we were in the back of the house when you called. We were gathering some vegetables to be cooked for dinner tonight. Come on in," was the invitation of Mang Isidro.

"Oh, I was about to leave, Mang Isidro. I thought there was nobody home.

How are you doing, Mang Isidro, and where is Aling Amanda?" asked David.

"Your Aling Amanda is still behind, getting some pepper leaves for our dinner tonight. We are both doing well. Come on in and let's talk," was the invitation of Mang Isidro.

David and Mang Isidro both entered the house. Mang Isidro offered David to sit, then excused himself to get Aling Amanda.

"Hey, Amanda, David is here. Please come here. Prepare something for him to drink!" yelled Mang Isidro. Aling Amanda was in the back of the house in their little garden.

"OK, I am coming. I got what I have to get. I am on my way," answered Aling Amanda.

Mang Isidro came back to the living room after he called Aling Amanda, and he sat across David.

"So, David, why are you here in our area? I thought you have missions in the south," asked Mang Isidro.

"Oh, I just came back to visit the grave of Rosemarie. I gathered some flowers along the way and brought them to her grave. I then offered her some prayers," answered David.

"That was a very nice gesture of a gentleman," responded Mang Isidro.

Aling Amanda came in carrying a tray of dessert and a glass of lemonade. She put the tray on the center table and greeted David.

"Hi, David, how are you?" asked Aling Amanda.

"I am doing fine, Aling Amanda. I just came by to say hello to both of you. It will be disrespectful if I am in the area and would not come to see you," answered David.

"Oh, taste our guava jam and lemonade. The ripe guava fruit and lemon came from our backyard little garden. We do not buy anything here. We cultivate them in our little garden in the back."

"Stay with us for dinner. I'll cook chicken adobo and chicken *tinola* for soup," said Aling Amanda.

"Yes, David, since it is getting late already for your journey, you may as well stay here overnight and leave early tomorrow morning," said Mang Isidro.

"Thank you very much, Mang Isidro and Aling Amanda. I may just as well join you for dinner and stay overnight since it is getting late already. It is going to be dark very soon," responded David with a smile.

"That is good. You take your horse, which you left in front of the house, and take it to a grassy area, then come back so that we can continue talking," said Mang Isidro.

David was a little concerned with the horse left in front of the house.

"Let me do that Mang Isidro and I'll be back after I have tied Lightning in a grassy area," answered David as he stood up and headed to the front door.

David rode Lightning to a nearby spring, close to their previous camp location, for the horse to have some drink. Then he led Lightning to a grassy area to eat. David just walked with all his things when he went back to the house of Mang Isidro and Aling Amanda. When David came back to the couple's house, dinner was ready.

"Come on, David, you just came on time. The table is ready for dinner.

Let's go and eat," said Mang Isidro. David was just coming in.

"Thank you. I am coming. I am really hungry," answered David. "Let me first wash my hand. I just brought my horse to a grassy area to eat, and my hands are dirty," requested David.

"Oh, sure, there is soap in the sink at the kitchen. You help yourself," answered Aling Amanda.

"Thank you, Aling Amanda," responded David as he headed to the kitchen.

The three ate together, exchanging stories. David mentioned to the couple that in the morning he had to leave very early, so when they finished eating, Aling Amanda showed David his room. The following morning, David woke up early. When David went out of his room, he was surprised that the couple was already awake and was busy cooking breakfast in the kitchen.

"Good morning, Mang Isidro and Aling Amanda," was the greeting of David.

"Good morning," was the response almost at the same time of Mang Isidro and Aling Amanda.

"Mang Isidro and Aling Amanda, I'll just go out to get my horse so that I can get ready to leave after breakfast," was the request of David.

"You go ahead. Do not stay long. Breakfast should be ready very soon," answered Aling Amanda.

"That's right, David. We will wait for you for breakfast," followed up Mang Isidro.

David proceeded to get Lightning from the grassy area near their old camp. On the way, he let Lightning have some drink in the spring to prepare him for the long journey they had to travel after breakfast.

"I am back," said David as he entered the unlocked front door.

"Oh, come on, David, the table is ready. Just wash your hands and proceed to the table," said Aling Amanda.

"Yes, Aling Amanda," responded David as he proceeded to the sink in the kitchen to wash his hands.

"Oh, come on, sit down, we have rice, fried eggs, fried bananas, and lemon tea for breakfast," said Aling Amanda. David was seated near Mang Isidro, who was seated at the head of the table.

"Thank you very much, Aling Amanda and Mang Isidro. This is a very rich breakfast. Where did you get the eggs and bananas?" asked David.

"Oh, we have some chickens we are raising here around the house. They just roam around. We also have some bananas planted behind our house. Here in our area, we have almost everything. We produce and raise them," said Mang Isidro.

"Wow, that's great. We also do that in our camp in the south, but we do not raise chickens because there are already wild chickens available in our area as one of our sources of meat in addition to the meat of deer and wild pigs that we could also get from hunting," answered David.

After eating his breakfast, David prepared his things to be taken to his trip, then asked permission from Mang Isidro and Aling Amanda to leave.

"Mang Isidro and Aling Amanda, I am heading back to our camp in the south. Thank you very much for everything, for your hospitality," said David on his horseback as he was ready to leave.

"You are always welcome here, David. Be very careful on your way back to your camp," said Mang Isidro, with Aling Amanda looking on and waving his right hand as David turned around to leave.

David while riding Lightning on his way back to his camp in the south could not stop thinking of his mixed feelings about everything that was going on his life. For the first time he fell in love with a beautiful woman, whom he worshipped with all his heart and soul, and just to lose her so suddenly without having the chance to nurture a relationship . . . The woman he loved, who gave him the miraculous medal that saved his life, made him feel as if she were still around watching him. He felt as if Rosemarie were just always by his side watching him so that he would be safe from any danger. The breeze that was blowing across the long span of the mountain range touching his face felt like the tender touch of Rosemarie. David was enjoying the sweet memories of his love for Rosemarie as he followed the path of his long journey to their camp in the south. The price tag of the freedom of Commander Borromeo, the father of the only woman he loved, was her precious life and their shattered dreams, faith, hope, and love.

When he arrived in their camp, David was so surprised to see that everybody was crowding in the quarters of Captain Lee, listening to the radio. The radio was so loud that everybody seemed focused and paying attention to the news. David hurriedly put away Lightning in the grassy area after he had given him something to drink, and he went straight to the quarters of Captain Lee and joined the crowding members of his group as they listened to the radio together, dialed to the international station.

> *The United States troops as part of a strategy aimed at isolating Japan from the countries it had occupied invaded Leyte, Province of the Philippines. The invasion of the province of Leyte deprived the Japanese forces and industry of vital supply of oil. The U.S. Sixth Army, supported by naval and air bombardment, landed on the eastern shore of Leyte. The decisive victory by the U.S. Navy, its Fast Carrier Task Force, its surface fleet, and its submarines effectively destroyed the remainder of the Imperial Japanese Navy. Four carriers of the Imperial Japanese Navy were sunk. The U.S. Sixth Army Division continued advances from the east of Leyte Province. The U.S. Fifth Air Force devastated the Japanese reinforcements from the western side of the island with air attacks and the support provided by the army's ground troops. When the American beachheads were established, the Leyte guerilla groups joined directly with the Sixth Army Corps and Division and assisted in scouting, intelligence, and*

*combat operations. General Douglas MacArthur and his staff landed in the beach of Dulag, Leyte.* (Wikipedia, the free encyclopedia)

After the radio broadcast, Captain Lee right away called the attention of all the members of his guerilla group: "Men, like what those guerilla units did in the province of Leyte assisting the coming U.S. military might, we will assist the Americans when they come to invade Manila. We have to help the Americans in mapping and clearing and fighting the Japanese. We have to move closer to the city of Manila. We will have a better view of the coming of the Americans in the part of Sierra Madre occupied by Commander Borromeo. From there we will watch the coming of the American forces when they invade Manila. Prepare everything. We will leave early tomorrow morning after breakfast."

Very early the following day, Angelo, Diego, Maria, and Anna woke up to prepare the breakfast for the group. They served heavy meals in preparation for a long journey northward of Sierra Madre to wait for the coming of the Americans invading Manila. They served rice, grilled meat of deer, and pork, served with tea extracted from lemongrass. After breakfast, everybody helped load their carts with the heavy military weapons, machine guns, ammo, and boxes of hand grenades. Angelo, Diego, Maria, and Anna after clearing and cleaning in the kitchen loaded their cooking materials into the cart. Julian, Marco, and Daniel helped load their food supplies into the cart. David, Kevin, and Alex helped hook the carts to their carabaos, cow, and horses. When everything was ready, Captain Lee ordered the crew to get on their horses, and in one signal from Captain Lee, the caravan started its journey northward of the Sierra Madre to join the guerilla unit of Commander Borromeo.

When the caravan arrived in the area controlled by Commander Borromeo, Captain Lee ordered his men to stay in the area where they camped before.

"Men, you all stay here for the meantime while I talk to Commander Borromeo. I would like to ask permission from him for us to occupy this area. David, Kevin, Alex, come on, let's see Commander Borromeo," requested Captain Lee.

When they reached the front of the house of Commander Borromeo, they got off from their horses and walked to see the commander. They were welcomed by Alfonso, who was guarding the house.

"Oh, Captain Lee, what can we do for you?" asked Alfonso.

"We want to talk to Commander Borromeo, please," answered Captain Lee.

Commander Borromeo heard the coming of Captain Lee, David, Kevin, and Alex, so he looked out the window.

"Hey, guys, come on in," was the invitation of Commander Borromeo. Alfonso opened the door, and Captain Lee and company entered the house.

"Have a sit please, gentlemen. Hey, Petra, please give us something to drink, for our visitors here!" yelled Commander Borromeo.

Aling Petra peeped out the kitchen door and answered, "Yes, sir."

"Oh, gentlemen, what can I do for you? You suddenly came here?" asked Commander Borromeo.

"Commander Borromeo, General MacArthur had landed in Leyte Province. The Americans are closing up in invading Manila. The last broadcast we heard from the radio, they have already landed in Bataan and have Corregidor already in control. We want to watch the coming of the Americans from your area here, which is very close to Manila, so that we can help them in mapping and fighting the Japanese. When the Americans invaded Manila, we will go down to the lowland, start mapping, and fight the Japanese. We have enough heavy weapons to defeat the Japanese after the punishing bombardment of the U.S. Air Force," explained Captain Lee while Commander Borromeo was listening.

"That is a very good Idea. Let us watch together the coming of the American military might, and after they have bombarded the lowland close to our camp, we will go down and attack the Japanese to overwhelm them. The Americans are coming from the north, and we are coming from the south. Great," responded Commander Borromeo.

"Gentlemen, have some dessert. I have prepared some young coconut salad and young coconut water. Please help yourself," said Aling Petra as she placed the tray of food in the center table.

"Thank you, Aling Petra," responded Captain Lee.

"So, where are your men now, Captain Lee?" asked Commander Borromeo. "We left them in the area where we used to camp when we were here. I would like first to ask permission from you for us to stay there," responded

Captain Lee.

"Oh, you are always welcome in our area. You can establish your camp there, and let us start watching from the edge of Sierra Madre overlooking Laguna Bay the coming of the American planes," replied Commander Borromeo.

"Thank you, sir, we will join forces in fighting the Japanese, starting from the province of Laguna as soon as the Americans invade Manila," recommended Captain Lee.

"Our guerilla unit here will be ready to join your unit to fight the Japanese. I'll not forget that you rescued me from the hand of the Japanese. We will fight together for the sake of democracy and freedom of our country," responded Commander Borromeo.

After eating their dessert, Captain Lee with David, Kevin, and Alex asked permission to leave so that they could start building shelters in their camp. They did not know how long they had to wait before the Americans could start invading Manila. They had to have a place to sleep and rest. Upon the return of Captain Lee to the site, he ordered the group to start building shelters to house all the members of the group. He ordered the gathering of the cogon grass to be tiled for roofing and sidings, bamboo trunks for flooring and sidings support, and woods for posts and braces. With their experience of building shelters, it did not take them long to build them using the power chain saw, bolos, and availability of nails. After they built the housing complex, they started watching along the edge of the mountain, hoping to see the coming of the American planes.

When the American military might entered from the north, the guerilla units under the command of Captain Lee and Commander Borromeo watched Manila with telescopes, from the edge of Sierra Madre, as a fiery hell with continuous artillery and bombardment from the American military might. The Japanese were giving the American military an intense resistance, causing great destruction and ruin of the city's buildings and monumental structures. With the continuous bombardment, artillery, and exchange of firepower between the Americans and the defending Imperial Japanese Army with their fierce resistance, the city of Manila was transformed into a sea of ruins.

The guerilla unit of Captain Lee and Commander Borromeo waited for the Americans to drop bombs on the Japanese military installation in the province of Laguna. When the American planes started bombarding the military installation in the province of Rizal, Captain Lee and Commander Borromeo ordered their men to prepare for the attack on the Japanese installation in the lowland of Laguna. In preparation for the mission to fight the Japanese as soon as the Americans started bombing Laguna Province, they discounted carrying the .50-caliber machine guns because of their weight. They assigned .30-caliber machine guns to guerillas by pair—one gunner and the other feeding the ammo and carrying the casing of the ammo during the forward advances of the group. Their plan was to move in a straight line, slow but thorough, without any chance of missing any target. The line of advancing guerilla must be followed by the ammo supplier on a cart towed by a carabao hiding behind any protected wall or object.

The time came when the bombing of the province of Laguna commenced. Using their telescopes, they watched the destruction of the bombs as they hit the different Japanese installations; buildings and structures with the Japanese flag were targeted by the low-flying bomber planes. They watched the explosions and devastation caused by the bombs dropped by the American airplanes. The Japanese soldiers were shooting into the air helplessly. They watched them get burned and run for safety.

When the bombing stopped, Captain Lee and Commander Borromeo signaled to their men to go down to the lowland and line up into formation, with David as .30-caliber gunner partnered with Kevin in the leftmost line. In the middle were Captain Lee as .30-caliber gunners and Alex as partner, followed by Commander Borromeo as .30-caliber gunner with Antonio as partner. In the rightmost wing was Julian as .30-caliber gunner partnered with Marco. In between the .30-caliber gunners were riflemen. Behind the line was a cart that carried the military supplies, more guns, ammo, hand grenades, bazooka, and .50-caliber machine guns. Their line moved toward the town of Cavinti and attacked the municipal building, killing most of the Japanese occupants. Then they moved forward, driving the escaping Japanese with their firepower until they had covered the whole town of Cavinti. They installed the Filipino flag in front of the Cavinti municipal building.

The group of Captain Lee and Commander Borromeo joined the Filipino soldiers of the Fourth, Forty-first, Forty-second, Forty-third, Forty-fifth, Forty-sixth, and Forty-seventh Infantry Divisions of the Philippine Commonwealth Army, the Fourth Infantry Regiment of the Philippine Constabulary, and the recognized guerrillas against Japanese forces in Laguna in mapping and clearing of the province against the Imperial Japanese Army.

With the fall of Manila and completed mapping of the entire country by the Americans with the help of Filipino guerillas from Luzon to Visayas and Mindanao, the country was liberated. General Masaharo Homma, who orchestrated the brutal treatment of Filipinos and Americans in the Bataan Death March, was tried, convicted, and executed. The war ended, but the country was left in ruins and was devastated. There was a huge casualty of war: Filipinos who were subjected to cruelty, brutality, and massacre; the Americans who fought the war and lost their lives to help liberate the country; and the Imperial Japanese Army, who were killed resisting the invasion of the American military might. The smokes of the gunfire and burning structures, houses, and buildings were gone, and the sun from the east started to shine. The people who survived the cruelty of war were looking forward to a new hope, a new beginning, a new life with great faith and optimism.

# Part II
## - Rebirth and Revenge
## - The Reincarnation of Love and the Fulfilled Destiny

# Chapter XVI

## A New Beginning

AFTER THE SUCCESSFUL mission of the guerilla unit headed by Capt. Joseph Lee and Cmdr. Artemio Borromeo, the group returned to the town of Cavinti. When they reached the town of Cavinti, Captain Lee talked to Commander Borromeo about going back to the mountain to clean their camp and to get Angelo, Diego, Maria, and Anna.

"Commander Borromeo, It has been nice working with you side by side fighting this war. We have finally worked together shoulder to shoulder fighting against our brutal enemies. Now, we are going back to the mountain to check the housekeepers in our camp, and at the same time we do not want to leave our camp in a mess. We will clean our camp before we come down here in the lowland to go back to our respective homes. We will probably pass by your house to say good-bye to you on our way home."

"Yes, Captain Lee, please come back here in our house so that we can celebrate together our successful mission and the liberation of the Philippines from the hand of the Japanese. I'll butcher a cow so that we can all eat and drink together with your men here in our house."

"By the way, Commander Borromeo, we will leave with you the cart of military weapons and the carabao towing it. We will not need them anymore," requested Captain Lee.

"I'll keep them with me. I'll take good care of them," replied Commander Borromeo. "Captain Lee, can I ask you a favor?" asked Commander Borromeo.

"What is it, Commander Borromeo?" asked Captain Lee.

"If it is OK with you if Alfonso can go with you so that he can get Petra from our house in the mountain. I would need her here."

"Sure, Commander," answered Captain Lee as he looked at Alfonso, who was standing with Commander Borromeo. "Come on, Alfonso, let's go," was the invitation of Captain Lee. Alfonso was just waiting to be called.

Captain Lee with his guerilla unit, including Alfonso, walked back to the mountain. When they arrived in front of the house of Commander Borromeo, Alfonso separated from the group.

"Captain Lee, you might stay longer here in the mountain. Aling Petra and I will just go ahead in going back to Cavinti," said Alfonso.

"Sure, you just go ahead and tell Commander Borromeo that we will follow you," answered Captain Lee.

Captain Lee and his unit proceeded to their camp to check on Angelo, Diego, Maria, and Anna. It had been several days that they had been out fighting the Japanese during their mapping operation in the province of Laguna with the guerilla unit of Commander Borromeo. When they arrived, they found Angelo and Diego busy cooking.

"Welcome back, guys," was the greeting of Angelo to the arriving members of the guerilla unit.

"You seem very busy cooking, as if you know we are coming," said Captain Lee.

"Oh yes, for some reason, a wild pig was roaming around near our camp, and Diego caught him. And yesterday a deer was passing by our camp, and Diego shot it on the leg and caught it, and we both dressed them up. I cooked some pork adobo, and I have grilled some deer meat. We will set the table. We are sure you are all very hungry," said Angelo.

"It was just my lucky day, yesterday and today. Sometimes you are hunting for deer or wild pig and you cannot find one. For some reason, the deer and the wild pig came around without being hunted. It was just plain luck," said Diego.

While Maria, Anna, Angelo, and Diego were busy setting the table to serve the food, David approached Captain Lee.

"Captain Lee, we have so much food, and since we are leaving for good, I would like to invite Mang Isidro and Aling Amanda to join us. This is probably our last meal here," requested David.

"Oh yes, go ahead and invite them so that we can meet them too," answered Captain Lee.

"Thank you, Captain Lee. I'll go and get them so that they can join us," replied David as he turned around to go to the house of Mang Isidro and Aling Amanda.

When David arrived in the house of Mang Isidro and Aling Amanda, they were in the front of the house, looking out.

"Mang Isidro and Aling Amanda, good that you are out here," said David. "Oh, we were just curious of the arrival of your guerilla unit. We would like to hear some news," replied Mang Isidro.

"The Philippines has been liberated. All the Japanese are gone, either killed or captured. We just came back to check on our camp. We will leave after we clean up. I'll report to our U.S. Army office in Manila and then go back to the United States," said David.

"Wow, that is good news. It is very hard here in the mountain because we have no radio and we do not know what is going on in the world," said Mang Isidro.

"Mang Isidro and Aling Amanda, I would like to invite both of you to eat in our camp so that I can introduce both of you to our guerilla unit," requested David.

"Sure, we will be honored to join you and your group," answered Mang Isidro.

David accompanied Mang Isidro and Aling Amanda to their camp, and David introduced both to Captain Lee and to all the members of the guerilla unit. Maria and Anna served Mang Isidro and Aling Amanda, who were so surprised to have pork adobo and grilled deer meat served. After eating, Mang Isidro and Aling Amanda talked to Captain Lee and asked permission to leave. Both of them then walked to David to let him know they were leaving. David escorted both of them back to their home.

"David, that was a very delicious dinner. Thank you for inviting us. We had the chance to meet Captain Lee and your guerilla unit," said Aling Amanda.

"I was thinking of that on our way back here, of how I can talk to both of you together now that the war is over," said David. Then he sighed and continued talking. "Mang Isidro and Aling Amanda, it has been a pleasure to know both of you. Thank you for everything, your hospitality and the nice accommodation you have accorded me during the time when I did not have a place to stay. After we finish cleaning our camp, we are heading to the lowland, and we will head home, and probably we will not see each other again. Thank you again for everything," followed up David.

"It is always our pleasure to serve and to show hospitality to our visitors, most especially someone like you, who is a foreigner in our country. We may also move to the lowland since the war is over. Maybe in the next week or two. So good luck in your journey back home, David," said Mang Isidro.

David hugged both Mang Isidro and Aling Amanda and left them, looking as he walked away going back to his camp.

After eating, everybody helped out cleaning up the camp. They did not want to leave the area in a mess. Captain Lee asked Simon and his men to dig a hole where they could bury their trash and garbage. Then he asked Andrew and his men to start loading things into the carts. They hooked one of the carts to a horse and the other cart to a cow. Then Captain Lee awarded one of the carts and a horse to Angelo and his Maria, and the other cart hauled by a cow, he awarded to Diego and Anna. Then he asked his guerilla unit to form a semicircle and told them to listen very carefully.

"Men, you have risked your life in this war. We fought together without fear. We risked everything we had and fought our enemies without hesitation or second thought. All of you must be entitled to benefits for the services you did in liberating this country. When everything is settled and the government of the Philippines is finally reestablished, look for me and Alex in the Philippine army headquarters.

Inquire where you can find me. We have to enlist you to the registry of all the guerillas who served this war. From here we must first all go home to check on our families. David, you will be reporting to the U.S. Army headquarters, most likely located in Manila. And, Kevin, you will also be reporting in the U.S. Marines office, also most likely located in Manila. Men, you are all brave, and I am much honored and very proud to have served with you in fighting this war," said Captain Lee. Then he started shaking hands with every member of his guerilla unit, one by one.

Captain Lee asked everybody to get on their horses, and after he was able to get on his horse, he signaled to start moving. The group went down the mountain, heading to the town of Cavinti to meet with Commander Borromeo. When they reached the street where the house of Commander Borromeo was located, Commander Borromeo was coming out from the gate, apparently seeing them coming from a distance.

"Men, get off from your horses and come on in. We have been waiting for all of you. The table is ready. Come on and let us celebrate our freedom!" yelled Commander Borromeo, apparently having already drank some liquor.

Led by Captain Lee, all the members of the guerilla group got off from their horses, secured their horses outside the fence of the house of Commander Borromeo, and they all went inside to join the celebration. There were lots of food, and most members of the guerilla unit of Commander Borromeo were there celebrating. The guerilla unit of Captain Lee joined the group, eating and drinking their native wine, called *tuba*. They celebrated until midnight, when everybody got drunk. One by one they looked for a corner to have some sleep. The following morning, Aling Petra with the help of Alfonso and Antonio served breakfast with some homemade bread, boiled bananas (plantains, called locally as *saba*), and coffee. One by one, they woke up, washed their faces and hands in the water pump, and ate breakfast. After breakfast, Captain Lee asked permission from Commander Borromeo to leave.

"Commander Borromeo, we will be leaving now. We still have long way to go. David, Kevin, and I will go to Manila, and most of the members of my unit will be heading to Bataan. Alex is heading to his hometown in Pampanga," said Captain Lee.

"Thank you very much for joining us in our little celebration. It has been great to have met you all. Thank you for your great service to our country and of course for rescuing me," said Commander Borromeo.

"Commander Borromeo, sir, if it is possible to leave with you my horse Lightning. I will not be able to take good care of him in Manila, and I am sure he will be taken care of here in your farm," requested David.

"So is my horse, Commander Borromeo. I am also going to Manila, and I'll not be able to take good care of my horse," said Kevin.

"You can just leave the horses with Alfonso, and he will take good care of them. He will take them to the farm. We have a barn there that was not destroyed by the Japanese and can be used as shelter for your horses," answered Commander Borromeo.

"David, Kevin, how will you go to Manila?" asked Captain Lee.

"We will hitchhike with the military trucks that travel from Southern Luzon to Manila," answered David.

"OK, let's go," commanded Captain Lee to his men, who were just standing around waiting for his command.

All the members of the guerilla unit of Captain Lee followed him out, as they one by one said thank you to Commander Borromeo. Captain Lee and his men rode their horses and left going to their respective destinations. David and Kevin after handing their horses to Alfonso walked to the main road and waited for a military truck from Southern Luzon traveling to Manila. After two hours of waiting, David and Kevin finally got a ride to Manila. On their way to Manila, they witnessed the ruins and the total destruction of so many structural buildings, the roads left by the ferocious fighting between the Imperial Japanese Army and the American military supported by the Filipino guerilla units. In Manila they separated, with David looking for the U.S. Army headquarters and Kevin looking for the U.S. Marines headquarters. When David found the U.S. Army headquarters based in Manila, he reported that he was a prisoner of war in the death march, escaped the death march, and became a part of the guerilla unit under Captain Lee. He also submitted an application for an honorable discharge from the army so that he could leave the service and be flown to the United States.

While waiting for his discharge papers, David served with the Sixth Division of the U.S. Army in the clearing of the city of Manila. When he received his honorable discharge papers, he flew back to the United States and landed at the Washington National Airport. From the airport, he took a taxi going back home. He would like to surprise everybody. When he reached the front of their house, David asked the taxi driver to let him out. He unloaded his luggage and just walked to the front door of their house and knocked on the door. It was Anne who opened the door and in shock yelled, "It is David, he is home!"

Dr. Scarborough, who was in his room, ran down. Martha, who took care of David, also came out. John, who was in the kitchen, ran to welcome David too.

"David, oh thank God you are back," was the expression of Dr. Scarborough as he came down from upstairs and hugged David, who was smiling and enjoying the moment of being back home with his family.

"It is nice to be home, Dad," replied David with all smiles. Then he turned around to Anne and Martha and hugged both of them and then shook hands with John.

"So, Dad, how is everything since I left?" asked David.

"Well, I decided to retire and just visit the hospital once in a while. I just work on a part-time basis just to get some mental and physical exercise," answered Dr. Scarborough.

"That's great. You are getting older anyway. You need some rest, Dad," responded David.

"How about you, David? How was your military experience? I was already worried when you were assigned in the Philippines. Then the Japanese invaded the Philippines. We were wondering where you were and what had happened to you during the war," asked Dr. Scarborough.

"I was one among the American and Filipino soldiers who became prisoners of war. I was part of the death march, but I was able to escape together with one American marine and two Filipino soldiers. We formed a guerilla unit in Bataan and fought the Japanese. We moved from Bataan to the top of the Sierra Madre Mountain Range. We did missions to attack the Japanese from our camp on top of the Sierra Madre. When General Douglas MacArthur landed in Leyte, we waited for the bombing and the attack of the American military on Manila. When the American airplanes started bombing the town close to our position on top of Sierra Madre, our unit went down to the lowland and helped the Americans in mapping and fighting the Japanese. The Japanese were no match to the firepower of the invading Americans. When the bombings, shootings, and mapping were completed, all the Japanese were either killed or held prisoner. Luckily, there was no casualty in our guerilla unit. We had a very smart Filipino officer who led us in all the missions," explained David.

"Wow, what an experienced. Meanwhile let me go to the kitchen and prepare the table so that you can eat," said Anne.

"Thanks, Anne. I'll join David in the dinner table please. Thank you," said Dr. Scarborough. Anne hurriedly went to the kitchen, followed Martha, who would like to help prepare the table.

"David, I'll take your luggage to your room," said John.

"Thanks, John," answered David.

"So, David, now that you are back, what are you planning to do?" asked Dr. Scarborough.

"Well, Dad, I would like to go back to school. I would like to take business administration. I think I have a good future in business than to stay in the military," answered David.

"That is good, David. I'll help you finish your career. There are many good universities here in our metropolitan area," said Dr. Scarborough.

"Dad, I'll probably rest for several days before I go around and check the different universities in the metropolitan area," responded David.

"By the way, do you know how to drive?" asked Dr. Scarborough.

"Yes, Dad, I learned how to drive during our commando training," answered David.

"We better get you a car so that you can get around," recommended Dr. Scarborough.

"How about the car of Mom? Is it still running?" asked David.

"No, it has been idle for quite a while and the engine got rusted, the tires were all flat and the oil was leaking. I had it towed to the junk shop. We will just get you a new one," answered Dr. Scarborough.

"Thank you, Dad," answered David.

"Dr. Scarborough, David, the table is ready," was the invitation of Anne to father and son.

The following day, David and Dr. Scarborough went to Mary Scarlet's grave to offer prayers. They brought flowers and lit candles.

David rested for several days and just took most of his time with John going fishing, which he missed since he left the country. David and John once again trailed the path going from their backyard to the Potomac riverbank to fish. He enjoyed the time spent grilling the caught fish with John, Anne, and Martha. But the image of the river made him remember Rosemarie, those days when they were walking hand in hand by the waterfalls. But he just gave a big sigh, for that was just a sweet memory, a memory he treasured in his heart.

When his dad got him a new car, David had the chance to go around and checked the different universities in metropolitan Washington DC. He visited Georgetown University, American University, Howard University, the George Washington University, and George Mason University. After a thorough evaluation, he decided to enroll at the College of Business Administration of the George Washington University. He liked GWU for its accessibility to all the tourist spots of Washington DC, the nation's capital. When he was younger, he did not have the chance to really enjoy going around the beautiful city of Washington and its tourist attractions. When he needed to do a research, the Library of Congress was a few minutes' drive away from GWU.

After he enrolled at the College of Business Administration of the George Washington University, he focused on his study. He had one thing in mind—he would like to return to the Philippines to be a part of the economic recovery of the country he served during the Second World War. He risked his life fighting the Japanese to help liberate the Philippines, and he wanted to help bring back the country to life. The county was in ruins when he left, and he believed that the country would come back to develop industries and hopefully once again could stand with other nations, trading, selling, and buying products that would lead to the country's self-sufficiency. He would like to be a part of that glory.

During the four years that he studied business administration at the George Washington University, he enjoyed driving around East Potomac Park, sitting in one of the benches, looking at the steady flowing current of the Potomac River. Under the shades of the trees, he would read and study his books. He would find tranquility and peace studying surrounded by nature. That had been his routine in life as a student of business administration. The only time when he had to break his studying with nature was when he had to go to the Library of Congress or the George Washington Library. And finally after four years of dedicated and focused studies in all his subjects in business administration, he finally graduated with honors. He graduated cum laude. His father was so proud of his only son.

After graduation, David talked to his father about his longtime intention since he came back to the United States. He would like to go back to the Philippines to invest in its economy, which was probably starting to grow. He would like to be a part of the growth of the Philippine economy.

"Dad, I would like to go back to the Philippines to invest in their industry. There is a very big potential for growth in that country after it had been ruined by war. There will be many countries that will invest to help that country, and soon the economy of that country will be booming. I would like to be a part of the growth of that economy, Dad," said David.

"Well, if you think there is a very good potential of growth in your investment in the Philippines, I'll support you. You can go ahead and prepare your plan, and I will back you up," said Dr. Scarborough.

"Dad, I have to go back to the Philippines to check the possibility of opening a business there. I would like to leave as soon as possible," said David with a feeling of anxiousness.

David left the United States bound for Manila, the business capital of the Philippines. He stayed in the Manila Hotel, which had been opened and remodeled after the war.

**A picture of the Manila Hotel, courtesy of Emerson Lot**

When he checked into the hotel, something caught his attention—a placard display that read, "Investment for Growth, Conference Meeting of the Philippine Chamber of Commerce." After he dropped his luggage in his room, he right away went down to the lobby of the hotel and observed the people who were coming and going. After a while, a gentleman dressed in *barong Tagalog* (Filipino shirt) approached him.

"Hello, sir, my name is Fernando Salazar, affiliated member of the Philippine Chamber of Commerce."

"I am David Scarborough. I just came in, and I noticed that there is a conference going on here on investments," said David.

"Yes, sir, we are inviting local and foreign investors to invest in our country to bolster our economy," explained Fernando.

"What kind of investment would you suggest that I should venture that you may be familiar with?" asked David.

"Right now, the best investment to start with is to provide our people with what they need, like investment on buy and sell. If you are interested to invest in our economy, I am willing to enter into a partnership with you. How do you like to invest in a haberdashery, a grocery store, and a coffee shop? We can start small. Then when we have generated enough capital, we can convert our investments into a department store."

"How can we explore your proposed business, that will convince me to make an investment?" questioned David.

"First, we will look for the location of our business. Then we will go to the drawing board of how we will operate the business. If you are convinced, we will have a lawyer write the articles of partnership for us, and then we will go to the bank and put yours and my investment. In the signature authorization in the bank, we will document that there will be no disbursement of five thousand pesos without both our signatures. What do you think?" asked Fernando.

"Well, it looks good to me. Can we start the exploration tomorrow?" asked David.

"Sure, I will pick you up tomorrow morning around 8:00 AM. Is that OK with you?"

"OK, I'll wait for you here in the lobby of the hotel," said David.

The two shook hands, and Fernando left, while David went back to his room, where he started unpacking his luggage, then took a shower to refresh.

The following day, Fernando arrived as agreed at eight o'clock in the morning in front of the Manila Hotel and picked up David. They drove to España Street, where they visited buildings with two vacant areas on the first floor open for lease.

"This is what I was telling you last night that is good for a small business like a haberdashery and a coffee shop," said Fernando as they parked their car in the back of the building and went around to the front.

"You see, this area is good for a haberdashery, and the next door we can open it for a coffee shop. As you can see along the road, there is a lot of traffic, which are potential customers. I would prefer a haberdashery because both of us are not familiar with women's clothes. We can do better with men's needs. A coffee shop goes well in this area because this is not far from the University of Santo Thomas. There are lots of students who are coming in and out of the university that would like to sit together over a cup of coffee. Our business will do very well in this location," explained Fernando.

"Let us go inside and investigate the area and let's see how we can plan the renovation to make it attractive to our prospective customers," said David.

"This area here that we can use as our haberdashery is wide enough to accommodate lots of merchandise. Here in front near the entrance, we can install an enclosed glass display window where we can dress two mannequins. We will also have glass shelvings for more merchandise and a wide mirror on the wall to make the area look bigger, attractive, and classy. We need to employ at least six employees here, two cashiers, two salespersons, and two management trainees who will be under our supervision and who will control and manage the inventory sales of the store, purchasing, and other needs. They will be working the morning and evening shifts," explained Fernando. David was eagerly listening.

"That is a very good idea. We can also add a glass display cabinet in the middle of the store to make use of more space," added David.

"We have to get a contractor for the renovation of this place, and in the renovation, we have to have a proper lighting system to make our merchandise stand out and be visible at night time. We will buy our merchandise from a wholesaler, who also delivers at no additional cost. We have to put a 100 percent to 110 percent price profit for every piece of merchandise to even our overhead. But we have to do sales of merchandise that have been in our inventory for some time," said Fernando.

"Let us see the area next door, and let's evaluate how we can make it attractive to more customers," requested David.

"In addition to the renovation to both of these business investments, we also have to make signs lighted, switched on and off with neon lights to make the name of our establishment attractive," added Fernando.

"OK, this coffee shop, we need to install chairs and tables for customers to sit. We also have to install mirrors on both sides of the wall to make the area look bigger and attractive," said David.

"Oh yes, and we have to hire people to operate this business—two cashiers, two food service clerks, a cleaner, and two management trainees under our supervision who will be working the morning and afternoon shifts. The cakes, breads, cookies, and other pastries can be delivered by a bakery shop at no additional cost. They do free delivery because we are patronizing their pastry products. We can order the renovation of both business establishments at the same time so we can start the operation at the same time," added Fernando.

"Well, I am excited to start this venture. How could we start the operation?" asked David.

"We have to first legalize our business. We have to get a lawyer to write the articles of partnership, which must be notarized and signed to make it binding. We have to go to the bank and deposit our initial investments. Then we have to register our business with the City Government of Manila. We have to make an appointment with the building owner to negotiate the leasing of the building, and then we both sign the contract, leasing the building for twenty years. We also have to ask permission to do the construction for the renovation of the building from the city government. We have many things to do before we can start the actual operation of the business. But to make our business rolling, let's go and see the office of Atty. Francisco Villegas at Escolta," explained Fernando.

As agreed in the articles of partnership, both David and Fernando would have a hand on the business. David, who was a graduate of business administration, would manage and administer the business, and Fernando, who was a certified public accountant, would do the financial management, accounting, and bookkeeping in the partnership. They were able to sign the lease of the building for twenty years and registered their business with the city and at the same time requested permission to renovate the building premises. While the shops were being renovated, the two started interviewing their prospective employees for both shops and also contacted wholesalers of products for the haberdashery and surveyed prospective bakery suppliers for the coffee shop. When the renovation was completed for both shops, they immediately met with their prospective employees and reviewed their respective responsibilities, then called their suppliers to start deliveries of their ordered products, and their business commenced operation. The Liberty Coffee Shop and the Liberty Haberdashery were born. David Scarborough, who was a veteran of World War II, became a businessman, a co-owner of the Liberty Partnerships.

# Chapter XVII

## The Birth of New Love

THREE YEARS AFTER they had established the business operations of the Liberty Haberdashery and the Liberty Coffee Shop, the businesses were doing very well, and David's investments on stocks doubled and tripled with the bolstering economy of the country. He also bought a piece of land, where he built an apartment for lease. He hired a live-in maintenance manager, who also collected the rent for him. David was no longer staying in the hotel. He owned a luxury condominium and was driving his own car and was very much focused on his business career. He still remained single and for quite a while had not seen any woman that would make him fall in love again. Rosemarie was still the woman that he idolized and loved, and he remained faithful to her. He wanted to immortalize his love for her. He did not want to fall in love again.

It was one hot summer that as he glanced through the glass window in their back office, David saw a lady come in, and he was puzzled. He closed and opened his eyes, and she was there. He did not know what to do. He looked again through the glass window, and he could see her selecting some shirts in the counter. He sat down and looked again, and he just did not know how to react.

"I cannot believe it. I think I am dreaming. That cannot be Rosemarie. I know we buried her. She is dead. How can it be possible?" murmured David to himself.

David looked again at the window, and she was still there. He sat down. Then with hesitation, he forced himself to walk to meet the lady. But when he came out to meet her, she was gone.

"I think I was just thinking too much of her. I must be just imagining. I know it is impossible that she will come back to life. I think I have to go to church to pray for her so that her soul will be at peace," murmured David to himself.

David decided to go to Quiapo Church to light a candle to dedicate for the repose of the soul of Rosemarie. Instead of driving his own car, to avoid too much traffic, he just took a jeepney from España to Quiapo Church. When he reached Quiapo Church, he bought a candle and lit one dedicated to the soul of Rosemarie. After lighting the candle, he knelt to offer a prayer for the peace of her soul. From Quiapo Church, he also took a jeepney going back to the Liberty Haberdashery and went straight to their back office.

**Picture of Quiapo Church by Karen Joy Reyes**

**Picture of Philippine Jeepney by Miguel Avelino**

When David reached his office, he sat down and was relieved, believing that everything would be OK and the soul of Rosemarie would be at peace. But when he stood up and looked at their glass window, there came again the image of Rosemarie. She was very much alive and well. She was beautiful as ever. This time he knew he was not imagining. But as he was going to step out, he felt numb and nervous. He would be facing the soul of Rosemarie. He inhaled and then composed himself, and with full intention of meeting the lady, he walked out of his office to confront the product of his imagination. At a distance, David called the name of Rosemarie. The lady was selecting and going through the displayed shirts.

"Rosemarie," was the very low tone of David's voice, with the expression of a little uncertainty and fear.

The lady, who was busy going through some shirts, apparently did not hear the call of David.

"Rosemarie!" This time the voice of David was a little louder, but still it had that expression of uncertainty.

The lady, who was looking at the shirts on display, heard the voice of David, with a little hesitation if she were the one being called. She turned around and faced David. When the lady turned to David, he almost sank onto the floor. The complete and actual face and features, from head to foot, of the lady faced him. He seemed stunned and surprised facing the live image of Rosemarie.

"Sir, were you talking to me?" said the lady, with an expression of surprise on her face.

"Rosemarie?" said David, with a little feeling of uncertainty.

"No, sir, you may be mistaken. My name is Rosalie, Rosalie Nuevavista," answered the lady, who was puzzled after being called Rosemarie.

"Oh, I am so sorry. You look like the one I knew, Rosemarie Borromeo," answered David with an expression of a little embarrassment.

"Sir, did you say Borromeo? My uncle's name was Artemio Borromeo," replied Rosalie.

"What did you say, miss? You are related to Artemio Borromeo?" asked David.

"Yes, sir, but he is already dead. He passed away last year," answered Rosalie.

"Miss, can I invite you to have a cup of coffee with me next door? I was with Cmdr. Artemio Borromeo during the war. I want to know more about him, please," was the emotional request of David.

"OK, sir," answered Rosalie.

"Please call me David. I am David Scarborough. I am not too old to be called sir," requested David.

"You can also call me Rosalie, fair and square, right?" Rosalie jokingly said.

The two walked together next door for a cup of coffee. David ordered the coffee, then asked Rosalie if she wanted any cake or pastry to go with it.

"Sir, what do you want to have today?" asked the server.

"Please give us coffee for the two of us," requested David. "Rosalie, do you care for cake, pastry?" asked David.

"No, David, coffee is fine with me," responded Rosalie. "Now, tell me what happened to Commander Borromeo?"

"He was a colonel in the Philippine Marines when he escaped from the death march. After the war, he was promoted to general. But the promotion in rank was not enough to make him happy. Last year because of loneliness he passed away. You see, he was by himself, and apparently, loneliness was too much for him to bear. All his property was willed to my mother. My mother was his only sister," explained Rosalie.

"Our guerilla unit with Commander Borromeo fought the war shoulder to shoulder. If you don't mind, I would like to pay respects to Commander Borromeo. Is it possible for me to meet you mother? I want to meet her, please," requested David.

"Well, you can call my mother and make an appointment. Her name is Josefina Borromeo Nuevavista. Just in case my father answered the phone, his name is Alfredo Nuevavista," answered Rosalie.

Rosalie wrote the names of her mother and father, the telephone number, and their home address on a piece of paper that she took from her handbag, and she handed it to David.

"By the way, what do you want to buy from the haberdashery next door? I saw you were selecting some shirts? Was it for your boyfriend?" asked David.

"No, I do not have any boyfriend. I was going to buy something for my dad. The first time I came there, I was not sure what color he wanted. I came back to get some light-colored shirts for him," answered Rosalie.

"OK, come on, let's go next door and select whatever you want. It will be charged to the house," requested David.

The two walked back to the haberdashery, and Rosalie selected two light-colored shirts, one light yellow and one light blue. David took the selected shirts from Rosalie and handed them to the salesclerk for wrapping. David gave the bagged shirts to Rosalie.

"How much do I owe you?" asked Rosalie.

"No, you do not owe me anything. Do you have a ride? I can drive you home," asked David.

"No, I do not need any ride. Our house is in Dapitan, just on the other side of this street, a few blocks from the University of Santo Tomas. I usually just walk around here," answered Rosalie.

"Well, if you do not want me to drive you home, please tell your mother I want to see her to pay respects, please," requested David.

"I will certainly tell her, and I will also tell her to expect a call from you anytime."

"Thank you, Rosalie, and it has been nice talking to you," replied David.

"Good-bye," were the farewell words of Rosalie.

When Rosalie arrived in their home, she anxiously told her mom about David while her dad was there listening.

"Ma, I met an American who was with Uncle Tim during the war, and he's apparently the co-owner of the haberdashery along España Street. He gave me two shirts for Dad. He wanted to meet you to pay respects. He said that they fought the Japanese shoulder to shoulder and asked permission from me if it is possible to see you. I said, 'If you want to see my mother, you have to make an appointment with her,'" explained Rosalie, with her father listening.

"What is his name?" interjected Mr. Nuevavista.

"David, David Scarborough."

"Well, let us just wait for his call and see what happens," replied Mrs. Nuevavista.

After work, David was anxious to call the mother of Rosalie to make an appointment. On his way home, he passed by a restaurant to eat his dinner and then proceeded home. He took a shower to refresh, then dressed in comfortable pajamas. He picked up the phone and dialed the number that Rosalie gave him. The phone rang in the house of Rosalie.

"Hello, this is Nuevavista residence!" answered Mrs. Nuevavista. "Can I speak to Mrs. Josefina Nuevavista, please?" requested David. "This is she speaking. How can I help you," asked Mrs. Nuevavista. "Ma'am, my name is David Scarborough. I met your daughter this afternoon in our store, and she told me the story about Gen. Artemio Borromeo. The then Commander Borromeo and we were together fighting the Japanese shoulder to shoulder during our mapping of the province of Laguna. Your daughter Rosalie told me that you are the only sister of General Borromeo, and I would like to make an appointment to see you to pay respects, if you don't mind," requested David.

"Well, when do you want to come? Our house is open to you," answered Mrs. Josefina.

"Is it OK this weekend, ma'am?" requested David.

"Why don't you come around 6:00 PM and join us for dinner," requested Mrs. Nuevavista.

"I'll be honored to join you for dinner, Mrs. Nuevavista. I will be there at six this coming Sunday evening."

"Do you have our address?" asked Mrs. Nuevavista.

"Yes, ma'am. I got your address from Rosalie. She wrote your address in a piece of paper when she came to our store."

"OK, David. We will see you this coming weekend, Sunday, at 6:00 PM."

"Thank you for your invitation. I'll be there at 6:00 PM this coming Sunday evening."

"We'll see you then, good-bye," replied Mrs. Nuevavista.

Sunday morning, David woke up very early and went to the gym. After an hour of exercise, he took a shower and went to a barbershop and had his hair trimmed. He went to a nearby restaurant and ate his brunch. From the restaurant he went to a card store and bought a sympathy card. After selecting the card, he went straight to a flower shop and bought a bouquet of white roses. He went straight home and filled up the card with a notation of sympathy for the passing of Gen. Artemio Borromeo and then attached his signature. At around 4:00 PM, David took his shower and dressed up in his white shirt and black striped necktie and black suit. He put on black socks and his well-shined black shoes. He put on his special cologne and combed his hair backward. He looked very neat, impressively tall, and handsome. At around 5:00 PM, he went down to his car, carrying the bouquet of white roses and the envelope with the sympathy card, then drove to the house of Mr. and Mrs. Nuevavista. He arrived in front of the house fifteen minutes too early, so he waited in front until it was about 6:00 PM, then left his car and proceeded to the house of Mr. and Mrs. Nuevavista. When he rang the bell at the gate, it was Rosalie who opened. Rosalie greeted him with a smile.

"Come in, David, we are waiting for you," was the welcome greeting of Rosalie, who was very impressed with the looks and gentleness of David.

"Thank you. Good evening," responded David as he entered the house. As David was coming in, Mrs. Josefina Nuevavista came to greet David, who was standing with Rosalie.

"Good evening, ma'am. I have with me a bouquet of white roses as a token of my respect for the passing of your brother, Gen. Artemio Borromeo," said David.

"Oh, thank you very much, David. Please come in and have a sit in the living room," said Mrs. Nuevavista as she received the bouquet of roses and the sympathy card from David. "Let me put away this bouquet of roses and the card. Rosalie, please attend to David," requested Mrs. Nuevavista as she headed to the dining room.

As David was heading to the living room, Mr. Alfredo Nuevavista came in and greeted him, who was escorted by Rosalie to have a seat.

"Hi, David, it is nice you can come. I am Alfredo Nuevavista, the father of Rosalie. Thank you for the two shirts you gave to Rosalie for me," was the greeting of Mr. Nuevavista as he shook hands with David, who was standing and ready to have a seat.

"Oh, it was just an expression of my respect to General Borromeo, who was with me during the war," answered David.

The three sat down around the center table, with Rosalie by the side of David and Mr. Nuevavista sitting down across. Rosalie could not help once in a while gazing at David, who looked very handsome. David meanwhile would sometimes look at Rosalie with a meaningful glance. As they were sitting down and were about to start the conversation, Mrs. Nuevavista came in and brought some appetizers, barbeque wings, and some spring rolls.

"Oh, David, please help yourself to some appetizers," said Mrs. Nuevavista.

David sat down by the side of Mr. Nuevavista.

"Oh, thank you very much, ma'am," answered David as he reached for a napkin and a buffalo wing.

"So you were together with my brother in Sierra Madre?" asked Mrs. Nuevavista.

"Yes, ma'am, we went down together to the lowland province of Laguna, and we did the mapping operation from the town of Cavinti to other neighboring towns. We cleared the areas from the occupation of the Japanese," answered David.

"That must be a very daring experience, fighting those brutal Japanese soldiers," said Mr. Nuevavista.

"We were all together fighting for the liberation of the country. We were lucky that in our unit, we did not have any casualty. The Japanese were running scared while we were running after them. We have killed some, and we have captured some, which we handed to the U.S. military group assigned to cover our area," replied David.

"My brother passed away last year. But a year before his death, we were together in his house in Cavinti. We even had a family get-together. We even had some paper signing with an attorney, but the year after, he passed away, maybe because of loneliness. He was retired and felt alone in the house," explained Mrs. Nuevavista.

"Who is now staying in the house in Cavinti?" asked David.

"Aling Petra is still there. She is still the housekeeper of the house. Once in a while we visit the house just to check what is going on. Alfonso is the one who takes care of the farm left by my brother."

"Mr. and Mrs. Nuevavista, is it possible to visit the grave of General Borromeo in Cavinti?" asked David.

"Sure, we will go with you whenever you want to go to visit the grave of my brother," answered Mrs. Nuevavista.

"How about next weekend, say, Saturday morning? Is it all right with you, ma'am?" asked David.

"Sure, I don't think we have any scheduled appointment next weekend," said Mrs. Nuevavista.

"How about you, Rosalie, it is OK with you to come with us to Cavinti this weekend?" asked Mrs. Nuevavista.

"I am coming, Mom. I do not have anything to do this coming weekend. I also want to get some fresh air away from the hustle and bustle of city life," answered Rosalie.

"Well, I will drive, and I'll pick you all up this coming Saturday around

7:00 AM. It is better to start early to avoid traffic," said David. "It is OK with us," Interjected Mr. Nuevavista.

They were having a very interesting conversation when the helper entered the living room and told them that dinner was ready in the dining room. The four stood up and proceeded to the dining room. Mr. Nuevavista sat at the head. By his right was Mrs. Nuevavista. Then seated to the right of Mrs. Nuevavista was Rosalie. David sat down on the left side of Mr. Nuevavista, across the table from Mrs. Nuevavista and Rosalie. They started with soup and then the main course of crispy pork, roasted chicken, and arroz valenciana (rice cooked with vegetable, shrimps, and meat). Everybody enjoyed the dinner, and David was very thankful for the hospitality of the family. After dinner, David asked permission to leave. On the way to the door, David could not help but look at Rosalie when their eyes met. David felt guilty and right away looked away and faced Mr. and Mrs. Nuevavista to say good-bye.

"Thank you very much for the very delicious dinner, Mr. and Mrs. Nuevavista, Rosalie, good-bye and I'll see you all on Saturday at 7:00 AM."

The whole week at work, David was so puzzled at the exact resemblance of Rosalie to Rosemarie. He was so confused with his feelings with Rosalie, who was the exact image of Rosemarie. At that moment, he did not know what to do and what role Rosalie would have in his life. He decided to let the situation dictate what was to come between him and Rosalie.

Friday evening, before the appointed date with the Nuevavistas, David went to a floral shop and ordered a beautiful floral arrangement to be brought to Gen. Artemio Borromeo's grave and a bouquet of red roses he intended to bring to Rosemarie's grave. He also bought some candles on his way home. When he got home, he packed some clothes and underwear in a suitcase just in case they would not be able to come back the following day. It was a weekend, and he also intended to visit Rosemarie's grave in the mountain, though he was not sure how he would be able to go up there.

At around 5:00 AM, David woke up and took his shower. He dressed up casually and prepared for the rugged trip if he would be able to go to the mountain. On the way to the house of the Nuevavistas, he passed by a coffee shop and had some breakfast. After breakfast, he proceeded to the house of the Nuevavistas. When he arrived at the gate, they were already waiting for him and were ready to go. David transferred the floral arrangement and the floral bouquet to the backseat, where Mrs. Nuevavista and Rosalie sat, and loaded the luggage of the family into the trunk of the car. Mr. Nuevavista sat in front in the passenger seat of the car. They proceeded traveling southward from the city of Manila, with Mr. Nuevavista navigating. They arrived at the house of General Borromeo in Cavinti before lunchtime. They were welcomed by Aling Petra.

"Come in, come in," was the welcome greeting of Aling Petra to the group. David started unloading the luggage from the trunk of the car and started carrying them up the stairs of the house. Mr. Nuevavista helped carry some of the luggage too. After they were able to unload the carry-on luggage, David asked permission to go to General Borromeo's grave.

"Mr. and Mrs. Nuevavista, I would like to first visit the grave of General Borromeo before I do anything if it is all right with you," asked David.

"Oh, let us just go together. Anyway, Aling Petra will still cook our lunch. Come on, let's go," advised Mrs. Nuevavista.

David drove the family to the cemetery where Gen. Artemio Borromeo's grave was located. In front of the cemetery, David parked his car and just unloaded his floral arrangement. He requested Rosalie to carry the candles. Then they just walked to General Borromeo's grave. David placed the floral arrangement in front of General Borromeo's grave, then lighted several candles. He then stood straight with his hands clasped together. He offered prayers for the soul of General Borromeo. The four went back to the car quietly, but Mrs. Nuevavista was surprised why the bouquet of flowers was left in the car. "Hi, David, did we forget this bouquet of flowers?" inquired Mrs. Nuevavista.

"No, ma'am, I would like to take that to a friend who was buried on the top of the Sierra Madre. I am not really sure how I would bring the flowers and candles to the grave. This would be my first time to be back in this area after a long time that I have been away," answered David.

"Well, anyway let's go back to the house. I am a little hungry already. Maybe Aling Petra has cooked our lunch already," replied Mrs. Nuevavista.

David took the driver's seat, and when the family was all seated and ready to roll, David started the engine and drove back to the house. When they reached the house, the table was ready. Without hesitation after washing their hands, they headed to the table. Aling Petra was so excited to see David back.

"Hello, Sir David, it is nice to see you back here in the country," said Aling Petra.

"Yes, Aling Petra, I feel at home here. As if nothing had changed," answered David.

After eating their lunch, David asked permission from the family to go to the farm to meet Alfonso.

"Sir, ma'am, and Rosalie, I'll just go to the farm to say hello to Alfonso. I used to know him when General Borromeo was still alive. I'll be back," asked David, and he headed out to go to the farm.

David drove his car to the farm, where he remembered leaving Lightning at the hands of Alfonso. After he parked his car in front of the farm gate, he just walked toward the farm and yelled, "Lightning!" Alfonso came out from the barn. He was then busy milking the cow.

"Hi, Sir David, what are you doing here? I thought you left for America after the war?" questioned Alfonso.

"Yes, but I came back. I am here to offer flowers to the grave of General Borromeo. We just came back from the cemetery. By the way, where is my horse Lightning?" asked David.

"Oh, he is in the back of the barn. You can go and get him," replied Alfonso.

David went to the back of the barn and saw his horse. When Lightning saw David, he jumped in celebration and made a hissing sound. David approached his horse and rode him. They rode around, and then he rode him back to the house of General Borromeo. When he arrived at the gate, he called the family to meet Lightning. The family led by Rosalie went down to see the horse.

"Sir, ma'am, Rosalie, please meet my horse Lightning. We used to work together during the war. Lightning and I fought against the Japanese during the war, and we had won several battles," said David. "Also, I would probably be late coming home tonight. I'll ride Lightning to the mountain to bring the bouquet of flowers and candles to the grave of a very close friend of mine. I'll be back as soon as I have brought the flowers, lit the candles, and offered some prayers," said David.

"Be very careful, David," said Rosalie with tenderness.

"Yes, I will," answered David as he looked into the eyes of Rosalie.

David turned around and rode Lightning going back to the farm to get the bouquet of flowers and candles from his car. He then rode Lightning tracing the path leading to the top of Sierra Madre. The trail had been familiar to him for the several times that they had travelled the path. He noticed that it was as if nothing had changed, except for more growth of vegetation, but the terrain remained the same. It was late afternoon when he reached Rosemarie's grave under the acacia tree. He offered the bouquet of flowers and lit the candles in front of Rosemarie's grave. He stood straight with his eyes closed and offered some prayers for the soul of Rosemarie. After his prayers, he looked intensely at the waterfalls and at the river that became the witness of their togetherness, walking along the edge of the river. He was in the middle of imagining those beautiful memories he had with Rosemarie when from nowhere came a Japanese soldier charging toward his direction, with a rifle pointed at him, with a fixed bayonet attached to the barrel, ready for the kill, shouting, "Banzai nippon!"

David was stunned and could not move in surprise. But when the Japanese soldier came closer under the acacia tree, it was as if he were tackled by an unknown force, with his head hammered to the ground, and the rifle he was carrying was thrown away. The Japanese soldier stood scared and ran downhill on the path toward the waterfalls. Scared and surprised, not paying attention to the steepness of the path, he tripped and fell to the ground and rolled down, then hit a rock at the edge of the path. He was bleeding and stood up disoriented, then ran toward the river and dived into the water, and he never came out. David waited for the Japanese soldier to come out from the water, but apparently he drowned.

> *(The spirits of Mary Scarlet and Rosemarie were there watching everything unfold. "What did you do to that poor Japanese soldier?" asked the spirit of Mary Scarlet. "Nothing, I just tripped him up, and his head fell on the ground, and he probably got disoriented and ran down to the waterfalls and stumbled and his head hit the rock. Then he jumped into the river," answered the spirit of Rosemarie.)*

David stood there under the acacia tree in disbelief. Who could have tackled that Japanese soldier who was charging toward him with a fixed bayonet at the barrel of his rifle, pointed toward him, with the intention to kill? The surface under the acacia tree was flat, and there was nothing that would have caused the Japanese to fall. He just fell to the ground head-on as if somebody lifted him up and dumped him.

With the big puzzle on his mind, David rode Lightning back to the farm of General Borromeo. David returned Lightning to Alfonso, who was waiting for his return in front of the farm. David kissed Lightning, then handed him to Alfonso. David drove back to the house of General Borromeo. It was already very late when he arrived, but the family had not eaten yet, worried about him. When David arrived, the family felt a little better and welcomed him, with Rosalie going down, worried about David.

"We were worried about you already," said Rosalie.

"Oh, it took me longer than I thought. It was a long journey. I feel so tired.

I think I have to take my shower first before I do anything," said David.

"OK, you go ahead. We will wait for you. We will eat together," said Rosalie.

When he came up the stairs, he greeted Mr. and Mrs. Nuevavista, who were busy helping Aling Petra prepare the table for dinner.

"Good evening, sir, ma'am, Aling Petra, I came a little late. It was a long journey. I will first take my shower. I feel filthy and dirty," said David, with Rosalie behind him.

"Go ahead, and we will wait for you," answered Mrs. Nuevavista.

David got new clothes and underwear from his suitcase and proceeded to take his shower. After shower, he dressed up and proceeded to join the family at the dinner table.

At the dinner table, David told the unbelievable experience he had on top of the Sierra Madre Mountains, with the Japanese charging toward him with a fixed bayonet at the barrel of his gun, pointed at him, who just fell to the ground head-on as if an unknown force tackled him. He told them that he watched everything unfold in disbelief. While he was telling the story, there were times his eyes and Rosalie's would meet, and they seemed to have a connecting sensation. David tried to fight the strong feelings within him, but he could not do it. His feelings surrendered to the truth that he felt something very strong toward Rosalie.

It was late before David went to bed, thinking of the very interesting experience he witnessed near Rosemarie's grave on top of the Sierra Madre Mountains. He asked himself questions: "Could it be the spirit of Rosemarie who tackled the Japanese soldier who tried to kill me? Was it the spirit of Rosemarie who tried to protect me from harm? I am now very confused with Rosalie coming to my life. I am not sure what to do." David was pondering those questions in his minds as he was going to bed.

Pondering those questions, it was already midnight when he fell asleep. In his sleep, he dreamt of traveling in an open space with white clouds. In the clouds, a little farther from him was the image of his mother waving at him. He wanted to reach his mother, but she disappeared in the clouds. He reached a beautiful place like a garden of paradise, with so many blooming flowers around. He saw a chair in the middle of the garden, and he sat there while admiring the beauty of his surroundings. Then while seated, a hand touched his shoulder tenderly. When he looked up, it was Rosemarie talking to him: *"David, I am in a different world as yours, and I am at peace with God. I am giving you the freedom to fall in love again. Please take good care of Rosalie."*

David stood and turned around to face Rosemarie and tried to reach for her hand, but the image of Rosemarie disappeared in the clouds. He ran looking for her in his dream. Then he woke up feeling tired.

"Oh, it was a dream. Rosemarie came to my dream to give me the freedom to fall in love again, and she mentioned the name of Rosalie." David pondered while seated on his bed.

David did not feel like going to sleep after the dream. He instead put on his rubber shoes and shorts and went down the house and jogged on the street in front of the house to the farm, then back to the house. He kept on running until it was dawn. Perspiring from running around, he went into the house and took his shower, changed to new clothes, fixed himself, and sat in the living room. Aling Petra heard David entering the living room. She offered him hot coffee.

"Good morning, Sir David," greeted Aling Petra.
"Good morning, Aling Petra," responded David.
"Sir David, you woke up very early. Please have a cup of coffee. Do you want sugar and cream?" asked Aling Petra.
"Oh no, Aling Petra, I want my coffee black. Thank you very much."

Aling Petra went back to the kitchen to prepare breakfast. She then set the dining table for breakfast. She cooked and served fried rice, fried eggs, their native sausage, bread, and coffee with sugar and cream. When the table was ready, Aling Petra called the family to let them know that it was time for breakfast.

One by one after using the bathroom, the family came into the dining room. Everybody was seated, while David was still in the living room. Aling Petra called David to tell him that the family was already seated in the dining room and waiting for him. David stood up and proceeded there.

"Good morning, everybody," greeted David.

"Good morning, David," was the simultaneous greeting of the family.

David sat down across from Mrs. Nuevavista and Rosalie, with Mr. Nuevavista at the head.

"Everybody had a good sleep?" asked David.

"Yes, we did," answered Mrs. Nuevavista.

"Yes, it is very nice here, fresh air, very quiet. I had a good rest," responded Rosalie.

"Do you have any more activities here in Cavinti, David?" asked Mr. Nuevavista.

"Oh, no, sir, my only intention of coming over is to see the grave of General Borromeo. We have fought the war together, and it is just fitting that as a soldier, I must pay respects to him," responded David, as he glanced at Rosalie, who was looking at him as he was talking.

David inhaled a little bit, then looked at the faces of Mr. Nuevavista, Mrs. Nuevavista, then Rosalie. When their eyes met, David felt a different sensation. He looked down and sighed, then looked at Mr. and Mrs. Nuevavista. Then without hesitation, he spoke: "Mr. and Mrs. Nuevavista, I hope you don't mind, I would like to ask permission from both of you."

"What is it, David?" asked Mr. Nuevavista.

"Sir, ma'am, with your permission, I would like to court Rosalie," replied David without hesitation.

When Rosalie heard what David said, she turned red. She blushed with David's unexpected declaration of courtship. But she remained composed and just smiled.

"Well, she is our only daughter. Please be very tender with her. You can come and visit her whenever you want. Our house is open to you. I think you are a fine gentleman. It is OK with us, right, Josefina?" answered Mr. Nuevavista as he turned to his wife.

"Thank you, sir. Thank you, ma'am, I'll always be gentle with Rosalie."

Rosalie remained quiet and did not say anything. She just looked away, trying to avoid the eyes of David in the presence of her parents. She pretended not to hear anything. She did not say a word. After the conversation about courtship, everybody seemed lost for a word to say. Everyone was waiting for a word to be spoken. David broke the silence as he looked at Rosalie.

"Rosalie, can I visit you in your house this coming Sunday afternoon?" asked David as he looked into her eyes, trying to read something from her body language.

"Our house is open to you. Yes, I'll be home on Sunday," responded Rosalie, who was still avoiding the eyes of David in the presence of her parents.

After breakfast, everybody prepared to leave. They started packing their things. Mr. Nuevavista and David helped bring down to the car their luggage and some boxes of fruits, vegetables, and other native and preserved Cavinti food prepared by Aling Petra, delivered from the farm by one of their workers. On the way, instead of going straight to Manila, David drove the family to Mount Makiling Restaurant in Calamba since it was almost time for lunch. David treated the family to lunch, and he also bought some native bakery products along the way and gave them to the family. David was starting to court not only Rosalie but also her family. David wanted to gain the respect and honor of the whole family to show that his intention toward Rosalie was pure and honest.

When they reached the house of the Nuevavistas, David helped unload the luggage and the boxes containing food from Cavinti.

"Thank you very much for letting me pay my respects to the grave of General Borromeo," said David to the family.

David shook hands with Mr. Nuevavista, then approached Mrs. Nuevavista and gave her a hug, then said, "Thank you, ma'am, for everything."

David approached Rosalie, held her by the hand, and then embraced her. Then he whispered to her, "I'll see you on Sunday afternoon."

Rosalie just smiled and did not say anything. David turned around and headed to his car and waved before he entered the car. He drove straight home, still wondering about the great experience he had during the travel, which seemed too long, with many things that happened. This time, he was facing a new chapter of his life, a new love.

The three remained standing at the gate in front of the house, watching David as he drove away. The family was in complete silence, when Mrs. Nuevavista spoke.

"He was a perfect gentleman. David is very polite, respectful, tall, and very handsome. What do you think, Rosalie?"

"I don't know, Ma. I am not sure," answered Rosalie with a smile. Then she walked back to the house.

# Chapter XVIII

## The Parental Courtship

DAVID LEARNED A lesson from his relation with Rosemarie. He was then so bold and anxious in declaring and insisting his love, and in a very short time he lost Rosemarie. This time David would like to be very careful. He would like to nurture his love for Rosalie with tenderness. He would like to learn more about her, her likes and dislikes, her family, and her views in life. He planned to be a part of the family as a part of his courtship. He would like to blend in with the family to learn more about them. If he was to establish a family, he would like to have a happy one; he would like to be sure of the life he was to enter, a new life without regret.

During the week before the first courtship visit of David to Rosalie, he still kept on thinking of the words that Rosemarie said in his dream: *"I am at peace with God. I am giving you the freedom to fall in love again. Take good care of Rosalie."*

David whispered to himself, "What a great love she had for me. She was willing to sacrifice for the sake of my happiness. Rosemarie, I will not fail you. I'll take good care of Rosalie. I promise." With a big sigh, he continued what he was doing in the store. With the birth of a new love, David was more focused on his job in the haberdashery and in the coffee shop and the apartment housing he had built. He paid attention to everything. He was more attentive to what he had to accomplish in life, looking forward to the big responsibility of falling in love.

Sunday morning, David dressed well and then drove to church to hear Sunday Mass. He was very thankful for everything that was coming to his life—the successful business and the new love that was burning in his heart. He would like to ask for more blessings and grace for the new venture he would face in loving Rosalie. He would like to ask for guidance in the new direction of his life. From church, he passed by a restaurant and got something to eat. Then he headed home and took his shower. He put on a sports shirt matched with white pants and leather shoes. He wore expensive cologne, then headed out to his car and drove to the house of Rosalie.

When he reached the house of Rosalie, he parked his car in front of the gate, then rang the bell. A little later, Rosalie came out from the front door and opened the gate for David.

"Come in, David," was the invitation of Rosalie as she opened the gate.

"Good afternoon, Rosalie," was the greeting of David.

"Good afternoon. Please come on inside," responded Rosalie, and she led David to the living room of the house. "Please have a seat," said Rosalie.

David sat down while looking around. One thing that attracted him was the piano in the corner of the house, but he did not say anything. He just got reminded of his mother when he was still small. His mother used to play the piano while he listened, and sometimes they sang together.

"Where are your parents?" asked David after seeing Rosalie was alone in the house.

"Oh, they are in the back of the house. They have a little garden in the back. They must be doing something there," answered Rosalie.

David took the advantage of Rosalie being alone and asked her some personal questions about her life.

"Rosalie, you are so beautiful. You actually stand out in the crowd. You are tall and different from other Filipinas I have been seeing every day as they passed by our stores. You look more like a Caucasian than Asian. You are different," asked David.

"Well, my grandparents were immigrants from Spain, so my father is pure Spanish. My mother is half Filipino and half English-Spanish. So you can say I am a half breed, I am a mestiza Filipina," responded Rosalie.

"How do you spend your leisure time? How do you keep yourself occupied?" asked David.

"Well, I keep on reading. I am in my second year in the College of Law at the University of Santo Thomas. I have been reading law books in preparation for the next semester. I would like to be sharp and well informed when classes start. We are in a summer break now. That's why I have time to relax. When I get tired of reading, I play the piano just to kill time," answered Rosalie.

"Oh really, you play the piano?" asked David.

"Oh yes, do you want me to play?" asked Rosalie.

"Can you accompany me if I sing "Because," the song from the movie *The Student Prince?*" asked David.

"I'll try," answered Rosalie.

David sang "Because" from *The Student Prince*:

> *Because, you come to me with naught save love*
> *and hold my hand and lift mine eyes above*
> *a wider world of hope and joy I see*
> *because you come to me*

The loud reverberating tenor voice of David sounded like a call to the ears of Mr. and Mrs. Nuevavista, who were in the back of the house. They could not help but run inside the house to have a glimpse of the singing sensation that was David, whom they had not heard before. When David finished singing, the couple could not help but clap their hands in joy.

"Can we hear another song, please?" asked Mrs. Nuevavista.

David turned to Rosalie and asked her if she could accompany him in singing "The Lord's Prayer."

"Rosalie, can you set the key for 'The Lord's Prayer'? Let's try and see if we can blend together," asked David.

Rosalie started the piano. Then David came in with an emotional song from the movie *The Student Prince*, "The Lord's Prayer."

*Our Father, who art in heaven*
*Hallowed be Thy Name*
*Thy kingdom come*
*Thy will be done on earth*
*As it is in heaven*

*Give us this day our daily bread*
*And forgive us our debts*
*As we forgive our debtors*
*And lead us not into temptation*
*But deliver us from evil*
*For thine is the kingdom*
*And the power and the glory forever*
*Amen*

"Wow, that was divine," commented Mrs. Nuevavista as she and Mr. Nuevavista clapped their hands.

"We did not know you know how to sing David," commented Mr. Nuevavista.

"Oh, my mother used to teach me how to sing when I was a young boy.

She also played the piano, and we sang together," answered David.

"Wow, you are something else, David. You have not stopped to amaze us.

You seem to have so many talents," commented Mrs. Nuevavista.

"Oh no, ma'am, I am just trying to share the little gift I learned through life," was the modest answer of David.

"Come, David, let's have a seat," was the invitation of Rosalie.

"Hey, Rosalie, how about going out with your parents? Let's take them out to Chinatown. I'll drive," asked David.

"Let us ask them," answered Rosalie.

"Sir, ma'am, let us go out and eat some Chinese food in Chinatown. I'll drive," asked David.

Mr. and Mrs. Nuevavista were unprepared to answer and were a little hesitant to speak, but Mrs. Nuevavista was signaled by Rosalie to say yes.

"OK, if you say so. Let me change. I should be ready in a few minutes," responded Mrs. Nuevavista.

"I'll change too. I'll be backed, David," followed up by Mr. Nuevavista. David and the family headed to Binondo, the Chinatown of the city of

Manila. David treated the family to the best Chinese restaurant in Binondo. David ordered Peking duck, special chow mein noodles, fried rice combination, and dumplings. He also ordered special *halo-halo* (Filipino native dessert). The family had a feast. David was so pleased with the development of his courtship with Rosalie. He was starting to gain the confidence of the parents. What David really wanted to do was to gain the trust and confidence of Rosalie's parents that his intention was honest and honorable. After dinner, David bought some Chinese pastries and handed the bag to Mrs. Nuevavista.

"Wow, David, you have already fed us, and you still got this bag of pastries for us," commented Mrs. Nuevavista.

"Oh, this is the first time I invited you here to Chinatown. I thought of getting something you can bring home," replied David.

"By the way, did you all enjoy the food?" asked David.

"Oh yes, I could hardly walk. I am ready to explode," answered Mr. Nuevavista.

David drove the family back to their home. Mrs. Nuevavista invited David to come up to have a cup of coffee. David did not want to decline the invitation of Mrs. Nuevavista, so he went with them inside the house to have a cup of coffee. David sat in the living room, facing Rosalie, while Mrs. Nuevavista went to the kitchen to prepare the coffee. Mr. Nuevavista followed Mrs. Nuevavista and helped put some Chinese pastries on a serving tray and served them in the center table in the living room.

David could not stop looking at the beautiful face of Rosalie, while Rosalie was trying to pretend not to notice David staring. There were times when their eyes would meet, and they would just smile. They seemed to feel the connection between them, but David did not want to rush anything. He wanted to court the whole family, not just Rosalie.

When Mr. Nuevavista came in with coffee cups, with Mrs. Nuevavista carrying the coffeepot, David asked Mr. Nuevavista if he was familiar with Pagsanjan Falls.

"Sir, are you familiar with Pagsanjan Falls?" asked David.

"Oh yes, that is the next town to Cavinti. Why?" asked Mr. Nuevavista. "Sir, let us have a picnic there. I heard that Pagsanjan Falls is beautiful."

"Oh, just let us know when you want to go. I'll navigate. I am familiar with the route going to Pagsanjan Falls," answered Mr. Nuevavista.

"How about next weekend?" said David.

"Well, Josefina, what do you think?" asked Mr. Nuevavista as he turned to his wife.

"Rosalie, are you available this coming weekend?" asked Mrs. Nuevavista as she turned to Rosalie.

"Ma, if you say I'll go, I'll go. I have no scheduled appointment next weekend," said Rosalie.

"So, it is OK. Let's do it on Saturday so that we could rest on Sunday," followed up Mrs. Nuevavista.

"OK, we are set next Saturday. I'll pick you all up at 7:00 AM. We should be in Pagsanjan Falls by lunchtime, I think," replied David.

"Yes, you are right, David. I think we should be in Pagsanjan Falls before lunchtime," followed up Mr. Nuevavista.

"OK, I think I have been taking too much of your time. I better head home to give you all time to rest," said David as he stood up.

"Thank you very much for treating us with the Chinese food in Binondo, David," said Mrs. Nuevavista.

"You are welcome, ma'am, sir, Rosalie. I am leaving now," said David as he headed to the front door. Rosalie followed him, and the couple was left in the living room.

Rosalie opened the door for David. David took the advantage of Rosalie being alone. He tenderly held her arms and embraced her. "Good night, I'll miss you. I'll be back on Saturday to be with you," whispered David to Rosalie as he stepped out of the door.

Rosalie looked tenderly into David's eyes and then smiled. David stepped out of the door, and Rosalie closed it. She then slightly opened the door and peeped to see David as he started his car and drove away.

The whole week while working, David was so anxious, looking forward to their trip to Pagsanjan Falls. He was imagining Rosalie wearing a bathing suit as they swim together in the pool below the waterfalls. He felt as if he would like to push the time to move faster so that they could already drive to Pagsanjan Falls. He already planned what he had to bring to the trip and prepared everything the day before. There were times when he would just sit down in the back office of their store imagining Rosalie. He was very much in love with Rosalie, but he had not expressed his love to her yet. He was looking for the proper timing, when her parents had complete trust in him.

Friday afternoon, the day before the scheduled trip to Pagsanjan Falls, David drove to La Loma, Quezon City. He ordered three pounds of roasted pork (*lechon*) and split-roasted chicken. From La Loma, he drove to Quinta Market near Quiapo Church and bought two pounds of sliced honey-baked ham. He went straight home and put all the meat in the refrigerator to keep their freshness.

The following morning around 5:00 AM, he woke up very early, took his shower, and dressed in a sporty short-sleeved white shirt, white short pants, white tennis shoes. He packed a swimming trunk, bath towel and underwear, and new clean clothes for the travel back. He put all the meat he bought the night before into a cooler and loaded everything into the trunk of his car. On the way to the house of Rosalie, he passed by a corner store that was open and bought bottled soda and bottled water and a bag of ice and put them all in the cooler to keep everything well preserved.

When he arrived in front of the house at six forty-five, the family was already waiting for him. David helped load their luggage and the container of food prepared by the family into the trunk of his car. Mr. Nuevavista went back into the house and checked everything and then came down and sat in the passenger side, while Mrs. Nuevavista and Rosalie sat behind them. It was almost 7:00 AM when they finally left, heading to Pagsanjan Falls. It was around

9:00 AM when they reached Calamba, Laguna, and David remembered seeing a bakery when they stopped over the last time they passed through Calamba. He drove around, and when he found the bakery, he went down and bought some freshly baked bread, rolls, and a cake. He asked Rosalie to hold the cake to prevent the icing from messing up due to the road bumps. Around eleven o'clock, when they arrived in the vicinity going to the town of Pagsanjan, to the amazement of David, Mr. Nuevavista, who was navigating, led them toward the town of Cavinti.

"Sir, are you sure we are going the right way? This road is going to the town of Cavinti. We passed this road before when we came here," questioned David.

"Yes, I know. Just drive ahead, and I will tell you where to turn," answered Mr. Nuevavista.

David followed the instructions of Mr. Nuevavista and continued driving. David was expecting that they were going to the house of General Borromeo, when suddenly Mr. Nuevavista gave him an instruction: "There, turn left on that road. That road is leading to the Picnic Grove, which they used to call Eco-Park. That is the place where we are going to eat our lunch."

David parked his car outside the entrance of the nature park, which they called the Picnic Grove. The family selected where they could eat their lunch before they went to the trail leading to Pagsanjan Falls. After the family selected the place where they would have a picnic, David got the cooler that contained the food he prepared the night before, including the drinks he got on the way to the house of Rosalie. He also helped Mr. Nuevavista in carrying the food that they brought with them. Mrs. Nuevavista with the help of Rosalie covered a park table with a clean tablecloth, and they started putting the food on the table. They put out the eating utensils, paper plates, plastic glasses, and plastic spoons and forks. They also brought out serving spoons for the food. Mrs. Nuevavista cooked and prepared rice, pork adobo, and chicken cooked in coconut milk. David brought out his crispy pork, split-roasted chicken, and ham. He also served the bread and cake they bought on the way. David and the family had a very good time eating in the scenic area of the nature park of Cavinti.

After eating their lunch, they sat around and enjoyed the beauty of the surroundings. Then Mr. Nuevavista warned everybody to get ready to head to Pagsanjan Falls.

"Well, it is time for us to head to Pagsanjan Falls from here. We all have to walk, but before we do that, we have to put our food back into the car, or else animals will have a feast on our food," said Mr. Nuevavista.

Mrs. Nuevavista and Rosalie put back the food into the containers and covered them properly. David and Mr. Nuevavista brought back to the car whatever was readied by Mrs. Nuevavista and Rosalie.

When they finished loading everything back into the car, Mr. Nuevavista advised the family to bring their swimming suits with them.

"OK, if you are all ready, come follow me," advised Mr. Nuevavista.

David and the family followed the path heading to Pagsanjan Falls. Along the way, they could not help but appreciate the lush forest. Then they went and descended to the magnificent Nakulo Falls. David was so amazed of the grandeur of the waterfalls, flowing like wide drapes, falling into a narrow basin. Then as they continued following the trail, they came to very steep steps with a metal railing leading to the waterfalls. Then they reached the perpendicular stairs going down to the edge of the Pagsanjan Waterfalls. David and the family walked along the river and appreciated the beauty of the waterfalls coming from around three hundred feet high, roaring like a lion as the water plunged with such strength, causing vibrations in the vicinity. David and the family paid to ride a raft going to the waterfalls to see the Devil's Cave behind. The water was cold, and Rosalie was holding the arm of David to maintain her balance as they rode a bamboo raft toward the waterfalls. They all got wet with the volume of water coming from the top, pouring in front of the Devil's Cave. After they had seen the Devil's Cave, David and the family sailed back to the side of the river and sat down, appreciating the beauty of the rushing water coming from the top of the hill three hundred feet away. Then David asked Rosalie to swim.

"Come, Rosalie, let's try the water. Let us swim," requested David.

"OK, let's go," answered Rosalie.

They just swam along the side of the river and did not go very far. They just played, wetting each other, and then they swam together. While they were swimming, Rosalie noticed the miraculous medal hanging on David's neck.

"David, what is that you are wearing around your neck? Is that a medal or something?" asked Rosalie.

"This is a miraculous medal. Without this I would not be here now. I would be dead. I was wearing this during one of my missions when a Japanese sniper shot me. The bullet hit me on the chest. With the force of the bullet, I was thrown from the horse. The force of the bullet was absorbed by the miraculous medal. I was not hurt," explained David.

"How did you get the medal?" asked Rosalie.

"Remember that time when I went to the mountain carrying the bouquet of flowers? I brought the flowers to the grave of Rosemarie. She was the one who gave me this medal. I courted her, and we had always been together, walking along the river, talking, holding hands under an acacia tree, but one day when I kissed her, she pushed me and told me, 'Let's talk about love after the war.' I was hurt. I left her and told her that I had to follow our guerilla unit in the south and that I had to see her the following morning to say good-bye. When I came to see her the following morning, she was there waiting for me in front of their house. I hugged her and said good-bye. Then I turned around to leave. But she called me and handed me a sealed envelope and told me to open the envelope when I reach my destination. When I reached our camp in the south and opened the envelope, It has her picture, and on the back she said, 'David, I Love you. Rosemarie.' I was willing to wait for her after the war, but his father was captured by the Japanese. She sent a messenger to our camp asking for help. We went back to their area in the mountain and planned the rescue. It was then that she gave me this medal when we were going to a surveillance mission. During the rescue, she insisted to come. After we rescued her father, she was shot by a Japanese soldier. She lost too much blood riding her horse back to the mountain. She passed away long before the doctor arrived," explained David.

"It is a very sad story of your love, David. She must be very beautiful," said Rosalie.

"Yes, as a matter of fact, you are the living image of Rosemarie. Rosemarie was born to life in you. I am not surprised. She is your first cousin. She was the only daughter of General Borromeo," added David. "Interestingly, that night after I had offered the bouquet of flowers to her grave, I dreamt of her, and she told me, 'I am in the other side of your world, and I am at peace with God. I am giving you the freedom to fall in love again. Please take good care of Rosalie.' The following morning after my dream, I asked permission from your parents to court you," followed up by David.

Rosalie was in complete silence while listening to David. Then she tried to avoid his eyes when David talked about courtship.

"The water is getting cold. Let's go to the side of the river and sit under the sun. I feel cold standing in the water," said Rosalie.

When Rosalie complained that the water was too cold, David took the arm of Rosalie and led her to the side of the river. Then they sat down together under the sun. As they sat down, David held Rosalie close to him.

"Are you still cold?" asked David.

"I feel OK now. It was cold in the water," answered Rosalie.

"Are you enjoying my company?" asked David.

"Yes, you are not biting me," jokingly answered Rosalie.

A little later, Mr. Nuevavista called the two so that they could experience riding the boat along the rapids.

"David and Rosalie, come on, let us try to ride the boat going up and down the rapids," asked Mr. Nuevavista.

David and Rosalie stood up. Holding hands, they walked to the direction of Mr. and Mrs. Nuevavista, who were waiting with the boatman. The two were already wearing safety vests. David and Rosalie also wore safety vests, and the four rode the boat going down the fast rushing current of the river, with Mrs. Nuevavista holding the arm of Mr. Nuevavista and Rosalie holding the arm of David. Sometimes Rosalie would even lean toward the shoulder of David, and David would hold her hand to make her feel safe. When they reached the bottom of the rapids, they rode back against the current. Rosalie enjoyed the company of David, all the time leaning toward his shoulder. David enjoyed the warm body of Rosalie as she leaned toward him, and sometime when the boat starts to zigzag in the rapids, David would embrace Rosalie to make her feel safe. David was very careful not to be misunderstood by the parents of Rosalie that he was taking advantage of the situation. That's why when the boat was running steady, he would release the embrace and just hold the arms of Rosalie.

After their boating experience, they headed back to the nature park. They once again climbed the steep vertical stairs and the diagonal stairs. During the climb, David stayed at the bottom just in case somebody would fall. He would be there to catch or prevent anybody from falling. After they had climbed the steep vertical stairs and the diagonal metal stairs, they followed the path leading to the nature park where they rested for a moment. While the family was resting, David got the cooler that contained the food and the drinks, and he served the family, who got tired with the journey.

"Come on, let's have something to drink and something to eat while we are resting," requested David as he opened the cooler.

David got the soft drinks and the bottled water and put them on the park table. He also brought out some meat leftover they had for lunch. He went back to the car and got the eating utensils, plates, and plastic glasses, and everybody enjoyed the food while resting in the park. While David was doing all these, Mrs. Nuevavista could not help but comment to Mr. Nuevavista her appreciation of David.

"David is a very find gentleman. I really like him," commented Mrs. Nuevavista.

"Well, he should show off. He has to work hard if he wants to be noticed," responded Mr. Nuevavista.

Rosalie just looked away as if she did not hear anything. When David arrived with the eating utensils, Rosalie stood up and served his parents and David with plates, cups, spoons, and forks. Everybody got their food served in the park table, which was arranged by Mrs. Nuevavista. Rosalie got her food too and sat by the side of David. David was starting to feel that he was gaining the trust not only of the family but also of Rosalie. After eating, Mrs. Nuevavista and Rosalie put away everything. They put back the food in the cooler, and David brought the cooler back to the car. Rosalie carried the bag of the eating utensils, and they all headed to the car.

David and the family headed on the bumpy road back to Manila. It was already late when they reached the house of the Nuevavista family. David helped unload all the food containers and luggage of the family. He also gave them the leftover of the crispy pork, the roasted chicken, and ham, including the leftover drinks. David helped them carry all the food to their kitchen so that they could put them in the refrigerator. After unloading the food, David headed to the door, then turned around and faced the family.

"Well, good night, sir, ma'am, Rosalie, and thank you for everything," said David as he stepped out of the door.

"Good night, David," was the simultaneous answer of Mr. and Mrs. Nuevavista.

Rosalie followed David outside the house up to the gate. David did not know that Rosalie was following him, so when he was closing the gate, he was surprised to see Rosalie.

"Oh, I did not know you were behind me," said David.

"I just want to see you go. That's all," answered Rosalie.

David looked around and saw if there was anybody around. Then he went to the gate and embraced Rosalie. He was going to kiss her lips, but she looked down, so he just kissed her forehead.

"Good night, Rosalie. I'll see you Sunday afternoon," whispered David.

"I'll be waiting for you. Good night and drive carefully," answered Rosalie.

The following Sunday afternoon, David visited Rosalie and invited her and the family to go to the movies. While they were seated in the living room, David asked Rosalie, "Rosalie, the remake of the movie *The Student Prince* is being shown now in the theaters. Let's take your parents with us and watch the movie?"

"I don't know with my parents. You can ask them if they want to go to the movies," answered Rosalie.

"Can I talk to your parents? I will ask them if they will go with us to the movies," requested David.

"Let me get them and ask them if they would be interested," answered Rosalie.

Rosalie stood up and went to see her parents, who were upstairs. Rosalie asked her mother and father if they were interested to go to the movies. Mrs. Nuevavista told Rosalie that they would just stay at home and the two of them could go ahead and watch a movie.

"I trust David. I know he is a fine gentleman. You will be all right with him," said Mrs. Nuevavista as she came down with Rosalie to talk to David.

"David, you can go ahead and watch the movie with Rosalie. You just bring Rosalie back after you finished watching, OK?" suggested Mr. Nuevavista.

"Yes, ma'am. You can trust me. I'll bring back Rosalie safely after we watched the movie," answered David.

"Can you wait for me for just a minute? I would like to change and fix myself," requested Rosalie.

"Go ahead, Rosalie, I'll be waiting," answered David.

David and Rosalie left the house, with Mr. and Mrs. Nuevavista watching from the window. Mr. and Mrs. Nuevavista had built their trust and confidence in David after the good manners and gentleness he had shown in the trips that they went on together. They saw how gentlemanly David was. He was open to share in any manner to make the occasion enjoyable. They loved the respect they had been accorded by David and the way they saw how she treated Rosalie with reverence.

When David and Rosalie arrived in the movie theater, David bought two packs of popcorn and gave one to Rosalie. David got the tickets, and both of them entered the movie theater. David showed Rosalie his gentleness and respect. They enjoyed watching the movie and whispered about what they were watching, but David was extra careful not to take advantage of the situation, remembering the experience he had with Rosemarie, when he was pushed away when he was too aggressive in their relationship. But in a gentle manner, he put his arm around the waist of Rosalie while they were watching the movie. Rosalie did not resist and just pretended to ignore the hold of David. Rosalie even leaned toward David, and David held Rosalie tight. David could feel the warm body of Rosalie, but David controlled his emotion and remained gentle until the end of the movie.

"You know, David, I think you sing better than Mario Lanza. You see, he was forcing his voice, while your voice is coming naturally," commented Rosalie on their way back home in the car.

"Wow, I am flattered," answered David. "By the way, how about if we go to church on Sunday to the ten o'clock Mass at the Manila Cathedral?" asked David.

"We will see. Let us talk to my parents before I commit going out with you," answered Rosalie.

When they reached the Nuevavista house, David went in with Rosalie to pay his respects to her parents. Mr. and Mrs. Nuevavista came out.

"Good evening, sir, ma'am, I just brought home Rosalie," was the greeting of David to the couple.

"Good evening, David. Did you enjoy the movie?" asked Mrs. Nuevavista. "Oh yes, ma'am. Mario Lanza is one of my favorite tenor singers. Thank you for asking," answered David.

"Sir, ma'am, I would like to ask permission from both of you if it is OK for me to take Rosalie to hear the Mass on Sunday at the Manila Cathedral at ten o'clock," requested David.

"It is fine with us. If you are going to church, you have our permission," answered Mr. Nuevavista, which was seconded my Mrs. Nuevavista.

"Sir, ma'am, Rosalie, I have to go now. It is getting late, and I am taking too much of your time," said David as he turned around. Then he said, "Good night," as he headed to the door.

Rosalie followed David to the gate. David turned around and whispered to Rosalie, "Good night. I'll pick you up around nine thirty Sunday morning." Rosalie was listening intently.

"I'll be waiting for you. Good night," answered Rosalie.

David embraced Rosalie and then turned around and headed to his car. Rosalie remained standing by the gate until David drove away and was lost from her sight.

**Picture of pig being roasted (lechon pork), courtesy of Milagros Timbingan Avelino**

**A picture of the Pagsanjan Water Falls, courtesy of Milagros Timbingan Avelino**

# Chapter XIX

## The Engagement

MONDAY, THE FIRST working day of the week, David delivered his black suit and white shirt to the dry cleaner. He also brought his special black shoes to the shoe-cleaning stand. He waited for the shoes to be shined and brought them back home before going to their store.

The whole week, while working in the shop, he had been thinking of the progress of his courtship with Rosalie. He believed that he had already gained the trust and confidence of her parents. This time he was decided to go with the second stage of his plan, to win the love of Rosalie. He would like to impress Rosalie and her parents that his intention was honest and honorable. With the new stage of his courtship, he would like to start with the hearing of the Mass together so that their love would be blessed and their relationship would be stronger with the grace and glory of God.

Friday afternoon, David passed by the dry cleaner and picked up his black suit and white shirt. The following day, he went to the barbershop and had his hair trimmed. He then went to the car wash on his way home.

Sunday morning, David woke up very early and took his bath, then ate his breakfast of coffee and cheese and ham sandwich and stood and prepared to fix himself. He wore his black suit and white shirt and a red with black stripes necktie. He put on a pair of black socks and his clean and shiny shoes, then checked himself in the mirror. He put on expensive cologne around his head and neck. He put moisturizing cream on his hand, then headed for the door. When he entered his car, he cleaned the seats and saw to it that the interior of the car was neat and presentable for his special guest. When he was sure everything was presentable, he started the engine and headed to the house of the Nuevavistas to pick up Rosalie.

When David reached the house of Rosalie and rang the bell at the gate, it was Mrs. Nuevavista who came out to open.

"Good morning, ma'am," greeted David.

"Good morning, David, come in. Rosalie is still upstairs. She will be coming down soon," answered Mrs. Nuevavista, and she headed to open the front door and let David into the house. "Have a seat, David. Rosalie should be down in a very short time," said Mrs. Nuevavista as she let David sit in the receiving room (foyer). "Oh, there she is. She is coming down, and it looks like she is ready to go," said Mrs. Nuevavista as she pointed to Rosalie, who was going down the stairs from the second floor of the house, wearing a fuchsia dress with a matching bag and shoes.

The heart of David almost jumped out of his chest when he looked up and saw Rosalie. She was so beautiful, with her hair flowing to her shoulders, glittering with rays from the lights. When she approached him, David was no longer stooping. Rosalie was almost six feet tall with the high heels and walked gracefully toward him. David seemed tongue-tied and for a moment just enjoyed looking at Rosalie. He just regained his senses when Rosalie spoke.

"Good morning, David," was the greeting from Rosalie.

"Yes, good morning," answered David, who seemed a little shocked after seeing Rosalie so beautiful coming close to him.

"OK, let us go. We might be late for the Mass," said Rosalie as she came close to David.

"Ma'am, we are going now. I might take Rosalie to lunch after church, so we might be a little bit late. Is it OK, ma'am?" requested David.

"It is fine with us. Drive carefully," answered Mrs. Nuevavista.

"Yes, ma'am, thank you very much," replied David as he turned around and walked with Rosalie to the door and through the gate. David went ahead and opened the passenger door for Rosalie. Then he went around the car and sat at the driver's seat and started the engine. "How are you this morning?" said David.

"I feel OK. How about you?" answered Rosalie.

"I feel good, most especially I am with the most beautiful lady I have ever met," responded David.

"I am flattered. Please do not start kidding me. We are heading to the church. Let us be serious to each other," said Rosalie.

"I was not kidding. I am just telling the truth. You are very beautiful," insisted David.

**The Manila Cathedral, courtesy of Karen Joy Reyes**

Rosalie just smiled and kept silent until they reached the Manila Cathedral. David looked for a parking space, then got out of the car and opened the door for Rosalie. David closed the door of the car, then offered his left arm to Rosalie, and they walked together to the main door of the cathedral. They arrived fifteen minutes before the Mass, so they were able to get good seats near the front. Rosalie knelt, and David followed. They were very quiet in the church from the beginning to the end of the Mass. After the Mass, David stood up and then held Rosalie by the hand, and they walked holding hands with the crowd, heading to the exit door of the cathedral. When they reached the parking lot,

David opened the passenger door and guided Rosalie to the passenger seat. He then went around the car and then sat on the driver's seat.

"How would you like to eat something different?" asked David.

"What do you mean?" asked Rosalie.

"Have you tried Ma Mon Luk's *mami* and *siopao*?" asked David.

"No, I have not tried those," answered Rosalie.

"Come on, let's try it. Ma Mon Luk is in Quiapo," replied David as he started the engine, and they headed to the Quiapo area, near the Quiapo Church. After David found a parking area, they just walked to Ma Mon Luk. The server greeted them at the door, then led them to a vacant table. David ordered their specialty mami and siopao for two. The mami (boiled noodles in chicken broth with boiled egg and fried brown garlic in the middle of the bowl) was served hot together with the siopao (steamed bun with meat stuffed inside).

"This is my first time to come to this place," said Rosalie.

"I thought so. I know you will not come to places like this. I just want you to experience something different," explained David as the order was being placed on the table in front of them.

"Oh, this soup is hot," said Rosalie.

"Yes, be careful not to burn your lips and tongue," commented David.

After they finished eating, they headed to the car, and when David started the engine, instead of driving Rosalie back home, he drove to Rizal Park. He looked for a parking area, then got out of the car and removed his jacket and put it back in the car. He then went around and opened the passenger door to let Rosalie out.

"What are we going to do here?" asked Rosalie.

"We will just walk around and enjoy the moment," answered David.

"That is very romantic!" jokingly commented Rosalie.

The two walked together holding hands, and when they reached a grassy area, Rosalie removed her high-heeled shoes and sat on the grass. David excused himself and walked to a vendor on the side of the road and ordered a box of popcorn. He went back to where Rosalie was seated and sat by her side and gave her the box of popcorn.

"Oh, we have just eaten. Why did you buy popcorn?" asked Rosalie. "That is a way to keep us busy, while we are seated side by side, right?" answered David.

David sat in front of Rosalie, took the box of popcorn from her hand, and reached for her left hand. He looked at the fingers of Rosalie (he was actually sizing her ring finger), then commented, "You have beautiful fingers." Then he kissed her hand.

"Oh, you caught me unguarded there. My hand smells like popcorn," said Rosalie.

"No, your hand smelled heavenly," said David.

"You're kidding me again," said Rosalie.

"You know, I just enjoy being with you. All week I have been looking forward to be with you. I always wanted the days to move fast so that I can be with you even just for a moment. I treasure those moments when I am with you," said David.

Rosalie just smiled and did not say anything. As they were seated, two monarch butterflies came by and caught the attention of Rosalie.

"Look, David, there are two butterflies as if listening to us," said Rosalie. "Oh yes, it looks like the butterflies would like to witness my real feelings toward you," said David.

Rosalie did not say anything and remained silent as she continued looking at the butterflies flying away from them.

"David, you better drive me home. My parents may be looking for us. We have been away too long already. They may be worried about us," said Rosalie, with a little concern in her voice.

"OK, let's go. Next Sunday afternoon I want to take you out again. Is it OK?" asked David.

"We will ask permission from my parents. If they permit us to go out, then I'll go with you," answered Rosalie.

"Promise?" asked David with a smile.

"Yes, I promise with the condition that my parents would let us go out again," replied Rosalie.

David helped Rosalie stand up, and she put on her high heels. Then they walked holding hands toward the car. When they reached the house of Rosalie, David opened the passenger door to let her out. He offered his hand to help her out of the car. David escorted Rosalie to the house, where her parents were waiting.

"Oh, did you have lunch already?" asked Mrs. Nuevavista.

"Yes, Ma," replied Rosalie, and she looked at David.

"Sir, ma'am, I hope you don't mind, I would like to ask your permission for us to watch the sunset in Manila Bay along Dewey Boulevard next Sunday," asked David.

"OK. Just drive Rosalie back here safely after sunset," answered Mrs. Nuevavista, with Mr. Nuevavista looking.

"Thank you, sir, ma'am. I'll see you all on Sunday afternoon," replied David with a smile as he turned toward the door. Rosalie followed David to the door, and as he closed the gate, she waved at him.

When David got home, the thing that he was imagining was the ring finger of Rosalie. When he was holding the hand of Rosalie when they were at the park, he was trying to figure out the size of her ring finger without her noticing his intention. During the week, after work, he would go around to different reputable jewelry stores looking for an engagement ring. He had finally decided to be engaged to Rosalie. He must first find the proper timing, and if the moment is right, the ring must be available at hand. He had been shopping and looking for a one-carat diamond engagement ring. During the week, he made up his mind on a solitaire one-carat diamond engagement ring, but there was something he would like to be very sure first—the exact size of the ring finger of Rosalie. That would be his mission on his next date with her, to get a fairly accurate size of her ring finger. He had to be tactful and discreet in getting the size of her ring finger. How he would to do it, he was not sure yet.

Sunday afternoon was the scheduled date of David with Rosalie. He dressed up casually with a white short-sleeved shirt, white pants, and white shoes. He would like to look clean and neat in this particular date with Rosalie. He arrived in front of their house around 4:00 PM, then rang the bell. Mrs. Nuevavista came to the gate and greeted David.

"Oh, you are early. I thought you are going to watch the sunset in Manila Bay?" asked Mrs. Nuevavista.

"Yes, ma'am. I thought of bringing Rosalie first to dinner before we go to watch the sunset in Manila Bay," answered David.

"Rosalie is not yet ready. She is still upstairs and fixing herself," explained Mrs. Nuevavista as she led David to the house.

"It is OK, ma'am. I'll just wait," answered David as he walked with Mrs. Nuevavista to the house.

"Have a seat first. Rosalie should be down in a minute," explained Mrs. Nuevavista as she walked upstairs to check on Rosalie.

David sat down quietly in the receiving room, planning the move he had to do to determine the size of the finger of Rosalie. He had two chances in his plan, at the dinner table and while watching the sunset. He was in deep imagination when Mr. Nuevavista came in, apparently from the back of the house.

"Oh, David, you are already here," said Mr. Nuevavista.

"Yes, sir, I came early. I would like to take Rosalie first to dinner before we proceed to Dewey Boulevard to watch the sunset in Manila Bay," answered David.

"I think Rosalie is still upstairs, fixing herself," explained Mr. Nuevavista. "Mrs. Nuevavista already went upstairs to let Rosalie know that I am already here," answered David.

A little later, Rosalie came down the stairs, as usual beautiful and stunning. David was holding his breath, anxious and excited, but held his cool and stood calm and gentle. He reached for the right hand of Rosalie as she came closer to him. Then he turned to Mr. and Mrs. Nuevavista.

"Sir, ma'am, we are going now. We will see you later," said David as he escorted Rosalie to the car.

"Drive carefully," advised Mr. Nuevavista, with Mrs. Nuevavista smiling as they both watched David open the passenger door for Rosalie. The two stayed watching the two until David started the engine and drove away.

"You came very early. I was not ready when you arrived," said Rosalie. "Yes, I intentionally came early to ask permission from your parents to take you to dinner before we go to watch the sunset in Manila Bay. We will go to a restaurant along Dewey Boulevard. From there we will watch the sunset," answered David.

David drove to Dewey Boulevard and looked for the restaurant he saw in the paper—the Flaming Chicken Restaurant. As he drove along Dewey Boulevard, he saw the restaurant. He drove around the restaurant and parked the car in the back parking space. He stepped out of the car and walked to the passenger door and opened the door. He offered his hand to help Rosalie as she stepped out of the car. The two, holding hands, walked to the restaurant. A waiter approached them and led them to a vacant table.

"Do you want anything to drink, sir?" asked the waiter.

"Please get me some iced tea," answered David. "How about you, Rosalie, what do you want to drink?" asked David.

"I just want cold water for me, please, thank you," answered Rosalie.

"Are you ready to make your order, sir?" asked the waiter.

"Yes, please give us two orders of your special flaming chicken. This is our first time here, please make it good," requested David.

"Yes, sir, we'll do that." And the waiter left to bring the order to the kitchen.

As the two were waiting for their order, David reached for the left hand of Rosalie, and she did not resist. David put his hand under Rosalie's hand and his thumb on top of her ring finger.

"You have beautiful fingers. You must be taking care of your hands very well," commented David as he massaged Rosalie's ring finger.

"Not really. I just wash my hands every day," kiddingly said Rosalie, not aware of the intention of David.

A little later, the waiter came to their side, carrying a table, and put two trays with the chicken split in half on top. He then poured liquor on top of the chicken and then set it on fire. The chicken was in flames, and when the flame was out, the waiter served the warm trays to them with the chicken smoking hot.

"Wow, this is something different. This is the first time I have seen a chicken on fire," commented Rosalie.

"Well, they say this should be very good," commented David.

They waited for the chicken to cool a little bit and then proceeded to eat. The two enjoyed the flaming chicken for dinner, and after David paid for their meal, they headed to the door. At the door, they picked up some mints. Then instead of heading to the car, they went across Dewey Boulevard and holding hands walked on the sidewalk overlooking the bay, looking for a place where they could sit, with a little privacy. Under a tree there was a bench. They sat there side by side and watched the sun as it started to hide from the clouds, giving different colors of red orange and yellow, with some rays coming out in between the clouds as if trying to reach out for something. David once again held the left hand of Rosalie and again felt her ring finger with his hand and thumb. So that Rosalie would not notice what he was doing, he kissed her hand. Rosalie smiled and said, "My hand still smells like flaming chicken!"

"No, when I kissed your hand, I felt as if I am in a different world," answered David.

David could not hold himself anymore and pulled Rosalie toward him and looked into her eyes and said, "Rosalie, I love you. I love you very much." Then David pulled her closer to him and kissed her on the lips. Rosalie totally surrendered her being to the craving of David. It was a long kiss, and when they opened their eyes, David said, "I have been waiting for this time to say I love you, Rosalie."

"I have been waiting for you to say you love me. I thought it will never come," answered Rosalie.

The two kissed once again as the sun set and the darkness started to cover the horizon, and the only thing that could be heard were the waves of the sea, hammering the rocks along the side of the bay. They felt as if there was no end to their treasured moment, when they realized that they needed to bring Rosalie back home, since the sunset was over.

"You have to take me home now. My parents would be looking for me. We have been out too long already. They may not let me out with you again if we abuse our freedom," commented Rosalie.

"Do not worry. We have an answer to that. Come on, let's walk back to the restaurant," said David.

When the two arrived in the restaurant, David made two orders of flaming chicken for Mr. and Mrs. Nuevavista.

"Please wrap the two orders with aluminum foil to keep the chicken hot," requested David.

"Yes, sir, we will see to it that when the bag of chicken arrives at your house, they are hot and delicious," answered the clerk.

They took the ordered chicken to the car. Then they hurriedly drove back to the house of Rosalie. Both Mr. and Mrs. Nuevavista were at the gate waiting for Rosalie when they arrived. All the time, Rosalie was holding the bag containing the ordered flaming chicken, and when David parked the car, he went around to let Rosalie out, holding her left hand while her right hand was holding the bag containing the food. David escorted Rosalie to the gate, which was opened by Mrs. Nuevavista. Rosalie handed the bag of chicken to Mrs. Nuevavista, which she eventually handed to Mr. Nuevavista.

"Good evening, ma'am, sir," was the greeting of David.

"Are you not going to come in, David?" was the invitation of Mrs. Nuevavista.

"It is all right, ma'am. I have to go. I have already taken too much of Rosalie's time and yours. I'll be back next Sunday to see you. Thank you, ma'am, and good night," said David as he turned around to head to his car.

The family, standing at the gate, waited for David to drive away. When David left, the three went in, carrying the bag of flaming chicken.

"What is in the bag? It is still very hot," said Mr. Nuevavista, who was holding the bag of chicken.

"Oh, we went to the Flaming Chicken Restaurant along Dewey Boulevard, and David ordered for you. He wanted you to taste the flaming chicken," answered Rosalie.

"Oh, David is very thoughtful. He is a very fine gentleman," commented Mrs. Nuevavista.

Rosalie just smiled and headed upstairs to change. Then she turned around as she was halfway up the stairs. "Mom and Dad, you better eat the chicken. David for sure would ask me if you liked it," said Rosalie to them, who were looking at her.

"Come on, Fred, let's go to the kitchen and taste the chicken. I am hungry anyway," requested Mrs. Nuevavista.

"OK, let's go," answered Mr. Nuevavista as he followed Mrs. Nuevavista.

Mr. and Mrs. Nuevavista enjoyed the flaming chicken with the additional sauce placed in the bag. Not satisfied with just the chicken, they ate it with steamed rice. When Rosalie went down to check on her parents, the two were very busy eating.

"Please tell David the flaming chicken tasted great. I could not have enough," said Mrs. Nuevavista.

"It is nice that you can enjoy," commented Rosalie with a smile as she turned around and left.

The first thing that David did after work was to go to the Gems and Diamonds Store located in Sta. Cruz, Manila, and look at the solitaire diamond engagement ring. After the store manager showed him the different sizes of the rings, he selected the size that he believed was the size that would fit the ring finger of Rosalie, based on his touch and observation the last three times with her. He then decided to order the beautiful one-carat solitaire engagement diamond for Rosalie, ready for pick up in the afternoon the following Friday.

Early Sunday morning, he woke up and took his shower, then wore his Sunday clothes and went to hear the eight o'clock Mass at San Sebastian Church. He knelt and prayed and asked for blessing for his intentions to be engaged to Rosalie. He hoped and prayed that his proposal would go well. Alone, he passed by a restaurant and ate his lunch, thinking of one thing—how was he going to give the ring to Rosalie? Was she going to accept the ring and his proposal for engagement? Then so many things went through his mind, remembering the bitter experience he had with Rosemarie when she pushed him away, when all the time he thought they were in love. After lunch, he went home and dressed casually—white short-sleeved shirt, well-ironed white pants, and white shoes. His hair was well trimmed, and he wore expensive cologne. He would like to look good on this very day when he had to make his proposal.

**A picture of San Sebastian Church courtesy of Karen Joy Reyes**

Unlike the previous Sunday, David arrived five o'clock in the afternoon at the gate of the house of the Nuevavistas. When he rang the bell at the gate, Mrs. Nuevavista came out to let him in.

"Rosalie is inside and has been waiting for you," said Mrs. Nuevavista. "Oh, I am sorry. I thought of just going straight to watch the sunset so that I would not take too much of your time and her time," answered David. When David entered the house, Rosalie stood up and walked toward David, and as she looked at her mother, she said, "OK, Ma, we are going now. I was ready to change. I thought David is not coming anymore." Rosalie had a little expression of displeasure.

David held Rosalie, and they walked together holding hands, with David not saying anything. Mrs. Nuevavista smiled as she watched the two walking together holding hands. David opened the passenger door for Rosalie and helped her sit comfortably, then went around to the driver's seat and started the engine. Before David drove the car, he looked at Rosalie, who was in complete silence.

"Are you mad at me because I did not come the usual time?" asked David. "I was waiting and waiting for you, and I thought you have forgotten our date. I thought you had something very important to do other than to attend to our date," said Rosalie in a very low tone, with a little expression of emotion. "No, you are the most important thing that has happened in my life. Later, I will tell you why I was late. I love you, and nothing can change that. I love you, and I love you very much," said David as he drove his car toward Dewey Boulevard.

Rosalie smiled and looked at David. David looked at Rosalie, and they both smiled. Rosalie touched the driving hand of David, and David put his left hand on hers.

"Rosalie, this is like a dream to me. It has been long that I have been holding my love for you, and now this is a reality. If I am dreaming, please do not wake me up," said David.

"I have waited for you to tell me you love me. I thought you were not serious about your courtship with me and you were just taking me for granted," replied Rosalie.

"No, I have been very careful with my courtship with you. I have a very high regard for the Filipino culture. I have learned in my guerilla experience a lot of the ways of life of Filipinos, their modesty, their hospitality, their respectability, and their love for their family. I decided that before I focus on courting you, I must first court your mother and father. I said that if I win their trust, I can easily win your trust and love," explained David as they were nearing Dewey Boulevard.

"We are almost here. Let us do something different this time," said David.

"What do you mean? What surprise do you have for me now?" asked Rosalie.

"You just watch. I still have to find what I am looking for," said David. Finally, David found a barbeque stand. He parked his car on the side and went out to buy some sticks of pork barbeque. David ordered four sticks of barbeque, two cold soft drinks, and two bottled water. He asked the vendor to wrap the barbeque sticks in aluminum foil to preserve the heat and smell of the meat. He then went back to the car and drove to the same place by the side of Manila Bay along Dewey Boulevard. David just parked the car along Dewey Boulevard near the place where they sat to watch the sunset in Manila Bay. As usual David, opened the door for Rosalie and led her to sit on a bench by the side of the bay.

"Rosalie, please wait here for a moment, and I'll get our food from the car," said David as he turned around to walk to their car.

David got a small bag from the trunk of his car and put their food and drinks in the bag. He also took some paper towels that they could use to wipe their hands from barbeque sauce. Then he walked back to where Rosalie was seated. He put out the food and drinks and the paper towels between them. David took one barbeque stick and gave it to Rosalie. David got one for himself. They ate together, once in a while looking at the sky, watching for the coming sunset. After eating each stick of barbeque, David invited to wash their hands using the bottled water and wipe them with paper towels. After cleaning their hands, Rosalie went back and sat to watch the beautiful change of colors in the sky. David wrapped the remaining two sticks of barbeque with aluminum foil and returned it back to the car together with the paper towels and bottled water in the bag. David went back to where Rosalie was sitting and sat by her side. Rosalie was in complete silence, looking at the sky, waiting for David to say anything.

"Rosalie, it is beautiful to watch the changing colors of the sky. The yellow color of the sky that changes to crimson red is like a defining moment of our life when we both discovered the hidden feelings within us. We finally opened our hearts to each other, which gave us the freedom to express our love," said David as he looked at Rosalie and kissed her tenderly on her lips while he was pulling out from his pocket the engagement ring. Rosalie closed her eyes and tenderly surrendered her lips to David, who was very thirsty for the taste of her lips. When David released his kiss with Rosalie, looking at her eyes, he took her left hand, without her knowing it. David then inserted the one-carat diamond engagement ring around the ring finger of Rosalie. Rosalie was so surprised, but before she could say something, David spoke. "Rosalie, would you marry me?" whispered David with tenderness and emotion.

"Can I say no? You have already put on the ring around my ring finger," answered Rosalie.

David held Rosalie close to him and kissed her tenderly and lovingly. The moment seemed endless to both of them. Then David stood up and invited Rosalie to go home.

"Come, let's tell your parents that we are engaged and we are going to get married as soon as possible," said David.

"David, I am not sure what will be the reaction of my parents," commented Rosalie.

"Well, they love you, and they will love anybody you love," answered David. "Come on, let's go. We will feed them with barbeque," jokingly added by David as he pulled Rosalie upward to come with him.

David embraced Rosalie as they walked toward the car. David opened the passenger door of the car to let Rosalie in. David walked around, then entered the driver's seat and drove the car fast as if he would like to reach the house of Rosalie quickly and meet her parents to tell them they are engaged.

"David, slowly please. Take your time. All the more that you are making me nervous. The quicker we get to our house, the more panicky I become about talking to my parents about us. I do not know. What will be the reaction of my parents when you ask for my hand, David?" asked Rosalie.

"Do not worry. I'll do the talking. Just be calm and listen. Our explanation would depend upon their reactions. For now let's think positive, right? This is what we will do. When we arrive at the gate of your house, I'll escort you inside the house and will greet your parents as if nothing happened. Then when we are inside, I'll give the sticks of barbeque to your parents. Then I'll tell them about us," explained David with an expression of surety.

Rosalie just kept quiet and listened to the suggestion of David with skepticism. This was the first time that Rosalie had been in love and the first time that a man would ask her parents about marriage. She was a little uneasy about the suggested plan of David, but she was just hoping for the best.

When the two arrived at the gate of the house, it was quiet. Apparently her parents were not yet expecting them to return that early. David opened the passenger door for Rosalie, who stepped out and headed to the gate and opened it. David followed and escorted Rosalie to the front door. Rosalie opened the door with her key and let David in. When they entered the house, Mr. Nuevavista heard the sound of the door and came out from the kitchen.

"Oh, you are back already," was the smiling greeting of Mr. Nuevavista.

"Oh yes, sir. We also brought you a couple sticks of barbeque," answered David as he walked toward Mr. Nuevavista to hand the barbeques wrapped in aluminum foil.

As David was handing the food to Mr. Nuevavista, Mrs. Nuevavista came out from the living room.

"Oh, you are back already," was the greeting of Mrs. Nuevavista as she looked at David and Rosalie.

When Mrs. Nuevavista looked at Rosalie, something caught her eyes. When Rosalie touched her hair to pull it backward, the one-carat diamond glittered as the rays from the light reflected from its facet.

"What is that glitter that I saw from your finger, Rosalie?" asked Mrs. Nuevavista.

Rosalie could not say a word and was tongue-tied and just looked at David. But David was quick to respond as he looked at Mrs. Nuevavista.

"Ma'am, Rosalie and I are engaged," said David to Mrs. Nuevavista, as he looked at Mr. Nuevavista to see what would be his reaction.

"What did you say, David?" was the clarifying question of Mrs. Nuevavista.

"Ma'am, Rosalie and I are going to get married," answered David.

The word "married" was like a dagger that slashed the heart of Mrs. Nuevavista. The baby that she nurtured and loved, the little girl that she groomed to become her beautiful princess, was getting married. For the first time in so many years, the baby that she nurtured would leave her. The baby she loved was to be with the man she loved. The reality was something hard for her to take, and the word "marry" shocked her. She retreated to a chair and sat down, then looked at Rosalie. Then tears started to roll out from her eyes. She did not say anything. She just sat and held her forehead and cried. Rosalie approached her mother and touched her shoulder in compassion. Mr. Nuevavista could not stand the tears coming from the eyes of his wife and turned around and headed to the kitchen. David just stood silently and was so shocked with the reaction of Mrs. Nuevavista.

> *The spirit of Maria Scarlet and Rosemarie, who were present watching as everything unfolded, could not believe what was happening. They both had been watching David for the love that they could not share. They were not so sure if Mrs. Nuevavista would accept the proposal of David to marry Rosalie.*

Mrs. Nuevavista was in deep anguish and kept on crying—something that nobody expected, with the fact that she gave permission to David to court Rosalie.

# Chapter XX

## Celibacy: The Test of Purity

MRS. NUEVAVISTA WAS in tears when she was told by David that he was going to marry Rosalie. She gave the permission to David to court Rosalie when they were in Cavinti, Laguna, visiting her brother's grave, but now that she heard the word "marry," it shocked her. It was hard for her to face the reality of the word "marry." The baby that she cared for and loved and nurtured to become a beautiful human being was going to get married, and she would leave her in loneliness. The reality of her daughter getting married was something very hard for Mrs. Nuevavista to take.

After a little moment of complete silence and distress, she changed her reaction. Suddenly the blood of a sister's general started to flow in her veins and overtook the emotion that earlier dominated her feelings. Mrs. Nuevavista stood up, wiped her tears, and with a determined voice called David and Rosalie.

"David, Rosalie, you come with me to the family room. Fred! Come here to the family room, and let's settle the affair of these children!" yelled Mrs. Nuevavista. Mr. Nuevavista was in the kitchen.

When they reached the family room, Mrs. Nuevavista was like a commanding officer, calling all the commands as she took the center seat. "Rosalie, you sit here at my right. And, David, you sit here at my left. Fred, you get a chair and sit right next to David and listen. We have to discuss this situation of the children," said Mrs. Nuevavista, and she turned toward David.

"David! Do you love my daughter, Rosalie?" asked Mrs. Nuevavista.

"Yes, ma'am. I love her very much," answered David.

"David, I hope you understand our culture. Married life is not like changing clothes that anytime you can change whenever you want to change. In our culture, you marry only once," explained Mrs. Nuevavista.

"Yes, ma'am, I understand the culture. Rosalie is the only woman I will marry. She will be my wife for life," answered David.

"Rosalie, do you love David?" asked Mrs. Nuevavista as she turned her questioning to Rosalie, who was trying to avoid the staring eyes of her mother.

"Yes, Ma. I love David," answered Rosalie, looking down with clasped hands, trying to avoid the eyes of her mother.

"David, are you sure you want to marry my daughter?" was the question of Mrs. Nuevavista, which came a little strong.

"Yes, ma'am. I am ready to marry her right now," answered David.

"Do you understand the magnitude of getting married? Do you know the responsibilities of the man who is proposing marriage in our culture? He takes all the financial responsibilities—all the expenses, the invitations, the church, the hotel, the reception, and all the preparations for the occasion. Are you ready to take all those responsibilities?" asked Mrs. Nuevavista, with a little stress on financial responsibilities.

"Ma'am, I will not enter into this commitment if I am not ready to take all the responsibilities you would want me to shoulder. I am ready for whatever you would want me to do," answered David.

"Are you a Catholic?" asked Mrs. Nuevavista.

"Yes, ma'am. I go to church every Sunday," answered David.

"Do you know the responsibilities of the couple that is going to get married in the Catholic church? They cannot just get married. They have to have a counseling to determine if the couple is ready to settle down. The counseling is a long process, to be conducted by a priest of the church where the couple will be married. Where do you want to get married? Have you decided on the church yet?" were the barrage of questions of Mrs. Nuevavista.

"I would like to have it in the Manila Cathedral. What do you think, Rosalie?" answered David, followed by a question to Rosalie.

"It is fine with me," answered Rosalie.

"OK, David, I would like to give you an assignment. Visit the Manila Cathedral and make an appointment for you and Rosalie. You and Rosalie talk about your plans of settling down. For now, you cannot schedule yet the date of your wedding. You have to have it approved by the priest who will conduct your counseling. I believe that the priest who will do the counseling will also be doing the wedding ceremony," explained Mrs. Nuevavista with her regular voice, showing that she apparently was calming down and ready to face the reality of the real outcome of getting married.

"Well, we will leave you alone here in the family room and talk about your plans. Please let me know if you have more questions. Come on, Fred, let's leave them alone so that they can talk about their plans," said Mrs. Nuevavista. Then she and Mr. Nuevavista headed out to give David and Rosalie a little privacy.

After Mr. and Mrs. Nuevavista left, David sat by the side of Rosalie and signed to her to be quiet, putting his pointing finger between his lips.

"I was so scared with your mom. I thought all the while we were in trouble. Good that she was able to recover and understood my honest intention. Now she is giving us the freedom to do what we want to do," commented David.

"I do understand the feelings of Mom. It hurts to see her daughter walk away from her care after we have been together so long. But my mom is always reasonable and just. She just sometimes comes very strong," commented Rosalie.

"What do you think of my answer to your mom to have our wedding in the Manila Cathedral? Is that OK with you?" asked David.

"That would be fine with me. So you still have to go there and make an appointment for us to see a priest. We will ask the priest how long or how many sessions the marital counseling is so that we can set the date of our wedding," suggested Rosalie.

"Yes, and also we would like to hire a wedding planner so that you will be relieved of so many things related to the wedding. All questions should be answered by the wedding planner. What do you think?" asked David.

"Well, I want to be involved in all the activities," commented Rosalie. "Right, you do not do the walking and the talking. That will be the duty of the wedding planner. The wedding planner will be under our supervision. Anything that he or she does must come from us. With that, you will not be bothered with anything, and you can only concentrate with what you have to tell the wedding planner. You do the planning, and the wedding planner does the execution of the plan," explained David.

"So after you have made an appointment with the priest, and when we are assured of the date of the wedding, we can hire the wedding planner," said Rosalie.

"Right, we cannot do anything now, not until we have discussed this with the priest who will eventually become our spiritual adviser," explained David.

"How are we going to pay the cost of the preparation of the wedding? This will be very expensive," commented Rosalie.

"Do not worry about the money. After we have made an appointment with the priest and we are assured of everything, we will open a joint account with the bank so that whenever you need money, you can just withdraw from our joint account," explained David. "What else do you think are our immediate concerns by now other than those we have discussed?" asked David.

"I think that's it for now. I could not think of anything else. We can ask the help of the wedding planner about the things we need to prepare and do. They are more experienced," explained Rosalie.

"OK, if you cannot think of anything anymore, I better go. I am taking too much of your family's time. Please help me ask permission from your parents to say good-bye," requested David as he held Rosalie by the arm, and they both stood.

David looked around, and when he was sure that they were alone, she held Rosalie close to him, embraced her, and kissed her lips. Rosalie accepted the kiss but right away tried to get separated from David, then signaled with her palm to be careful as they walked out of the room.

"Ma, Dad, David is leaving. He would like to say good night." Mr. and Mrs. Nuevavista came out and faced David and Rosalie.

"Oh, David, when would you be back? I want to know if you have made an appointment with a priest in the Manila Cathedral," asked Mrs. Nuevavista.

"I'll be back Sunday afternoon to talk about my meeting with a priest in the Manila Cathedral," answered David.

"OK, good night and drive carefully," said Mrs. Nuevavista.

"Good night, David," followed up by Mr. Nuevavista.

"Good night, sir, ma'am. I'll see you on Sunday afternoon," said David as he headed to the door.

Rosalie followed David to the door and to the gate. At the gate, David stopped and pulled Rosalie and kissed her lips. Rosalie just closed her eyes and then whispered, "You better go. My parents may see us, please."

David released Rosalie, and he stepped out of the gate, still looking back to Rosalie, who was standing by the gate watching him. David drove away, and Rosalie was left alone looking. She then locked the gate and went back to the house and locked the front door. Rosalie was heading upstairs to her room when her mother called her.

"Rosalie, come down and let's talk," requested Mrs. Nuevavista.

"Yes, Ma," answered Rosalie as she turned around and went down to talk to her mother.

"Rosalie, you listen very carefully. Are you sure of your decision to marry David?" asked Mrs. Nuevavista.

"Yes, Ma. We did our initial preparation for the wedding as you suggested."

"Well, do you really love David?" was the sincere question of Mrs. Nuevavista.

"Yes, Ma, I love him very much," answered Rosalie.

"Well, if that is what you want and you are happy, I will give you the liberty and freedom to make your decision. You are old enough. However, if you encounter any problem, please let me know. I will always back you up. You are my only daughter, and I have to protect you from harm. For any problem that you may encounter in settling down, please let me know. I'll be here," explained Mrs. Nuevavista.

Rosalie could not hold back her tears. She embraced her mother and kissed her.

"Thank you, Ma. I know you will understand me."

"OK, go ahead and rest. It is getting late," were the motherly and warm words of Mrs. Nuevavista.

When David arrived home from the house of Rosalie, he called his business partner, Fernando Salazar, right away.

"Hi, Fern, this is David."

"Yes, David, what's up? How can I help you?" answered Fernando.

"I have a very important favor I would like to ask you," said David over the phone.

"What favor do you want me to do?" asked Fernando.

"I have a very important thing to do tomorrow. I have to go to the Manila Cathedral to meet a priest," explained David.

"Hey, why are you going to see a priest? Are you going to make a confession?" jokingly asked Fernando.

"No, Fernando, I have to see a priest to schedule a marital counseling. I am going to get married," explained David.

"What? You are going to get married? Wow. Of the all persons I knew, I did not expect you to find a girl. You have been dedicated to your work," commented Fernando.

"Well, I have been going out only on weekends. I never abuse my work schedule," said David.

"OK, I'll cover for you tomorrow at the store and the coffee shop. Do not worry. Do whatever you want to do tomorrow. I'll be at our business establishment the whole day tomorrow," was the assurance of Fernando.

"Thank you very much. I'll see you tomorrow at the store as soon as I am done with my schedule. Bye," were the parting words of David as he headed to rest for the night.

Monday morning, instead of heading to the stores, David headed to the office of the Manila Cathedral to see a priest. When he arrived, he was attended by a receptionist.

"Hello, ma'am, my name is David Scarborough, and I would like to inquire about premarital counseling?" asked David.

"Have a seat, sir, and I will call you as soon as I have a priest available to talk to you," said the receptionist.

David took a seat in the receiving area and waited for a priest to come out. He took a magazine to read while waiting. A little later, a middle-aged priest came to approach him.

"Hello, sir, I am Father Benjamin de Gracia. The receptionist told me that you are inquiring about premarital counseling, right?" asked the priest.

"Yes, Father. My name is David Scarborough, and I am planning to get married and would like to inquire about your premarital counseling here in the Manila Cathedral," explained David as he extended his hand for a handshake.

"Well, there are some paperworks that you and your future wife have to complete. You have to register to attend the premarital counseling. Premarital counseling usually takes seven weekends. We hold the classes every Saturday,

4:00 to 5:00 PM. The last session on the seventh weekend, there will be questions and answers, blessings, and the issuance of the certificates. Our class will start next Saturday. I'll be teaching. Why don't you and your future wife come early one hour before our class next Saturday so that you can register and complete the paperworks?"

"Father, where shall we go to register, and what are the paperworks that we have to complete?" asked David.

"I'll leave the registration and all the required paperworks with the receptionist, and after you have filled them out and signed, you can just give all the signed documents to her. She will also tell you where to go to attend the classes. It will be just in the conference room in the back office. I have here with me the topics that we will discuss in the next seven weeks."

Seven Sessions for Premarital Counseling (4:00–5:00 PM on Saturdays)

| | |
|---|---|
| First Two Sessions | — Sacrament of Matrimony |
| Third Session | — Morality and Sexuality in Married Life |
| Fourth Session | — Communication, Relationship, and Commitment |
| Fifth Session | — Stewardship and Finances |
| Sixth Session | — Planning and Parenting |
| Seventh Session | — Questions, Blessings, and the Issuance of Certificates |

"Thank you very much, Father. I'll see you on Saturday," said David as he stood to say good-bye.

"I'll see you and your future wife on Saturday afternoon. Come at least an hour before our session so that you can complete all the required paperworks, OK?" explained Father de Gracia.

"Yes, Father, we'll do that. Good-bye, Father," said David as he headed to the door.

From the Manila Cathedral office, David proceeded to their haberdashery to meet Fernando.

"Well, I am back. I can take over. Was there any problem while I was away?" asked David.

"No, everything seemed under control here by your people. How was your meeting?" asked Fernando.

"Everything went well. We have to attend the premarital session for seven weeks 4:00 to 5:00 PM every Saturday starting this coming Saturday," answered David.

"Wow, it is just like going to school," commented Fernando.

"Yes, as a matter of fact there is a certificate of completion issued at the end of the session," said David.

"Well, good luck. Just let me know if you need anything else. I am always here to help," said Fernando.

"Thank you, Fernando," answered David.

"Since you are already here, I'll be going back to my office. You can just send the end-of-the-day bank reconciliations and receipts through your store manager to my office," requested Fernando as he headed out the door of the store.

After Fernando left, David sat down in his office and called Rosalie. "Hello, this is David."

"Hi, David, this is Rosalie. How are you?"

"I have been to the office of the Manila Cathedral, and I talked to Father Benjamin de Gracia, and he told me for us to be there on Saturday afternoon an hour before their session at four to five if we have to start our premarital sessions. We have to be there early to register and complete some paperworks. Do you have anything to do on Saturday?" asked David.

"No, there is nothing special that I have to do. I'll be available this coming Saturday. You can pick me up around two or two thirty, so that we will be at the cathedral by around 3:00 PM," suggested Rosalie.

"I'll tell my mom. I am sure she will be happy to hear the news. She has been waiting for this information," said Rosalie.

"OK, I'll see you on Saturday afternoon around 2:00 PM. I love you," said David.

"I love you. Bye," answered Rosalie.

After David called, Rosalie called her mother right away.

"Ma."

"Yes, Rosalie," answered Mrs. Nuevavista.

"David called."

"What did he say?"

"Ma, we can start our premarital counseling this coming Saturday in the afternoon."

"What time is the session?" asked Mrs. Nuevavista.

"He said 4:00 to 5:00 PM, but we have to be in office of the Manila Cathedral an hour before the session. He said we have to register and there are paperworks that we have to complete," replied Rosalie.

"Well, prepare your birth, baptismal, and confirmation certificates and ID picture and put them all in a brown envelope. I am sure you will need those in your paperworks. I think if I remember it right, the only sacraments that you will be required before the sacrament of marriage are the sacrament of baptism, the sacrament of confirmation, the sacrament of confession, and the sacrament of Holy Communion, and you have done those. So you should have no problem in completing the paperworks required for your premarital counseling."

"Thank you, Ma. I'll prepare those documents and put them in a brown envelope," said Rosalie.

"What time is David coming on Saturday?" asked Mrs. Nuevavista.

"He said around 2:00 or 2:30 PM," answered Rosalie.

"You better get dressed and prepare before then so that you will not be delayed."

"Yes, Ma. I will. Thank you," replied Rosalie.

Saturday morning, David woke up early and ran around their area, then took a shower. He ate breakfast and dressed up to go to the library to read something about premarital counseling and preparations for a wedding. He discovered that some Catholic church that offered premarital counseling needed a copy of baptismal and confirmation certificates. He discovered that he had a problem—his baptismal and confirmation certificates were in the United States, and it would be too late to do anything.

"I'll just explain to Father de Gracia that I'll produce the certificates later. They are in the United States. I hope he accepts that so that we can proceed with the premarital counseling." David was talking to himself.

After lunch, he rested a little bit, and around one thirty, he drove to the house of Rosalie. He arrived at the gate before 2:00 PM. He rang the bell, and Mrs. Nuevavista came out.

"Good afternoon, ma'am," was the greeting of David.

"Good afternoon, come in. Rosalie should be coming out soon. She is just getting the brown envelope where she placed the needed documents in completing the required paperworks," answered Mrs. Nuevavista.

"Thank you, ma'am. I'll just wait here. We may be late for our appointment," answered David.

"Oh, there she comes. OK, you can go now so that you will not be late," advised Mrs. Nuevavista.

Rosalie kissed her mother, then went out with David. David opened the passenger door of the car to let Rosalie in, with Mrs. Nuevavista observing and smiling. David went around and took the driver's seat, started the engine, opened the passenger window, and glanced at the gate, where Mrs. Nuevavista was standing.

David waved his hand to Mrs. Nuevavista. Mrs. Nuevavista waved back, smiling. Rosalie looked at her mom and smiled. David drove away, with Mrs. Nuevavista waving and smiling.

"Hey, your mom looks very happy," commented David.

"Yes, I hope it continues," answered Rosalie.

When David and Rosalie arrived in the office of the Manila Cathedral and entered the reception area, they introduced themselves to the receptionist.

"Hello, ma'am, good afternoon. My name is David Scarborough, and she is my fiancée. Father de Gracia should have some paperworks for us?" said David.

"Oh, yes, sir. I have the registration forms and documents that both of you have to fill up and sign. I have prepared them on a clipboard for your convenience," said the receptionist as she handed the two clipboards containing the documents to be completed.

As the two were completing the forms, Father Benjamin de Gracia came out to meet them.

"Hello, David, welcome back. It is nice to see you both," was the greeting of Father de Gracia as he came closer. David stood up.

**A picture of the Manila Cathedral, courtesy of Karen Joy Reyes**

"Father, she is my future wife, Rosalie. Rosalie Nuevavista. We will attend your first session at four. By the way, Father, I do not have my baptismal certificate with me. It is in the United States. Is that going to be a problem," asked David.

"No, go ahead and fill out the forms, and we will take care of the supporting documents later. We can easily request the documents from the archdiocese of your state in America. That should not be a problem.

What is important is you take the premarital counseling classes so that you can get married," answered Father de Gracia.

David and Rosalie attended the premarital counseling. The two enjoyed the discussion, and they learned a lot, most especially on the topics of communication, relationship and commitment, planning, and parenting. They took notes on the sacrament of matrimony and just listened and did not make any comments nor discussed during the session on sexual morality in married life. On the seventh week of their premarital counseling, they were blessed by Father de Gracia and were issued a certificate of completion. Father de Gracia congratulated the couple for completing the course. After the dismissal of the class, David and Rosalie approached Father de Gracia.

"Father, we intend to get married here at the Manila Cathedral. We have not yet decided on the date of the wedding, but we would like you to celebrate the Mass for our wedding ceremony since we have known you very well," requested David, with Rosalie listening, smiling, and nodding.

"Oh, definitely, if that is what you wish, I can do it. Just let the receptionist know and give her the invitation so that I can prepare. Anyway you will still have to come to schedule your wedding with us. We can talk about it when you are ready," answered Father de Gracia.

"Thank you, Father, we also want you to be our spiritual adviser if you don't mind."

"Oh, sure, I'll pray for your successful married life." Father de Gracia approached David and Rosalie and put his hands on the foreheads of the couple and said his prayers and blessed them.

"Thank you, Father," was the simultaneous answer of David and Rosalie.

When David and Rosalie were in the parking lot of the cathedral, he suggested to Rosalie to invite her parents to dinner to celebrate their completion of their premarital classes.

"What do you think? Let's get your ma and pa. Let's take them to dinner tonight to celebrate our completion of our classes, and at the same time we could discuss the date of our wedding," requested David. Rosalie was listening and thinking.

"Well, let's see. We just go and tell them. Then if they say yes, where are you going to take us?" questioned Rosalie.

"Well, you see, I am thinking of having our reception at the Manila Hotel, so we may just as well see what they have to offer. We can also ask the opinion of your parents. We can also discuss our wedding plans. What do you think?" said David.

"OK, let's go," answered Rosalie.

The two left the parking lot of the cathedral and headed to the house of Rosalie. When they arrived at the gate, David stepped out and opened the door for Rosalie. Rosalie went straight to open the gate, but as she was doing it, Mrs. Nuevavista came out from the front door, so Rosalie just stood and waited for her mother.

"Ma, David wants us to go to dinner together to celebrate the completion of our classes. Can Pa and you come with us?" asked Rosalie.

"Well, we still have to change. We are not ready. Can you wait?" asked Mrs. Nuevavista.

"Yes, ma'am, we will wait for you," answered David, who was standing by the side of Rosalie.

"So please come in first and have a seat while we are dressing up," answered Mrs. Nuevavista. She then turned around to tell her husband of the invitation.

David and Rosalie went in and sat in the receiving room while waiting for Mr. and Mrs. Nuevavista. David could not stop looking at Rosalie, who pretended not to notice it.

"Rosalie, are you excited that we have finally completed our premarital classes."

"Yes, definitely, that is one out of the way. Now we have to start preparing for our wedding. We have to set the date, hire a coordinator, prepare invitations, think of the people we have to invite, the reception. There are a lot of things that we have to attend to. Are you ready for this, David?" asked Rosalie.

"I am not worried about those things, Rosalie. We can handle those things easily with the help of a wedding planner or coordinator. After we hire a wedding planner or coordinator, he or she will take over the walking and talking about our wedding. What I am looking forward to is our honeymoon," answered David, and he stood and approached Rosalie, touching her hair while sitting.

"David, take it easy. My parents may come down and see us. Everything can wait. Please do not embarrass me in the presence of my parents, please!" requested Rosalie as she felt that David was about to kiss her again, taking advantage of the situation.

David returned to his seat and smiled.

"You are right. We can have our time without putting you in an embarrassing situation with your parents. I understand the Filipino culture. I do not want to be in trouble with your ma. She is very tough. I should really be very careful with her," explained David.

After a few minutes of waiting, Mr. and Mrs. Nuevavista came down well dressed. Mr. Nuevavista was wearing a barong Tagalog, and Mrs. Nuevavista was wearing a matching Filipina dress.

David stood up and headed to the car.

"Rosalie, I have to go ahead to the car to open the doors," said David.

Rosalie was watching her parents coming well dressed.

"Ma and Pa, you both look great," commented Rosalie.

"Well, we are ready wherever you will take us," commented Mrs. Nuevavista, with Mr. Nuevavista just standing and smiling. "Patricia!" yelled Mrs. Nuevavista to their housekeeper.

"Yes, Mrs. Nuevavista," answered Patricia, who just came out from the kitchen.

"We are leaving now. Please lock the door and the gate. You do not need to wait. We have the keys. Please lock everything. We will be back shortly," said Mrs. Nuevavista, and they stepped out of the door, with Patricia following them.

David was standing by the door of the backseat of the car.

"Ma'am, you and Rosalie sit in the back, and Mr. Nuevavista will sit in the passenger seat," said David.

"Well, if you say so. You are the driver. We will go wherever you want us to go. Tonight, you are the boss," jokingly commented Mrs. Nuevavista.

David let Mr. Nuevavista to the passenger seat, and they started to roll.

"Where are we heading, David?" asked Mrs. Nuevavista.

"Ma'am, we are going to the restaurant at the Manila Hotel. We were thinking of having our reception there, so let us see what they have to offer," answered David.

When they reached the restaurant at the Manila Hotel, David requested to talk to the manager. He told him that they were selecting a place for their wedding reception and they were checking their restaurant as one of the possible locations. The manager of the restaurant of the hotel showed them the reception area and the menu. After they had seen the reception area, David requested for a square table or a round table so that the four of them could be closer to discuss their wedding preparations. Before and during the dinner, David and Rosalie presented their plan for the wedding—about hiring a wedding coordinator, who would manage the planning and the execution of the wedding. David presented the research he made in preparation for the wedding:

"We have at least six to twelve months to prepare for the wedding, with the following things we have to accomplish. We have to announce the wedding, locate and buy the rings, hire a wedding planner or a wedding coordinator. We have to set a wedding date, then search for a reception hall, which may be this hotel. We have to book the ceremony site—that is, the Manila Cathedral. We have already talked to Father de Gracia to officiate the wedding. We have to determine how many guests we have to invite. We have to set hotel arrangements for out-of-town guests. Set up the music for the wedding and reception, then decide who will be in the bridal party. We have to start looking for the wedding dress, formal tuxedo, bridesmaid dresses, and formal wear for the groomsmen. The photographer, we have to check their work. Then obtain our marriage license if we want to have it before the wedding. With all these that we have to accomplish, I think we need more than six months. Rosalie dear, tell me, what month do you want us to get married?"

"Well, I want to be a June bride. Do we have a calendar for next year?" asked Rosalie.

"OK, let me go ask the manager. I am sure they have next year's calendar." David went to ask for the June 1954 calendar from the restaurant manager.

"OK, here is the calendar for June next year. You can select the date," said David.

| Calendar for the Year 1954<br>Month of June | | | | | | |
|------|------|------|------|------|------|------|
| Sun | Mon | Tue | Wed | Thu | Fri | Sat |
|  |  | 1 | 2 | 3 | 4 | 5 |
| 6 | 7 | 8 | 9 | 10 | 11 | 12 |
| 13 | 14 | 15 | 16 | 17 | 18 | 19 |
| 20 | 21 | 22 | 23 | 24 | 25 | 26 |
| 27 | 28 | 29 | 30 |  |  |  |

"I like the second week of June. That will be June 12. What do you think?" asked Rosalie, looking to David.

"That is our wedding, your very special day. Whatever you say is OK with me," answered David.

"What is your comment, Ma, Pa?" asked Rosalie, looking to her mother and father.

"Well, that is your day. If you like it, we are with you," commented Mrs. Nuevavista.

"OK, to start everything rolling, Rosalie and I will go to the bank on Monday morning to open our joint account. So that she has the liberty to spend what has to be spent for the wedding," said David as he turned to Rosalie.

"Sure, I'll be ready when you come to the house Monday morning," answered Rosalie.

"Rosalie, you have to start looking for your wedding dress. We also have to hire a wedding planner or coordinator, who can help us prepare and execute our plans quicker than us doing the walking," suggested David. "We can start that also on Monday," answered Rosalie.

"Ma'am and sir, you have to start listing your prepared guests for the wedding, and I'll do the same. Rosalie, you also have to start selecting your maid of honor and bridesmaids, while I'll be looking for my best man and groomsmen. We need a ring bearer and a flower girl. We also have to select our wedding sponsors. Those are the things that we have to do that the wedding planner cannot do. If we do our work, the other area can be handled by the wedding planner, of course with consultation with us," explained David.

"David, how about your family. Are they coming?" asked Mrs. Nuevavista. "Ma'am, my mother had already passed away. My father,

I'll see to it that he will be here one week before the wedding. I'll make a reservation for him in this hotel for him," answered David.

After dinner, David brought the family back to their house. When he got home, he called his partner, Fernando.

"Hello, Fernando, this is David."

"What's up, David?" answered Fernando.

"I need your help. I would like you to cover the stores the whole of next week. I have some personal things to do for my wedding. Is it OK with you?"

"Sure, I'll cover you the whole of next week," answered Fernando.

After David's conversation with Fernando, he went to bed wondering about the big dilemma he was facing. Who was he going to get as his best man, and who would be his groomsmen? He didn't know where Captain Joseph was nor Lt. Alex Torres. But he had a week to find them. He decided to prioritize the needs of Rosalie. Rosalie needed financial support to start her wedding preparations rolling.

The following morning, December 14, 1953, he woke up very early and took his shower, ate his breakfast, and dressed well to pick up Rosalie to go to the bank. When he arrived at the house of the Nuevavistas, Rosalie was already at the gate waiting for him. When Rosalie saw David coming, she went to the front door to announce to her parents that David had arrived and she was leaving. Then she closed the front door. She also closed the gate as she walked to the car of David, with David holding the door of the passenger seat to accommodate her. They went straight to the Philippine National Bank, the personal bank of David. They were welcomed by the receptionist, then were asked to sign the visitor's registration form and asked to wait for the next available bank professional. A little later, their names were called, and they were led to a closed office for interview.

"How can I help you this morning?" greeted the bank professional.

"I am David Scarborough, and this is my fiancée, Ms. Rosalie Nuevavista, and we would like to open a joint account, please."

"OK, I need both your ID pictures so that I can fill out the form for you."

"Sir, I have a personal account in this bank, from which I would like to move some money to our joint account," said David.

"Let me check your records. This will take me a moment," said the bank professional.

When the bank professional came back, he had David's bank records.

"How much money do you want me to transfer from your personal account to your joint account, Mr. Scarborough?" asked the bank professional.

"I want the amount of one hundred thousand pesos transferred from my personal account to our joint account." When Rosalie heard the amount, she put her hand to cover her mouth in disbelief, but she did not make any comment.

"OK, Mr. Scarborough, I have done it. Now I need both of you to fill out the signature cards and sign them. The signature cards will be our basis for any signed check disbursed from your account, so please use your customary signature for our clear and authentic reference. I am also giving you this booklet of checks for your temporary use. We still have to print a couple of booklets of checks for your joint account," explained the bank professional.

When they had completed their transaction with the bank, they both shook hands with the bank professional, and they headed out. Outside the bank, as they were walking together, Rosalie could not help but say something.

"David, that was a very big amount you entrusted to me."

"Rosalie, that is our money. You need that so that you can start working on your preparations for the wedding," said David. "With that amount, you have the freedom to buy whatever is necessary to make our preparations for the wedding smooth. You do not need to call me every time you have a transaction to pay," explained David.

David went straight to the passenger side of the car and opened the door. When Rosalie was about to enter the car, David pulled her and embraced her and kissed her lips. Rosalie closed her eyes in total submission to David, then opened her eyes and whispered, "David, I am lucky to have you. Thank you for coming to my life." Then she leaned down to enter the car.

"Rosalie, I love you," replied David as he closed the passenger door, with Rosalie smiling.

When David entered the car, he thought that it was still early and they could do another thing in preparation for the wedding. As he turned around to Rosalie, without starting the engine of the car he said, "Rosalie, since it is still early, why don't we proceed to the office of the Manila Cathedral and book our wedding schedule? What do you think?"

"Let's do that. That will be one task out of the way," answered Rosalie.

When they reached the parking lot of the office of the Manila Cathedral, they met Father de Gracia, who was ready to leave.

"Father, good morning, it is nice that we met you here. We need to book our wedding," said David.

"Hello, Rosalie," was the greeting of Father de Gracia. Rosalie was standing with David. "So you will arrange to book your wedding. The secretary of the cathedral will arrange to book your wedding. I think there is a certain fee to book a wedding. Go and see the receptionist, and she will tell you what to do," explained Father de Gracia.

"Thank you, Father," answered David, and he and Rosalie turned around and headed to the office of the Manila Cathedral.

When they entered the office and told the receptionist their intention, she led them to the office of the secretary. The secretary of the cathedral booked their wedding, Saturday, June 12, 1954, at 10:00 AM, to be officiated by Father Benjamin de Gracia.

After booking their wedding with the secretary of the Manila Cathedral, they finished two of their planned schedules and were still early to eat lunch. With Rosalie happy and smiling with the development of the preparations for their wedding, David drove with the plan of going to Chinatown to eat, but when David saw a motel, he parked the car in front of it.

"David, why did you park the car here?" asked Rosalie.

"Rosalie, it is still early. Let's go up and have some rest just for a few minutes," requested David.

"David, NO! NO! We have just finished our premarital classes, and you are already thinking of something that will violate the rules we learned from our class sessions. No! I do not want to embarrass myself when I go to confession with Father de Gracia that I went with you in bed before our wedding date. No! David, no!" was the very strong and emotional statement of Rosalie, who was almost crying.

"There is nothing wrong with that. We will just go to bed and rest. There is nothing to it," insisted David.

"David, I know what is in your mind, but I want to be virgin and pure on the date of my wedding. I want to be clean with no stain of sin when both of us are blessed before the altar. David, you can do whatever you want to do with me after the wedding. I will be your slave, and you will be my king," was the very well-stressed comment of Rosalie, looking away from David, trying to avoid his eyes.

"My love, maybe you meant I will be your king and you will be my queen, right?"

Rosalie did not say anything and remained silent. She was emotional, and her eyes were reddish and ready to cry, looking away from David.

"I am sorry, Rosalie. I did not expect you to react that way. I love you, and I do not want to hurt your feelings. Come on, let's go somewhere, OK?" said David, with Rosalie looking away and remaining silent, with two tears starting to roll from her eyes.

David drove to Dewey Boulevard and parked on the side of the place they used to visit, where they first kissed and fell in love. He opened the door for Rosalie to get out. Rosalie remained seated, with tears in her eyes, which she wiped as David looked at her and held her hand.

Rosalie felt insulted and hurt. After she was entrusted the big amount of money, the man that she loved and cared for wanted to take her to a motel. She felt belittled and degraded, her principles of purity and dedication to the Christian teaching of morality violated. Sex between a man and a woman must be holy for they generate a new breed of humanity, a new creation of human life, and therefore must be within the concept of the Christian doctrine. Rosalie could not believe that the man she loved would dare to drag her to commit a sin before their scheduled marital rites. Before their scheduled marital rites, both of them must go to confession. She felt insulted and ashamed just to think that David would dare to lure her to commit a sin before their scheduled confession—defiance to the teaching that they had just learned in their premarital counseling. Sex outside the marital rites is a mortal sin. It is lust and adultery, against the purity of human conscience, and an insult to human dignity.

# Chapter XXI

## The Wedding Planning

"ROSALIE, PLEASE FORGIVE me. I am sorry if I hurt your feelings," said David. Rosalie stood up, and she took the offered hand of David to assist her to get out of the car.

Rosalie walked toward the bay and stood in front of the concrete barrier, looking at the water. David followed her and held her by the shoulders and whispered to her ears.

"Rosalie, I love you. Please forgive me. Please!" said David, and he turned Rosalie toward him, then kissed her on the lips. Rosalie did not resist and submitted to the kisses of David. After David kissed her, David whispered, "Are you OK?"

Rosalie nodded but still avoided the eyes of David.

"Come on, let's go to lunch. I am already hungry," said David, with a lower tone, an expression of humility.

When Rosalie looked at David, David whispered, "I love you." Rosalie looked at David and smiled.

David escorted Rosalie to the car, and they drove to Binondo to eat Chinese food. While eating in the restaurant, they discussed their wedding preparations. With the exchange of opinions and ideas,

Rosalie's emotional misery started to evaporate. She started smiling and was back to normal.

"By the way, David, in two weeks would be Christmas. It is already December 14, and Ma wanted you to spend Christmas with us."

"You know what, I have been very busy with my schedule, and I totally overlooked the coming of Christmas. We have to buy gifts for your parents. We have to go out as soon as possible. Do you want us to do that now, so that we will have that out of the away?" asked David.

"We may just as well do it. It is very hard to find time. Let's do it now while we have time," said Rosalie.

After eating, David and Rosalie drove to a jewelry store at Escolta, and David pointed to a cultured freshwater pearl for her mother and an Elgin watch for her father.

"What do you think of those two gifts for your parents?"

"They are both beautiful. I am sure they will love those."

David ordered the cultured freshwater pearl necklace and the Elgin watch and asked the clerk to Christmas-wrap the gifts, with a card attached to each. When the gifts were completely wrapped, the clerk gave the gifts to David, and David gave both gifts to Rosalie.

"Rosalie, here are the two gifts. Please sign your name and my name in the cards. The gifts are from both of us. Put away the gifts, and we will give them on Christmas Day, OK?" said David, and Rosalie nodded.

"Ma'am, I have a bag here where you can put those gifts," offered the salesclerk.

"Oh, thank you. Thank you very much," replied Rosalie as she received the bag and put the wrapped gifts for her parents into it. Then she faced David and said, "David, I will keep the gifts for you. I'll take them out on Christmas Day when you are in the house."

"OK, let's go, I'll drive you home," instructed David.

> *(The spirits of Mary Scarlet and Rosemarie, who watched everything unfold, was so pleased with the strong stand of Rosalie on purity. They were very happy that the test of the relationship between David and Rosalie was healed by the spirit of Christmas. The gifts that David bought for the parents of Rosalie made Rosalie feel sincerity of the heart of David.)*

David drove Rosalie straight home. When they parked the car in front of the gate of the house, David helped Rosalie out. David kissed the lips of Rosalie as she stood coming out from the car, then whispered into her ears, "I love you."

"Are you not coming in?" asked Rosalie.

"No, I still have something to do for our wedding preparations. I still have to look for my best man and my groomsman. By the way, please have only one bridesmaid. I do not know many people here in the Philippines yet to match your bridesmaid . . . Please say hello to your ma and pa, OK? Bye," said David. Rosalie was standing by the gate, who later waved her hand. Then David entered the car and left. Mrs. Nuevavista, who heard the car of David leaving, stepped out of the front door and walked toward the gate to let Rosalie in.

"What happened? Where is David? Why did he leave right away?" asked Mrs. Nuevavista, with a little difficulty understanding the sudden departure of David, who would usually come by.

"He left already, Ma. He is very worried because he has no best man and groomsman yet. He has to look for them he said," answered Rosalie.

"OK, come in. You stayed out almost the whole day. You must be very tired."

"I am OK, Ma. Thank You," answered Rosalie.

"What do you have in that little bag, Rosalie?" asked Mrs. Nuevavista. "Oh, David got this for me and wanted me to keep these for him," answered Rosalie.

"Can I see what is in the bag?" asked Mrs. Nuevavista.

"No, Ma, David said to keep it as secret until Christmas," answered Rosalie.

Mrs. Nuevavista did not insist anymore and changed the conversation.

"How was your day with David?" asked Mrs. Nuevavista.

"Oh, everything went well, Ma. We opened our joint bank account with the PNB, and we have already booked our wedding with the Manila Cathedral. Then we went to eat in Chinatown. Then we shopped around, and he drove me home," answered Rosalie.

Meanwhile, David drove straight home to look for Capt. Joseph Lee and Lt. Alex Torres. He had to make calls to locate their military assignments. The two were the only hope he had for a best man and a groomsman. He started to locate the telephone numbers of the different military camps in the Philippines. After a long search and several calls, finally he was connected to the line that knew Joseph Lee.

"Sir, we do not have Capt. Joseph Lee here, but we have Lt. Col. Joseph Lee," said the operator.

"Yes, that's him. We used to be together during the Second World War eight years ago," said David.

"Hold on, sir, let me connect you to his line," instructed by the operator.

Then David was connected to the line of Lt. Col. Joseph Lee.

"Hello, this is Lt. Col. Joseph Lee, may I help you."

"Hello, Lieutenant Colonel, this is David Scarborough. How are you?"

"Hi, David, it has been a long time since we went different ways. I am good. How are you doing?" answered Joseph Lee.

"Can I call you Joe? I need your help. I need a best man. I am going to get married here in the Philippines, and I want you to be my best man."

"Yes, you can call me Joe. We had a long friendship as soldiers. I am very willing to help with whatever you want me to do. Yes, I can be your best man," answered Joe.

"There are other things I want from you, if you don't mind?" requested David.

"What is it, David? I am willing to help. Just let me know."

"I want Alex to be my groomsman. I also want our guerilla unit to be a part of our wedding. Would that be a very hard task for you?" asked David.

"No, I can help you on those. Since you are appointing me as your best man, I will do whatever task you would want me to do. However, we have to meet in a certain place so that we can plan our action, the military way, the way we were doing things during the war," said Joe.

"Yes, that is a very good idea. Can we meet tomorrow, say, at 10:00 AM, in the restaurant of the Manila Hotel?" asked David.

"Sure, I'll be there at 10:00 AM tomorrow morning," answered Joe.

"Can you take Alex with you? I want to see him too. It has been a long time that I have not seen him. I want to get him as my groomsman," said David.

"I'll contact him and tell him about your forthcoming wedding. I am very sure he will be very happy to receive the news. By the way, he was recommended for promotion. He will be promoted to major as soon as the order comes down," answered Joe.

"Please tell Alex congratulations. I'll see you then in the restaurant at the Manila Hotel tomorrow at 10:00 AM. Thank you. Good-bye," was the parting statement of David.

After David confirmed his appointment with Joe and Alex, he called the Manila Hotel right away to make a reservation for their 10:00 AM meeting.

The following day before 10:00 AM, David was already at the lobby waiting for Joe and Alex. He was sitting in the lobby when he saw the two military officers coming. He would like to be sure that they were Joe and Alex before he stood and walked to their direction. They were in military uniform, and he had not seen them in eight years. David approached Joe and Alex and embraced them one by one.

"Wow, I could hardly recognize both of you in uniform. Both of you are very handsome and good looking in military uniform. Come in to the restaurant. I have made a reservation for the three of us," commented David.

"Congratulations, David, I heard you are going to get married," said Alex as they walked to the reserved table.

"Yes, it would be next year, Saturday, June 12, 1954, at 10:00 AM, and I would like you to be my groomsman. Would that be OK with you?" asked David as the three of them were seated at the table.

"Sure. Can I say no with the friendships we developed together during the war? Whatever you say, I am game."

"By the way, congratulations on your forthcoming promotion. Joe was telling me that you will be promoted soon to major," said David.

"Yeah, that's what they said, but I do not have the papers yet. I'll believe them when I got the appointment," commented Alex.

"Joe, thank you for bringing Alex, and now we can start working with my plan," said David.

"What is your plan, David?" asked Joe.

"Well, I want to invite Mang Pedro and Aling Bertha, the couple we stayed with in Bataan, and all the members of our guerilla unit to my wedding. They have been part of my journey through life and in the war. I want them to witness my wedding. I do not know how to go to the house of Mang Pedro, so I need your help," asked David.

"When do you want to go?" asked Alex.

"As soon as possible, say, tomorrow, would you be available?" asked David. "Sure, we just have to report to our unit that we have to accompany you to Bataan. There should be no problem," said Joe.

"That's right. We need to make an official confirmation of where we are going," added Alex.

"I'll drive. I just need a navigator. Where shall I pick you up?" asked David. "You can pick us up tomorrow at around 9:00 AM at the gate of Camp Aguinaldo. You do not need to enter. We will wait for you at the gate," answered Joe.

"OK, that is a deal," commented David.

After eating their brunch, the three walked together to the parking lot of the hotel. David walked with Joe and Alex to their car. Joe and Alex drove together, with Alex as the driver. After they shook hands, the two entered their car and drove away. David walked to his car and drove home feeling good about his accomplishment. He got a best man and a groomsman. Now he had to prepare to go to Bataan with Joe and Alex, to invite their guerilla unit to his wedding. He decided to bring some extra clothes and some underwear just in case he had to stay overnight.

The following day, David woke up very early in the morning. After taking a shower and eating his breakfast, David dressed up, took his luggage to his car, and drove to a gasoline station. He filled his tank to be sure he had enough gas and bought some snacks and drinks for the trip. He picked up Joe and Alex in front of the gate of Camp Aguinaldo around 9:00 AM. Joe sat at the passenger side to do the navigation, and Alex sat in the back. After almost four hours of driving, they finally reached the front of the house of Mang Pedro.

The three got off the car and walked through the gate, and at the bottom of the stairs looking up, they called for Mang Pedro and Aling Bertha.

"Mang Pedro, Aling Bertha?" called Joe as he looked around, thinking they might just be in the vicinity.

Mang Pedro and Mang Bertha came out from the house and greeted them.

"Hi, Joe, Alex, and David, come here upstairs," invited Mang Pedro. The three went upstairs to the house and had a seat, while Aling Bertha went to their kitchen to prepare something.

"Oh, what can I do for the three of you? You came without any announcement," said Mang Pedro.

"Mang Pedro, David wanted to talk to you," said Joe.

"Yes, Mang Pedro, I want to invite you and your wife to my wedding next year. It would be Saturday, June 12, 1954, at 10:00 AM. I know that you know all the men that we recruited here during the war. I also want to invite them to my wedding," explained David.

"Sure, let me get somebody to call your recruited men here in our area, and we can assemble here in the house tonight. We can probably have a little get-together, an after-the-war celebration," commented Mang Pedro.

While the four were discussing the invitation of David, Aling Bertha was very busy in the kitchen preparing their lunch. She later brought some fried egg rolls for appetizer and some glasses of soft drinks.

Later in the afternoon, one by one all the members of Joseph Lee's guerrilla unit arrived. Angelo and his wife Maria, Diego and his wife Anna, Simon, Andrew, Jim, Tomas, Martin, Jun, Juan, Felipe, Roberto, Ted, Patrick, Pablo, Victor, Carlos, Julian, Marco, Daniel and Isaac all came in to say hello to their officer, Captain Lee. David, Joe, and Alex hugged them and shook hands with them. But to the surprise of David, Joe, and Alex, behind the house of Mang Pedro, there were already tables set by all the members of their guerilla unit. Before coming to the front of the house to meet David, Joe, and Alex, they had already gone to the back of the house to bring lots of newly cooked food, including two roasted pigs and gallons of their native wine and locally produced gin. After all the members of the guerilla unit met with David, Joe, and Alex, they invited them to the back of the house of Mang Pedro and started their celebration. That was the first time since the end of the war that the whole guerilla unit under Capt. Joseph Lee celebrated their victory together as a unit. Captain Joseph made a speech to the crowd, thanking them for their bravery and loyalty to the unit for the sake of freedom. He then introduced David to speak about his wedding. David invited all the members of the guerilla unit, including Mang Pedro and Aling Bertha, who were instrumental in the recruitment of all the members of the guerilla unit from their village in Bataan.

Lieutenant Colonel Lee, during the celebration, talked to the members of the guerilla unit to participate in the celebration by wearing a white shirt, white pants, white shoes, and a white bandana. They also had to bring their knives during the wedding to be used in their formation as the bride and the groom walk out of the church. Lieutenant Colonel Lee called the unit to form two columns facing each other, four arm's length between each column. The distance between the members of each column must be one arm's length. Each member of the columns must stand straight, looking very firm forward. After the columns were formed, Captain Lee said, "When the groom and bride are coming out, close to around ten feet from the columns, I would command the following:

> "Prepare, meaning each member of the columns will hold
> the handle of his knife, looking straight forward with a
> firm look, no movement.
> "Draw. I mean each member of the columns will draw the
> knife and have a straight body, looking forward, with no
> movement. The knife in the sides of each member of the
> column must be pointing forward.
> "Present arms. I mean each member of the column will
> elevate their arms, pointed upward in a sixty-degree angle,
> honoring the newlyweds.
> "At the end of one column would be Maria in a Filipina
> dress, showering petals of roses to the newlyweds.
> "At the end of the other column would be Ana, who would
> also be wearing a Filipina dress and will be showering rice
> to the newlyweds."

Lt. Col. Joseph Lee reviewed the formation several times, and when he was satisfied with the result of the practice of the column formation, he asked the members to continue the celebration and later said to the group:

"My brother fighters for freedom, we will practice again the formation during the rehearsal a day before the wedding. All of you will have a reservation at the Manila Hotel, where the reception will be held. For your transportation to the Manila Hotel, in the morning of the eleventh, the day before the wedding, you will be picked up by two military trucks to be brought there, where you will check in. You will have two days' reservation in the hotel—the night before the wedding, which would also be the night of the wedding rehearsal at the Manila Cathedral, and the day of the wedding. You will check out the morning after the wedding and will be picked up by two military trucks to bring you all back here to Bataan. Do you have any questions?"

After the brief speech of Lt. Col. Joseph Lee, he encouraged everybody to continue the celebration. David took the opportunity to go around to each member of the unit, shaking hands and saying thanks for their full support in his coming wedding. At around midnight, Lt. Col. Joseph Lee delivered his last speech to the group:

"My beloved fighters for freedom of our country, thank you for your services to our unit in fighting our enemies, for risking everything you have for the love of our country. We gathered today to reach out among each other and to celebrate our longtime unity in liberating this country. But most of all, we come back today to show our loyalty to one of our brothers in blood to participate in his forthcoming wedding, David, who was very instrumental in all the battles that we fought and won. It is getting late, and tomorrow, we still have a long travel to do back to Manila. David, Alex, and I have to get some sleep to prepare for our long trip tomorrow. We will see you all on the morning of June 11. Please continue the celebration. Thank you to all of you and good night."

The following morning, David, Joe, and Alex woke up very early to get ready for their long travel back to Manila. When they woke up, Mang Pedro and Aling Bertha were already awake and were in the kitchen, with the breakfast ready on the table.

After breakfast, the three drove back to Manila. David dropped Joe and Alex at the gate of Camp Aguinaldo, where they were picked up by their respective drivers. David drove home and arrived 1:00 PM. He quickly fixed and ate a sandwich for lunch, took a shower, dressed up neatly, then called Rosalie.

"Hello, this is the Nuevavista residence, may I help you?"

"Rosalie, this is David. I just came back from my trip, and I have to see you right away."

"Where have you been?" asked Rosalie.

"From Bataan. I invited my brother members of our guerilla unit to our wedding. You dress up. We have lots of things to do. Please have your checkbook with you ready when I arrive. Also, I want to talk to your parents if we could use your house to call applicants who are applying as our potential wedding planner. I love you," instructed David.

"I love you too. I'll wait for you. Bye," answered Rosalie.

When David arrived at the house of Rosalie, she was already waiting for him, with the brown envelope containing their checkbook. When David rang the bell at the gate, Rosalie ran, opened the main door, and went to open the gate for him.

"Come in, David," Rosalie said as she opened the gate.

David followed Rosalie to the house. Then Rosalie called her mother and father.

"Ma, Pa, David wants to talk to both of you!" yelled Rosalie.

Mr. and Mrs. Nuevavista came out from the family room and walked to the receiving room, where David and Rosalie were standing.

"Yes, Rosalie?" asked Mrs. Nuevavista.

"Ma'am, I would like to ask your permission to use your place to make calls to applicants to our potential wedding planner. I am sure Rosalie would not want to come to my place to do our search for our wedding planner."

"Sure, you are always welcome here in our house," answered Mrs. Nuevavista.

"Yeah, you are always welcome here," followed up Mr. Nuevavista.

"I am taking Rosalie with me. We have to book our reception hall for the wedding, and we also have to book rooms for our guests and for us in the Manila Hotel," said David.

"OK, go ahead. Do not stay too late on the road," suggested Mrs. Nuevavista.

"Come on, Rosalie, let's go," said David as he turned toward the door. "Ma, Pa, we are going now," were the parting words of Rosalie to her parents.

David drove to the Manila Hotel to book the reception hall and rooms for their guests and their families. On their way to the hotel, "It is good that you remembered to book the reception hall now before it is too late," said Rosalie.

"Yes, we hope that the reception hall has not been reserved yet by anybody for the twelfth of June next year. We really should have done that last week," said David.

"How many rooms are we going to book at the Manila Hotel?" asked Rosalie.

"We will book twenty- four rooms and three suites for now. Those are for the people that I know would come," answered David.

"Wow, that's a lot. Who are those that we have to accommodate?" asked Rosalie.

"Twenty members of our guerilla unit, one for my best man, one for my groomsman, one for Mang Pedro and Aling Bertha, one for your Tito Isidro and Tita Amanda. And the three suites will be one for your father and mother, one for my father, and one for us after the wedding," answered David.

When they arrived in the registration area and talked to the salesclerk about reserving the reception hall, the desk clerk called the sales manager, who later came from the side of the front desk.

"Hello, sir, ma'am, I am Mika, the sales manager of this property."

"I am David Scarborough, and this is my fiancée, Rosalie Nuevavista," was the salutation address of David.

"I was told that you would like to reserve the reception hall. You follow me, Mr. Scarborough and Ms. Nuevavista. Let's talk inside my office," asked Mika.

Inside the office, the sales manager asked the details of the reception they would like to have. The sales manager looked at the booking of the reception hall, and they were lucky that June 12, 1954, was not booked. David right away offered to reserve the reception hall for June 12 for a wedding party. The sales manager gave the contract agreement to David and Rosalie and invited the two to a room to complete the said agreement. David asked Rosalie to complete the agreement under his guidance. Before the sales manager stepped out of the room, David asked her to also book twenty- four rooms and three suites.

While Rosalie was completing the contract agreement, David went with the sales manager to book the twenty- four rooms and three suites for the June 12, 1954, wedding event.

"Mika, I want those rooms reserved with their names so that they will know where to go when they check in. OK?"

"Yes, we can do that," said the sales manager.

"Mika, here are the names of our twenty- four guests. The suites would be one for Mr. and Mrs. Nuevavista, one for Dr. Frederick Scarborough, and the last one is for me."

"OK, Mr. Scarborough, I will handle this from here. You can go back to your fiancée."

"Oh, another thing, Mika, do you have a list of wedding planners that you might have worked with in the past that I may use for our wedding preparation?" asked David.

"Oh yes, I'll give a listing when you finish completing the contract. I still have to research on that," answered Mika.

"Also if you have any information of a hotel that you could recommend in Baguio for our honeymoon, I'll really appreciate it, please," asked David.

"I'll also give you a list of the hotels in Baguio City, which you can call as soon as we are done with our transactions," answered the sales manager.

David went back to check on Rosalie. They both checked the agreement, and when they were satisfied with everything stated in the contract, they both signed the documents and went to see the sales manager. They were required to pay a deposit fee for the reception area and the rooms and the suites that they reserved. After they paid the deposit, Mika gave them a listing of wedding planners they dealt with before and some brochures of hotels in Baguio City. It was almost 5:00 PM already when they stepped out of the hotel, so David just invited Rosalie to dinner. After dinner, David drove Rosalie back to her house.

"Rosalie, I have to talk to your parents for us to start calling these listed wedding planners tomorrow. We have to set appointments to see them one by one. We have to ask for proposals that they must submit during the interview," explained David.

"Yes, let's do it together. I don't think my parents will say no. They like you," answered Rosalie.

"Thank you."

When they arrived at the gate of the house, Rosalie did not wait for David to open the passenger door. She right away stepped out and opened the gate for David. Rosalie and David went together inside the house.

"Ma, Pa. we are back!" yelled Rosalie.

Mr. and Mrs. Nuevavista came out and welcomed the two.

"So how did it go? Were you able to book what you had to book?" asked Mrs. Nuevavista.

"Yes, ma'am, we have done what we had to do. But tomorrow, I would like to ask permission for me to come here to work with Rosalie to start calling our wedding planner applicants. We also have to book a hotel room in Baguio City for our honeymoon."

"Yes, you are welcome here, David. You can feel at home here," answered Mrs. Nuevavista, seconded by Mr. Nuevavista.

"Thank you very much, ma'am, sir. I have to go now. It is getting late. It has been a long day for me. I'll see you tomorrow," said David as he turned around and headed to the door.

Rosalie followed David to the gate.

"David, I love you," said Rosalie as she opened the gate for David. David embraced Rosalie and kissed her on the lips. And he whispered, "I love you. See you tomorrow."

David drove home, changed to his pajamas, and went straight to bed. He was very tired after that long driving from Bataan and dealing with hotel transactions. He really felt the fatigue of travel and the pressure of his forthcoming wedding. He woke up early after a very nice long sleep. He right away went through the brochures of the hotels in Baguio, which he got from the sales manager of the Manila Hotel. After going through the brochures, he made some push-ups, then took his shower. He ate breakfast with coffee and toast, brushed his teeth, dressed up, and headed to his car to go to the house of Rosalie. They first decided on the hotel where they would like to have their honeymoon. Then David made the reservation. They then started calling the numbers of the wedding planners, doing both phone interviews and asking for a presentation of what they had already done so far in terms of wedding preparations. They set appointments the following day for the interviewed applicants, with the required submission of their respective wedding proposals. At around 11:00 AM, David asked to leave for a few minutes. He went to Chinatown and ordered some Chinese food. He went back and asked Rosalie to set the table so that her parents could also eat lunch.

"David, you should not do that. You are in our house, you are our guest, and we already have food cooked for you," said Mrs. Nuevavista.

"Ma'am, it is a big hassle for you. We are already using your home, and we still bother you for something else," answered David.

"David, you are going to get married to Rosalie. You will be my son through Rosalie, so feel at home here. OK? Come on, let's go to the dinner table and eat," said Mrs. Nuevavista.

"Come, David. Let's go to eat so that we can finish what we are doing," said Rosalie.

David stood and followed Rosalie to the dinner table. After eating, David and Rosalie went back to their work and continued calling their prospective wedding planners. It was almost 5:00 PM when they finished interviewing by phone. David told Rosalie he had to go.

"David, you may as well stay for dinner with us," suggested Rosalie. "No, I have already took too much of your family's time. I still have to be back tomorrow to meet those we have interviewed over the phone. Please reserve dinner for me some other day," said David.

"Ma, Pa, David wants to leave now," Rosalie called her parents.

When the parents of Rosalie came out, "David, why are you leaving? Why don't you join us for dinner?" suggested Mrs. Nuevavista.

"No, ma'am, I have already taken too much of your family's time. Please reserve dinner for me some other time. I still have to come back tomorrow to continue our work searching for our wedding planner. Thank you for the offer," said David as he turned around, heading to the door, with Rosalie following him.

Rosalie felt that David was very tired already, with the so many things he had been attending to for their forthcoming wedding. Rosalie was starting to feel the real connection between her and David. She no longer felt strange toward every move and word of David. She was starting to read his heart and mind. When David was about to exit the gate, Rosalie touched him by the shoulder and whispered, "David, take good care of your health. I could feel that you are very tired. Have a good rest, good sleep. I love you."

"Rosalie, I have to do this for us, for our future. I love you," whispered David, then kissed the lips of Rosalie and headed to his car and left.

The following day, David went back to the house of Rosalie. The whole day, they did face-to-face interviews of the applicants and reviewed each of their proposals. At the end of the day, they decided to hire Meredith Gomez as their wedding planner. David asked Rosalie to call Meredith Gomez to start searching for a professional photographer, florists, a wedding cake, music, and transportation providers, and they would like to see their work. Before David left the house of Rosalie, he told her that the following day, Monday, he was going back to work, but he would call her later in the afternoon after work to check on things.

The whole day of Sunday, David just stayed home and rested. It was already late in the afternoon when he looked at the 1953 calendar and started to panic when he noticed that it was already Sunday, December 20, and he had no gift yet for Rosalie. He right away dressed up and went to his car and drove to a jewelry store at Escolta and selected something that Rosalie would wear. Something attracted him, a matching one-carat diamond pendant. He bought it and had it wrapped beautifully and put it in a personalized bag. He went home very happy, ready for Christmas.

Monday, December 21, David was back to work in his office at the haberdashery. He asked the managers of the haberdashery and the coffee shop to have Christmas décors and lights in their respective stores. He also called the building manager/maintenance of his apartment rental building to remind him of Christmas lights and decoration in the property. He just realized how behind he was on things because he was focused on Rosalie too much. But he believed that he did not neglect anything except the feeling of Christmas that he seemed to overlook. Since David went back to the Philippines, the only thing he focused on was to get rich. His total attention was on his business investments, his real estate investments, stock exchange investments, and partnership with Fernando. When he met Rosalie, he focused only on courting her, on his business, and nothing else. But when Rosalie became part of his life, the word "Christmas" from the lips of Rosalie opened to him the world around him, and suddenly he recognized the meaning and color of Christmas—that Christmas was a message of giving. He convinced Fernando to give their employees Christmas bonuses.

That afternoon after work, he went straight home to have a good rest. He could still feel the fatigue in his body from the preparations for his wedding, trying to squeeze everything in a very small period of time, forcing things to be completed as planned. When he got home, he called Rosalie to check on Meredith.

"Hello, this is David."

"Hi, David, this Rosalie, how was your day," asked Rosalie.

"Still tired, with the hectic schedule I had last week, but I always feel better whenever I talk to you. So what is the development on our assigned work to Meredith?" asked David.

"Well, she has been contacting prospects, and since it is Christmas week, everybody is very busy. She said she will get back to me after Christmas. I suggested that she come to our house either Saturday the twenty-sixth or Sunday the twenty-seventh of December so that you can be present during our meeting," explained Rosalie.

"Good work, Rosalie. By the way, what is your plan on Christmas Eve, this coming Thursday, the twenty-fourth? Are you going to hear the midnight Mass?" asked David.

"I want to. What is your plan? Can we go together to hear the midnight Mass?" asked Rosalie.

"Sure, I'll pick you up around 8:00 PM with your parents. Let's hear the Mass at the Manila Cathedral?" asked David.

"I'll tell my parents. I am sure they will like it," answered Rosalie.

Wednesday afternoon, December 23, 1953, during the change of shifts in their stores, David came dressed as Santa Claus and distributed bonus envelopes to their employees. He also declared December 24 and 25 as paid holidays so that their employees could have time with their families and enjoy the spirit of Christmas.

On the evening of December 24, Mr. and Mrs. Nuevavista joined David and Rosalie for the midnight Mass. During the midnight Mass, Rosalie prayed that her relationship with David would not be dominated by material and physical things but by love and spiritual feelings between them. She prayed that all the things they had to overcome in their forthcoming wedding be resolved with the guidance of His mercy and grace. She said that David was a gift to her life and prayed that he be a good husband to her and that she be a good wife to him.

After the midnight Mass, David drove the family home. Rosalie insisted for David to come in and join them to celebrate Christmas together. When they got into the house, Mr. and Mrs. Nuevavista with the help of their housekeeper prepared the dinner table. While they were busy preparing the food, Rosalie played "Silent Night" on the piano, and David sang the song. Then with the accompaniment of Rosalie, David sang "O Holy Night." Mr. and Mrs. Nuevavista could not help but leave what they were doing and listen to the tenor voice of David. Then when Rosalie played "Joy to the World" and "Hark! The Herald Angels Sing," Mr. and Mrs. Nuevavista joined the singing. Then Mrs. Nuevavista called for a break for them to eat their Christmas midnight dinner together.

After eating, they all went to the family room for the opening of gifts. Rosalie first gave the gifts for his father and mother. The two were happy to see that their gifts were from David and Rosalie. Then Rosalie gave her gift for David, and David gave his gift for Rosalie. Mr. and Mrs. Nuevavista then gave their gifts for David. Mr. Nuevavista brought out his camera for the opening of the gifts. They all opened their gifts together. Mr. Nuevavista was so pleased with his Elgin watch. Mrs. Nuevavista was dancing in front of the mirror with her freshwater pearl necklace. When David opened his gift from Rosalie, it was expensive cologne for men, and the gifts from Mr. and Mrs. Nuevavista were two sets of cuff links and necktie clips. One set was gold plated, and the other set was silver plated. When Rosalie opened her gift, everybody was just amazed when she raised it up. The diamond of the pendant glittered like her diamond engagement ring. David took the pendant and put it around her neck. Then David kissed her on the forehead, with her parents looking. Rosalie smiled.

"Thank you, David," said Rosalie tenderly.

"Thank you for everything," answered David.

Morning of Saturday, December 26, Meredith called that she was coming to the house of Rosalie to present several works of photographers. Rosalie called David right away to come over to their house so that they could meet with Meredith. David and Meredith arrived almost at the same time, with Meredith a little ahead. Meredith presented on the table all the sample works of photographers and their respective album proposals. When David arrived, all the samples were already spread on the table, and Rosalie was already looking through them. After they had gone through all the presented work of the photographers, they unanimously decided to hire Metro Manila Photography.

After making the decision of which photographer they would hire, Meredith invited the two to visit several florist shops whose specialty was weddings. The whole afternoon of Saturday, they went through different shops, with Meredith driving around. They liked the floral arrangement of the Garden Florist Professional and did sign a contract with them.

Sunday, December 27, Meredith came again to the house of Rosalie and picked up the couple to drive them around to look for specialists in making wedding cakes and the bands who would provide the music during the wedding. At the end of the day, they had hired and signed contracts for the wedding cake and the band that would provide the music. Before Meredith left for the day, she advised Rosalie that the following day, she would be coming back to work on her wedding dress. She was coming back with different books and magazines on wedding dresses designed by famous fashion designers.

Monday, December 28, Rosalie wanted her mother to help her decide which design of wedding dress she would wear. Not only did Mrs. Nuevavista want to help select the wedding dress for Rosalie. She wanted to pay not only for the wedding dress but also for what the bridesmaid, the flower girl, and the ring bearer would wear— all of whom were also from the Nuevavista family. Mrs. Nuevavista commented, "David must take care of the groom's side of the wedding party, and we will take care of the bride's side. Rosalie is our only daughter. We will spend even how much money to make her happy."

Meanwhile, David went to the Philippine National Bank and transferred another one hundred thousand pesos from his personal account to his joint bank account with Rosalie.

In the afternoon of December 31, in the Nuevavista residence, David, Rosalie, and Meredith reviewed their wedding preparation lists to determine the things that needed immediate attention. They talked about the color for the wedding and decided that everything must be in white. Meredith said that men instead of suits should wear barong Tagalog, all white, because the month of June is a warm month. The flowers would be all white—white roses and sampaguita as the dominant centerpiece for their beauty and fragrance. In their review, Meredith said that in the first week of January, they had to shop and select the wedding rings, the invitations, and the announcement notes and stationaries and order the men's attires. Meredith also had to confirm their honeymoon reservation and arrange for the honeymoon travel details. Meredith also emphasized that six to eight weeks before the wedding, the wedding invitations must be mailed and the portrait must be ready for newspaper publication. David reminded Rosalie not to forget to send an invitation to Mang Isidro and Aling Amanda in Cavinti, Laguna. After they had completed reviewing their wedding preparation lists, Meredith left, and David was also getting ready to leave, just helping Rosalie to organize the notes and things left by Meredith.

"David, tomorrow is New Year. I want you to be with me. I want to welcome the New Year by your side, please. Do not leave. Let's welcome the New Year at midnight together," was the emotional request of Rosalie.

"If that's what you want, I'll be by your side. Come with me and let's get some champagne. Let's also buy some Peking ducks so that we will be flying in everything we plan to do in the coming year. Let's buy fruits that are all round, like apples, grapes, and oranges to bring financial stability to us in the coming year 1954. Come on, let's go!" said David.

"Ma, Pa, David and I are leaving, please lock the door!" yelled Rosalie to her parents.

Mr. and Mrs. Nuevavista came out and locked the door, and they watched the couple at the window depart to go to Chinatown in Binondo.

When David and Rosalie came back, carrying all the things they bought, Mrs. Nuevavista recommended that they wait for the New Year in the family room and to watch TV. David and Rosalie sat side by side, and across the center table were Mr. and Mrs. Nuevavista, also seated side by side as they watched TV, waiting for midnight, for the global celebration of the coming year 1954. In the middle of the table were the Peking ducks, apples, grapes, and oranges. Mrs. Nuevavista also added fish to the table. She said it was so that they all would be able to swim around any barriers that might obstruct their path. There were glasses of champagne on the table. David and Rosalie were holding hands as the clock started to tick to almost midnight. When the bell rang for the New Year, David kissed Rosalie on the lips for the first time in the presence of her parents, but this time she gave it all. She surrendered her lips totally to David with no shame. It was a New Year, a new life with David, a new beginning of a different journey, looking forward to having a family of her own. After they kissed, they tossed the champagne, and they hugged one another—the end of another chapter of life for the year 1953.

Sunday afternoon, February 14, 1954, David dressed very well and went to the florist and bought a bouquet of red roses. He also bought a big chocolate bar from the supermart and drove to the house of Rosalie. When he arrived at the gate and rang the bell, Rosalie came out, expecting him because it was Valentine's Day. She rushed to the gate, almost running to meet David. David was also as exited and could hardly wait to hand the bouquet of red roses and big chocolate bar and to kiss Rosalie. When Rosalie opened the gate, David almost forgot the roses and the chocolate bar. He right away embraced Rosalie and kissed her lips tenderly and lovingly. The heavenly feeling seemed endless.

When they separated, they were almost breathless, and David handed the bouquet of roses and big chocolate bar to Rosalie.

"David, come in. I have been waiting for you. I know you are coming, and I had been waiting at the window, looking for any car that was passing. It is very hard to be in love," said Rosalie with sincerity and emotion.

"Rosalie, you know how much I love you. I will not fail you, most especially on this very special day, Valentine's Day."

The two went into the house, and they sat at the receiving area, Rosalie appreciating the beautiful bouquet of red roses, which made her feel very special.

"Rosalie, are your parents here today?" asked David.

"Oh yes, would you like me to call them," asked Rosalie.

"Yes please. I would like to make a long-distance call to my dad, and I want to introduce you and your parents to my dad," said David.

Rosalie stood up, and instead of just calling her parents, a little bit excited, she went to get them.

"Ma, Pa, David wants to see both of you. He is going to call his dad in the United States by long distance to introduce us to him," said Rosalie with a little excitement.

"OK, let's go and talk to David," answered Mrs. Nuevavista.

"Hello, ma'am and sir, I will be calling my dad in the United States, and I would like to introduce all of you to him. He is Dr. Frederick Scarborough," said David to the family.

"Sure, we will be happy to hear from him," answered Mrs. Nuevavista. David dialed the number of Dr. Scarborough in the United States while the family was looking and excited to hear from him.

"Hello, who is this?" asked Dr. Scarborough in the other line.

"Hello, Dad, this is David. Did you receive our invitation to our wedding?"

"Oh yes, congratulations! It was a big surprise to me. I thought you will not get married anymore," said Dr. Scarborough. "Do you have enough money to spend for the wedding?" asked Dr. Scarborough.

"Yes, Dad, I have more than enough, thank you for asking."

"Well, let me know if you need help. I'll send you money by bank transfer," offered by Dr. Scarborough.

"No, Dad, I am financially OK. Dad, I mailed your plane ticket Pan Am flight 101 arriving at the Manila International Airport afternoon of June 8, 1954. I'll pick you up at the airport," David said to his dad.

"Oh yes, I already looked at the itinerary, and I am very excited to meet your future wife," said Dr. Scarborough.

"Dad, it is Valentine's Day today, and she is with me. I would like you to talk to her. Her name is Rosalie Nuevavista," answered David.

"Good, give her the phone and let me talk to her," anxiously asked Dr. Scarborough.

"Hello, Doctor, I am Rosalie, the fiancée of David. How are you, sir?" asked Rosalie.

"I am good. Thank you for asking. I have received the invitation and the plane ticket a couple of weeks ago. I'll be there to meet you and your family personally," said Dr. Scarborough.

"We will look forward to see you here in the Philippines during our wedding, Doctor," said Rosalie.

"Yes, I will ask David to make the arrangement to invite you and your family to a dinner in my suite when I arrive in the Philippines so that I can meet you and your family personally before the wedding. Please hand the phone to David so that I can confirm that arrangement with him right away," Said Dr. Scarborough.

"It's nice to hear from you, Doctor," said Rosalie.

"It was a pleasure talking to you, Rosalie," answered Dr. Scarborough.

"David, your dad wants to talk to you," said Rosalie as she handed the phone to David.

"Hello, Dad," said David to his father.

"David, would you please make a dinner arrangement with the Manila Hotel in the suite where I would be staying so that I can invite the family of your fiancée to meet them personally before the wedding. A day or two after my arrival would be fine. That will give me enough time to recover from jet lags," requested Dr. Scarborough.

"Yes, Dad. I'll do that. Dad, I would like you to talk to Mrs. Nuevavista, the mother of Rosalie. Please hold on," said David as he handed the phone to Mrs. Nuevavista.

"Hello, Doctor. How are you? I am Josefina Nuevavista, the mother of Rosalie, the future wife of David."

"Mrs. Nuevavista, nice to hear from you. I told David to make arrangement with the Manila Hotel so that you can join me for dinner so that I can meet you all before the wedding. David is my only son, and I will be there to support him on his wedding day," said Dr. Scarborough.

"Doctor, we will be looking forward to meeting you personally here in the Philippines. Doctor, you have a safe travel coming over to our country, the Philippines," said Mrs. Nuevavista.

"Yeah, it is a very long trip by air. I heard it is more than twenty hours in the air, but I'll be all right. I told David to give me enough time to recover from jet lags," answered Dr. Scarborough.

"Doctor, here is my husband, Alfredo Nuevavista. He wants to talk to you," said Mrs. Nuevavista as she handed the phone to Mr. Nuevavista.

"Hello, Dr. Scarborough, I am Alfredo Nuevavista, the father of Rosalie.

How are you?" was the introduction of Mr. Nuevavista.

"Hello, Mr. Nuevavista, I am doing fine. I am anxious to meet you all there in the Philippines. David said that you have a very good, decent, and very traditional family. I told David to invite you to my suite for a dinner so that I can meet the family," said Dr. Scarborough.

"Thank you, Doctor. I think we should be the one inviting you to our house. You are just visiting our country. We will make an arrangement with David to have you in our house to join us for dinner before the wedding. It is nice if you see our house so that when you come to visit the Philippines, you do not need to stay in the hotel. You can stay with us, Doctor," said Mr. Nuevavista.

"Oh, that's very nice of you. I am looking forward to meeting all of you, the whole family. Thank you very much for the offer," said Dr. Scarborough.

"Doctor, here is David. He wants to talk to you," said Mr. Nuevavista.

"OK, Dad, you got your ticket. Your travel arrangement is prepared. You will be staying at the Manila Hotel, and I will make dinner arrangements in your suite so that you can meet the family of Rosalie personally. I will pick you up at the Manila International Airport in the afternoon of June 8. Is everything OK with you, Dad?" asked David.

"Yes, I'll see you then in the afternoon of June 8," said Dr. Scarborough.

"Thank you, Dad, good-bye," were the parting words of David.

"Wow, David, it is nice we were able to talk to your Dad," said Mrs. Nuevavista.

"Thank you for talking to my dad. He was anxious to meet you all personally. I'll arrange your meeting in his suite for a dinner days after his arrival," said David.

"David, your dad sounded good. I am very anxious to meet him," said Rosalie.

"I am sure you will like him. He is a very nice man," said David.

Monday morning, March 1, 1954, David, Rosalie, and Meredith met again in the house of Rosalie. They once again went through their checklist of wedding preparations. The wedding dress was already made. They already had the wedding rings, the invitations and announcements were ready, the notes and stationeries were already ordered, all the men's attires were done, and they had already finalized the guest list. They had finalized the honeymoon details and reservations and travel. The dress of Mrs. Nuevavista was ready, together with the dress of the bridesmaid and the flower girl and the attire of the ring bearer.

Monday morning, April 12, 1954, David, Rosalie, and Meredith met again in the house of Rosalie and once again went through the checklist of their wedding preparations. Since their meeting of March 1, they had already confirmed the details with the food service of the Manila Hotel. They had already prepared maps and directions for the ceremony and reception. They had selected the wedding guest book, set the dates and times of the rehearsal, designed and printed the invitations, confirmed the photographer, confirmed the florist, finalized the accommodations of the out-of-town guests, confirmed the rehearsal dinner, and confirmed the wedding cake details.

Monday morning, May 3, 1954, David, Rosalie, and Meredith met again in the house of Rosalie and once again went through the checklist of their wedding preparations to verify if everything that they were to execute had been done. They prepared the mailing of the invitation, Meredith made arrangement for the formal bridal portrait, and they selected gifts for the attendants, set appointments for the hairdressers and makeup artists, and finalized the transportation.

Monday morning, May 17, 1954, David, Rosalie, and Meredith met again in the house of Rosalie and once again went through the checklist of the wedding preparations and additions to what they had accomplished. They had finalized with the food service of the Manila Hotel reception hall the menu for the reception. They had already bought the gifts for the groom and the bride. They had already fitted the dresses and attires for the wedding, purchased the apparel to wear when leaving the reception hall, confirmed the photographer, confirmed the florist, planned the seating arrangement, prepared the placement cards, and selected the music for the wedding ceremony and reception.

Monday, May 31, 1954, Meredith made arrangements to have the wedding gifts moved to the house of Rosalie in Dapitan and prepared the wedding announcement for the newspaper and other local media.

Monday, June 7, 1954, Meredith reviewed and finalized the seating arrangement for the reception hall; reconfirmed the honeymoon reservations and transportation; reminded David and Rosalie of packing for the honeymoon; called the guest who had not responded; finalized the place cards for the reception; reviewed and finalized the details with the photographer, florist, baker, and food service; wrapped the wedding party gifts; and finalized the rehearsal dinner.

# Chapter XXII

## The Wedding

TUESDAY, JUNE 8, Dr. Frederick Scarborough arrived at the Manila International Airport. David picked him up and checked him in at the Manila Hotel.

*(The spirit of Mary Scarlet brought the spirit of Rosemarie to the airport and followed Dr. Scarborough and David to the Manila Hotel.*

*"Rosemarie, that man with David is Dr. Frederick Scarborough. He was my husband when I was still alive. He is a very fine man. He has been very faithful to our love. He did not fall in love since my death."*

*"Mary Scarlet, I think David is also a very fine man."*

*"Oh yes, David is a very fine man. I love him and watched him all the time growing up. David would have not fallen in love with anybody if you did not give him the freedom to fall in love again.")*

David after he checked in his dad at the front desk of the hotel led him to his suite in the upper floor of the hotel. David showed him everything.

"Dad, for anything that you need, you can just call the front desk. They will take care of you."

"David, this room is very big."

"Dad, this is a suite. You are the father of the groom. You have to be comfortable."

"Did you make the dinner arrangement with the hotel so that I can invite the family of your fiancée? I want to meet them personally."

"Dad, they invited us to dinner to their house tomorrow. You will see the family personally."

"That is fine, but I want to invite them too, here, to join me for a dinner."

"That would be fine, Dad. We will host the dinner on Thursday, June 10.

They will be coming here. By the way, Dad, we should be all in white on the wedding day, and I ordered for you a barong Tagalog and white pants. Would you please fit them?"

"Sure, let me have them."

Dr. Scarborough put on the pants and the barong Tagalog.

"David, the shirt is too big for me, and the pants are too long."

"Oh, I am sorry, Dad. I miscalculated your size. You may have shrunk with age."

"No! But I cannot wear the outfit. I will look funny with this."

David right away called Meredith on the phone with a little concern.

"What's up, David?" answered Meredith. "Meredith, we have a very big problem."

"What is it?"

"The outfit of my dad is too big for him."

"Oh, don't worry. I'll get a tailor to his suite to get his measurements, and we will fix the outfit.

I'll call you from the lobby when I come back so that you can open the door for us."

"You are great, Meredith. Thank you."

Meredith under pressure drove to a professional tailoring shop and talked to one of the tailors and hired him to fix the outfit of Dr. Scarborough. He drove the tailor back to the hotel, and after she parked the car, they ran to the front desk and called David.

"David, we are on our way. Open the door for us so that the tailor can take the measurements of your dad."

"Great. Thank you. Meredith, you have not stopped to amaze me," said David.

Meredith ran, took the elevator, and rushed to the suite of Dr. Scarborough, where David was waiting at the door. David introduced Meredith to Dr. Scarborough, while the tailor took the measurements of the doctor and then took the outfit with him.

"Sir, I have to take this outfit with me so that I can fix this. I'll rush fixing this and bring this tomorrow morning," said the tailor.

"OK, David, Dr. Scarborough, we have to go. I have to drive the tailor to his shop. Nice meeting you, Doctor," said Meredith.

"Oh, thank you, ma'am. It was nice talking to you," returned by Dr. Scarborough.

In the afternoon of Wednesday, June 9, David drove his dad to the residence of the Nuevavista family. At the gate, they were met by Rosalie.

"Dad, this is Rosalie," said David.

Rosalie walked forward and kissed Dr. Scarborough on the cheek.

"It is nice you could come, Doctor," said Rosalie.

"Thank you, Rosalie. David, Rosalie is very beautiful," commented Dr. Scarborough.

"Yes, Dad, and I love her," answered David, which made Rosalie smile. Rosalie led David and his dad to the house, where they met Mr. and Mrs. Nuevavista. Mrs. Nuevavista offered some appetizers of egg rolls, while Rosalie played the piano, and David sang songs. After the merry welcome to Dr. Scarborough, they all went to dinner. It was late when David and his dad went back to the hotel, exchanging stories, and the long conversation made the night fascinating and interesting.

The following day, Thursday, June 10, Dr. Scarborough hosted a dinner in his suite for the family of the Nuevavistas. David and Rosalie were very pleased that Dr. Scarborough and Mr. and Mrs. Nuevavista were enjoying each other's company and the conversation.

"Come and visit me in the United States," was the invitation of Dr. Scarborough to the couple.

"We just want to stay here in the Philippines. We do not know anybody in the United States. But if you visit here in the Philippines, please do not stay in hotels. Stay with us. Just give us a call, and we will pick you up from the Manila International Airport," responded Mr. Nuevavista.

"You are very kind. Thank you very much," answered Dr. Scarborough.

It was evening, June 11, 1954. Joe with Alex was very busy practicing his guerilla unit columns at the entrance of the Manila Cathedral, while David was talking with Father de Gracia near the altar about the rehearsal.

"OK, you form into two columns facing each other with arm's length from the man in your left or right. Remember your position between the columns, where the bride and groom will pass on their way out, must be at least seven feet. David is tall. You might poke his head, so watch out and be very careful. When the bride and groom are closing to us from the altar, I'll call ATTENTION. When I call attention, all of you must stand still looking forward. When I say PREPARE, without movement hold on to your knife. When I say DRAW, pull out you knife and keep the knife at your side, pointing forward in full attention. When I command PRESENT ARMS, raise your arm at a sixty-degree angle. At the end of columns would be Maria and Ana. Maria, you will shower rose petals to the newly married. And, Ana, you will be showering rice. You continue showering them until they reach the limousine." They repeated the execution several times. Then Joe gave them a break. Joe and Alex were standing and talking to each other at the entrance of the cathedral when Joe saw a lady in white with a white veil getting off from a car. The light focused on her that her dress seemed to glitter.

"Alex, do you see what I am seeing? That is a ghost, we buried her in the mountain. This cannot be," said Joe.

"What are you talking about, Joe?" asked Alex.

"Look at the ghost, she is coming," said Joe.

When Alex looked at the lady who was walking in their direction, Alex right away pulled Joe and ran inside the church. Joe followed Alex, running to the altar to get David and talk to him. The members of the guerilla unit were stunned and surprised to see Joe and Alex running toward the altar.

"David, David, the ghost of Rosemarie is coming. What are we going to do? The ghost may give us trouble," said Alex.

When the lady entered the church in full view of everybody, Joe and Alex hid behind David, and Alex said, "That is the ghost. We buried her in Sierra Madre, remember?"

David smiled and said, "Relax, guys, she is Rosalie, the living image of Rosemarie. They look exactly the same. Rosemarie is dead, and Rosalie is my future wife," explained David.

Joe and Alex sidestepped and pretended that there was nothing that caused them to run to David. Joe asked David to introduce them to Rosalie. When Rosalie came closer to David,

David said to Rosalie, "Please meet Lt. Col. Joseph Lee of the Philippine army, and this is Alex Torres. He is going to be a major in the army."

"Glad to meet you, gentlemen," said Rosalie, and she just nodded to Joe and Alex.

Under the close supervision of Father de Gracia, the rehearsal went very well, including the exit passage of the bride and groom between the two columns and the showering of the rose petals and rice under the command of Lt. Col. Joseph Lee.

**The Manila Cathedral, courtesy of Karen Joy Reyes**

In the morning of June 12, 1954, at 10:00 AM, the wedding of David and Rosalie began with the wedding march music, and everybody stood looking at the door to see who was coming in. Everybody was dressed in white. Father de Gracia was standing in front of the altar waiting for the procession to start. The first to enter the door was the best man, Lt. Col. Joseph Lee, followed by the groomsman, Maj. Alex Torres, followed by David, who walked to the right of the kneeling stand. Then the mother of the bride, Mrs. Josefina Nuevavista, was escorted by the father of the groom, Dr. Frederick Scarborough, followed by couples of wedding sponsors; then the bearers of the candle, the veil, and the cord; then a child ring and coin bearer; then a child Bible bearer; followed by the flower girl; followed by the bridesmaid; then the maid of honor. Then there was a little suspense. Then came Rosalie dressed all in white, with the face covered with the veil, escorted by Mr. Alfredo Nuevavista. When Rosalie and her father reached the altar, David met them, and the three of them faced Father de Gracia.

Father de Gracia asked, "Who will give away the bride?"

And Mr. Nuevavista answered, "I do." Then Mr. Nuevavista gave the hand of Rosalie to David, then went to sit by the side of Mrs. Nuevavista.

The Bible bearer walked to the altar and held the Bible in front of standing David and Rosalie. Father de Gracia blessed the Bible. Then David and Rosalie put their hands on the Bible, and they were blessed by Father de Gracia. The couple knelt together in the bride and groom kneeling stand in front, facing the altar.

Father de Gracia then started the rite of the holy Mass with the greeting prayers. He then led the congregation in reciting the Penitential Rite and invocation.

The choir sang "Glory to God in the Highest."

Lt. Col. Joseph Lee did the first reading—a reading from the First Letter of Saint Paul to the Corinthians:

> *If I speak with the tongues of men and of angels, but do not have love, I have become a noisy gong or a clanging cymbal. If I have the gift of prophecy, and know all mysteries, and all knowledge; and if I have all faith, so as to remove mountains, but do not have love, I am nothing. And if I give all my possessions to feed the poor, and if I surrender my body to be*

*burned, but do not have love, it profits me nothing. Love is
patient, love is kind and is not jealous; love does not brag and
is not arrogant, does not act unbecomingly; it does not seek
its own, is not provoked, does not take into account a wrong
suffered, does not rejoice in unrighteousness, but rejoices with
the truth; bears all things, believes all things, hopes all things,
endures all things. Love never fails.[1]*

Major Alex Torres did the second reading—a reading from the
First Letter of Saint Paul to the Ephesians:

*As the church is subject to Christ, so also the wives ought to
be to their husbands in everything. Husbands love your wives,
just as Christ also loved the church and gave Himself up for
her, so that He might sanctify her, having cleansed her by the
washing of water with the word. Walk in the way of love, just
as Christ loved us and gave himself up for us as a fragrant
offering and sacrifice to God. As the church submits to Christ,
so also wives should submit to their husbands in everything. In
this same way, husbands ought to love their wives as their own
bodies. He who loves his wife loves himself. However, each one
of you also must love his wife as he loves himself, and the wife
must respect her husband.[2]*

The deacon read the Gospel—a reading from the holy Gospel
according to Matthew. Everyone answered, "Glory to you, O Lord."

*Now it came to pass, when Jesus had finished these sayings
that He departed from Galilee and came to the region of Judea
beyond the Jordan. And great multitudes followed Him, and
He healed them there. The Pharisees also came to Him, testing
Him, and saying to Him, "Is it lawful for a man to divorce his
wife for just any reason?"*

*And He answered and said to them,*

*"Have you not read that He who made them at the beginning
'made them male and female,' and said, 'For this reason a
man shall leave his father and mother and be joined to his
wife, and the two shall become one flesh'? So then, they are*

> *no longer two but one flesh. Therefore what God has joined*
> *together, let no man separate."*[3]

Father de Gracia said the homily and talked about David and Rosalie about their relationship and their future responsibilities as parents.

Father de Gracia led the congregation in recitation of the Profession of Faith.

Father de Gracia started the liturgy of the Eucharist and led the congregation in praying the Eucharistic Prayer.

The choir sang "Gloria in Excelsis Deo" (Sanctus).

The candle sponsors walked to the altar and lit the two side candles representing two lives and two spirits joined together. David and Rosalie each got a small candle and lit the big unity candle, which symbolized their new life together. David and Rosalie knelt back on the bride and groom kneeling stand.

The veil sponsors walked to the kneeling David and Rosalie. The female veil sponsor pinned the right side of the veil to the shoulder of David, while the male veil sponsor pulled the veil to cover the head and shoulders of Rosalie and pinned the left end of the veil on her left shoulder.

The cord sponsors walked to the kneeling David and Rosalie and put the eight-figure cord over the veil over the heads and shoulders of Rosalie and David.

Father de Gracia continued the Mass by reciting the Eucharistic Prayer. He then proceeded with the Communion rite, where he invited the congregation to pray the Lord's Prayer. Father de Gracia continued the Mass by breaking the bread. Then the choir joined by the congregation and together sang, Lamb of God.

Father de Gracia recited the Communion rite: "This is the Lamb of God, who takes away the sins of the world. Happy are those who are called to his supper."

The congregation answered, led by Father de Gracia, "Lord, I am not worthy to receive you, but only say the word and I shall be healed."

Father de Gracia gave the Communion to David and Rosalie, and with the help of a deacon, the Communion was distributed to the congregation.

The cord sponsors walked to the kneeling David and Rosalie and removed the cord around their heads and shoulders and walked back to their seats.

The veil sponsors walked to the kneeling David and Rosalie and removed the veil and walked back to their seats.

Father de Gracia started the rite of marriage and spoke: "In the presence of Christ, I ask you your intention."

Father de Gracia asked Rosalie, "Rosalie, did you come here on your own free will, to bind yourself with David in the sacrament of marriage?"

Rosalie answered, "Yes, Father."

Father de Gracia turned to David and asked him, "David, did you come here on your free will to bind yourself with Rosalie in the sacrament of marriage?"

David answered, "Yes, Father."

Father de Gracia talked to both David and Rosalie. "David and Rosalie, will you promise to love and honor each other as husband and wife for the rest of your life?"

David and Rosalie both answered, "Yes, Father."

Father de Gracia asked David and Rosalie, "David and Rosalie, will you accept children lovingly from God and bring them up according to the law of Jesus Christ and His church."

David and Rosalie answered, "Yes, Father."

Father talked to David and Rosalie. "David and Rosalie, since it is your intention to enter into marriage, join your hands and declare your consent before God and His church."

David faced Rosalie and held her hand. "I, David, take you, Rosalie, as my lawful wife. To have and to hold, from this day forward, for better or for worse, for richer or poorer, in sickness and in health, until death do us part." Rosalie faced David and held his hand. "I, Rosalie, take you, David, as my lawful husband. To have and to hold, from this day forward, for better or for worse, for richer or poorer, in sickness and in health, until death do us part."

The ring bearer stood and walked to the altar for the rings to be blessed. Father de Gracia blessed the rings. Then David got the bride's ring and put it on Rosalie's ring finger. Rosalie got the blessed groom's ring and put it on the ring finger of David.

The coin bearer walked to the altar and presented the coins to Father de Gracia. Father de Gracia dropped the coins into the waiting hands of David. Then David dropped the coins into the waiting hands of Rosalie. Rosalie put her hands above David's hands and dropped the coins. David then dropped the coins into a plate held by the acolyte.

Father de Gracia looked at and addressed the congregation: "By the authority of the church, calling all here present as witnesses, I confirm and bless this marriage, which you have contracted, in the name of the Father and of the Son and of the Holy Spirit. Amen."

When the wedding rites were completed, Father de Gracia pronounced David and Rosalie as husband and wife. Father de Gracia congratulated David and Rosalie. David pulled up the veil covering the face of Rosalie and kissed her lips tenderly, and everybody clapped their hands.

*(The spirits of Mary Scarlet and Rosemarie were witnessing the wedding of David and Rosalie. After David and Rosalie were pronounced husband and wife by Father de Gracia, Rosemarie asked Mary Scarlet, "Mary Scarlet, are we leaving this Mother Earth now that David and Rosalie are married?"*
*"No! Not yet, Rosemarie. David is going to meet the man who killed me. I want to see to it that he is safe," answered Mary Scarlet.*
*"How did you know that?" asked Rosemarie.*
*"David unintentionally asked to meet the man who killed me from the shooting star. We better go now to the United States. It is in Washington DC where David will meet the man who killed me. Come on, let's go."*
*"Yes, Mary Scarlet, I am behind you.")*

David with Rosalie on his right, with her left hand around his arms, turned away from the altar and marched the aisle toward the door of the cathedral and passed through the waiting two columns of the guerilla unit, with their knives pointing sixty degrees upward under the command of Lt. Col. Joseph Lee. As the two walked out of the columns, Maria and Ana showered them with rose petals and rice. The two paused in front of the church for pictures.

They eventually went back to the altar of the cathedral to have more pictures taken with parents and all the wedding participants.

After the newlyweds' pictures were taken with all the participants at the altar of the cathedral, the couple rode the limousine, waving to the crowd, and headed to the Manila Hotel. David and Rosalie were met by Meredith at the lobby of the hotel and were escorted to a holding room, where they were also holding the other wedding participants. They waited until most of the wedding guests were seated. Then they started the program by serving the cocktails to the guests and proceeded with the introduction of the parents of the bride, Mr. and Mrs. Nuevavista.

The moderator introduced the parent of the groom, Dr. Scarborough. The moderator then introduced the maid of honor escorted by the best man.

The moderator introduced the bridesmaid escorted by the groomsman.

The moderator introduced all the sponsors.

The grand introduction of the moderator—the introduction of David and Rosalie, where David escorted Rosalie to the bridal table, where both of them were seated.

When everybody was seated, Father de Gracia did the blessing, and after the blessing of Father de Gracia, Lt. Col. Joseph Lee, the best man of David, stood and offered a toast.

David and Rosalie stood and offered a toast.

The parents of Rosalie, Mr. and Mrs. Nuevavista, offered a toast.

The father of David, Dr. Scarborough, also offered a toast.

Then the dinner was served.

After David and Rosalie finished eating, they went to each table and had a photograph taken with the guests in each table. They had a special picture taken together with Lt. Col. Joseph Lee and Maj. Alex Torres, with Mang Isidro and Aling Amanda, with Mang Pedro and Aling Bertha, and the members of the guerilla unit, with Maria and Ana seated on the left and right of David and Rosalie, who were seated in the middle. David and Rosalie had a picture where all the wedding gifts were in the background. All the wedding gifts were later ordered by Meredith to be transferred to the Nuevavista residence.

After the dinner, David and Rosalie cut their wedding cake, and they fed each other in the mouth to the laughter of everyone. They then distributed the cut pieces of wedding cake to the guests.

Then the special moment for Rosalie and David—to have their first dance on their wedding day. They embraced closely to the sound of sweet music, which they selected together. When Rosalie went back to her bridal table, Mr. Nuevavista took her to the dance floor, and they danced together, while Dr. Scarborough approached Mrs. Nuevavista, and they danced together. With the change of music, David approached Mrs. Nuevavista, and they danced together. Everybody was enjoying dancing with the music in the dance floor.

They stopped the music for a moment, and they called all single ladies assembled, and with Rosalie's back facing the group of single ladies, she tossed the bridal bouquet, and a lucky lady caught it. Then they assembled single men, and like what they did with the tossing of the bridal bouquet, Rosalie tossed her garter to the single guys. Then they continued the dancing on the dance floor.

David and Rosalie entered the center of the dance floor and danced to the sweet, slow tempo of the music. The guests made noise by beating their glasses with spoons, inviting the newlyweds to kiss. David and Rosalie kissed tenderly. When the other guests of the wedding party joined David and Rosalie, David whispered to Rosalie, "Rosalie, we have to skip the dance floor and go to the suite of your parents and transfer your suitcase to our suite. You have to sleep with me tonight. We have to leave early tomorrow morning to go to our honeymoon in Baguio."

"Yes, we have to do it in a way that the party will not be disrupted. We will let them enjoy the celebration as long as they are allowed by the hotel. By then we are already in our suite. Let us have Meredith take over after we exit. She knows what to do after we are gone," responded Rosalie.

(1) The First Letter of St. Paul to the Corinthians, 13:4–13; The Breaking Bread 2013, pp. 68–69

(2) The First Letter of St. Paul to the Ephesians, 5:21–32; The Breaking Bread 2012, p. 206
(3) The Holy Gospel according to Matthew, 19:13–12; The Word Among Us, Aug. 16, 2013, p. 138

# Chapter XXIII

## The Night of the Wedding

ONE HOUR BEFORE their designated end of the wedding party, while everybody was enjoying dancing and drinking, David and Rosalie exited from the reception hall and proceeded to Rosalie's parents' suite and took her luggage to be brought to their honeymoon and brought them to David's suite. David after escorting Rosalie to his suite left her to talk to his dad.

"Rosalie, I have to leave you for a moment. I have to talk to my dad. I will have no time to talk to him anymore. We have to leave early tomorrow morning for our honeymoon in Baguio City."

"Go ahead, David, I'll wait for you," answered Rosalie.

David left Rosalie in his suite and was almost running to reach the reception hall for fear that his dad might already go back to his suite. But fortunately, Dr. Scarborough was still seated in the presidential table, enjoying his drink and the music. He sat by the side of his dad and in a low tone said,

"Dad, I am leaving tomorrow morning for our honeymoon, and I may not see you. Do you have everything? Do you need anything?"

David had an expression of concern just thinking that that was the first time of his father in the Philippines.

"No, David, I am OK. I'll leave tomorrow afternoon."

"Dad, your suite is already paid. You do not need to check out."

"Don't worry about me. I can manage," said Dr. Scarborough.

"Dad, we may come to visit you in the United States."

"Good, the earlier you come to our house, the better for me."

"OK, Dad, I'll see you soon in the United States and thank you for everything."

"Just come home. You stay with me in the United States."

"Yes, Dad, we'll do that. Thank you and good-bye," were the parting words of David to his dad as he rushed back to his suite with Rosalie left alone.

When David opened the door of his suite, his eyes almost fell to the floor seeing Rosalie having nothing on.

"Come on, David. Now that we are married, I am your slave," were the daring words of Rosalie, with David standing in surprise.

David was stunned with the change of events. He put off the light and undressed. He was afraid of scaring Rosalie upon seeing him naked. He then took Rosalie by the hand and brought her to the shower. In the shower, they embraced very tightly. When David entered Rosalie, Rosalie felt the pain that sank deep into her being. She felt that unbearable pain, which seemed to tear her apart as her virginity was broken. The blood that oozed from her and the tears of pain from her eyes were washed by the rushing pouring water from the showerhead. She held on hard to David to ease the pain, but the pain later changed to an exciting feeling within her. The sensation that she never felt before was heavenly. When they separated, they both went out of the shower, and David dried her whole body. Then Rosalie went to bed, while David stayed and continued drying himself. David stepped out of the bathroom and proceeded to their room and lay down beside Rosalie, who was wearing nothing. They both slept side by side with nothing on.

A little later, Rosalie woke up with a burning sensation inside her private part. She could feel a tear inside her, and she could not sleep. She hoped that she would heal faster before David could have another session with her. She hoped that she could bear another painful penetration of David, which seemed to kill her during their first lovemaking. But she had to bear the pain to satisfy the yearning and desire of David. She could remember what she said to David before their wedding: "I will be your slave, and you will be my King." She thought of what was to come in her life now that she was a wife. She thought of her parents. She felt different now that the feeling of dependability on her parents was no more and replaced with the feeling of responsibility as a wife with a countless duty to a husband. With the many questions and thoughts in her mind, she fell asleep.

At around 5:00 AM, David woke up and gently touched the body of Rosalie, then kissed her tenderly, which woke her up. David put his body on top of Rosalie, and they made love. Rosalie felt a little slashing pain at the beginning, but it was later turned to excitement and a heavenly sensation, which numbed the pain that she endured as they reached the climax of their embraces. She felt like dreaming, then suddenly brought back to reality. When she opened her eyes, everything was over. She was lying down quietly, then felt dirty and stood up and rushed to the shower.

Rosalie went back to the room and saw David was sleeping, so she went to get her luggage, pulled a chair, and went to the bathroom so that she would not bother David, who was snoring and sound asleep. She used the mirror of the bathroom as her dresser. She got her cosmetics from the luggage for their trip to Baguio City, then put them on the counter of the bathroom. She rubbed her entire body with moisturizing cream and applied body lotion. She shampooed her long hair, then used a blower for her hair to dry. She fixed her makeup and her eyebrows. For the first time in her life, she watched herself in the nude. She had been very conservative and always covered herself. Even from the shower she would wrap herself with a towel and then dressed up. Now with nothing on, she had that feeling of freedom.

Rosalie was so too engrossed in what she was doing, watching herself in the mirror, adoring her beauty. Then she remembered to check on David. She went to the room where David was sleeping and saw David with nothing on—the first time she saw a man lying down with nothing on. She approached David and sat by his side for a moment. She kept on looking at him. Then she felt that craving for that heavenly sensation. She moved closer to David and started kissing him on his lips. David woke up and pulled Rosalie down and put his body on top of her, when the phone rang.

"Mr. Scarborough, this is your wake-up call. It is seven o'clock in the morning."

David jumped out, to the surprise of Rosalie, and went to the bathroom and took his shower. Then he went back to where Rosalie was and said, "We have to leave soon for our honeymoon. The car that will take us to Baguio will be waiting for us. You better dress up quick."

Rosalie dressed up very quickly and put all her things in her suitcase and waited for David, who was still gathering all his things and putting everything in his luggage.

As they were leaving their suite, David talked to Rosalie.

"Rosalie, did you enjoy last night?"
"You almost killed me in the shower. Good thing there was water relieving my pain. But the second time was heavenly. I really wanted more, but the phone rang," said Rosalie.
"Well, you can have more in our honeymoon," answered David.

When the couple reached the lobby of the hotel, they did not know that most of the guests were there waiting for them, and when they saw them coming, they clapped their hands and were yelling in celebration. Mrs. Nuevavista was there worrying about her baby, Rosalie, about the first night, but when she saw her smiling and seeming happy and walking straight, she smiled. She knew her baby survived the pain of the first night. She was OK.

David and Rosalie boarded the car bound for Baguio City for their honeymoon. There were cans and bottles tied to the end fender of the car, and on the back window, there was a big poster: JUST MARRIED. The cans and bottles were making noise as the car rolled toward their destination, while David and Rosalie were looking forward to more enjoyable nights in their honeymoon in Baguio City.

# Chapter XXIV

## The Honeymoon

DAVID AND ROSALIE came from the hotel lobby waving and being cheered by their guests from their wedding party the night before. David opened the left side of the backseat of the sedan and let Rosalie in, and then he went around the sedan and entered the other side. When they entered the sedan at the back of the driver's seat, they were amazed. The backseat was like a small private room, where they could not see the driver but there was a sound system to talk to him. There was a table in front of the seat, and there were magnetic plates with a serving of hot breakfast eggs, bacon, bread, bottled milk, and bottled orange juice. There was a small refrigerator, which contained some apples, grapes, oranges, some soft drinks, and bottled water. There was also a thermo bag, which contained roasted chicken and a covered container with mashed potatoes and brown rice. The silverware were magnetized so that they would not fall. There was also a bottle of hand sanitizer. The sedan that was rented to them was exclusively rented to honeymooners.

"Rosalie, I did not expect all of these. Meredith did an excellent job. This is the first time I have seen a car like this, and it is very elegant and neat," commented David.

"Well, whatever it is, let's eat. I am very hungry," said Rosalie.

After eating, Rosalie felt so sleepy, she leaned on David's shoulder, and David put his arm around her and also closed his eyes. Both of them did not get enough sleep the night before, and their bodies seemed to need some rest. They slept almost all the way, and after three hours of travel, Rosalie woke up, and so she woke up David.

"David, I am hungry, let's eat."

"Yes, I am hungry too. Let's open this thermo bag and take out the roasted chicken, mashed potatoes, and brown rice."

After eating their early lunch, Rosalie ate some grapes, and David ate an apple. They took a bottled water and soft drinks from the refrigerator and enjoyed the cool drinks as they became closer to their destination.

It was past noon when they arrived at the Burnham Suite Hotel. Their limousine parked in front of the main door of the hotel, where a bellman approached the driver of the car and received the luggage of David and Rosalie. He loaded them on a cart and rolled the cart to the front desk of the hotel. David and Rosalie followed the bellman to the front desk, where they presented their reservations. They were registered and checked into a suite, and the desk clerk gave the keys to the bellman. The bellman rolled the cart carrying their luggage, and David and Rosalie followed him. The bellman opened the door of their suite for them and rolled the cart carrying their luggage inside. The bellman showed them around the suite—the control of the lights, the thermostat, the refrigerator, and the kitchen equipment.

After a short presentation of the suite to David and Rosalie, he handed the keys to both of them. David gave the bellman some tip. Then he left and locked the door. David chained the door and approached Rosalie and said, "Shall we continue our unfinished business?" Rosalie was smiling.

"What unfinished business do you mean?" asked Rosalie.

"Let us take our shower together?" recommended David.

"Well, if that is what you want, let's do it," replied Rosalie.

The two removed their clothes and went to the shower nude. They embraced under the rushing water from the showerhead. Like the first time when they made love under the shower, Rosalie remembered when she was in too much pain. This time she was ready and eager, and with a little slashing pain, she took everything that David had to offer. She embraced David and gave everything she had. They kissed and made love, enjoying the moment of their first time in Baguio City. After they finished making love, they left the shower and dried each other's body smiling.

From the shower room, they picked up their clothes and their suitcases and brought them to their room. They opened their luggage and put the things they might need on top of their dresser. They hanged the clothes that they might use in touring around in the closets. Then they both lay down in the bed with nothing on. They did not seem to have enough of each other. They had the urge of making love anytime their skin touched, and they could not resist the temptation of enjoying the moment. They closed the outside world from them, and they just focused on each other and spent the time of their honeymoon together, savoring the unguarded moments alone, thinking of nothing but love until they each could not give anything more. Tired and exhausted, they both fell asleep.

It was almost 7:00 PM. Rosalie woke up very hungry.

"David, wake up, please."

"Yes, love, what do you want?" said David, who was still disoriented waking up.

"David, I am very hungry," said Rosalie.

"OK, let me call food service. You better dress up before the food service arrives here," said David. Rosalie had nothing on.

David called food service and ordered, while Rosalie dressed into her nightgown. After calling food service, David also dressed into his pajamas. Then they both got out of the room and waited at their dining table. A little later, somebody knocked at the door.

"This is food service."

"Yes, I am coming," answered David.

The food service deliveryman pushed his food cart into the suite, and David gave the food service deliveryman a tip. When the food deliveryman stepped out of the door, David closed the door and put the door chain. He pushed the food cart near their dining table, and Rosalie took over, putting the food on the table. David, instead of sitting across the table, sat by the side of Rosalie, and they ate together, enjoying the food together. David would feed Rosalie, and Rosalie would feed David. Their eyes looking at each other with tenderness, smiling as they enjoyed not only the food they ate but also the connection in between them in their hearts and souls. They had finally found the true meaning of love, not only for the physical aspect of it, but also for caring and understanding and good communication in silence even without the use of words. They had felt the connection spiritually and mentally. Their honeymoon gave them the chance to know each other's souls as they looked through their eyes and kissed. They could feel the throbbing sensation of truthfulness and purity of heart and of their love.

David finished eating first. He went to the bathroom and brushed his teeth, then approached Rosalie, who was still eating, and kissed her cheek.

"Good night, love. I'll go ahead and sleep some more. I need to recharge.

You're exhausting me," said David, looking at Rosalie. Rosalie only smiled.

When Rosalie finished eating, she put back all the plates and utensils on the food cart and pushed it outside their suite. She again locked their suite. She proceeded to the bathroom and took a shower, brushed her teeth and fixed herself, put body lotion on her entire body, and put back her nightgown. She wanted to always look nice and clean in the presence of David. She then went back to their room and lay down by the side of David, who was fast asleep. Rosalie, while lying down by the side of David, still wondered about the fast changes in her life the past days. She was now a wife and in a honeymoon and was asking herself, "What would be next?" Rosalie fell asleep thinking of many things, including her parents, whom she loved very much and who took care of her since she was born, and for the first time in her life, they were very far away from her.

Around seven o'clock in the morning, David woke up hungry and noticed that Rosalie was still sound asleep. He walked out of their room and from their living room called food service. After calling, something caught his attention on the center table of their suite, a tourist attraction brochure in Baguio City. He perused the pages of the brochure and got attracted to the different sites in Baguio. He decided that when Rosalie woke up, he would take her around Baguio city to look at those different sites. He proceeded to take his shower and fixed himself to get ready so that when Rosalie woke up, they could eat together and leave. A little later, there was a knock at their door.

"This is food service."

David opened the door and pulled the food cart inside their suite and gave the food service deliveryman a tip. Rosalie woke up with the sound coming from the door.

"Who is that, David?" asked Rosalie.

"That is the food service delivery guy. He is already gone."

David pushed the food cart toward their dining table, while Rosalie went straight to take her shower. David transferred their food from the cart to their dinner table and sat and waited for Rosalie.

Rosalie took a little longer than David expected. She was putting body lotion on her entire body and fixed herself to look beautiful. David patiently waited and was smiling when Rosalie came out of the bathroom.

"I thought you fell asleep already in the shower," jokingly said by David.

"No, I fixed myself to always look beautiful for you," answered Rosalie. "That's why I love you. Come on, let's eat. The food is getting cold," said David.

"You are dressed. Where are we going?" asked Rosalie.

"After eating, you dress light. We are going around to see Baguio City," answered David.

"OK. After we eat, I'll dress up. Good that I brought my flat shoes. I feel uncomfortable wearing high heels. My feet ached during our wedding, wearing high heels. I do not usually wear high heels because I am tall," said Rosalie.

"I have been looking at the tourist attraction booklet, and I realized that Burnham Park is just a walking distance from here. Let's find out what we can see there. We will bring our camera to take some pictures," said David.

"Sure, I like that so that we'll have some souvenirs of our visit here in Baguio City."

**A picture of the entrance to the Burnham Park, courtesy of Majella Zosa**

**A Picture of the Burnham Park Lake, courtesy of Majella Zosa**

After eating their breakfast, David and Rosalie headed to Burnham Park. The first area they visited was the man-made Burnham Lake, where they rented a boat. But before they boarded the boat, they asked the operator of the boat to take their picture, with the lake and the boat as their background. They rode around the man-made lake, which was actually in the center of the park itself, and when they finished, they headed to the Botanical Garden. One of the attractions in the Botanical Garden was the Rose Garden. They were fascinated with the different type of roses planted, of varied colors. They had their picture taken with the bust of Daniel Burnham, located in the center of the Rose Garden. They then proceeded to see the Orchidarium, where they saw different varieties of orchids and other beautiful flowers. In the Botanical Garden, they also visited the Igorot Garden, where they had their picture taken with the statue of the five Igorot tribes of the Mountain Province.

It was almost noontime when they finished going around Burnham Park, and David feeling hungry convinced Rosalie to go to Lower Session Road, located at the center of the city of Baguio.

They took a taxi and got off at Lower Session Road to look for a restaurant. After eating their lunch, David and Rosalie walked around Lower Session Road and enjoyed just seeing a lot of things at the center of the business in Baguio City. Around 3:00 PM, Rosalie felt feverish and asked David to go back to the hotel.

**Picture of Session Road in Baguio city, Courtesy of Majella Zosa**

"David, I am not feeling well. Let's go back to the hotel. I want to rest," requested Rosalie.

"OK. Let me get a taxi," said David, at the same time touching the cheek of Rosalie by his palm. "Love, you have a fever. We do not have medicine in the hotel. I saw a clinic on this street. Let's go back and find it. It is Dr. Bautista's clinic (OB/GYN)," said David as they turned back, looking for the clinic.

When they found the clinic, they knocked at the door, and they were let in by the receptionist.

"Good afternoon, can I help you?" was the welcome statement of the receptionist.

"My wife is not feeling well, and we want to see a doctor," said David. Rosalie just let David talk to the receptionist and sat on one of the chairs, leaned back, and closed her eyes.

"Sir, do you have an appointment?" asked the receptionist.

"No, ma'am, we are tourists, and we were just going around when my wife felt ill. We do not have a doctor in the hotel. That's why we came down."

"Please have a seat, and I'll call the doctor so that she can check on your wife. She seems very sick," said the receptionist.

The receptionist stood from her reception desk and walked to the back office to talk to the doctor. A little later, the doctor came out from the door by the side of the reception desk.

"Hello, sir, I am Dr. Imelda Bautista, and it looks like your wife is not feeling well," said the doctor.

"Doctor, I am David Scarborough, and she is my wife, Rosalie, and she is not feeling well. We just got married last Sunday. She was OK the whole time until a few minutes ago after we have walked for more than three hours here in this area," said David.

"Let me check on her . . . She has a high temperature," said Dr. Bautista. Rosalie opened her eyes.

"Hello, Mrs. Scarborough, how do you feel?" asked Dr. Bautista. Rosalie was leaning on the back of the sofa.

"I feel sick, Doctor," said Rosalie in a very low tone.

"Can you stand? Can I take you inside to check on you?" asked the doctor. "Yes, Doctor," said Rosalie as she stood and walked with Dr. Bautista to her examination room.

"Mrs. Scarborough, I am an obstetrician, and since you are newly married, I could feel the reason of your illness. Tell me, you are in pain, right?"

"Yes, Doctor."

"Tell me if this part of your abdomen is painful," asked the doctor as she pressed Rosalie's lower abdomen.

"It hurts, Doctor," answered Rosalie.

"I have to examine you internally, OK? Remove your underwear, and you lie down on this examination bed, and I have to look at the inside of your private part," said the doctor.

The doctor took her medical visual vaginal examination instrument to look at the inside of the vagina of Rosalie, and as she suspected, she had a swollen laceration in the opening and inside of her organ. Dr. Bautista took some samples from the inside of her vagina and brought it to the back lab for analysis. Then she came back and talked to Rosalie.

"Mrs. Scarborough, you have a severe inflammation inside your female organ. There are lacerations that need to heal before you can have relations with your husband. The way I look at it, you must be a virgin, and this is your first experience with a man. Right?" asked Dr. Bautista.

"Yes, Doctor."

"Well, your husband must not touch you one or two days to let the laceration heal. I'll give you some sample medicine to ease the pain, to heal the wound, eliminate your temperature, and prevent infection, OK? But first I have to talk to your husband. Meanwhile please take this medicine now. Here is a bottle of water," explained Dr. Bautista.

"Ma'am, here is the result of the lab work for Mrs. Scarborough," said the medical technician who just came in after her complete test of the sample taken from Rosalie.

"Mrs. Scarborough, we did not find any diseases or virus in your system. Everything looks OK, and what we only need is for the laceration to heal. You stay here for a minute. I have to call your husband," said Dr. Bautista as she walked to get David, who was waiting in the reception area.

"Mr. Scarborough, please come in and join us in our conversation," asked Dr. Bautista. David stood and walked into the examination room.

"Mr. Scarborough, I was right in my expectation when you said that you just got married last Sunday. Your wife has inflamed lacerations in her vagina that is causing her pain in her lower abdomen and fever. Mr. Scarborough, if you love your wife, do not touch her for a day or two. Let her heal, OK? She was a virgin on your first day you had a relationship, and you may have more than worsen her laceration. You have to let the laceration heal because she may get infected, and that would be worse. OK?" advised the doctor.

"Yes, Doctor," answered David, who was very concerned with Rosalie.

"She has already taken some painkiller medication to ease her pain and fever. So she should be all right for now. I have here some sample medicines that she has to take to help the healing of her inflammations and to avoid infections," said the doctor.

Rosalie was listening silently, looking at what would be the reaction of David.

"You can go now and see the receptionist. Please give me a call if you have any more problems, OK?" said Dr. Bautista as she stood up. David and Rosalie headed to the exit door.

"Thank you, Dr. Bautista," said David. He held Rosalie by the arm and helped her stand from the chair of the examination room, then turned toward the door.

"Thank you, Doctor," said Rosalie as she followed David.

David and Rosalie went out the examination room and proceeded to see the receptionist, who presented to them the bill. After David paid the bill, he made an appointment for Rosalie.

"Ma'am, I would like to make an appointment for her to see Dr. Bautista."

"When do you want to see Dr. Bautista?" asked the receptionist.

"How about on Thursday, June 17, at 10:00 AM. Would that be all right?"

"OK, Thursday, June 17, at 10:00 AM. It is done, sir."

"Thank you."

David and Rosalie took a taxi back to the hotel. When they arrived in their suite, David right away called food service and ordered dinner. Rosalie went straight to their room and rested. After David called food service, he entered their room and looked after Rosalie.

"David, I am so sorry I have this problem. I promised you the last time that you can do whatever you want to do to me when we got married. David, I want to make you happy. I am ready to bear the pain. I want you to enjoy our honeymoon. I'll shoulder the pain," said Rosalie with tears in her eyes.

"Rosalie, your pain is my pain. You are my wife, and I love you. Today and tomorrow are not the only days for us. We have many more days to enjoy our love together. I'll wait however long it takes. I want you to be healthy and happy. We are in this together. I love you," said David, wiping the tears in the eyes of Rosalie.

"Thank you, David, for loving me," said Rosalie, still crying.

"Love, do not cry. I have a very good plan for us," said David.

"What is it, David?" asked Rosalie.

"I'll take you to America. We will live in America," said David.

"David, how about your businesses here in the Philippines?" asked Rosalie. "We will ask your pa and your ma to manage my business. It is that simple," answered David.

"David, they do not know how to manage businesses like yours. They do not have the experience to run a business," said Rosalie.

"Well, they will learn how to run the business. I'll teach them before we leave the country."

"David, I hope you know what you are doing. But I trust you because I love you," said Rosalie.

"That's what I want to hear, you love me, and you stop crying, OK?" said David, smiling, pinching the cheek of Rosalie.

A little later, there was a knock on their suite.
"This is food service."

David went to the door and met the food service delivery person. He pulled the food cart to their suite and paid the food delivery person, then closed and chained their door. He pushed the food cart to their dinner table and transferred the food. Rosalie came out of their room and joined David at the dinner table.

Before, David was so aggressive in their lovemaking. But this time he understood what Rosalie was undergoing. He also felt the pain the way Rosalie felt the pain. When Rosalie went to bed, David lay by her side, embraced her, and kissed her and said, "Good night."

"Are you sure you can stand without enjoying me?" asked Rosalie.

"Rosalie, my love for you is more than physical. It is spiritual. It is more than your body that I need in my life. It is your heart, your love, and nothing more. I need your love, and that will not change. I will never forget my sworn promise to you in front of the altar: 'I take you as my lawful wife to have and to hold, from this day forward, for better or for worse, for richer or poorer, in sickness and in health, until death, do as part.'"

"David, I love you."

David embraced Rosalie tightly and kissed her. Then he went to sleep.

Rosalie turned toward David and embraced him and went to sleep.

The following day after breakfast, David was scanning the brochure for touring Baguio City. Rosalie told David that she was feeling better and wanted to go out and have some fresh air.

"David, I saw in the brochure the Baguio Cathedral. I want to visit it," said Rosalie.

"Are you OK now?" asked David.

"Yes, I think so. Let's go and visit the cathedral," requested Rosalie.

"OK, let's dress up and visit the cathedral. Please let me know when you are not feeling well so that we can come back so that you can rest, OK?" said David.

"OK, I will now go and dress up," answered Rosalie.

**Picture of the Baguio Cathedral, courtesy of Majella Zosa**

David and Rosalie took a taxi going to the Baguio Cathedral. They called it Our Lady of Atonement. As they were approaching the Baguio Cathedral, grandly standing on top of Mt. Mary Hill, they could not help but be amazed at the majestic structural beauty of the cathedral. The two went inside the cathedral. Both knelt, admiring its beauty and the grandeur of the altar.

Rosalie prayed with tears in her eyes, thanking God for having David as her husband, who had been caring and understanding to her. She further prayed:

"Mother Mary, please guide our hearts in everything we have to do. Please help me to be a good wife to David and David to be a faithful, loving husband to me. Please lead us the way in all the things we will undertake in our journey through life. We ask this in the name of your Son Lord Jesus Christ. Amen."

After prayers, they took some pictures inside the cathedral and some pictures in front. They then took a taxi to the business section of Session Road to eat their lunch. After eating their lunch, they took a taxi going to the Mansion House, the summer residence of the president of the Philippines. They took some of their pictures using the mansion as their background. From the mansion, they took a taxi going back to their hotel.

**A picture of the Mansion summer residence of the President of the Philippines, Photo by Majella Zosa**

The following day, David suggested to Rosalie to stay in so that Rosalie could rest in preparation for her appointment the following day. David wanted to be sure that Rosalie was fully healed and not aggravated by too much walking in touring the city. But at around four in the afternoon, Rosalie asked David to go to the cathedral to attend the novena for the Mother of Perpetual Help. They both dressed up and took a taxi going to the cathedral and arrived just as the five o'clock novena for the Mother of Perpetual Help started. Rosalie once again begged Mother Mary for guidance for their marriage and to lead David in whatever decision he had to make regarding his business. She asked further that if it would be her parents who would manage the business, to give them the knowledge and the skills that would be needed to make the business profitable. David knelt by the side of Rosalie and held her other hand and prayed for her quick healing. He prayed that she heals well without any complications, that he be more compassionate and understanding to Rosalie, and that he be a good husband to her.

Very early the following morning, David and Rosalie ate their breakfast together. After breakfast, Rosalie took her shower and cleaned herself very well, knowing that she would be examined by Dr. Bautista physically. She applied body lotion on her entire body and fixed herself very well to look beautiful and healthy. After Rosalie finished using the shower, David took his shower, while Rosalie was getting ready for her physical. She checked all the medicines the doctor had given to her, and the remaining extra she brought with her, to ask the doctor if she had to continue taking them. After David took a shower and dressed up, they went down to the lobby, and in front of the hotel, they took a cab that was parked. They arrived around 9:30 AM at the doctor's office, and the receptionist asked them to take a seat. A little later, Dr. Bautista came out and greeted David and Rosalie.

"Good morning, Mr. and Mrs. Scarborough. The nine thirty scheduled appointment was cancelled, so I can start with you, Mrs. Scarborough. Mr. Scarborough, I'll take with me Mrs. Scarborough for examination, and I'll call you later. OK?" said Dr. Bautista. David stood when Dr. Bautista came out.

"Yes, Doctor. You can take her. I hope everything goes well," said David with a smile.

Dr. Bautista asked Rosalie to remove her underwear and to lie down on the examination bed. Dr. Bautista covered Rosalie's lower part of the body, and with the use of her medical visual vaginal exploratory instrument, she examined Rosalie thoroughly. Dr. Bautista was so pleased with her findings. Rosalie was fully healed, and there was no sign of any complications. After the examination, Dr. Bautista asked Rosalie to put her underwear back and asked her to have a seat. Dr. Bautista then called David, who was reading some magazines in the reception area. When David entered the examination room, Dr. Bautista asked him to sit down.

"Mr. Scarborough, Mrs. Scarborough is fully healed. Now that you are newlyweds, sometimes you get excited toward each other very quickly. It is very important before you engage with each other that Mrs. Scarborough is ready to receive yours. You know what I mean. She must be fully ready before you engage. You have to start kissing, touching. Get Mrs. Scarborough excited and ready before you engage. OK? Mrs. Scarborough, you have to reciprocate his loving and get stimulated so that you will not get hurt. Is that very clear to both of you?"

"Yes, Doctor," answered David, with Rosalie looking down, trying to avoid the eyes of the doctor.

"Do you have any further questions?" asked Dr. Bautista.

"No more, Doctor," answered Rosalie.

"Thank you very much for your professional advice," said David.

"OK, you can go now, and give me a call if you have any more medical problems. Good-bye and you have a safe trip back to Manila," were the parting words of the doctor to the couple.

"Thank you very much, Doctor," said David as he shook the hand of Dr. Bautista before turning to the door with Rosalie. Rosalie hugged Dr. Bautista before she followed David to the door.

**Picture of busy Session Road in Baguio City, courtesy of Majella Zosa**

From the doctor's office, David and Rosalie walked and shopped along Session Road, buying some souvenirs. They also took their pictures on Session Road and then ate in a restaurant before heading to their hotel. When they got into the hotel, David felt romantic with Rosalie. David remembered what the doctor said. He must be very careful and must take his time with Rosalie. They kissed and embraced, feeling each other's readiness. David saw to it that Rosalie was very much ready before they made love. David was very careful and slow in entering Rosalie. David made love with Rosalie with such tenderness and lovingly embraced her, giving the fullness of his love with such gentleness that it made Rosalie feel like she was in a different world, savoring the heavenly feeling. When the two were done, they felt as if they had been to a long journey, running to the space of infinity and just back to reality. They both stayed lying down without a word. Then David turned around to Rosalie.

"Rosalie, was there any pain? Is everything OK?"

Rosalie smiled and said, "I want more. Do you have some more to give?"

"Let's do it later. You just got healed. We must not abuse it. We may irritate it again, and we are going to have problems," answered David, as he kissed

Rosalie on the lips so tenderly.

The following day, after breakfast the two went out to see more of Baguio City. They went to see the Mines View Park. They passed the Mansion on their way. When they reached the Mines View Park, they were amazed at the spectacular view of Benguet's gold and copper mines. From the top of the ridge, they took their picture, using the verdant Cordillera Mountains as their background.

**Picture of the Baguio Mines View Park, courtesy of Majella Zosa**

They visited the Good Shepherd Convent and bought some strawberry and purple yam jams and other goodies to be brought back home as giveaways to Mr. and Mrs. Nuevavista when they come back to Manila. They also bought some wood carvings as souvenirs from the place.

**A picture of the entrance to the Good Shepherd convent, courtesy of Majella Zosa**

**A picture of the statue of the Virgin Mary in the entrance of the Good Shepherd Convent, photo by Majella Zosa**

Friday, June 19, 1954, David woke up very early in the morning to get ready for their last day of touring Baguio City. They scheduled to go see the Bridal Veil Falls. He called food service so that they could eat before leaving. While he was scanning the tourist brochure for Baguio City, the food service deliveryman called.

"This is food service."

"I am coming," said David as he walked to the door.

"Who is that, David?" asked Rosalie, who just woke up.

"It is the food service deliveryman. Come on so that we can eat," said David.

David opened the door and pulled the food cart inside the suite and paid the food service deliveryman. Rosalie walked from her bed and went to use the bathroom. After using the bathroom and cleaning herself, she went to their dining table to join David for breakfast. After breakfast, David and Rosalie dressed up for their trip to the Bridal Veil Falls.

"They said that if you inhale the mist from the Bridal Veil Falls, you will have a very flourishing and lucrative relationship in your marriage," said David.

"Oh, I like that. The more I am getting eager to visit the Bridal Waterfalls," said Rosalie.

The two were excited to see the waterfalls. They took a taxi going to Kennon Road. From Kennon Road, they could see the grandeur of the Bridal Veil Falls. The two crossed the bridge, hanging around eight hundred meters from the Rocky River. The Bridal Veil Falls was so beautiful, like a bride's hair coming from the mountain, the stream of water falling strongly, gushing down the smooth boulders and forming a cool mist. They took their pictures on top of the rock by the waterfalls and enjoyed the mist coming from the gushing water down from the top of the mountain, falling several feet away from them. In their hearts were hopes and prayers that their love for each other would thrive, prosper, and last forever. David and Rosalie stayed till sundown to watch the sunset along Kennon Road.

**A picture of the Bridal Veil Waterfalls showing the hanging bridge, photo taken by Majella Zosa**

Saturday, June 20, 1954, the last day of their honeymoon in Baguio City. David woke up early and ordered their breakfast from the food service of the hotel. David was busy organizing the things they had to bring back home to Manila when food service knocked at the door.

"This is food service."

"Yes, I am coming," said David as he walked toward the door.

David pulled the food cart inside their suite after he paid the food service delivery person. He chained the door again and pushed the cart toward their dining table.

"Who was that, David?" asked Rosalie, who just woke up.

"It was the food service delivery. Come on, let's eat," was the invitation of David. Rosalie was walking out of the room.

"Wait, I'll just brush my teeth. You can set the table, and I'll join you in a few minutes."

After Rosalie brushed her teeth, she joined David at the breakfast table.

"Well, this is it, our last breakfast here in Baguio City. Get ready with all your things. We will be picked up by our driver around 11:00 AM. We have plenty of time. When we arrive in Manila, I have to work for your visa so you can come with me to the United States. We have to tell your pa and ma to manage our business. I'll train your pa. If he will have any problems, he can call us long distance to our house in the United States. I'll have to hire a real estate management agency to manage our twenty apartment units so we will have better control of the whole renting business."

"David, you have a very big plan for us. You have a big task that you have to accomplish. With all those things you have to attend to and negotiate with, when do you think are we going to leave for America?"

"I don't know yet, but I have to work on it. My dad is getting old and alone. He needs us, and we will come to stay with him. We are the only family he has," answered David.

After breakfast, David convinced Rosalie to make their last day memorable. "Love, come, let's make our last day here in Baguio City very memorable."

"What do you mean, David?" asked Rosalie.

"You undress and let's take a shower together," said David.

"OK. Let's take a shower together. I'll rub your back, and you rub my back," answered Rosalie.

Both David and Rosalie undressed, and they both went to the shower together. David was reminded of what Dr. Bautista told him: "Take it easy with your wife." David started kissing Rosalie on the lips, and she tenderly embraced him. David kissed the neck of Rosalie, which made her so excited. David was very gentle in making love with Rosalie. David made love with Rosalie with such tenderness and compassion that she responded with such emotion, giving everything she had to offer to make David enjoy the moment. They made every minute memorable for their last lovemaking on their honeymoon in Baguio City. When they reached the pinnacle of their excitement, they embraced so tightly, but after they reached the peak of that heavenly sensation, it was as if they were brought back down to earth, and everything was over. They released their embrace and let the water wash their tired bodies, and they leaned and hold on to each other. David turned off the shower, and they both stepped out. David dried the entire body of Rosalie with a towel, and Rosalie dried the back of David. Then she gave the towel back to him. She then faced the mirror to start fixing herself. She applied body lotion and moisturizing cream on her entire body while David was watching and admiring her nude Venusian beauty. When David felt excited, he stepped out of the bathroom so as not to mess up Rosalie, who was fixing herself and getting ready for their checkout from the hotel.

David went to their room, where he dressed up. He had been very careful with Rosalie, who had been very tender. He did not want to hurt her. He had to be slow on her and not abuse her weakness. After dressing up, he started putting all the bags of souvenirs, giveaways, and his luggage near the door, ready for pickup. Then he went to the bathroom and talked to Rosalie.

"Love, are you ready?"

"Almost, I am dressed up already. I am just fixing my hair. I'll be out in a second," answered Rosalie.

"Shall I put your luggage near the door for pickup?" asked David.

"Not yet. I still have to put my cosmetic bag inside my luggage. I'll be done shortly."

After Rosalie was done fixing her hair, her eyebrows, and putting her lipstick, she put everything into her cosmetic bag and put the cosmetic bag inside her luggage. She put her used clothes in a laundry bag and put the bag in her luggage. Rosalie rolled her luggage near the door together with the other bags and luggage. David meanwhile was checking all the drawers—in their room, in the kitchen, the bathroom, checking every corner to see to it that they had not forgotten anything.

"I think we are all set. I'll call the bellman to load our luggage to take to the front desk so that we can check out. We will just wait for our pickup in the lobby," said David.

"I think that is a very good idea. We just check out and wait for our pickup at the lobby," replied Rosalie.

David called the bellman, and in a very short time, he came knocking at their suite. The bellman loaded all the luggage and bags into his cart. David and Rosalie followed the bellman to the front desk, where David checked out and paid their bills. They waited in the lobby for their pickup, which was part of the honeymoon package David paid through Meredith.

It was past eleven o'clock when their limo pickup arrived. The driver of the limo came into the lobby and asked for David Scarborough. David and Rosalie stood and identified themselves.

"Sir, ma'am, come on, let's go. I am going to take you back to Manila," said the driver to the couple.

"Yes, we have been waiting for you," answered David as the bellman pushed the cart containing their luggage and loaded them into the trunk of the limo.

David went to open the left side of the backseat of the limo and let Rosalie in. David gave a tip to the bellman and then entered the right backseat of the limo. The setting of the backseat was the same as the limo they took coming to Baguio. They had a table in front of their seat and magnetized plates and utensils on the table. There was a small refrigerator and a thermo bag containing food for their lunch. A little later, as they started their journey back to Manila, David asked Rosalie.

"Love, are you hungry?"

"I am. How about you, are you hungry?" asked Rosalie.

"OK, let's eat. Let's see what they prepared for us in the thermo bag?" said David.

David opened the thermo bag, which contained warm roasted pork, mashed potatoes, tasty bread, brown rice, and tiny bags of ketchup, salt, and pepper. They had soft drinks and bottled water in the small refrigerator. The two ate their lunch and put their leftovers in the thermo bag. They also had a small waste can at the backseat of the limo for their trash. There was also a small bottle of sanitizer, which they used to clean their hands before and after eating.

After eating, Rosalie leaned back and closed her eyes. David put his arms around the shoulders of Rosalie and pulled her close to him, then closed his eyes too.

Their first journey together in life was their honeymoon, where they learned not only the intimacy of sex but caring for each other. Rosalie with tears in her eyes, in spite of the pain, offered her body to David to make him happy—a promise she made before she got married, that as a wife David could do whatever he wanted to her. David wiped the tears in her eyes and lovingly spoke his love, his concern, that they had many more days they could enjoy together, that her pain was his pain and he was willing to sacrifice whatever it took for the sake of their love. For two days David and Rosalie sacrificed their honeymoon without making love, a test of their passion and their desire for each other. Compassion and empathy for each other overcame their lust for physical satisfaction. Their honeymoon brought them closer to God, praying in the Baguio Cathedral to be a good husband and a good wife, asking for blessing and guidance from the Mother of Perpetual Help in their very long journey through their marriage life.

**A Close view picture of the Bridal Veil Waterfalls, courtesy of Majella Zos**

# Chapter XXV

## The Tears of a Mother

DAVID AND ROSALIE were aboard the limo from their honeymoon in Baguio City and woke up when they entered Manila, awakened by the noise and the heavy traffic. It was 3:30 PM when the couple was dropped in front of David's condominium. The driver of the limo unloaded their luggage and bags of gifts and wood carvings, and David and Rosalie brought all their carry-ons to their condominium. David showed his condominium around to Rosalie. This was the first time that Rosalie ever entered the condominium of David. They did not stay long in the condominium. After they had unloaded their luggage and put their dirty clothes in the washer, then dried them in the dryer, they sorted their souvenirs and selected the things they had to bring to Mr. and Mrs. Nuevavista. Rosalie told David to bring some extra clothes because they might stay overnight in her parents' house because of the gifts that they had to go through and respond to. Rosalie also warned David of the Filipino culture of kissing the hand.

"David, our culture here in the Philippines for newly married couples like us, who just came from a faraway place, must kiss the hands of the elders for a blessing. When I kiss the hand of my mother and father, you follow me, OK?" advised Rosalie.

"I'll just follow you. I'll watch you and just imitate you," answered David. "OK, let's go and see my parents," said Rosalie as they both went down to their car and drove to the Nuevavista residence, with their extra clothes and their giveaways from their trip to Baguio.

When David and Rosalie arrived in front of the gate of the Nuevavista residence, Rosalie right away got off and walked to the gate and rang the bell. Mrs. Nuevavista came out of the main door smiling, followed by Mr. Nuevavista, and they opened the gate, excited to see the newlyweds.

"Good that you are back," was the greeting of Mrs. Nuevavista. Rosalie went to kiss the hand of her mother. David followed Rosalie and kissed the hand of Mrs. Nuevavista. Rosalie kissed the hand of her father. David followed Rosalie, and he also kissed the hand of Mr. Nuevavista.

"Come on, let's get in. You must be tired from the trip," said Mrs. Nuevavista as she led the newlyweds inside their house, followed by Mr. Nuevavista.

"David and Rosalie, we have all your gifts from your wedding stored in the family room. You can go through them while we are fixing the table so that we can eat together," said Mrs. Nuevavista as she accompanied the couple to the family room and then headed to the kitchen, followed by Mr. Nuevavista.

"Wow, we have a lot of things to do. We have to go through all these gifts, and then we have to send them thank-you cards," said David.

"Oh yes, that is the first thing that we have to do before anything else. We have to collect the greeting cards from each of the gifts that we will open and record the name and gift into our wedding remembrance notebook. We have to write the name of the guest who gave the gift and the content of the box. This is what we will do. You remove the name tags and open the gifts while I will write the name of the guest and the gift in our wedding remembrance notebook. Is that OK with you?" said Rosalie.

"OK, let's do it," answered David.

David started reading the guest's name written on the gift tag, then opened the gift to see the content of the box, while Rosalie recorded everything into their wedding remembrance notebook. They were not even halfway done when Mrs. Nuevavista came to see them.

"Rosalie and David, you first leave what you are doing and let's eat. I know you are already hungry. It is already 6:30 PM. Come on, let us go and eat now," said Mrs. Nuevavista to the couple.

"Come on, David, let's go and eat," said Rosalie, as she stood to follow her mother.

"OK, let's just continue this later," said David.

David and Rosalie left the recording of wedding gifts and went to dinner with Rosalie's parents. At the dining table, David presented Mr. and Mrs. Nuevavista the plans he discussed with Rosalie while they were in Baguio. He also presented the way he would want to call Mr. and Mrs. Nuevavista.

"Ma'am, sir, I am your new member of the family. Would it be all right if I call you Mama Fina instead of ma'am and Papa Fredo instead of sir?" suggested David.

"That is sweet, David. That would be fine with us," said Mrs. Nuevavista. "Papa Fredo and Mama Fina, I would like to tell you that Rosalie and I will be leaving for United States," confided David.

"When are you planning to leave for United States?" asked Mrs. Nuevavista.

"Very soon. I still have to work with the U.S. embassy for Rosalie's visa.

She also needs to apply for her passport," replied David with assurance. "How about your business here in the Philippines? Who will manage them?" asked Mrs. Nuevavista.

"I am thinking of Papa Fredo to manage my business, with your assistance. I have to train both of you, and if you have any problem, you can ask my partner, Fernando. For my apartment units, I'll hire a real estate management agency so that you will not be bothered by any problems that may occur in the operation of the building. Tomorrow, from church we will go around and visit my establishments so that you will be familiarized with the area," said David.

"It looks like you have already well planned your departure to the United States. But you still have a lot of things to do. By the way, you just stay here tonight. You sleep in Rosalie's room so that you can continue your work with the opening of your wedding gifts," suggested Mr. Nuevavista.

"Yes, Papa Fredo, we can just go together to the ten o'clock Mass tomorrow," suggested David.

After dinner, David and Rosalie worked a little bit opening and recording their wedding gifts. They then went upstairs to Rosalie's room, and they went to sleep. They were so tired from their journey to Baguio, and their work on their wedding gifts was enough to make them a little drowsy. They slept right away as soon as they lay down on the bed. Rosalie woke up first and proceeded to take her shower, then went down to check with her parents, who were busy with their house helper, preparing breakfast.

"So, Rosalie, how is the feeling of a newlywed?" asked Mrs. Nuevavista.

"We are doing fine, Ma. David is very nice and caring. I do not have any complaints. I am very lucky to have him as my husband," answered Rosalie.

"What is your feeling about going to America?" asked Mrs. Nuevavista. "I am not sure yet, Ma. I have mixed feelings because I will miss you and Pa. Even in our honeymoon, I was thinking of you. But I guess I have to learn to adjust. It is the decision of David that I have to follow. He is my husband, and I have to respect what he wants for both of us," answered Rosalie.

"Do not think of us, Rosalie. You are already married, and whatever David wants, you have to listen to him. I am sure what he wants is what is best for both of you," answered Mrs. Nuevavista.

As they were talking and busy setting the breakfast table, David came, who just finished taking his shower.

"Good morning, everybody," was the greeting of David as he came to the breakfast table.

"Good morning," was the almost simultaneous answer of Rosalie and Mr. and Mrs. Nuevavista.

"Come on, have a seat, so that we can eat our breakfast. You are the only one we are waiting for," commented Mrs. Nuevavista.

"We will attend the 10:00 AM Mass at the Manila Cathedral," reminded Rosalie.

"Yes, I remember, and after the Mass I am planning to show Papa Fredo our business establishments. At the same time, I can familiarize him of the environment and what to expect in every establishment that he will manage," explained David.

"That would be good, David," said Mr. Nuevavista, while Rosalie was just looking in silence.

"By the way, Papa Fredo and Mama Fina, Rosalie and I will probably stay here temporarily while we are processing our departure for the United States. I have to vacate my condominium so that it will be rented while we are away," said David to Mr. and Mrs. Nuevavista.

"That would be fine. This is also your second home. The home of Rosalie is also your home. You are always welcome here," answered Mrs. Nuevavista.

"Thank you, Papa Fredo and Mama Fina," was the respectful answer of David.

After breakfast, the family headed to the 10:00 AM Mass at the Manila Cathedral, with David driving the family.

"Papa Fredo, you sit here in the passenger seat so that after the Mass I can show you the properties that you are going to manage. We are not going to get off. I'll just show you the locations," said David to Mr. Nuevavista as he opened the backseat door and let Rosalie in.

"Love, please sit by the side of Mama Fina in the backseat, OK?" said David to Rosalie, who sat with her mother in the backseat of the car.

It was past eleven when the Mass at the Manila Cathedral was finished. From the cathedral, David drove the family to each of his properties.

"Papa Fredo, this is my two-floor condominium. The first floor is the living room, dining, and kitchen, and the second floor are two bedrooms. We are going to have this managed by a real estate management agency. The only thing that you have to check is to see to it that the rental of the property less the operation cost is deposited into our bank account. You will receive a monthly report on the rental of the property," explained David as he drove toward his building with twenty rental units.

"Papa Fredo, this is the building that house my twenty rental units. I have a building manager/maintenance residing in the building for free. His name is Nestor Go. He is under my payroll now, but as soon as the real estate management agency takes over, I will take away his name from our payroll. But we will let him stay in his apartment for free. He can do minor maintenance in the building, and the major maintenance would be taken over by the agency," explained David as he drove toward the Liberty Haberdashery and Coffee Shop.

"Papa Fredo, this is our Liberty Haberdashery and Coffee Shop. Your office will be in the back of the haberdashery. You have the morning and evening shifts in both. You have managers for both haberdashery and coffee shop. You have to support what the shops need in operation. The payroll and accounting of the shops are handled by my partner, Fernando Salazar. I will tell more in detail of what to do when I train you for the job, OK? For now let's go and get something to eat," said David as he drove toward Dewey Boulevard.

Rosalie was reminded of those beautiful memories she had with David, during their courtship, when they dated near the bay, most especially the first time she was kissed by David and the unexpected putting of the engagement ring around her ring finger. David drove to the back of the famous Max's Restaurant. David got off from the driver's seat and opened the door for Rosalie and held her arm as she got off the car, while Mr. Nuevavista opened the door for Mrs. Nuevavista and helped her out of the car. The four enjoyed the afternoon luncheon at Max's Restaurant, and after their luncheon, they went straight home.

"Papa Fredo, tomorrow morning I will introduce you to my partner, Fernando Salazar, in the haberdashery. He will be there to meet us. We must be there around eight thirty in the morning. The store should be opened by then by the store manager. Please dress with your shirt and tie," said David.

"Sure, I'll be ready when you are," answered Mr. Nuevavista.

David and Rosalie right away went upstairs and changed clothes and went down to complete the opening and recording of their wedding gifts. After they finished opening and recording all their wedding gifts, they prepared the thank-you stationaries and prepared them for mailing. It was already late when they finished preparing the mailing of the thank-you notes.

"Love, please you do the mailing of all the thank-you notes tomorrow. Papa Fredo and I will go to the office so that I can introduce him to Fernando. Also please put together your personal information, the one you have prepared for our wedding. We have to get your NBI clearance. We have to apply for your passport, which can be handled by our travel agency, and your visa, which we have to get from the U.S. embassy. Thank you," said David, and he kissed her on the lips.

"I will do, sir, at your command," jokingly responded Rosalie with a smile.

David and Rosalie went upstairs hand in hand and went straight to their room, thinking of the things they had to do the following morning. Rosalie went to the restroom before going to bed, while David picked up the phone and called Fernando.

"Hello, Fern."

"Oh, David, you are back from your honeymoon?" answered Fernando. "Yes, we came back yesterday afternoon, and I have a very important thing to tell you. Rosalie and I are planning to go to the United States, and I am planning to have my father-in-law manage our partnership. I'll introduce him to you in our office in the haberdashery tomorrow morning. Is that OK with you?" asked David.

"Sure, I'll be there tomorrow morning to meet your father-in-law," answered Fernando.

"The salary of my father-in-law would be 10 percent higher than our store managers and should be charged to my interests in our partnership. Is that OK with you?" asked David.

"That would be fine with me. I'll include him in the payroll starting tomorrow," answered Fernando.

"The name of my father-in-law is Alfredo Nuevavista. I'll see you tomorrow. Thank you very much for everything," said David.

"I'll see you both tomorrow morning, good-bye," responded Fernando.

The following morning after breakfast, David and Mr. Nuevavista went straight to the haberdashery to meet Fernando. When they arrived, David introduced Mr. Nuevavista to the staff of the store and then went to the coffee shop and introduced Mr. Nuevavista to the personnel there. The two went back to the office at the back of the haberdashery, and David started briefing him on the operation of the business. David showed the safe where the cashiers drop their sales reconciliation of money collection. He opened the safe and showed each Manila envelope that contained the starting banks of the cashiers each day.

"Papa Fredo, your responsibility here is to give the opening bank to the cashier at the start of the shift. At the end of the shift, the cashier drops his/ her bank together with the cash sales and reconciliation sheet in the safe."

He explained that cash management, accounting, and payroll are the responsibility of Fernando. That his responsibility would be to see to it that the business was properly managed, all the bills were sent to the office of Fernando, and all he had to do was pick up the phone for any needs of both stores. David was talking to Mr. Nuevavista when Fernando arrived.

"Good morning," was the greeting of Fernando as he entered the door. "Hi, Fern, good morning. Please meet my father-in-law, Mr. Alfredo Nuevavista," David introduced Mr. Nuevavista to Fernando.

"Nice to meet you, sir, I am Fernando Salazar, the partner of David," answered Fernando.

"It is nice to meet you, Mr. Salazar. David had already started telling me the things that I have to be responsible for just in case he left for the United States. He also told me that you are responsible for the cash management, payroll, and all bills related to the business and that my job will be just to manage the business."

"Right, Mr. Nuevavista. Also if you have any problem, you can just give me a call, and I will always be available to give you a hand. Do not be afraid of anything. We can resolve any problem together, OK?" was the assurance of Fernando to Mr. Nuevavista.

"So, David, when are you planning to leave for the United States?" asked Fernando.

"Oh, we still have lots of things to do, with Rosalie and my other business investments. I have no specific date yet. Everything takes time. I'll let you know when we are ready to leave the country," said David.

"OK, I'll let you and Mr. Nuevavista work together. I am heading to my office. It is nice talking to you, Mr. Nuevavista. By the way,

David, please ask Mr. Nuevavista to fill out the personal information form, the tax forms, and all the forms required for new employees, which have to be completed and signed," said Fernando as he left to go to his accounting office at Escolta.

"Sure, we'll do that," answered David.

The whole day, David oriented Mr. Nuevavista on managing the haberdashery and the coffee shop. David saw to it that Mr. Nuevavista understood the whole operation of the business. When he had a little break from the training, he took an opportunity to canvas for a possible real estate management agency that could manage his condominium and the twenty rental units. He was able to select the three most popular and biggest real estate management agencies. He called the three offices and provided them the addresses of his rental properties and asked each representative to submit a proposal.

Meanwhile, Mrs. Nuevavista accompanied Rosalie to get an NBI clearance. After they secured that, they took a taxi to the World Travel Agency along Dewey Boulevard, which would handle their travel to the United States. David called the travel agency to help Rosalie get her passport and secure her visa from the U.S. embassy. When Rosalie and Mrs. Nuevavista arrived in the office of the travel agency, they were welcome by the receptionist.

"I am Mrs. Rosalie Scarborough, and my husband told me to come here for our travel abroad," said Rosalie to the receptionist.

"Oh, yes, Mrs. Scarborough, Mr. Scarborough just called to arrange for your travel to the United States. Let me give a ring to the agent who will handle your travel. Please have a seat for a minute," said the receptionist.

"Hello, Ms. Medina, Mrs. Scarborough is here to talk to you," said the receptionist over the phone.

A little later, Ms. Medina came out from the side door and approached Rosalie and Mrs. Nuevavista.

"Hello, Mrs. Scarborough, I have just talked to your husband. I am Sharon Medina. I will handle your account."

"Nice meeting you, Ms. Medina. Please meet my mother, Mrs. Josefina Nuevavista," was the introduction of Rosalie to her mother.

"It is nice meeting you, Mrs. Nuevavista," was the greeting of Ms. Medina.

"Please come both of you to my office so that we can discuss the things you have to do for the passport and the U.S. visa," said Ms. Medina as she turned around to lead Rosalie and Mrs. Nuevavista into her office.

When the two entered the office of Ms. Medina, Rosalie right away pulled out from the brown envelope all the documents necessary for her applications for her passport and visa and handed them to Ms. Medina.

"This is great, Mrs. Scarborough, It looks like you got all the documents I need to processes your applications for passport and visa. But I still want you to complete these application forms that should accompany your documents. I'll just attach to them my endorsement, and you should be good," explained Ms. Medina.

Rosalie filled out the application forms with the help of her mother, and after completing the forms, Ms. Medina went through all the entries and then accepted them.

"Also, Mrs. Scarborough, I have made an appointment with Dr. Victorina Valencia just next door to our office this coming Wednesday, June 23, at

10:00 AM, for your medical and physical examinations for your visa to enter the United States. I have made two applications for you—one a tourist visa for you to enter the United States as soon as possible and the other visa is for your permanent residence. Your permanent residence visa may take a while, but the tourist visa will let you enter the United States right away," explained Sharon Medina.

"Thank you very much, Ms. Medina, you are very helpful," said Rosalie as she stood, ready to go.

"You are welcome, Mrs. Scarborough. Mr. Scarborough has been our client, and we have records of his travels. We will just mail to your current address the passport and the visa as soon as we receive them," answered Ms. Medina.

"Thank you again, Ms. Medina, you have a pleasant day. Bye," said Rosalie as she headed to the door with Mrs. Nuevavista.

"Bye, Mrs. Scarborough and Mrs. Nuevavista," said Ms. Medina.

David met in person the three representatives from the different agencies. He went through all the proposals, and after a thorough study of the proposals and the interviews with the representatives, he decided to hire the Fil-Am Real Estate Management Agency, represented by Bob Wagner. He called Bob Wagner to tell him the news.

"Mr. Wagner, I am happy to tell you that you won the bid to manage our properties."

"Wow, thank you very much, Mr. Scarborough, for giving us the trust and confidence to manage your properties," answered Mr. Wagner.

"Mr. Wagner, I want to meet you in our house in the afternoon this coming Saturday. Would that be OK with you? We will drive to the rental property, and I want to introduce you to my building manager residing there for free. He is still in my payroll. But after next month, I'll take him out of my payroll, and you will take over the property, but I still want him and his family to stay there for free to do minor repairs. For big repairs, you take over, and the costs will be added to your management fee."

Wednesday, June 23, very early in the morning, David and Mr. Nuevavista drove to the Liberty Haberdashery to continue the training. At around 9:00 AM, Rosalie and Mrs. Nuevavista took a taxi from their home to the clinic of Dr. Victorina Valencia for Rosalie's medical and physical examinations. It was already 11:00 AM when the medical and physical examinations were completed. Rosalie and Mrs. Nuevavista took a taxi going home. David and Mr. Nuevavista arrived from training after five in the afternoon, while Rosalie and Mrs. Nuevavista with their house helper were busy preparing for their dinner.

Friday afternoon, June 25, David left his office at the haberdashery and went to visit his building manager in his rental property. David was still parking his car when Nestor Go came to see him.

"Hello, Mr. Scarborough, it is nice to see you," was the greeting of Nestor to David.

"Nestor, I would like to let you know that I am leaving for the United States. And I am going to have this rental property managed by the Fil-Am Real Estate Management Agency," was the sad news that David related to Nestor.

"Sir, do you mean to say that I have to leave the property when the agency takes over?" asked Nestor.

"No, Nestor, you will still live here for free. You can do minor repairs you can afford to do, and any major repairs would be done by the agency. The only difference now is you will not receive any salary from me, and the rental collections will be taken over by the agency."

"Thank you very much, sir. When do you expect the agency to take over the property?" asked Nestor.

"The Fil-Am Real Estate Management Agency will take over effective July 1, 1954. I'll give you your three months' salary as incentive for your good job while managing this building. You will be paid for the month of July, August, and September," answered David.

"Thank you very much for letting us stay here for free and for the three months' salary in advance. That would be a very big help to my family," answered Nestor.

Saturday afternoon, June 26, Bob Wagner came to the Nuevavista house to meet with David, who had been by the window waiting for him. When Bob parked his car in front of the house, David right away went to open the gate and let Mr. Wagner in.

"Good morning, Mr. Wagner," was the greeting of David.

"Good morning. Please just call me Bob," answered the real estate agent.

"Come in, Bob, and please have a seat," welcomed David.

"Thank you, David," was the respectful answer of Bob.

"OK, Bob, before we visit my properties, there are things I would like to clarify with you. First, my condominium must be painted, and you have to make repairs if there are things to be repaired. I still have my things in there. I have to clear everything in the condominium before you can start painting the place so that we can have a higher rental rate. I want the painting in white or beige or any light color to reflect light so that it will look roomy. Second, in my rental units, I have my building manager staying in the building. I want him and his family to stay in one of the units for free. He will do minor repairs for the building, and for major repairs, you will take over. Your agency will take over first day next month. We have already collected the rental fee for July. You have to take over the collection of the rental fee for the month of August. We always collect the monthly rental fee in advance. Your monthly deposit to my bank account would be the total rental collection minus your management fee minus cost of repairs if any. You just mail all the paperwork to my accountant at Escolta. The address is in the deposit slip. Attn: Fernando Salazar. Do you have any questions?" asked David.

"No. I think I got everything written," answered Bob.

"By the way, here is a booklet of deposit slips to our account with the Philippine National Bank. Please make a separate deposit for the rental building and for the condominium so that I have a better accounting of my properties for tax purposes. Let's go so that you can meet the building manager in my rental property building," said David.

"OK, let's go. Let me drive to the property," requested Bob.

When they reached the rental property building, Nestor was in front of the property watering the plants and the grass around the building. When Nestor saw David coming with the real estate agent, he stopped what he was doing and came to see them.

"Good afternoon," was the greeting of Nestor.

"Good afternoon. I am Bob with the Fil-Am Real Estate Management Agency," was the response greeting of Bob.

"Glad to meet you sir," responded Nestor.

"Nestor, I have already told him what we have agreed yesterday that you will stay in one of the units of the building for free. You will make minor repairs, and for major repairs, his company will take over. His agency will also take over the collections and deposits of the monthly rentals of all the rental units. You are relieved of any responsibility in the management of the building except minor repairs. If in the future you elect to leave your unit, please just let Bob know, and he will take over. So far do you have any questions?" was the explanation, followed by a question, of David.

"No more, sir. Thank you for everything, Mr. Scarborough," responded Nestor.

"It is nice meeting you, Mr. Go. I'll see you soon," said Bob.

"Bye, Nestor," were the parting words of David.

"Bye, sir," responded Nestor.

Bob drove David back to the Nuevavista residence. When Bob parked his car in front of the gate of the house, Rosalie came out and opened the gate for them. David got off the car, and Bob drove away. David walked to the gate, where Rosalie was waiting. David kissed Rosalie on her waiting lips. Then they walked hand in hand to the house.

After two weeks of intensive training, David seemed very happy with the progress of the performance of Mr. Nuevavista. He had been letting him do the job alone and just checking him once in a while. He took those breaks to move all his things from his condominium to the Nuevavista residence. The only things that he moved were his clothing and personal items, and he left all the furnishings and appliances so that the rental would be for a well-furnished housing, a better rental rate.

And finally after the third week of training, when David could feel that Mr. Nuevavista could be left alone and his condominium was prepared and ready for rental by the Fil-Am Real Estate Management Agency, he called for a meeting in the office of Fernando Salazar. In the meeting were David, Fernando Salazar, Atty. Francisco Villegas, Bob Wagner, and Mr. Nuevavista.

"Gentlemen, I called this meeting to tell you officially that I am leaving the country. My wife Rosalie and I will be heading to the United States. All accounting functions and questions, taxes, finances related to my business must be directed to Mr. Fernando Salazar, our accountant. All legal questions, issues with the city, national government, or with private citizens must be directed to Atty. Francisco Villegas, our corporate lawyer. Mr. Wagner, if you have any issues with our tenants regarding nonpayment of rent, evictions, or vandalisms in our property, please consult with Atty. Villegas. Mr. Nuevavista, if you have any issues with our employees, you consult with Mr. Salazar. Terminations of employees or vandalism of our property must be reported to our corporate lawyer, Atty. Villegas. Is everything very clear to everybody? Mr. Wagner?"

"Yes, Mr. Scarborough, everything is very clear to me," answered Bob Wagner.

"How about you, Mr. Nuevavista?" asked David.

"I understood everything. I do not have any further questions," answered Mr. Nuevavista.

"Mr. Salazar, are you in agreement of what we have talked about, your responsibilities in my absence?" asked David.

"Yes, everything as we have agreed is OK with me," answered Fernando.

"How about you, Atty. Villegas, what can you say?" asked David.

"Well, if there are legal issues related to your business properties, just present them to me, and I'll take action," answered Atty. Francisco Villegas.

"Do you have any further questions or comments?" asked David.

"If you have no more questions, I declare that this meeting is adjourned," was the final statement of David in the meeting.

In the morning of Friday, July 23, 1954, one month after Rosalie took the medical and physical examinations, they received a registered brown envelope from the World Travel Agency containing her passport and tourist visa to the United States. Rosalie was so excited when she received and opened the brown envelope and found her passport and visa and right away called David, who was with her father in the Liberty Haberdashery.

"This is David speaking," answered David.

"David, I have very good news for you. We received my passport and visa from the travel agency," was the excited news of Rosalie.

"Well, congratulations. We can schedule our departure to the United States as soon as possible," answered David.

"OK, David, I'll start preparing. I am excited just to think that this will be my first time to fly in an airplane," was the excited answer of Rosalie.

After the call of Rosalie to David, David right away called the World Travel Agency.

"Hello, this is the World Travel Agency," answered the receptionist. "This is Mr. David Scarborough. Can I talk to Ms. Medina please?" said David.

"Certainly, sir, please hold on," responded the receptionist as he connected his call to Ms. Medina.

"This is Sharon Medina speaking."

"Ms. Medina, this is Mr. David Scarborough. Can you get us a flight to the United States in three weeks? For my wife Rosalie and myself, from the Manila International Airport to the National Airport, Washington DC. I should be ready to leave the Philippines by then," asked David.

"OK. Let me see my record for the availability of a sitting arrangement with you and your wife. Is August 14, Saturday, OK with you, Pan Am flight 47 to San Francisco departing from the Manila International Airport 10:00 AM and connecting flight 77 to Washington National Airport, and you will have two hours' waiting time for your flight 77 to Washington National Airport?" asked Ms. Medina.

"That would be fine with me. I'll come by your office this afternoon after work and pick up our tickets and itinerary and pay you the cost of our travel and your services. Thank you for your help," said David.

"You are welcome, Mr. Scarborough. I'll expect you this afternoon. Bye," said Ms. Medina.

After work from the Liberty Haberdashery, with his father-in-law riding with him, he picked up their tickets and the itinerary of their travel and paid the World Travel Agency for the tickets and the services they did to secure the passport and visa of Rosalie. When they got home, Rosalie and Mrs. Nuevavista were in the kitchen, helping out with cooking for their dinner. David signaled to Mr. Nuevavista to just keep quiet and not to say anything. David left the brown envelope containing their tickets and their itinerary of travel on top the dining table and went upstairs, while Mr. Nuevavista proceeded to greet the two, who were busy in the kitchen.

"Oh, you are home" was the greeting of Mrs. Nuevavista.

"Yes, we just arrived," said Mr. Nuevavista.

"Where is David? I thought you were together?" asked Mrs. Nuevavista.

"He went upstairs. He thought that Rosalie was upstairs," said Mr. Nuevavista.

Rosalie went out of the kitchen to see David upstairs, when she noticed something on the dining table. She knew there was nothing there when she cleaned and cleared the dining table. Out of curiosity, she took the envelope and opened it.

"David! David! We got our tickets!" yelled Rosalie as she ran upstairs.

Rosalie ran to David and hugged him, kissed him, and showed him the itinerary and the tickets for both of them.

"David, I am surprised. Why are these on the dining table?" asked Rosalie.

"I put them there to surprise you," answered David.

"You are naughty," responded Rosalie as she kissed David on his lips and pinched him on the side of his belly.

The following Monday, July 26, David sent an official letter to the Fil-Am Real Estate Management Agency, to the office of Fernando Salazar, to the law office of Francisco Villegas, and a copy of the letter posted on the shops of the Liberty Haberdashery and Coffee Shop, announcing their official departure going to the United States on August 14, 1954.

Rosalie was so excited with her forthcoming departure to the United States. In the open, Mrs. Nuevavista was showing her smiles, but when she was left alone, behind closed door, she could not hold her tears. Rosalie had been her little angel, whom she nurtured and loved for many years, and she grew up like a beautiful princess under her care, and she would be leaving. Her departure was very painful for her but was something she had to accept. She was no longer her little girl. Somebody owned her love. She had to let her go. She wiped her tears and pretended to be happy and excited, but her heart was aching and crying. But the happiness of Rosalie was her happiness. So she had to give way for the sake of the love of Rosalie to David.

One weekend, two weeks before the scheduled departure of David and Rosalie, David heard the cry of his mother-in-law as she was talking with Rosalie in the kitchen. He slowly came close to the door to hear their conversation.

"Rosalie, I'll miss you. I have been crying since that day I knew you were leaving us," said Mrs. Nuevavista, as she continued crying, holding the hands of Rosalie.

"Ma, do not worry. We will come to visit you, and better, you can come to visit us in America," said Rosalie as she tried to appease the sadness of her mother.

David slowly went away so that the two would not notice that he was listening to their conversation. David went upstairs and waited for Rosalie to come up. He had to plan something to take his mother-in-law's mind from the forthcoming departure of Rosalie. A little later, Rosalie went upstairs looking for David.

"David, I was looking for you. I thought you were in the family room watching TV?" asked Rosalie.

"No, love, I am thinking about Mama Fina. She will just be lonely, alone in the house. How about if I ask her to work in the coffee shop just to keep her mind busy. What do you think?" asked David.

"I am not sure. Let us ask her if she would like to work in the coffee shop," answered Rosalie.

"Come on, let us ask her, and if she agrees, we can have her start on Monday," replied David.

David and Rosalie hurriedly went down to see Mrs. Nuevavista, who was still feeling sad after she conversed with Rosalie.

"Ma, David was suggesting if it is OK with you to work in the coffee shop so that you will not get bored in the house when we leave for the United States," asked Rosalie.

"I don't know. I have no experience in selling. I do not know if it would work?" answered Mrs. Nuevavista.

"Well, the only way to find out is to try it. Let's try it on Monday and see if you would like to work in a coffee shop?" requested David.

"OK, I'll try," answered Mrs. Nuevavista.

That evening, David called his partner, informing him that his mother-in-law would be working in the coffee shop. He also told Fernando to charge her salary to his interests in their partnership.

The following Monday, David while driving toward the stores told Mr. Nuevavista to put out all the necessary papers to be filled out by a new hire, Mrs. Nuevavista, and after dropping Mr. Nuevavista at the haberdashery, he accompanied Mrs. Nuevavista to the coffee shop. David introduced Mrs. Nuevavista to his coffee shop manager, Benito Sarmiento.

"Benito, please meet my mother-in-law, Mrs. Nuevavista. She is going to work with you to help you out in the coffee shop."

"Nice meeting you, Mrs. Nuevavista," was the greeting of Benito Sarmiento.

"Nice meeting you," responded Mrs. Nuevavista.

David introduced Mrs. Nuevavista to all the employees of the coffee shop. Then he invited her to his office to fill out all the necessary papers for a new employee.

"Papa Fredo, please give all the necessary papers to be filled up by Mama Fina as our new employee. Please help her if she has some questions," said David.

"Sure, David, I'll do that," answered Mr. Nuevavista.

After giving Mrs. Nuevavista all the forms to be completed, David went back to the coffee shop and talked to Benito and told him the reason why he wanted his mother-in-law to work there. He told Benito to be nice to her and to let her get involved in a lot of things in the shop. "Give her the liberty to talk to customers and do whatever is necessary to make her happy." David then returned to his office in the haberdashery and checked the forms completed by Mrs. Nuevavista. After going through the completed and signed forms, David accompanied Mrs. Nuevavista to the coffee shop and handed her to Benito. David left her and stayed in his office and once in while would look into the coffee shop and check on her. Apparently, Benito did a good job. Mrs. Nuevavista seemed happy with what she was doing and was happy talking to her co-workers and customers. David was relieved of his problem with his mother-in-law.

One week before the departure of David and Rosalie, David talked to his father-in-law about driving.

"Papa Fredo, do you know how to drive?" asked David.

"Yes, but I have not driven in a long time. But I guess you do not lose the skill," answered Mr. Nuevavista.

"Papa Fredo, when we leave the country, I have to leave to you my car.

You have to learn how to drive it," asked David.

"Well, I can try. I think I can still remember how to drive," replied Mr. Nuevavista.

"Come on, let's see if you can still remember how to drive," said David.

"Josefina, Rosalie, David, and I are going to drive around!" yelled Mr. Nuevavista.

"OK, be careful," answered back by Mrs. Nuevavista.

David let Mr. Nuevavista sit on the driver's seat and let him start the engine. But David was ready if it were necessary for him to extend his long legs to step on the brake just in case Mr. Nuevavista did a wrong move. But to the surprise of David, Mr. Nuevavista still retained his careful driving skills. They drove around. They even tried the heavy traffic going around Quiapo Church, sometimes even overtaking jeepneys stopping to pick up passenger. David was so satisfied with the driving skills of his father-in-law.

The last project that David did to make the departure of Rosalie was not so painful to her parents was to have Mr. Nuevavista drive the three of them to Dewey Boulevard along Manila Bay. On weekdays, in the afternoon, David would pick up Rosalie from home and drive back to the parking lot at the back of the store. David would get Mr. and Mrs. Nuevavista from the store, and he would let Mr. Nuevavista take the wheel, with Mrs. Nuevavista sitting on the passenger side while he and Rosalie stayed seated on the backseat. David would ask Mr. Nuevavista to drive to Dewey Boulevard. After Mr. Nuevavista parked the car along the side of the boulevard by the Manila Bay, the four would walk by the bay side, and David would buy some barbeque sticks and soft drinks, and they would sit on a bench and enjoy the fresh air from the bay. They did this routine every day until the day when David and Rosalie were about to leave for the United States.

Saturday, August 14, very early in the morning, David and Rosalie woke up and checked their luggage, their carry-on bags, their travel itineraries and plane tickets, visas, and passports. David, Rosalie, Mr. Nuevavista, and Mrs. Nuevavista ate their breakfast together. David was watching his in-laws if there would be a little expression of sadness, and it looked like what he did worked a little bit. Mrs. Nuevavista was telling about her experiences with the coffee shop, and Mr. Nuevavista was telling about his experiences in the haberdashery, and David was just smiling. But that happy breakfast was short-lived. When David and Rosalie were about to enter the security area of the airport, when Rosalie and David said good-bye, Mrs. Nuevavista started crying uncontrollably. Rosalie had to stay for a moment to calm down her mother. Then when Rosalie felt that her mother felt all right, she entered the security area, waving to her mother, who had tears in her eyes but was waving and smiling.

It was very painful for Mrs. Nuevavista to see her daughter leave their care. For so long, from birth, she tenderly cared for and loved her. Through the years, she watched her grow to a beautiful young lady, and now that she found the man she loved, they would be left lonesome and abandoned. But she had to give way to Rosalie's love because her happiness was their happiness. She cried with the feeling of giving up to the wishes of her beloved daughter, with the hope of her happiness in her new life to face as a wife. She waved her hands with tears in her eyes. Her heart could feel the pain of seeing her beloved daughter go, but with her hands waving to Rosalie and David, with a wish to them of a more bountiful tomorrow in the life that they had to face together.

# Chapter XXVI

## The Fulfilled Destiny

AFTER DAVID CHECKED into the counter and loaded their luggage onto the belt for transport to their flight, David led Rosalie to the customs area. Then they walked to the waiting area of the Pan Am. Seated in the waiting area, Rosalie could not help thinking of her mother crying. For the first time, her excitement to reach America changed to loneliness from missing her parents. She could not hold tears coming to her eyes as they rolled down her cheeks. David noticed the tears on the cheeks of Rosalie, and he wiped them with his hand and tenderly embraced her and whispered to her.

"I love you, Rosalie. We will see them soon. Do not worry. They will be all right. We have to test their ability to live a life without you around. You have your own life to live."

"Yes, I know. I have to be strong. I know they would be all right. It is that feeling of sadness of a daughter going away from her family. It is that daughter's emotion of seeing her mother crying, which made me feel sad. But we have to face the reality that I took the responsibility to be your wife, and I have to be with you wherever you want to take me. You are my husband," said Rosalie as she embraced David tightly.

David had his right arm around the shoulders of Rosalie, trying to comfort her, making her feel all right to leave her parents alone for some time. There would be more days to come and that they would come back someday to see her parents again. Then . . .

"Pan Am flight 47 ready for boarding!"

"Love, come on, we have to board the airplane. Are you ready?" asked David.
"Yes, I am coming, let's go," answered Rosalie.

David and Rosalie boarded Pan Am flight 47 to San Francisco as their port of entry and flight 77 from San Francisco to Washington National Airport. When the plane soared upward to gain height, Rosalie felt the deafening sound of the engine, and a little later, she felt as if everything around her was rotating.
"David, I am not feeling well. I think I am going to throw up," was the very low voice of Rosalie as she leaned back into her chair.
David stood and called the attention of the stewardess.
"Ma'am, please I need help. My wife is not feeling well. She is about to throw up. Can I have a brown bag please?" begged David.
The stewardess right away went to the end of the plane and got a brown bag and handed it to David.
"Thank you very much. Do you have by any chance any Bonamine or any tablet for motion sickness," asked David.
"Yes, sir. Let me get a couple for her to take," answered the stewardess. But before the stewardess could come with the medicine, Rosalie vomited and felt so weak and fell asleep after.
"Love, I have medicine for you to take. Please wake up," asked David. "No, David, I do not want to move my head. Please leave me alone for a while. Let me have some sleep, please," begged Rosalie as she leaned away from David and closed her eyes.

When dinner was served in the airline, David tried to wake Rosalie up, but she refused to move her head.
"Love, we have here your food still hot. Please eat something," begged David.
"No, David, please. I'll just be throwing up again. I better not eat anything. Let me sleep some more. I feel better with my eyes close, please," begged Rosalie.
David did not insist anymore and let Rosalie stay leaning back, which made her comfortable until they landed at the San Francisco

Airport. David let all the passengers get off before he woke Rosalie up, to give her more time to rest and recover. When Rosalie woke up, David had a glass of water ready for her.

"Love, wake up. We are here in America already," said David. A couple of stewardesses were watching them, concerned about the status of Rosalie.

"Oh, I have a headache," said Rosalie.

"Love, please take this medicine to relieve your headache," said David.

Rosalie took the medicine and drank a glass of water. David slowly guided the hand of Rosalie as she stood slowly. A stewardess helped put down their carry-on luggage from the top compartment and led them out to the door of the plane. Rosalie was finally able to regain her bearings and was able to walk straight while David was pulling their carry-on luggage to their port of entry. From the passport checkpoint and customs, David had to pay attention to Rosalie, who felt very weak. He had to hold on Rosalie as he led her to their waiting area for their next flight to Washington DC. In the waiting area, Rosalie just leaned back onto a chair and closed her eyes. After an hour, Rosalie finally was able to feel a little better. She woke up and felt hungry.

"David, I am hungry. Do we have something to eat?" asked Rosalie. "Do you feel better? Come on, let's walk to that restaurant across so that you can have some soup," suggested David.

David guided Rosalie across to the restaurant, and they ordered some soup. Rosalie felt better after she was able to have some warm soup.

"Do you want some bread?" asked David.

"No, thank you, this soup is fine with me," answered Rosalie.

After their soup, the two went back to the waiting area for their next flight to Washington DC. Rosalie felt a little better after eating some soup from the restaurant.

"I am so sorry, David. I am giving you so much trouble. This is my first time to board a plane, and my system is not ready for it. I hope you understand?" asked Rosalie in a tender voice.

"Love, you are under my care. I understand your feeling. You will be all right," said David.

They boarded flight 77 to Washington National Airport, and in the air, Rosalie felt very much better after taking Bonamine, given by the stewardess from flight 47 of Pan Am. But still she had that sense of instability and weakness, so she closed her eyes, leaning on David's shoulder, both her hands holding the arm of David. It was a sunny afternoon when they arrived at the Washington National Airport. David woke Rosalie up, but they waited until most of the passengers were all out before they stood, to give Rosalie time to recover from her long sleep. From the airplane to the baggage claim, Rosalie felt better and seemed to recover from the long flight. After they claimed their luggage from the long running belt, David led Rosalie outside of the airport and took a waiting taxi in front.

"Sir, we are going to PG County, but I would like to show my wife the tourist spots here in the DC area."

"Sure, sir," answered the taxi driver.

"David, did you tell your Dad that we are coming today?" asked Rosalie. "No! I would like to surprise him. That's why I want you to first see some beautiful scenery here in the nation's capital," said David, and they drove around to the Washington Monument, the Lincoln Memorial, the Jefferson

Memorial, the Washington Capitol Building, and the Potomac Park.

"David, let's go straight home. I want to rest. My head is aching. I have not fully recovered yet from the jet lag, please," begged Rosalie.

"OK. Sir, please can you take us to our house in PG County. Take 325 to 295, then to Indianhead Highway, and from there I'll guide you where our house is. Thank you," said David.

**The Scarborough Residence**

When David and Rosalie arrived at the beautiful mansion of the Scarborough family, Rosalie could not help but appreciate the well-cared-for flowering plants around, the well-trimmed grass so green, and the sprinkler that kept on showering water around. The taxi parked in front of the mansion, and the taxi driver unloaded their luggage. A little later, just after the taxi driver drove away and David was about to carry the luggage, John came from the back of the house, as he heard the sound of the taxicab.

"Hi, David, you are back. We did not know you are coming," was the greeting of John as he right away took the luggage and carried them to the mansion.

"John, this is my wife, Rosalie. She is still not feeling well, with the jet lag from our long flight from the Philippines," said David.

"Welcome to America, Mrs. Scarborough," was the greeting of John.

"Nice meeting you. Thank you," responded Rosalie.

John led the couple to the main door of the mansion, and when they opened the door, Anne and Martha came from the kitchen.

"Oh, David is here, welcome home!" was the simultaneous greeting of surprised Anne and Martha.

"Meet my wife, Rosalie, Anne and Martha," said David.

"It is nice to meet you," was the respectful answer by Rosalie.

The voices of Anne and Martha were heard by Dr. Scarborough, who was upstairs. He rushed to look downstairs to see David and Rosalie.

"Oh, David, Rosalie, you did not let us know you are coming. Anne, Martha, you set the table. I am sure David and Rosalie must be very hungry," was the instruction of Dr. Scarborough.

Dr. Scarborough walked down the stairs and greeted David and Rosalie.

He embraced Rosalie, who smiled in spite of her not feeling well.

"Welcome to our home here in America," was the greeting of Dr. Scarborough.

"You have a beautiful home. I am your new daughter in the family, Dad," was the confident response of Rosalie.

"This is your home. You are welcome here. How was your flight?" asked Dr. Scarborough, but David answered right away.

"Dad, we had a rough flight, a lot of turbulence, and Rosalie had to throw up, and she has not fully recovered yet. I have to take her to our room so that she can change to a more comfortable dress. Is that OK, Dad?"

"Sure, go ahead, I'll wait for both of you so that we can eat together," replied Dr. Scarborough.

David led Rosalie to their room, followed by John carrying all their luggage. After John left their room, "David, I want to take a shower to feel a little better to relieve my lightheadedness, please," asked Rosalie.

"Sure, we have a separate bathroom, toilet, and shower in this room. You get your clothes from the luggage, and I will prepare the shower for you. I'll set the right temperature of water so that you can just open the faucet and you will be set. OK?" said David.

Rosalie opened her luggage and pulled out her dresses and put them on top of the bed and selected the dress that she would like to wear, together with her underwear. She took her selected dress and new underwear to the bathroom. David showed her how to use the faucet and how to set the water temperature of the shower. Then David went out and let Rosalie enjoy the fresh water to relieve her headache. David went down to get the telephone directory for the metropolitan DC to look for the names of his classmates. After going through the names, the only name that he could find was the telephone number of the law firm of Robert Haynes. David wrote the telephone number of Bert Haynes and went back to their room to check on Rosalie.

"Love, are you OK?" asked David as he approached the door of the bathroom.

"Yes, I feel better," answered Rosalie as she opened the door and stepped out of the bathroom dressed in a nightgown.

"Good, come on, let's go down so that we can join Dad at the dinner table," said David as he held Rosalie on his arm to guide her to the door of the room and down to the first-floor level of the mansion.

At the dinner table, Dr. Scarborough was seated and waiting for the arrival of the couple.

"I have been waiting for both of you. The food is getting cold already," said Dr. Scarborough.

"Rosalie had to take her shower first to relieve her headache, Dad," answered David.

"Well, you both have a seat and enjoy the dinner," replied Dr. Scarborough.

"Thanks, Dad," answered Rosalie.

"By the way, Dad, I want to invite some of my high school classmates here to the house for a sort of reunion, so that Rosalie would at least meet some of my classmates and their families," said David.

"Super. I like that. I have not heard joyous music in the house since the death of your mom. Let's do that. Let's bring joy once again to this house," answered Dr. Scarborough.

"After dinner, I have to call Bert. He was my close friend in high school.

I'll find out where our other classmates are residing now," said David.

After dinner, David escorted Rosalie to their bedroom. He showed the controls of the room temperature (the thermostat), the switches, the closets, the beddings.

"Love, you have a good rest. You sleep well. I am going to call my classmate and see if we can have a reunion here in the house so that you will meet their families. I want you to have friends here in America," said David.

"OK. Do not stay long. I'll wait for you," said Rosalie.

"I still have to call him. I hope he's still in his office. It is almost 5:00 PM already. I'll be back," said David, and he kissed Rosalie tenderly on her lips, then rushed down to call Bert Haynes.

"This is Robert Haynes Law Office, may I help you?" answered the receptionist.

"Yes, can I talk to Bert Haynes, please?" asked David.

"Yes, sir. Hold on please," requested the receptionist.

"Yes, this is Bert Haynes, may I help you?" answered Robert Haynes. "Bert, this is David, your classmate in high school. I just came back from abroad, and I want to invite our classmates to have a reunion in the house," said David.

"David, welcome back. I have not heard from you since we graduated from high school. Come down to my office so that we can have a long talk," suggested Bert.

"Where is your office?" asked David.

"You will not miss it. My office is behind St. Matthew Cathedral. You have to take Eighteenth Street from Penn Avenue, right on N Street. N Street is one-way. The only townhouse with a wide window, you will see me. I'll work late and wait for you," explained Bert.

"I think I know the place. I'll see you in an hour. Thank you and good-bye," answered David.

"See you. Good-bye," was the final reply of Bert.

After David put down the phone, he went upstairs and talked to Rosalie. "Love, I have to go out to see my classmate Bert. You just go to sleep, and

I'll be back soon. OK?" said David.

"Do not stay long. I won't be able to sleep without you by my side. OK?" said Rosalie.

"OK, love, I'll try not to stay long," said David as he headed downstairs to talk to his dad.

"Dad, can I borrow your car? I have to meet my classmate Bert downtown. I should not stay long."

"Sure, here is the key. Drive carefully," advised Dr. Scarborough.

"Thank you, Dad," was the respectful answer of David.

It was around 6:00 PM when David headed toward downtown DC. From Penn Avenue he turned right onto Eighteenth Street, then made a right at N Street. He right away saw the building, but he had to look for a parking spot along N Street. After he parked the car, he walked toward the building, when he saw, inside the lighted office, Bert with his hands up and a man pointing a gun at him. David was stunned.

*("Mary Scarlet, David is going to the building with that robber pointing a gun at his friend. What shall we do?"*
*"Rosemarie we have to think quickly. I have to make that stone near him glitter so that it will call his attention to use it as a weapon.")*

**A picture of the stone seen by David as he was running towards the office of Bert Haynes.**

David was going to rush to the aid of his friend when he noticed a stone that was glittering. He picked up the stone and ran to the entrance door of the building and up to the floor where the office of Bert was located, and he slowly opened the door. The gunman turned to David, but before he could pull the trigger of his gun, David had already thrown the stone, hitting him on the forehead. The gunman fell on his back on the floor like a heavy log. Bert was shocked of what he witnessed.

"Bert, are you OK?" asked David.

"Yes, I am fine. You just came on time. Thank you for saving me," said Bert as he knelt to check the pulse of the gunman.

"He is dead, David. We have to call the police to report the incident," said Bert.

Bert called the police and reported what happened.

"I did what I was trained to do," said David as he knelt to check the dead man.

After he checked the pulse, something called his attention—the scar under his left eye, the mole on the right nose, a birthmark between his eyes, thick lips, big nose, and the deformed right ear. Then in his emotional jubilation, he yelled, "Mother, I killed him. I killed Brutus Diablo!"

"What did you say, David?" asked Bert, who was so curious with the reaction of David.

"Bert, he was the man who shot my mother. I killed him," answered David.

When the police arrived, they started the investigation. The detective took pictures of the site of the crime, the dead gunman, and the location of the stone, the gun and then put the gun in a bag. The detective asked questions while the police was processing the scene of the crime.

"Sir, you tell me what happened," said the detective.

"Sir, I am Robert Haynes. This is my law office. I was working when this man came and held me up. My friend came and hit him with a rock on the head. When we checked his pulse, he was already dead," explained Bert.

"Sir, my name is David Scarborough. When I was coming to see Mr. Haynes, I saw from outside of the building this gunman holding up Mr. Haynes. I picked up a stone and rushed upstairs, and before he could fire the gun at me, I was able to throw the stone, hitting him on the forehead."

"Mr. Robert Haynes and Mr. David Scarborough, you have to go with us to the police station. We have to continue the investigation in our headquarters," was the invitation of the police investigator.

The DC police and detectives escorted Bert and David into their cruiser, and the two were driven to the police headquarters for further investigation.

# Chapter XXVII

## The Reunion

IN A POLICE cruiser escorted by two police cars, David and Bert were brought to the DC police headquarters for questioning to continue the investigation for the death of the gunman in the law office of Robert Haynes. The lead detective, Henry Davis, after taking all personal information from David and Bert, started questioning Bert Haynes.

"Mr. Haynes, let me start with you," said the detective. "You were in your law office working when the guy came into your office with a gun?"

"Yes, Detective," answered Bert.

"What did you do when he came with the gun? Was the gun pointed at you?" asked the detective.

"He came into my office and pointed his gun at me, so I raised my hands.

He was demanding money," answered Bert.

"So what happened? Did he do something else?" asked the detective.

"Everything went so fast. All I remember as I was looking at the man, the door opened, and he looked at the door and was about to point the gun at the door, but before he could react, a stone hit his forehead, and he fell backward on the floor. When Mr. Scarborough came in and I checked the pulse of the man, he was already dead," explained Bert.

"Thank you very much for your statement, Mr. Haynes," said the detective. "Mr. Scarborough, how did you know that your friend Mr. Haynes was being robbed?" asked the detective.

"I was on my way to see Mr. Haynes, when from the window, I saw a man pointing a gun on him, and Mr. Haynes's hands were both raised. I picked up a solid rock and rushed to the building and to his office, and when I opened the door and the man was going to point the gun on me, I went ahead and threw the stone, hitting him on the forehead. He tumbled backward and fell on his back. When Mr. Haynes checked his pulse, he was already dead. That was the time when he called the police."

"Thank you very much for your statement, Mr. Scarborough," said the detective. "For this time, I am going to release you in your own cognizance. I have no reason to hold both of you this time, but I may call you anytime to continue our investigation further. For now I will let both of you go. I may call you in the next couple of days after we finish the investigation of the man killed. We have to determine if it is a homicide, self-defense, or murder. We will let you know the result of our investigation," explained the detective, and he called one of the policemen.

"Officer Marvin, please drive them back to their cars, near the crime scene, so that they can go home. Thank you, Officer Marvin," said the detective.

Officer Marvin with another policeman drove David and Bert to N Street, near the law office of Bert Haynes. Inside the cruiser, David and Bert were in complete silence, not talking, which might complicate their situation in the presence of two police officers. David got off the cruiser, followed by Bert.

"David, there is an Old Tavern Hotel and Restaurant not far from here.

Come on, let's have some drink," was the invitation of Bert.

"Sure, let's take away the stress from us. I am sure we can get through this," said David.

"Yes! I know. In the next couple of days, we will find out what is going to happen," replied Bert.

The two walked to the Old Tavern Hotel and Restaurant, which was along N Street. When they entered the tavern, a lady waitress approached them.

"Just the two of you?" asked the waitress.

"Yes, please," answered Bert.

The lady waitress led David and Bert to a table. And after they had been seated, the waitress gave them the menu.

"Do you want something to drink?" asked the waitress.

"Give us two of your imported beers please?" said Bert.

"David, they have a very good steak here. Would you like to try their version of steak?" asked Bert.

"Sure, I may just as well try their specialty. Thank you," said David.

Bert turned to the waitress and made the order.

"Miss, we want two of your specialty steaks, medium rare, and mashed potatoes to go with it. Please give us a serving of your peanuts to go with our beer. Thank you," ordered Bert.

"So, David, what's up? You just returned from the Philippines?"

"Yes, Bert, and I want to have a reunion with our friends and their families in our house. Remember Arthur Silver, Steven Cohen, and Vincent Brown? I went through the directory, and I did not see their names. I just got married, and I want my old friends to meet my wife. Do you remember Kevin Smith, that little boy when we were in our first year in high school?"

"Yes, I remember him," answered Bert.

"He has grown very tall and was drafted by the marine. We met in the death march. He saved me when I was going to be attacked by a Japanese soldier. I fell on the ground helpless, and before a Japanese soldier could get to me, David snatched me from the ground and carried me on his shoulders for almost two hours. When I gained consciousness, we escaped from the death march and joined the guerilla headed by Capt. Joseph Lee. It was a very long story, but I'll try to find Kevin. I think he is in New York," explained David.

"Wow, you really had an adventure in the Philippines. So when are you intending to have the reunion?" asked Bert.

"As soon as I find the families of our classmates. I have more than a month to work on it, so my initial plan is to have it the Sunday before Columbus Day, which is this coming October 10. Columbus

Day is the second Monday in October, which is the eleventh. After the reunion, everybody has enough time to travel back to their homes."

"That would be great. Give me a call as soon as you have contacted our classmates. I will certainly bring my family to join the party," said Bert.

"Certainly, you had been my best friend in high school. I want you and your family to be there," answered David.

After having a couple of drinks, David and Bert headed out to the car of David, and David drove Bert to the parking lot where the car of Bert was parked.

"Thanks, for giving me a lift," said Bert.

"Thank you for the dinner. I'll keep in touch. Bye," were the parting words of David.

"Bye," said Bert as he entered his car, while David drove away, going back home.

After David arrived in their mansion and parked the car in the garage, he entered the door leading to the living room and was surprised to see his dad waiting for him.

"Oh, Dad, you are still awake?" asked David.

"Yes, I was waiting for you. This is your first time back here in the United States, and you stayed very late. I was kind of worried already," answered Dr. Scarborough.

"It is a long story, Dad. I met my classmate Bert in a very unusual situation. He was being held up in his law office, and I came to his aid, and I accidentally killed the bad guy when I threw a stone, hitting him on the forehead. He fell backward and never regained consciousness. He died on the spot. We were brought to the police headquarters for our sworn statements and were released at our own cognizance. Do you know, Dad, the guy whom I killed? It was Brutus Diablo, the man who killed Mom."

"What?" was the surprised word of Dr. Scarborough.

"Yes, Dad. I do not know if there will be a case against me for killing him. But I am confident that what I did was self-defense. I hit him with the stone before he could squeeze the trigger of his gun as he pointed the barrel at me. We will see what happens. Bert is a lawyer. I am sure he will help me if it comes to litigation. He was the sole witness of the case," explained David.

"Whatever happens, I'll back you up on this, David," replied Dr. Scarborough.

"Thank you, Dad. You go to sleep now. I am home safely, and I am heading to our room," said David.

"OK, David, good night," said Dr. Scarborough, and he also headed to his room.

"Good night, Dad," said David.

When David entered their room, expecting Rosalie to be sleeping, as she was complaining of her jet lag, he was surprised to see Rosalie sitting on a chair, waiting for him.

"Love, why are you not sleeping yet? Are you not tired from our trip? You said you have jet lag and you were lightheaded," questioned David.

"I could not sleep without you by my side. Since I could not sleep, I just sat down and waited for you," answered Rosalie.

"Let me just take my shower, and I'll be with you, OK? I smell dirty. I do not want to sleep by your side with a bad smell," answered David as he headed to the shower.

The following day after breakfast, David right away started looking for a possible private detective agency that he could hire to find his other classmates. The one that attracted him the most was the Miller Private Investigating Agency, owned by Anthony Miller, who used to work with the CIA and was a retired marine. He dialed the number of the agency.

"This is the Miller Private Investigating Agency. May I help you?" answered the receptionist.

"Can I talk to Mr. Anthony Miller please?" said David.

"Yes, sir, may I know who is calling?" answered the receptionist.

"This is David Scarborough, and I would like to talk to him regarding people I want him to look for," answered David.

"Hold on please," answered the receptionist.

"Hello, this is Anthony Miller speaking," said Mr. Miller on the other line. "Yes, Mr. Miller. I am David Scarborough, and I want to hire you to find some people for me," answered David.

"Sure, please come to my office so that we can discuss the details of what you want me to do. OK?" said Mr. Miller.

"Can I see you this afternoon?" asked David.

"Let me see my schedule first. OK, how about around 2:00 PM?" asked Mr. Miller.

"Sure, I'll see you at 2:00 PM."

"Do you have my address?" asked Mr. Miller. "Yes, sir, I got it from your ads in the directory."

"OK, I'll see you at 2:00 PM. Good-bye," said Mr. Miller as he put down the phone.

That afternoon, David met Anthony Miller in his office and gave the names of his classmates—Arthur Silver, Steven Cohen, and Vincent Brown. They all graduated from the Bishop McNamara High School. He also added the name of Kevin Smith, who was a marine before and during the Second World War and was part of the death march. David wanted their telephone numbers and addresses. They agreed on the cost of the search, payable upon accomplishment of the job.

When David arrived that afternoon after meeting with Mr. Anthony Miller at the Miller Investigating Agency, "David, a certain Henry Davis from the DC Police Department called. He said he will call again. He did not leave a message," said Dr. Scarborough.

"I do not have his number. I'll just wait for his call," answered David as he went straight to his room to see Rosalie.

"How is my love?" said David. Rosalie was sitting in front of the dresser fixing herself. She just took her shower.

"I am OK. How was your day so far?" asked Rosalie.

"It has been good. I have been to an investigating agency to locate some of my classmates in high school. I want to invite them here into the house for a sort of reunion. As a way of introducing them to you so you will have some people that you would know here in the United States," answered David.

"I am already happy with you by my side," replied Rosalie.

"We do not want to live a lonely life. We have to socialize. We have to meet people. OK?" answered David.

They were in the middle of their conversation, discussing the intention of David to invite his classmates, when the telephone rang.

"David, you have a call!" yelled Dr. Scarborough.

David went down to answer the phone.

"Hello, this is David Scarborough speaking."

"Mr. Scarborough, this is Detective Henry Davis of the DC Police Department. We have identified the man that you have accidentally killed in the law office of Robert Haynes. His name is Brutus Diablo, an escaped prisoner from jail. He had a very long list of crimes committed against society and was a wanted when you accidentally killed him. We will not file any case against you and would declare your case closed. So you have nothing to worry about coming to our headquarters. Your name will be cleared of killing Mr. Brutus Diablo."

"Thank very much, Detective Davis, for everything," answered David. "Do you have any further questions, Mr. Scarborough?" asked Detective Davis.

"Do I have to do anything, Detective?" asked David.

"No. We have cleared your name of any criminal responsibility," answered Detective David.

"Thank you, Detective Davis," said David.

"You are welcome, Mr. Scarborough, and good-bye," were the ending words of Detective Davis.

"Bye, sir," responded David as he put down the phone.

David right away called his best friend, Bert. "Yes, can I help you?" said the receptionist. "Can I talk to Mr. Haynes please?" said David. "Hold on please," answered the receptionist. "This is Robert Haynes speaking."

"Bert, this is David. I got a call from Detective Henry Davis. My name was cleared. The man I accidentally killed was an escapee from prison and had a long list of crimes. He was wanted by the police when I accidentally killed him," explained David.

"That is a great news, David," answered Bert.

"Also, I have already hired a detective agency to look for our classmates. I am looking forward to having our reunion on October 10. Cross your fingers," said David.

"Well, I'll be there with my family, David. Thank you for the update and the good news," replied Bert.

"Well, I'll expect you and your family at the party. It should be a good one. OK, I just wanted to update you on things, Bert. I'll talk to you later," said David.

"Bye, David," replied Bert.

Wednesday, September 8, 1954, Mr. Anthony Miller completed his research on the names and addresses of the classmates of David, including the telephone number and address of Kevin Smith. Mr. Miller right away called David.

"Hello, can I talk to Mr. David Scarborough?"

"Yes, this is David. How can I help you?" said David.

"Mr. Scarborough, this Anthony Miller. I have completed the project you assigned for me to accomplish. You can come to my office so that we can clear your account," said Mr. Miller.

"Sure, Mr. Miller, I am going to your office right away," said David. David right away went to the office of the Miller Investigating Agency and met with Anthony Miller. Mr. Miller presented to David the telephone numbers and addresses of his classmates, including the phone number and address of Kevin Smith in New York City. After paying Mr. Miller the agreed costs of services, David went straight home to talk to his dad.

"Dad, I got the phone numbers and addresses of my classmates. I'll be calling them to invite them to our house for a reunion. Is that OK with you, Dad?" asked David.

"Sure, go ahead so that we can play some music around here."

"Thank you, Dad," said David, and he started calling his classmates.

"Hello, Arthur, this is David Scarborough, your classmate at Bishop McNamara High School."

"Oh, it has been a long time that I have not seen you, David. I am here in California, teaching in middle school," answered Arthur Silver.

"Yes, I know. I hired an investigator to look for you, and I would like to invite you and your family to a family reunion at our house—your wife and your children. How many children do you have?" asked David.

"I have two children. How about you?" asked Arthur.

"I just got married and want to introduce her to the families of my high school classmates. I will schedule the reunion on the tenth of October, and make reservations for you and your family at the Hilton for two nights at downtown DC. I'll send you the invitation together with your plane tickets from California to Washington DC."

"Wow! That would be great. That would be a chance for my kids to see Washington DC," replied Arthur.

"I'll arrange all this scheduling in the next couple of weeks. Thank you very much and expect my invitation in your next mail. Good-bye, Arthur."

"Bye, David."

David also called Dr. Steven Cohen, who was practicing in the state of Ohio, and Engr. Vincent Brown, who was employed by the Engineering Company in the state of Texas. Both of them agreed to come with their families to the reunion. After calling Dr. Steven and Engr. Vincent, he turned to Capt. Kevin Smith of the New York City Police Department.

"This is Kevin Smith, may I help you?" answered Kevin on the phone. "Kevin, this is David Scarborough. How are you?"

"David, long time no see. I am doing fine, how about you?" asked Kevin. "Kevin, I finally got married, and I am going to have a party at our house in Maryland, and I want to invite you and your family so that you can meet my wife," said David.

"Oh, that is good. When are you going to have the party?" asked Kevin. "It would be on the tenth of October, the Sunday before Columbus Day," said David.

"Well, that is great. That is a long weekend. Sure, that is an easy drive from New York," answered Kevin.

"I'll send you an invitation together with your two nights' reservation, October 9 and 10, at the Hilton in downtown DC. So that you can have some time to go around tourist spots in DC, and then you come to our party the night of the tenth with your family. How many children do you have?" asked David.

"No. We don't have children yet. It is just me and my wife, Pam. We will surely want to see you and meet your wife," said Kevin.

"So, Kevin, I expect you to come to our party on the night of the tenth of October," asked David.

"Yes, definitely, Pam and I will drive from New York to DC and will check in at the Hilton. I'll wait for the invitation. OK, thank you," was the assuring answer of Kevin.

"Thank you, Kevin. Good-bye," were the closing words of Kevin as he hung up the phone. Then David came to see his dad.

"Hi, Dad, we are all set. All my closest friends and their families are coming for the reunion. The reunion would be scheduled on the tenth of October. That is next month, Sunday, before Columbus Day, at seven in the evening," said David.

"Well, we have to hire a band to play the music, and we have to have lighting around the mansion. We have to order fresh flowers for the occasion so that everything would look nice and beautiful. We have to select a good caterer to serve good food to the guests. We have to set tables for each family. We have to prepare programs to make the occasion lively. There will be dancing, and you can ask each of your friends to speak about their journey from the time they left high school," explained Dr. Scarborough.

"That is a very good Idea, Dad. For the meantime, I have to get the help of Rosalie in designing a nice invitation. Thank you, Dad," said David as he rushed to see Rosalie.

"Love, I need your help," asked David.

"What help do you need?" asked Rosalie.

"I need your skills on designs. I have to go to the printing press to print for us some beautiful and personalized invitations. I want you to come with me and help me select the best design for an invitation for our reunion," begged David.

"Sure, whenever you want me to go, I am available."

David and Rosalie went to the printing press to select and order the printing of invitations for the reunion. Rosalie helped pick the style of the invitations, which was not only beautiful but also attractive. From the printing press, they went straight to the World Travel Agency and bought the round-trip tickets for the families of Arthur Silver, Dr. Steven Cohen, and Vincent Brown. After they had secured the tickets and travel itineraries for the three families, they went straight to Hilton downtown and made reservation for the ninth and the tenth of October for the families of Arthur Silver, Dr. Steven Cohen, and Engr. Vincent Brown and for Kevin and his wife, Pam. Rosalie and David went home feeling good after they had accomplished everything on their schedule. They just had to wait for the printed invitations, which should be ready in a couple of days.

When David and Rosalie got home, David called Bert.

"Bert, this is David. How are you?" asked David.

"Hi, David, I am fine. What's up?" asked Bert.

"Well, my mission is accomplished. All our closest friends will be coming to the reunion. I expect you to be there. I will send you the invitation, which should be ready in a couple of days. Expect it in your mail," said David.

"Thank you. I'll expect it," said Bert.

"I'll talk to you later, good-bye," said David.

"Bye, David," replied Bert.

After a couple of days, David picked up the printed invitations from the printing press. From the printing press, they passed by the office supplies store to buy some brown envelopes for the mailing of the invitations, tickets, travel itineraries, and hotel reservations for those out of town. They sent an invitation and hotel reservations to Kevin Smith and his wife and an invitation to Bert and his family.

One week before the reunion, David called each of the invited guests to confirm their arrival. David also confirmed the band that would provide the music for the occasion, the caterer, the furnishing and lightings, the flower arrangements, and the sound system. In addition, David hired a party moderator, who would make announcements of the program. Dr. Scarborough had also invited some of his friends and previous co-workers in the hospitals and some prominent dignitaries in the State of Maryland and Washington DC.

On October 9, the day before the scheduled party, John was already very busy clearing everything to give way to the arrival of tables and chairs, the installation of the stage, and the dance floor. The electricians installed all the lighting system and the sound system, and they also put a provisional kitchen in the back area of the mansion to warm the food if necessary.

The morning of October 10, the florist delivered the flowers. Each table had a bouquet of red roses and also at the entrance of the mansion, at the gate, and around the first floor. The first floor of the mansion was set for hard drinks, soft drinks, hot coffee, ice water, and tables for appetizers. The side door of the mansion led to the dancing area, where they installed the stage and tables and chairs for the guests.

At around seven in the evening of October 10, the visitors started to come one by one. At the door of the mansion were Dr. Scarborough,

David, and Rosalie. Dr. Scarborough would welcome his visitors and introduce them to David and Rosalie. Then the names were announced by the program moderator, and they were given their table number and were led to the appetizer area. David would welcome his visitors and would introduce them to Rosalie and to Dr. Scarborough. The names were also announced by the program coordinator using the mike, and they were also given the number for their table as they were led to the appetizer and drinks area. When all the expected visitors of Dr. Scarborough were already in the mansion, he left David and Rosalie at the door. The families of Arthur Silver, Engr. Vincent Brown, and Bert Haynes had already come in and were already introduced by David to Dr. Scarborough and Rosalie. David had led them to the appetizer area, then to their tables. Then he went back to the side of Rosalie. When Dr. Steven Cohen and his family arrived, David introduced them to Rosalie. Their arrival was announced by the moderator, and David momentarily left Rosalie to lead the family to get some appetizers and drinks and then led them to their table.

Rosalie was left alone at the main door of the mansion to welcome the incoming visitors, when Kevin and his wife, Pam, arrived. When Kevin looked at the main door of the mansion and saw Rosalie with the lights coming from her back, it looked like she was floating in the air, all dressed in white. Kevin's eyes almost fell down from their sockets, and he almost run scared.

"Kevin, where are you going? There is a lady at the door receiving guests," said Pam to a scared Kevin.

"No. That is a ghost. We buried her in the mountain. I was there. What is she doing here? We better leave now," said Kevin.

"No. Kevin, we are already here. Why should you be afraid? You stay here, and I'll come to see her. We traveled a long way, and I'll not just go away," insisted Pam.

Kevin was hesitant to approach the door of the mansion, where Rosalie was standing. When Rosalie saw the couple at the gate, she was going to approach them, when David came from behind.

"What's wrong, love? Where are you going?"

"There are two guests there at the gate that are hesitant to come in. I am not sure why," said Rosalie.

When Kevin saw David side by side with Rosalie, Kevin could not believe what he was seeing. Pam walked toward David and Rosalie, and Kevin walked behind Pam.

"Welcome, Captain and Mrs. Kevin Smith," was the greeting of David.

Kevin still could not believe what he was seeing.

"Please meet my wife, Rosalie," was the introduction of David.

"David, I thought she was Rosemarie. I was so scared when I looked at her with rays of light coming from her back. I thought I was seeing a ghost."

"Yeah, Kevin, my wife Rosalie is the first cousin of Rosemarie. Rosalie's mother is the sister of Cmdr. Artemio Borromeo. They both look exactly the same. They are like twins. OK, come on, let's get inside and enjoy the food and the music. We have a long night to talk about many things," said David.

When all the invited guests were already inside the reception hall, they started serving the food while the music was playing. They had string instruments of violins, a cello, a bass string, a piano, an accordion, and trumpets.

After dinner was served, Kevin stood up and requested everybody for a toast as he announced, "Friends, ladies and gentlemen, let's rise and hold on to our glass of champagne and have a toast for the strong bonding love of David and Rosalie, to wish them a long-lasting happiness together in their long journey of building a blissful family." Everybody stood up and had a toast dedicated to David and Rosalie's successful married life.

After the toast, the coordinator started the program. Each classmate of David went to the stage to speak about their journey from high school to where they were residing.

Arthur Silver said that they moved to California from Washington DC because his wife was tired of winter and just wanted to live in a state where there are only sunny and rainy seasons.

Dr. Steven Cohen took his medical career from the Ohio State University, and he decided to practice his profession in the same state.

Engr. Vincent Brown graduated from the University of Maryland, College of Engineering, but got a job offer in the state of Texas, so he decided to just live there.

Robert Haynes graduated from Georgetown College of Law and decided to practice his profession in the Washington DC area.

Capt. Kevin Smith talked about his experience in the death march in Bataan and how he escaped with David and became a member of a guerilla unit that trained on the top of Mount Mariveles in Bataan, mastering the precision killing of their enemies in seconds. He explained that they were taught the art of killing like dancing, where you have a partner that you have to kill in seconds without any sound. They became the Silent Killers, whose mission was to overtake Japanese sentries silently during the ungodly hours after midnight.

Dr. Scarborough spoke that David was very much loved by his mother. That David was the apple of her eyes. That the first thing Mary Scarlet was looking for when she got home from work was David and David was so down after the death of his mother. He also mentioned how proud he was to have Rosalie as his daughter-in-law. That her parents were so nice and hospitable and they loved Rosalie very much.

David spoke about the courtship with Rosalie. He said that he asked permission from the parents of Rosalie to court her and without hesitation was given that. He explained that although he was visiting Rosalie, his strategy was to first court the parents. He said that when he was able to gain the trust and confidence of the parents, he started courting Rosalie. But when they discovered that they were engaged and wanted to get married, the mother became hysterical. And when she regained herself, she threw on him a barrage of questions, as if he were being tried in court. (Everybody laughed and clapped their hands.) David further mentioned that eventually he was able to win back the trust and confidence of Rosalie's parents, and they let them get married.

After the program, the moderator declared that the dance floor was open for everybody. David and Rosalie danced together with the other members of his class.

"Love, are you happy tonight socializing with everybody?" asked David. "Yes, definitely. This is the first big event that I ever attended. Thank you for the experience," answered Rosalie.

"Love, you know how much I love you, and I'll do whatever is necessary to make you happy," said David.

"David, you call me 'love.' I call you David because that is the name that I have learned to love, the name that had been printed in my heart, and the name that I will love forever. I am happy and lucky to have you as my husband for life. Thank you for coming to my life. David, I love you," said Rosalie with tenderness and sincerity.

"Rosalie, I love you," responded David as he kissed Rosalie on the lips, while everybody in the crowd clapped their hands and yelled in celebration, hitting their champagne glasses with their spoons.

> *(The spirits of Mary Scarlet and Rosemarie were watching the whole event, and when they thought that they had already accomplished what they had to accomplish with David, Mary Scarlet said, "Rosemarie, we could see that both David and Rosalie are very happy. We have together watched David in his journey, and now that they are settled and ready to raise a family, our mission here is over. Rosemarie, we have to leave the Mother Earth and just wish David and Rosalie happiness and that their love for each other will last forever."*
> *"Yes, Mary Scarlet, we have to wish them love for each other, the love that both of us could not share with David."*
>
> *The spirits of Mary Scarlet and Rosemarie left this Mother Earth hand in hand, with their hearts filled with* Love That They Could Not Share.*)*

# Glossary

Acacia Tree – A big shade tree very common in the Philippines. They can be found in parks, along the riverbanks, and farms. In the story, under the acacia tree was the meeting place of the main character David and Rosemarie, where the two fell in love.

Binondo – The Chinatown in the city of Manila, the center of Chinese businesses, restaurants, and retail and wholesale stores, believed to be the oldest Chinatown in the world.

Bataan – The province along Manila Bay, which served as the frontline battlefield during the Second World War.

Baguio City – The summer capital of the Philippines, located in the northern part of the island of Luzon, around 244 kilometers, or over 151 miles, from the city of Manila—a travel time of three hours and thirty minutes.

Bayan Ko - A Filipino song famous in the Philippines during and after the Second World War. The song was composed and popularized by artist Freddie Aguilar. The message of the song is my country, the Philippines my beloved.

Calabasa – Yellow squash native in the Philippines, raised and cultivated in farms for food.

Carabao – Water buffalo native to the Philippines, sometimes called Philippine beast. They are strong animals commonly used to plow the fields for farming.

Caldereta – Native Filipino spicy dish cooked from goat meat, commonly served in the villages of the Philippines.

Cavinti – A town in Laguna Province close to the Sierra Madre Mountain Range. It is the hometown of Cmdr. Artemio Borromeo in the story.

Chicken Labuyo – Wild chicken commonly found in the wilderness of the Sierra Madre Mountain Range, hunted for their delicious meat. In the book, they also hunted for wild chicken labuyo for meat in addition to wild pigs and deer.

Commander – The title given to Artemio Borromeo in the story as he headed the group of guerilla occupying the Sierra Madre

Mountains, overlooking the province of Laguna. Commander Borromeo formed a community made up of a non-offensive guerilla unit on the top of the Sierra Madre Mountains, because they did not want to be under Japanese rule.

Death March – The line of Filipino and American prisoners after the Fall of Bataan, forced to walk the over seventy-five-mile distance from Mariveles, Bataan, to the prisoners' concentration camp in San Fernando, Pampanga. The journey was characterized by Japanese brutality, death by execution, and beheading of the exhausted, hungry, and thirsty prisoners.

Deliverance – The rescue operation planned and successfully accomplished by the guerilla unit to free Commandeer Borromeo, the father of Rosemarie in the story.

"Dungawin Mo Hirang" – A popular serenade song in Tagalog during the early days, asking a sweetheart to look out the window to see who is serenading.

Emancipation – The liberation of the Philippines from Japanese rule. The cost of liberty, with thousands of lives wasted—Filipinos, Americans, and Japanese—and the country was left in total ruin. Capt. Joseph Lee and Commander Borromeo led their guerilla groups to emancipate the province of Laguna, starting from the town of Cavinti.

Entrapment – The military operation applied by the group led by Capt. Joseph Lee by luring the greater number of enemies to a line of firepower. The guerilla group would burn a small Japanese sentry after they had killed all the guards. Then the group would wait for the Japanese reinforcement in a line formation along the road, ready for the kill.

Guava Leaves – Foliage of guava trees boiled in water to make tea.

Jeepney – A modified military jeep made to accommodate more passengers in the back of the driver, used to transport traveling passengers for a certain fee.

La Loma – A place in Quezon City famous for their roasted pig, locally called *lechon*, around three kilometers away from the city of Manila.

Lechon – Whole pig stuck and tied to a rotating pole, roasted above burning charcoal until it becomes crispy and cooked.

Lightning – The name of the horse that David trained and used in his missions to attack the Japanese in revenge for the death of his beloved Rosemarie.

Makapili – Filipino spies who worked for the Imperial Japanese Army to report guerilla activities during the Japanese occupation of the Philippines.

Manila Cathedral – The Roman Catholic Basilica, also called the Manila Metropolitan Cathedral or the Cathedral Basilica of the Immaculate Conception, which is located in Intramuros, in the city of Manila, where the wedding of David and Rosalie in the story was celebrated.

Manila Hotel – The oldest prime hotel in the city of Manila, overlooking the scenic view of the Manila Bay, where the reception of the wedding in the story was held. There were several scenes in the story held at the Manila Hotel.

Mariveles – The southernmost town of the province of Bataan along the Manila Bay. It was the dead end of the Bataan Provincial Road during the Second World War. It was the center of the fierce battle during the Japanese invasion of the Philippines.

Masaharo Homma – The Japanese lieutenant general who commanded the transport of the prisoners of war in the death march, forcing the prisoners to walk the more than seventy-five miles under the vicious and cruel hands of his soldiers. He was later found guilty at the end of the war and was executed by firing squad.

Miraculous Medal – A medal with the picture of the Virgin Mary, believed to protect and save from danger those who would wear it all the time. It was the gift of Rosemarie to David on his way to a surveillance operation at the Cavinti municipal building, where Commander Borromeo was held prisoner.

Mestiza – Half-bred Filipina mixed with another foreign breed, like Spanish or English. Usually taller than ordinary Filipino women. Rosemarie and Rosalie in the story were both mestizas.

Molotov Bomb – The bomb used in the story was made of a bottle filled with gasoline, sealed tight with cloth at the bottle neck, with a string as a wick.

Pagsanjan Waterfalls – The famous waterfalls located in the province of Laguna, a tourist spot around 123 kilometers, or 76 miles, from the city of Manila, with a travel time of over two hours. It took a much longer travel time in the story because of the bumpy and uneven roads, and the cars then were slower.

Pampanga River – Runs from the Sierra Madre Mountains to Manila Bay. Around 260 miles long, used by the guerrilla unit headed by Capt. Joseph Lee as guide to reach the top of the Sierra Madre Mountains as they escaped the province of Bataan.

Papaya River – The river located in Mount Mariveles, which the guerilla unit led by Capt. Joseph Lee in the story used as supply of freshwater, on whose banks they built their shelters during the initial training of the guerilla unit.

Partnership – Refers to the legal agreement between David Scarborough and Fernando Salazar to establish a business together, with David Scarborough as administrator and Fernando as the finance officer. The two formed the Liberty Partnership together.

Premarital Counseling – The preparation of the couple to be married to give them a sense of direction in their relationship as husband and wife, within the bounds of morality, and for them to develop their outlook regarding parenthood. In the story, both David and Rosalie attended premarital counseling before they got married.

Quiapo Church – A very famous church located in the very heart of the city of Manila, popularly visited because of its miraculous Black Nazarene.

Quezon Province – The province that covers the southernmost part of the Sierra Madre Mountain Range.

Retribution – The vengeful reaction of David after Rosemarie was killed by the Japanese. David was almost killed in his last mission to avenge Rosemarie's death.

Sacrament of Marriage – The Catholic church requires a couple to have the sacrament of baptism, the sacrament of confession, the sacrament of Communion, and the sacrament of Confirmation before the rite of marriage could be performed.

Sierra Madre Mountain Range – Covers ten provinces, with the province of Cagayan in the northernmost part and Quezon Province in the southernmost part of the mountain range. It is the source of the Pampanga River, which runs southward 260 miles, draining into Manila Bay.

Silent Killers – The guerilla unit trained to kill their enemies fast and swift by matching their enemies one-on-one and attacking them from behind by slashing the throat and stabbing the heart during the ungodly hours of the morning.

Tarak Ridge – A point or section on top of Mount Mariveles that was mentioned in the story, used as the training ground of the guerilla unit headed by Capt. Joseph Lee.

Tinola – A ginger and garlic based soup with chicken as the main ingredient, cooked with pepper leaves and green young papaya.

W Housing Complex – The design of the lodging quarters built by the guerilla unit headed by Capt. Joseph Lee in a W shape, with the center tip of the letter as their kitchen area. Each member of the group occupied a separate individual quarter in the housing complex. It was built like a resting house to give each member of the group the break they needed after their very fierce battle with the Japanese. The housing complex was built along a river and a spring to have a ready supply of freshwater. The restroom was built separate and away, located in the back of the housing complex.

# List of Contributors

1. Avelino, Amado – for the pictures of Tarak Ridge, Papaya River, Dunsulan and Sibul River in Bataan
2. Avelino, Joseph – provided financial support in the amount of $ 200.00 for the photographic trip to Baguio City. Total cost of the trip amounted to P 10,030.85 Philippine pesos.
3. Avelino, Miguel – for the pictures of jeepney in the Philippines
4. Avelino, Milagros Timbingan – for the pictures of roasted pig (lechon) and Pagsanjan Falls
5. Lot, Emerson – for the pictures of Manila Hotel and San Sebastian Church façade
6. Peras, Rossel – translated from English to Japanese the command of the Japanese lieutenant general to his officers in the Death March.
7. Reyes, Karen Joy – for the pictures of Quiapo Church, Manila Cathedral, and San Sebastian Church
8. Ruhlmann, Lilimar Avelino – for the picture of Scarborough Residence
9. Whidden, Edythe – She evaluated Chapters XXIII and XXIV to determine the acceptability of the contents of the two chapters to the current standard social norm.
10. Zosa, Majella – for all pictures taken in Baguio City, which include the Bridal Veil Falls, the Mansion, Burnham Park, Session Road, the Five Tribes of Igorots, and the Baguio Cathedral.

# Lists of illustrations Tables and Pictures